DEAD PETALS

ALAN I'ANSON

Dead Petal Press

ISBN-10: 1790923506
ISBN-13: 978-1790923502

Any references to historical events, real people, or real places are used fictitiously. Names, characters, and places are products of the author's imagination.

Published by Dead Petal Press

Cover design by GermanCreative.

First Print Edition 2019.

http://www.alanianson.co.uk
https://www.facebook.com/authoralanianson
https://www.instagram.com/alanianson/
https://twitter.com/Alaneye72
https://www.amazon.co.uk/l/B07H28RVLK

Acknowledgments

"Write with the door closed, rewrite with the door open."

–Stephen King

Quite a few people were generous enough to help me during the writing of this book, from reading earlier drafts and offering encouragement, to letting me bounce ideas off them while they asked questions that I was forced to answer. My thanks go to my wife, Debbie, who made me make a better ending, my sons, Alan and Mark, my old school pal, Lynne Payne, who made me question the killer's motives, Sarah Beth and Joe Kelly, who listened patiently while I constructed the story, and to everyone who read the earlier drafts and offered so much advice and encouragement: Leanne I'Anson (then Brown), Debby Wilson, Bex Wilson, Dave 'Dodge' Tattersall, Linda Hamilton, Ste and Ben Melling, and my sisters Maureen and June. I'd also like to say a special thank you to Donise Sheppard for all her help, encouragement, and unceasing enthusiasm. Last, and most certainly least, to Neil and James, for keeping it real – and no, there are still no dinosaurs.

Dedicated to mum and dad.

The murdered do haunt their murderers, I believe. I know that ghosts have wandered on earth. Be with me always -- take any form -- drive me mad! Only do not leave me in this abyss, where I cannot find you!

EMILY BRONTE, *Wuthering Heights*

Prologue

There wasn't anything special or unusual about the day Hannah Reid disappeared. It was just a plain old March Thursday. A school day. Rain had drizzled from an indifferent grey sky all afternoon; Hannah had scored a B+ in a spelling test, chomped down burger and chips for tea, and had spent an entertaining evening with Mandy and Liz at Liz's house, fooling around on social media and listening to music.

At 8:56pm, she set off on the short walk that would get her home for nine o'clock precisely. Her parents were great and everything, but they did insist on this unbreakable curfew: home by nine, and not a minute later.

Hannah grabbed the gatepost and cheerfully swung around it, while Liz and Mandy leaned dangerously out of the bedroom window, shouting and waving.

"See you tomorrow, Han," they called.

"See yas!" Hannah called back.

She headed home, the low heels of her court shoes tapping the pavement like water dripping in the empty night. Three new texts from a boy she liked at school made her stomach do a happy little twist and shout, her heart skipping like a smooth stone on a pond.

She typed in a reply, oblivious to her surroundings, the high-resolution display illuminating her face as her thumbs flew over the keys.

The attack was fast and powerful. A strong arm across her chest, a smothering hand over her mouth. The phone flew from her grasp, the screen shattering on the pavement, as her unseen assailant dragged her from the lights of the road and into the seclusion of the dark footpath that bisected the estate.

A man's breathy, excited voice next to her ear warned that if she screamed or struggled, he would cut her throat. The arm around her body briefly released its grip to show the knife held in his hand.

Her mind conjured an unfathomable image of herself stumbling around in panic, blood splashing onto the ground from her open throat.

The man asked her if she understood. Hannah nodded that she did.

He squeezed her tightly to him, his face buried in her hair, breathing its fragrance. She'd washed it the night before - mango and peach shampoo - last night when the world was safe and cosy.

Then he was dragging her backwards down the path, the heels of her shoes barely skimming the ground. The crushing hand mashed her lips painfully against her teeth, the coppery taste of blood on her tongue.

Her eyes darted left and right, searching the backs of the houses that lined the path. Curtains were drawn, blinds pulled. People were watching TV and thinking about getting up for school or work in the morning. No one was going to help her.

How can this be happening to me?

Then she recalled a story she'd seen on the news, about a girl who had gone missing from a nearby town. She remembered it because the girl had been Hannah's age, and had been remarkably like herself, with similar blonde curly hair and fresh face. The girl's bewildered parents, their weary faces white in the stark flash of the photographer's bulbs, offered a heart-

2

rending plea: *please come home, we love you*.

The realisation that this might soon be the fate of her own parents was too much to contemplate.

He stopped beside a white van that had been backed into the other end of the alley.

Oh no, she thought, *he's going to take me away*.

Letting go of her with one arm, he released the van's sliding side door and rolled it back.

He spun her around to face him, pressing her against the van and quickly covering her mouth again with his bitter, sweaty palm. He stood taller than she, thin and wiry and deceivingly strong. The lights from the street cast him in silhouette, but she could make out a dark beanie hat and jacket. He warned her again not to make a sound or he would kill her, but this time he continued the threat, telling her that after she was dead he'd go to her house and kill her parents, her brother, and their little dog, Jasper too.

Hannah stared in terror. *How did he know so much about her?*

He uncovered her mouth and she sucked in a gulp of air, wetting her lips and unsticking them from her teeth. She could taste blood. "Please..." she started to say, but he covered her mouth again and silently threatened her with the knife.

When he was sure she understood to be quiet, he took away his hand and just looked at her. Hannah stared back at him, her chest rising in little gasps of stress and fear, pinned like a butterfly under scrutiny. Then he scooped her up and threw her into the van, quickly hauling himself in after her and closing the door behind him.

Working swiftly and excitedly, he duct-taped her wrists and ankles together.

Once she was securely bound, he gazed at her again, his breathing laboured. He leaned over her and gently swept a few locks of hair from her terrified face.

"You're so beautiful," he whispered. "Don't be afraid. I'm not going to hurt you. I love you."

He smoothed a final piece of tape over her mouth and clambered between the seats into the cab. The engine started, gears shifting, and the van eased quietly onto the deserted street.

Hannah watched in despair as blue slate roofs and streetlights slid by. She caught a glimpse of a football scarf in an upper window and realised they were on her street! That was Jimmy Calder's room. He was friends with her brother and came around sometimes to play. Her house was just a little further down here on the right.

She prayed that her parents would see the van, that *anyone* would see the van, and realise she was in trouble. But a moment later, the van leaned into a left turn and they were leaving the estate. The engine snarled and pitched up as they joined the main road and picked up speed.

Just a few minutes ago she'd waved good-bye to her school friends. How could everything turn on its head so quickly?

High sodium lights bathed the van in their strange yellow glow. Her home and family were growing smaller behind them, all hope of rescue fading with them. Her mother would be at the window, watching for her as she always did. The kettle would be boiling water for some bedtime hot chocolate. Her pyjamas would be warming on the radiator while her father read the newspaper or watched sport on TV, unaware of what was happening to his daughter.

Behind the strip of tape, Hannah began to cry, and the man told her to be quiet.

Chapter One

While Hannah Reid lay bound and terrified in the back of a grimy, nondescript van, Gary Wright spent his usual hour or so at home on his Mac, following up the day's work and replying to emails. His wife, Fiona, was curled on the armchair reading a novel, while their eleven-year-old daughter, Charlotte—or Charley as everyone called her—was upstairs in her bedroom.

Gary tapped his pen on the dining table, smiling and nodding at the figures on the screen.

Fiona placed her novel face down on the chair arm and stretched out like a cat. "I'm going to make some supper for Charley," she said. "Do you want anything?"

"Erm..." Gary muttered.

Fiona padded to the bottom of the stairs, her bare feet whispering on the deep-pile carpet. "Charley? Get your PJs on. Time for bed!"

"She won't hear you," Gary said.

"Won't?"

"She'll have her earphones in. She's just discovered *Evanescence*."

Fiona sighed and hauled herself up the stairs to Charley's room at the end of the landing. A ceramic plaque on the door's centre panel read 'Charley' diagonally across the face in funky blue script. A tiny hand-painted beach scene adorned the bottom right corner, while a smiling cartoon sun—complete with shades—shone ever-widening rays of cheer from the top left. A beachfront artist had painted it for her when they holidayed in Greece the year before.

Fiona opened the door to find Charley lying stomach-down on the bed, listening to music through her earbuds, and leafing through a glossy magazine. She saw her mother and tugged out an earpiece by the wire.

"It's gone nine," Fiona said. "PJs on. You want toast or crumpets?"

"Um... toast... no, crumpets."

"Okay," Fiona said.

"Can I have jam?"

"Strawberry or blueberry?

"Um, strawberry... no, blueberry!"

Fiona smiled. "Make your mind up, fuzzy-head. Ten minutes, okay?"

"Yep."

Gary glanced at her when she came back down. "Evanescence?"

"I didn't ask." She stopped and massaged his shoulder. "Are you nearly done? It's gone nine already."

Gary glanced at his watch and stretched. "Sorry, Fee. Yeah, I'm done."

As she moved off, he snagged her hand. "Hey, Fee, AppTech is doing well. And I mean, *really* well."

"Yeah?"

"Yeah. Last quarter was way above expectations, and this month's figures alone are killer." He chuckled. "Michelle and Ed are going to have to eat their words. 'Too early to think about a sister company', eh? New contracts are coming in, and WebTech clients are going crazy for phone app versions of their websites. Lance can't keep up with the server stuff." He frowned. "Which reminds me, I need to get him some help with

6

that." He made a note on the legal pad beside the Mac.

"How is Lance?" Fiona asked. "I haven't seen him in a while."

"He's good. Busy, but good."

"We'll have to invite him over for dinner."

"Yeah," Gary agreed, but his attention had already returned to the screen.

"Hey!" Fiona said.

Gary looked up.

"You are aware that it's Charley's birthday party on Saturday, aren't you?"

"Of course I am," Gary scoffed. "Haven't I already ordered the marquees and the food and the bouncy castle and everything?"

Fiona crossed her arms and tilted her head at him. "What time does it start?"

Gary rubbed an eye with his knuckle. "Erm... three?"

"One o'clock! Honestly, Gary, if it's not work or an application these days, it doesn't even appear on your radar. Does it?"

Gary laughed and pulled her to him. "I'm sorry, Fee. Everything's so crazy right now. I can hardly keep up. Clients to see. Back-to-back meetings. Ed isn't scheduling the work very well, and Michelle corners me every time she sees me, to complain about the ever-tightening deadlines."

"Michelle corners you, does she?" Fiona asked, arching a well-shaped eyebrow. "I bet you don't complain too much about that."

"Hmm." He thumbed his chin and pretended to think about it for a moment.

Fiona lightly thumped his forehead with her fist.

"Hey!" Gary protested.

"Does that help you think more clearly?" she asked. "Maybe you should get Michelle to write you an app that tells you what's happening *outside* of work."

"Michelle's Creative Director, Fee. And she's two months pregnant."

"Whatever," Fiona dismissed. She started to get up, but Gary pulled her back to him.

"I'm not really that bad, am I?"

"Sometimes."

He kissed her. "You're so patient with me."

"I know I am. If I wasn't, we'd be divorced by now."

"Harsh," Gary grumbled, his attention drawn back to some detail on the screen in front of him. He tapped the keyboard, making some adjustment.

Fiona shook her head and went to make supper.

A moment later, Charley sauntered into the dining room. She'd changed into her pink pyjamas with 'Missy!' printed diagonally across the front in big puffy white letters. Beneath the text sat a fat cartoon-cat, licking its paw. She'd ditched the iPod, her attention now focused entirely on the magazine. She slid onto the dining chair opposite Gary and carefully laid the magazine on the table top, smoothing the pages and taking a moment to hook a lock of mousey brown hair behind her ear.

Gary glanced at her as she scanned a few pictures, then turned the page. Something held her attention. Gary peered over. It was a piece about a boy band.

"Whatcha reading?"

"Um... nothing," Charley said without looking up.

Gary frowned. "Yeah you are. I can see you reading something, right there."

"Huh, well that's what you think. I'm looking at the pictures, if you must know."

Gary raised his eyebrows. "Oh, you are, are you?"

"Um, ye-eh."

Gary snatched the magazine from the table.

"Hey!" Charley protested. "Give it back!"

"What is this anyway?" He flipped the magazine closed to

8

read the cover, "*Teen Vogue*?"

"Give it back," Charley whined. She lunged over the table to grab it, but he kept it beyond her reach.

"*Mum!*"

"Should you even be reading this? It's for *teeeen-agers*."

"So? I'm nearly a teenager."

"In a year and three days."

"So?"

He flipped through the pages. "Oh, this is just trash. Why do you read this rubbish?"

"It's not rubbish. Give it back. *Muuuum*!"

"What?" Fiona called.

"Tell dad to give back my magazine."

"Stop teasing her, Gary. Give it back."

Charley smiled smugly and held out her hand.

"Hmmm," Gary mused. "I'm not sure what kind of father I would be if I let you read trashy magazines for *teenagers*."

"Da-ad," Charley whined.

Gary looked at the photo of the boy band on the cover, all hairstyles and photoshopped faces. "You have a poster of these on your bedroom wall, don't you?"

She nodded, her smile all cheeky and mischievous.

"Well it can't be their music you like, so I'm guessing it's one of the band members."

"Their music's good."

"Yeah, right. So, who do you like the best then?"

Charley slumped in a sigh. "Deville, of course, he's dreamy."

"*Deville*? Seriously? First name Cruella?"

Charley giggled, "That's *De Vil*."

"Whatever," Gary said. "And what do you know about dreamy, anyway? You're eleven. Which one's Cruella?"

"*Deville*. The one in the middle. And I'm not eleven, I'm nearly twelve!"

"Same difference," Gary said and pretended to look closely at the photo. "This one here? The one with the silly hairstyle and the flat face?"

"He does not have a flat face," Charley said.

"He does. Look..." Gary showed her the photo and while she studied it, he pushed his pen clean through the middle of the singer's face, from the back of the page.

Charley's eyes widened, and her mouth dropped open. "OMG! I can't believe you just did that! That's three ninety-nine you owe me!"

"Three ninety-nine? For a magazine?" He grinned. "It was worth it though, just to see the look on your face."

Charley's eyes sparkled with mischief, her mouth set in a determined line as she scanned his things on the table. She lunged over and slapped the lid of his Mac closed.

This time it was Gary who was all wide-eyed and open-mouthed. "Hey, that's expensive!"

"Yeah, yeah," Charley said, with a little flip of her head. She slid her butt off the chair and casually yanked out the Mac's power cord too as she walked by.

"Right!" Gary roared, jumping to his feet.

Charley squealed and took off into the hall.

Gary plugged the cord back in, then gave chase, entering the hall in time to see Charley grasp the kitchen door frame and swing through.

"Mum! Tell him!" she squeaked.

Fiona leaned against the sink, watching with amusement as Charley found refuge behind the kitchen island. "What's going on?" she asked. "What did she do?"

"Nothing!" Charley cried.

Gary grasped the sides of the island, his shoulders hunched and his eyes on Charley. "She's been cheeky again."

"He made a hole in Deville's face," Charley countered.

"She closed the lid on my Mac *and* pulled out the power cord, putting hours of work at risk."

10

"You hit 'save' about every ten seconds," Fiona told him.

"You're missing the point," Gary said, faking a lunge.

Charley screamed and laughed.

"Isn't it about time you grew up?" Fiona asked, but she was smiling as she said it.

"Never," Gary replied.

Charley made a dash for freedom, but Gary caught her, wrapping his arms around her belly and shaking her up and down until she squealed with laughter. He scooped a handful of soapsuds from the basin and slopped it into Charley's face, making her scream even louder.

"Right!" Fiona said. "That's enough!"

A second later, she too was spluttering through a face full of suds.

"Gary!" she wailed. "My make up!"

"Oops," Gary mumbled.

If there was one thing you didn't mess with, it was Fiona's makeup. He set Charley on her feet and glanced sheepishly at Fiona as she wiped the suds from her eyes.

She blinked at him. "Have you smudged my mascara?"

Gary's mouth made torturous contortions as he tried not to laugh at the black smears and drips.

"You look like the Joker!" Charley laughed, her face all pink and wet.

Fiona tore off a sheet of kitchen roll and carefully dabbed around her eyes. "Honestly, Gary," she sighed. "You're *worse* than a child sometimes."

Gary looked guiltily at Charley and pushed out his bottom lip. He nudged her and asked, "Why so serious?"

They both cracked up at the Dark Knight quip.

"And why is that so funny?" Fiona asked.

"Cos it's what he says in the movie," Charley laughed.

"The Joker," Gary explained. "Y'know, it's what he says when he..."

11

Fiona turned her attention to him and folded her arms.

"Come on, Fee, it's not the end of the world is it?"

"No, but I'm going to have to take this off properly now."

"You should leave it off," Gary said.

"Leave it off?"

"Yeah, leave it off. You look just as gorgeous without it."

Fiona smiled shyly. "I do not. I look a mess."

He grinned and moved in closer, his hands slipping around her waist. "Is that a blush I see?"

"I do not blush."

"Blushing and denial," Gary noted. "What a gorgeous combination."

He pulled her closer and kissed her.

"Ew," Charley interrupted. "I'm outta here, before you two start *doing it*."

Gary and Fiona exchanged shocked glances, waiting while Charley flounced from the kitchen, before sniggering together like teenagers.

Later, when Charley was tucked up in bed, and Gary munched a piece of toast, Fiona decided to approach a delicate subject.

"You know how we've been stuck for something to get Charley for her birthday?"

"I thought you'd got her... that thing?" Gary replied.

"Thing?"

"Yeah. You know, that...pink...girly thing."

If only they'd had a boy as well as a girl, then he could have mooched around Toys "R" Us looking at action figures and train sets instead of the girly stuff.

Fiona let it go. "We have, but I've been thinking..."

"Uh-oh," Gary said.

"...you know what Charley would really like?"

"The new Deville album?"

"No, a kitten."

Gary stopped eating. "Oh no, not the 'K' word."

"Come on Gary, you've been a grouch about this for far too long. It's good for a child to have a pet."

Gary popped the last piece of crust into his mouth and dusted his hands onto the plate. "I never had a pet," he said.

"Yes, and look how you turned out."

Gary shot her a hurt frown, which she promptly ignored.

"It would be such a surprise for her. She would never be expecting a kitten."

"It's not exactly what I was expecting either."

"I know, but she's wanted one for so long."

Gary gave a deep sigh.

"She would absolutely *love* you for it. *And,* even though it's my idea, I'll let you take the credit. She knows you're the only reason she can't have one."

Gary closed his eyes and made a grimace of indecision. "But it's a *cat*. Cats have needs. It'll whine to go out and whine to come in."

"It can't be any worse than listening to your whining," Fiona said, with a wry smile.

"And it'll crap everywhere."

"Cats don't do that, they poop in their litter trays."

"Yeah, and then someone has to *empty* the litter trays."

"Charley and I will do all the dirty work," Fiona said. "Oh, come on Gary, *please*?"

She tried her best pitiful, doe-eyed look and he finally caved.

"Oh, all right."

Fiona clapped her hands excitedly. "Yes!"

"But I'm warning you," he said, pointing a finger for emphasis. "I don't want it bothering me."

"It won't."

"Especially when I'm working."

13

"Promise."

"And also, when I'm relaxing."

Fiona wriggled with excitement.

"And I'm not taking it for a walk," Gary added.

Fiona laughed. "You don't take cats for a walk, you just let them out."

"Well, I'm not letting it out either."

Fiona picked up her phone.

"And I'm not feeding it or giving it milk or whatever."

Fiona half nodded, half shook her head as she typed on her phone.

Gary pointed toward the hall. "And I'm not picking up any dead birds it brings in either, so don't be pulling any of that squeamish crap on me when it happens, because it will."

Fiona nodded all the way through, but it was obvious she was no longer listening to him.

"Who are you texting?" he asked

"Stacy," Fiona said. "I'm letting her know that operation 'talk him around' has been a success and was actually much easier than expected."

"What?" Gary asked.

Fiona tapped 'send', then put her phone down. She slung both arms around his neck and gave him a crooked smile. "Stacy's cat had a litter and I asked her to save one for me...us."

Gary began to splutter a protest, but Fiona covered his mouth with a long, sensual kiss. When she pulled away, he had to catch a breath.

"You're just about the only person who can manipulate me, you know that?" he asked.

She smiled smugly. "Hmm, I see it more like getting the best out of you."

Gary laughed, and they kissed again.

"How about we go up to bed?" Fiona whispered close to his ear. "And if you're lucky, maybe I'll manipulate something else."

"Hmm," Gary mused. "Maybe getting a cat isn't such a bad idea after all."

Fiona smiled and kissed him again, then pulled away, taking his hand and leading him towards the stairs. Gary followed willingly, enjoying her taking the initiative, as she sometimes did.

It made him recall the night he met her. He had been out on the town with Lance and a few friends. She'd caught his eye on the crowded dance floor, whooping it up with her friends while dancing to the Communards' *Never Can Say Good-bye*.

Lance had knocked on his head and said 'Hello, McFly?' and pointed out that while they had all drunk up, he was still holding onto the best part of a pint. Gary had nodded absently, wondering if he should try his luck and go speak to her.

He'd about made up his mind to do just that, when Lance broke the spell, telling him they were moving on.

Gary shook the crazy notion away, downed most of the pint, and slid the glass onto the bar. Reluctantly, he followed Lance through the throngs, casting regretful glances back at the girl on the dance floor. She was out of his league, he assured himself. He'd be punching way above his weight, as his mates no doubt would have keenly advised him.

But at the doors he'd stopped. The bouncer had looked him up and down. "You coming or going, mate?"

Gary had looked back at him and said, "I'm gonna ask her." The bouncer had grinned and given him an encouraging wink as if he knew exactly what he meant.

Lance held out his hands in exasperation whilst Gary told him he'd catch them at the next bar.

He found her still on the dance floor, surrounded by her friends. His heart hammered, and even though he knew it could end in humiliation, he drew in a deep breath and pushed through the crowds, walking right up to her.

She was even more beautiful up close, her brown eyes sparkling. For a few moments, he could only stand with his mouth open and stare at her like an idiot.

She had shown him that cheeky, crooked-smile of hers and raised a perfectly arched eyebrow...*yes*?

"Gary," was all he could manage.

"Gary?"

"My name."

"And?"

"And, well, I was wondering if you migh-"

Before he could finish, she covered his mouth with her fingers, took his hand, and led him to the bar.

"Well? Are you going to buy me a drink or not?" she asked, when he'd just stood there looking lost.

"Oh, yeah." He fumbled his wallet out of his pocket and managed to drop it onto the sticky floor.

He offered an awkward smile, then stooped over, groping around in the darkness. He came back up without the wallet, his face red from the bending, and found her standing with her arms folded, the elusive item clutched in her hand.

"You know," she said. "You're going to have to get your act together if you're hoping to take me out."

Gary had blinked at her a couple of times, unsure if she was serious or setting him up for a fall.

Then she had giggled, and he offered her an embarrassed chuckle.

She handed him the wallet. "So, are you going to buy me a drink then?"

He almost had to punch himself in the head a couple of times to pull himself together. He asked what she would like to drink, and she told him a white wine and soda.

As he turned to order she said, "And, Gary? It's Fiona by the way—just in case you never get around to asking."

He smiled at the memory of the wickedly mischievous grin

she'd favoured him with, and still gave him to this day.

Fiona teased him sometimes about their first meeting, but he liked to point out how he *had* gotten his act together. He had started WebTech, the huge success of which had led to the new sister company, AppTech.

He had dated Fiona for a while, and when the guys finally met her, they told him he was punching way above his weight. All except Lance. Lance had just grinned and shook his head and muttered, "You lucky sod."

Eighteen years later, they had fourteen years of happy marriage behind them, a successful business, a beautiful daughter, and a wonderful, if busy life.

Sometimes he wondered where fate might have taken him had he not changed his mind that night and decided to go back to speak to her.

It seemed there are key moments in everyone's lives when the decisions they make, both good and bad, help shape their destinies.

The decision to go back that night had been an excellent one, the best, and he had made a good many more over the years. But soon he would make another decision. The worst decision of his life. One that would change everything.

Chapter Two

Despite Friday's usual glut of progress reports and back to back meetings, Gary had still insisted he'd find time to call the companies hired for the party and confirm the bookings, delivery times etc. Fiona had conceded but had warned him not to forget.

He knew his controlling nature tried her patience at times, but she made allowances. She was a good manager. He'd tried to tempt her into taking a role at AppTech, but she had already chosen her career path—working in various management roles—until she settled on a position at the New Royal Gableton hospital, built after the old one burned down in the terrible blaze of '96, killing hundreds of patients and staff.

At lunchtime, he grabbed a Styrofoam cup of soup from the kitchen and browsed the BBC News website while he ate. The main headline concerned a missing girl. He skimmed the story: *... twelve-year-old Hannah Reid...missing while returning from a friend's house last night...police appeal for anyone who knows where she is to come forward...urge Hannah to call home...*

He clicked the 'technology' link and read about Microsoft's latest *Surface* tablet and the much-rumoured *Apple Watch*. A few of the guys at work had something called a *Pebble,* a sort of plastic wristwatch that allowed their phones to pass information such as SMS text messages and news updates to its screen. It was kind of cool, but they had been, so far, unable to browbeat Gary into getting one and joining their 'club'. With techies, there was always a new club to join, or a new challenge to rise to, whether it was working all afternoon in a beanie hat or taking the Pringle Challenge (how many Pringles can you cram into your mouth and eat in one go).

He drank down the soup dregs and grimaced at the vaguely plastic flavour at the bottom of the cup, wondering—as he always did—if the accumulated effect might be doing him any harm.

He closed the BBC website and continued working until five-thirty when he packed away his Mac and took the twenty-minute drive home.

They ordered takeaway for dinner, special Chow Mein, sweet and sour chicken, and dumplings from Mister Chen's. The dumplings always came in an odd number, and Gary always teased Charley that he was having it.

While they ate, Charley told them about the task they'd had to complete in English class that day.

"Okay, so we had to choose someone, past or present, living or dead, and pretend we were on a plane that was going to crash and there was only one parachute."

"Ah, yes!" Fiona said, through a mouthful of noodles. "I remember doing this at school. You have to give reasons why you should be the one to survive?"

Charley nodded.

"Who did you choose?" Gary asked. He quickly sucked up a noodle strand, making it flick around and splatter his chin with gravy. It never failed to make Charley laugh.

"Louis Pasture," Charley said, giggling.

Fiona dabbed Gary's chin with her napkin. "Good choice," she agreed. "Microbiologist."

"Yep, he invented immunisation."

"Did you win?" Gary asked.

19

"Um, well, first we all had to read out why we thought we should be the one to live. Then the class voted and the top five had to read them out again."

"And you were in the top five, of course," Gary boasted.

Charley grinned. "Of course."

"Who were you up against?"

"Um." She counted them off on her fingers. "Winston Churchill, Wayne Rooney, Gandhi, and Justin Bieber."

Gary laughed, "A motley crew if I ever heard one. And did you win?"

Fiona shushed him. "Gary, just let her tell the story!"

"Well, I want to know if she won!"

"You'll know in a moment," Fiona scolded. "Let her build it up. Go on, sweetie."

"So we did two rounds in alphabetical order, and I *really* listened to what all the others had to say." She grinned mischievously. "Then when I read mine the second time, I went through all the others one-by-one and gave reasons why I didn't think it mattered if they lived or not, and that the class should vote for me."

Gary stopped eating. "You character assassinated *Gandhi*?"

"Ha! He was easy. Justin Bieber was the hard one."

"Justin Bieber? How come?"

"Cos the class is full of *Beliebers*," she said, rolling her eyes.

"So how did you convince them?"

"I said if not for my immunisations, he probably would've died as a baby and wouldn't have made any music at all. And what a sadder world it would have been without him."

Gary laughed at her morose tone. "And it worked?"

"Ha! Tina Simmons was nearly crying just at the thought of it. And yep, I won!"

Gary laughed so hard he nearly choked. He held up his hand and she gave him a high five.

"That's my girl," he grinned.

20

Fiona smiled at their antics and shook her head.

After they'd cleared up, they talked about the party arrangements. Charley was bursting with excitement about having her own bouncy castle for the day. They finally got her to bed at nine-forty while Gary and Fiona turned in at eleven.

"Did you see the news today?" Fiona asked, brushing out her long blonde hair at the vanity table.

"No?" Gary replied as he unbuttoned his shirt.

"Another young girl has gone missing."

"Oh yeah, I did see that actually," he remembered. "*Another*?"

"Yes, don't you read the news?"

"Just the technology pages usually. The news is far too depressing." He shook out his trousers and carefully hung them over the chair on his side of the bedroom.

"Well, a girl went missing about four months ago—Linda something—it was all over the news for a time, and then it just seemed to fade out. I don't think they found her though. Now there's another one."

"I'm sure people go missing all the time," Gary said. He slipped under the covers and picked up the dog-eared copy of *Bravo-Two-Zero* he'd borrowed from Lance.

"Yes, but don't you think it's a bit of a coincidence? Two young girls from nearby towns. They looked alike too, if I remember rightly."

"I'm sure she'll turn up," he murmured, scanning the page for his place in the book. "Probably run away with her teacher or something."

"Maybe." Fiona slipped in beside him. "I hope nothing's happened to her. She looked such a sweet thing."

"She'll be okay. The police'll find her."

Fiona watched him as he read, already lost in the book. *How can you be so sure*? she wanted to ask. Gary was always so sure of himself and his convictions. It was one of the reasons why she loved him so. Yet occasionally it annoyed her, because sometimes, like now, he seemed almost dismissive in his certainty.

"Not too long tonight, huh?" she reminded him. "Tomorrow's going to be a long day, I expect."

"Half an hour. Tops. I left it at a good bit."

Fiona kissed him and turned onto her side, thinking about the missing girl, Hannah. Perhaps Gary was right about her. It had happened before. Girls falling for teachers and teachers falling for their students. But this girl was Charley's age, so even that scenario was sinister. Maybe she'd argued with her parents and run away. She might just be at a friend's house, safe and sound, as runaways mostly were.

She tried to remember the faces of the other two girls. They'd both had blonde hair and fresh complexions; the same age, but from different towns. Fiona wondered if the police had picked up on the similarities.

She was still thinking about it when Gary's bedside lamp clicked off.

"Night," he mumbled as he settled down.

"Night," she whispered, and stared into the darkness, the shadows creating spooky faces everywhere she looked.

Chapter Three

The first van pulled through the gates early on Saturday morning, with a team of guys to erect two marquees on the expansive back lawn. Fiona had argued for just one, but Gary had noted more than the usual number of cold, rainy days that month and wanted to play it safe.

The bouncy castle arrived mid-morning, a huge pink and purple affair with a Disney Princess theme. Gary showed them where to site it, and the morning soon echoed with the chug of the compact-compressor. Even before the towers had fully inflated, Charley was leaping and bouncing around on it like a crazy girl.

Gary inspected the castle and wasn't happy to find that, while the princesses printed on the walls *looked* like Disney princesses, they weren't genuine. The print quality wasn't great and there were no Disney logos or copyright notices printed anywhere. He brought it up with the deliverymen but received vacant glances in response.

"We just deliver it, mate," one of them told him.

Gary made a mental note to check how the website had advertised it later.

After the caterers had set up the free bar and food in the marquees, Gary and Fiona disappeared into the house to get changed. Gary emerged looking smart in a sweater and jeans, paired with a charcoal grey, wool-flannel jacket. Fiona wore a knee-length cream dress and Jimmy Choo strappy sandals. She'd put her hair up and tussled five minutes before coming down, but it still looked stunning.

She stepped out onto the porch, just as her parents, Frank and Audrey arrived; a good half an hour early, by Gary's watch.

Gary eyed Fiona appreciatively. "You look ravishing, Mrs. Wright."

She gave him her crooked grin. "You don't look half bad yourself, Mr. Wright." Then her face broke into a sparkling smile as she greeted her parents.

Gary prepared himself for one of Frank's bone-crushing handshakes and was not disappointed. When he let go, Gary flexed his fingers and Frank laughed.

"Too firm for you, Son?" he asked.

"Oh, Frank, I do wish you'd stop that!" Audrey admonished.

"Not too bad, Frank. Only a couple of fractures this time."

"I still have a boxer's grip," Frank laughed, and gave Gary's shoulder a slap, hearty enough to stagger him.

Gary rolled his eyes at Fiona, who had an amused little smile in her eyes.

She tweaked her father's misshapen nose. "When are you going to get this fixed, Dad?"

"Same time as I fix these," he grinned, flicking the lobes of his cauliflower ears.

Audrey shook her head. "You're wasting your time, Fiona. He loves them. He's like a silly old soldier with his war wounds. No doubt he'll have his shirt off later, showing off his muscles. You wouldn't think he was sixty-three."

"If you've got it, flaunt it, eh?" Frank laughed. "What do you say, Gary?"

Gary forced a smile.

Frank gestured around the garden. "You certainly know how

to put on a party, Son. I'll give you that."

Gary smiled modestly, but the corners of his mouth twitched. He could never be quite sure if Frank really was complimenting him, or getting in a sly dig.

"If you've done all this for her twelfth birthday, what on earth are you going to do for her eighteenth, eh?"

"Oh, I don't know, Frank," Gary said. "Maybe *two* bouncy castles?"

Frank leaned back to eye him for a second, then laughed and threw a rough arm around Gary's shoulder. "Ha! *Two bouncy castles*! Sharp as a tack this one. What do you say, Fiona?"

"I didn't just marry him for his good looks," Fiona said, all the time smiling at Gary, who looked about as comfortable as a mouse at a cat show.

"You can say that again," Frank joked. "I've seen better heads on a boil." He grinned at Gary. "Aw, just pulling your leg, Son. Have I upset him?" he asked the others. "What do you think?"

Gary performed a skilful little ducking side-step out of Frank's grasp and pointed in the direction of the bar. "Get yourselves a drink, Frank. There's beer, ale, lager, whatever you want." He lowered his voice, "And there's a bottle of single malt back there too, but you have to tell the barman I sent you."

Frank looked at him and Gary gave him a wink.

"Didn't I say he knew how to put on a party?" Frank said, "Didn't I?" He tapped the side of his nose and winked back. "We'll save that for later. Come on, Audrey, this could get messy."

"All being well," Gary said and watched them head off down the path toward the marquees.

"Single malt, eh?" Fiona noted. "A masterstroke."

"Well, we mere mortals have to offer sacrifice to appease the Gods."

Fiona nudged him. "Oh, come on. He's not that bad."

"No," Gary sighed. "He really is."

Fiona laughed, "I don't know why you get all regressive around him."

"Because he makes me uncomfortable, Fee. He calls me 'Son' for Christ's sake."

"Aw, I love when I get to peep behind the curtain of the Great and Powerful Oz, to see the little man pulling the levers."

Gary shot her a glance. "Where do you get that stuff?"

"What stuff?"

"Like that thing you just said. How do you think them up?"

Fiona smiled. "It's called a metaphor, dear. They only live in the playground of the *creative* mind, which is probably why you struggle with them."

Gary frowned and shook his head, watching as Frank stopped to greet someone he knew, mildly crushing their hand, before feigning a few playful punches to their midriff.

"Just don't leave me and your dad alone together for any length of time, huh? Cause there's every chance *that* could get messy."

"Don't worry," Fiona promised. "I'll come save you if it's looking dangerous." She gave him a quick kiss and headed off to meet and greet.

Lance arrived at one o'clock on the dot, as expected. He brought with him a gift for Charley, and flowers for Fiona.

"Good idea with the marquees," he said. "Weather's been sketchy."

"Well, you know me. Heard anything from Max?"

"Not today. He wasn't happy when I left yesterday."

"No, he said as much in the project meeting. He's struggling with this one."

"He'll be fine," Lance said. "It's the server stuff you need to worry about. There's a lot of work involved."

"I'm working on it."

Lance grinned. "Well, while you work on it, I'm going to get a drink. Where...?"

As Gary pointed him in the direction of the drinks marquee, Fiona's friend, Trixie, arrived with Sylvia in tow. Trixie was dressed in her usual eccentric flair; a colourful swirling-print dress swathed in layers of black net; her hair burgundy, wildly twisted, with red and blueish-purple highlights. Her famous spiked leather ankle boots completed the ensemble. They were creased and scuffed but she refused to throw them away. They didn't go with the dress at all, and yet they worked because it was Trixie.

"You both look stunning," Fiona gushed.

Trixie smiled. "Thanks. Just hope it doesn't rain."

"Weather has been taken into consideration," Gary said, with a sweeping gesture.

Trixie followed his direction. "Ooo, marquees!" she squealed. "You're such a show-off, Gary."

"Where's the birthday girl?" Sylvia asked.

Fiona nodded toward the bouncy castle. "Been on it since they blew it up."

"A few drinks and we'll be on that. Won't we, Sylvia?"

"In this dress?" Sylvia laughed. "I don't think so."

"Get yourselves a drink, ladies," Gary offered, gesturing toward the drinks marquee.

Trixie caught his arm instead and linked it with hers. "How about escorting us over there, Mr. Wright?" She leaned in close and gazed up at him, batting her eyelashes. "You know I've been searching for you my entire life, don't you?"

Gary rolled his eyes. "Don't you ever get tired of that one, Trix?"

Trixie gave Fiona a satisfied smirk. "I only say it to aggravate him. You'd think someone so smart would have realised that by now. Come, Gary, introduce me to some people so I can embarrass you."

Gary gave Fiona a 'help me' look, but she only laughed and watched as she dragged him across the garden.

Trixie kept him occupied for half an hour, insisting he introduce her to just about everyone they met, even people she already knew.

She'll be lining them up for some paranormal stories later, he thought, as he escaped in time to greet Michelle and her husband, Nigel. Michelle wasn't showing much of a bump yet, but Fiona made a fuss of her all the same.

By two-thirty, everyone had arrived, and the party was well underway. The day was cool, but not as chilly as it had been, and the rain seemed to be holding off. The sun even managed to peek through the cracks in the clouds occasionally.

People stood in groups in the garden, but many had taken to the marquees, chatting and drinking. Kids screamed and leapt about the bouncy castle and at least two of the younger ones ended up in tears. Two bouncy castles might not have been a bad idea after all, Gary thought, one for the youngsters and one for the more rough-and-tumble kids. Charley, of course, was in the centre of it all and loving every second.

When he got a moment, Gary slipped away to call Max, who had declined the party invitation because of his workload. His mobile battery was low, so he went to his study and called from the landline.

Balancing business and home life was a constant battle. In many ways, the two were inextricably woven together, no matter how much Fiona might protest about it. Deep-down though, she understood that one couldn't exist without the other.

"Max, it doesn't matter, it doesn't matter," Gary was saying. "We need to push them on this release date."

Fiona popped her head into the study and tilted it as if to say, *really? Even at your daughter's birthday party?* Gary sighed. She seemed to have a radar for these things. He focused on the phone again.

"Have you spoken to Lance? Well you should. He said it's

28

going to be a struggle to get the server-side up in time. Michelle? Michelle's working on the City app assets and she isn't even going to be able to look at what you need until the end of next week." He paused, listening. "I know what we said, but it was way too optimistic. And I said that at the time if you remember, but Ed had already committed."

Fiona flapped a hand at him and when she had his attention, she mouthed that they were ready to bring out the birthday cake. Gary nodded, holding up two fingers.

"Just do what you can, Buddy. Even a week will help. Offer them a sweetener. I dunno... tell them Sophie will do a lap dance for the CEO or something." He laughed. "No, no, Fiona had to do it last time."

Fiona gave him a reproachful look, but she was smiling. 'Hurry up' she mouthed and left.

Gary wound up the call and made some notes. He closed and straightened his diary, carefully placing the pen parallel to the blotter, and re-joined the others.

He grabbed a drink from the marquee and spotted Lance standing on the patio, people-watching and drinking from a bottle.

Gary wandered over. "You driving?"

"Where've you been? Fiona's looking for you."

"She found me," Gary said. "Cake and 'Happy Birthday' song imminent."

"Ah. And yeah, drinking. I'll grab a taxi and pick the car up tomorrow. If that's okay?"

"Of course," Gary said. "Me Casa."

"Been speaking to Max?"

"Yeah," Gary said, wondering briefly how Lance knew he'd been speaking to Max. "Ed really needs to stop throwing his finger in the air when estimating project delivery times. We're pushed to the limit as it is right now, which is good, but then he's taking on more work and giving clients unrealistic completion times. He needs to speak to the teams more and get a better understanding of the workflow."

Lance swigged some lager. "He's bringing in the work though, Gary. You have to give him that."

Fiona waved from the conservatory and pointed over at Charley, who had taken a break from bouncing around. The time was nigh.

"Ed's pretty good," Gary conceded. "But I'm still going to have to rein him in."

Lance grinned. "Yeah, good luck with that."

Gary looked back as he walked away. "Hey, Fiona was saying you should come over for dinner soon."

"Sure, just say when."

"Next week? It's been a while since we got together."

Lance tipped his bottle and Gary went to collect Charley.

After some organisation and less-than-subtle hand signals, one of the caterers rolled in an impressive realisation of Charley's favourite Disney villain, Maleficent, made from cake and icing. Everyone sang happy birthday and Charley blew out all twelve candles in a single breath.

While everyone cheered, Fiona slipped away to get the main present.

Gary raised his hands and called for quiet. "I'd just like to say a quick 'thanks' to everyone for coming today..."

"Any excuse for a speech!" someone heckled, gaining a round of laughter from the crowd.

Gary grinned. "Who let that guy in?"

"God help us when she gets married!" someone else called.

Gary patted his breast pocket. "Got the speech written already, all ten pages of it."

"Dad!" Charley exclaimed and gave him a thump.

As the laughter subsided, Gary glanced over at the door, where Fiona waited. She gave him the thumbs up and Gary continued, "But truly, thanks everyone, you've all made it a really special day for our birthday girl." He turned to Charley. "Speaking of which, finding a gift for the girl who has everything has not been easy, but, and I have to say your mum had to just about twist my arm until it broke to make me agree to this, we have something that I know you've been wanting for a while now."

Charley looked around, her bright eyes brimming with expectation.

"Fee?"

Fiona brought the kitten into the room and, as if on cue, the assembled guests all gave out a big *ahhhhhh.*

Charley's jaw dropped, and her eyes grew wide. She covered her open mouth, then her eyes, and then began sobbing.

"Aww, Sweetie," Fiona said.

She turned to her father and hugged him tightly. "Thank you, Dad! Thank you! Thank you!" She smothered his cheek with kisses and then ran over to meet her new friend.

Gary touched his face and looked over at Fiona in surprise. He knew she wanted a kitten, but he hadn't expected that reaction. Fiona gave him her crooked little smile that said, 'told you so'.

Charley bundled the kitten into her arms. "Oh, she's gorgeous!"

"He," Fiona corrected.

"What you gonna call him?" Gary asked.

Charley held the kitten at arm's length, so she could get a proper look at him. His legs dangled comically. "Hmm," she mused. "Mister Whiskers."

"Mister Whiskers?" Gary asked. "Not Simba?"

Charley gave him a reproachful look and cuddled the kitten back to her chest. "Simba's a lion, Dad. This is Mister Whiskers, the kitten."

Gary looked around the room at his laughing guests and shrugged at his apparent lack of logic.

Charley was quickly surrounded by a squabble of children, all wanting to pet Mister Whiskers. Fiona intervened before it got out of hand and the kitten became overwhelmed by all those well-meaning hands. She moved them to another spot in the room, arranging it so the children could take turns at petting Mister Whiskers.

With the cake and present now over, the official part of the day was done. Everyone dispersed throughout the house and the gardens again, gathering in groups, meeting new people and reacquainting with old friends and family.

Gary spotted Brian, one of the WebTech developers, leaning against the kitchen wall, looking at his phone and frowning. He shook his head and looked up as Gary sauntered over.

"What's up, Brian, your share prices falling again?"

Brian smiled but there wasn't much humour in it.

Gary leaned against the wall beside him. "What's up?" he asked more seriously.

"Just reading about that girl who went missing on Thursday. But I'm sure you don't want to hear about that today, though."

Gary thought about Fiona mentioning it the previous night.

"What's happened? Have they found her?"

"No. They think it's linked with two other girls who went missing in the past few months."

"Really?" Gary said. "That's shocking. How sure are they?"

"Pretty sure, I think."

"Were they all from the same place?"

"All different."

"So why do they think they're linked?"

"All the girls were around the same age and have blonde hair. The media is already calling him the Goldilocks Kidnapper."

Gary made a face. "*Goldilocks Kidnapper*—I hate that media stuff."

"They're just young kids," Brian said through gritted teeth. "Makes me sick to my stomach."

Before Gary could say anything more, Charley grabbed his hand. "Dad! Dad! Singstar! Hakuna Matata!"

"Okay, okay!" Gary said, and in a single moment, the news was out of his mind.

Father and daughter had a ball performing the song for everyone, leaning together as they do in the movie, and walking around in a circle chanting *Hakuna Matata, Hakuna Matata*. When it was over, the room exploded with cheers, whistles, and riotous applause. Gary held out his palm for Charley to slap, then lifted her for kisses and hugs.

The whole thing was captured in photographs and videos, and Gary was promised more than once that he was destined for YouTube.

"Trixie was right," Fiona said, laughing and shaking her head. "You are a show-off."

Gary showed his palms. "What can I say?"

He kissed her, and she playfully pushed him away.

After grabbing a bottle of lager from the fridge, he wandered into the back room where he found Trixie regaling an audience with another supernatural encounter. Gary perched on a chair arm, next to a girl who was listening intently.

"My mother and I were at my Nan's house sorting out her things after she died two years ago," Trixie was telling them. "You know my Nana's house, don't you, Sylvia?"

Sylvia nodded. "Oh yes, it was big and old and very spooky," she said. "I always expected Dracula to step out from behind a curtain and kiss my hand."

"So, I was upstairs with my mother, sorting through all these old clothes," Trixie went on. "She was in one room and I was in another. There must have been ten bedrooms in that place, most of them rotten to the core. I was thirsty and thought I'd go down to the kitchen to get a drink. When I came out onto the landing, I just caught a glimpse of what I thought was my mother taking the old servant's stairs to the kitchen. I followed

33

her down, but when I walked into the kitchen, she wasn't there. I was like 'what?' how could she have disappeared so quickly? I called out for her…" Trixie paused for dramatic effect and looked around at the expectant faces. "…and my mother answered… *from upstairs.*"

"Oh my God," the girl next to Gary gasped. "There was no one else in the house?"

"Nope, just the two of us." Trixie raised a hand to her chest. "Well, I got such a chill. I went back upstairs and there was my mother, still in the other room sorting through my Nan's clothes."

"So, who had you followed downstairs?"

"Well, that's just it. I don't know who it was."

"Do you think it was your Nana?" someone asked.

"Well, that's what's strange. I don't think it was my Nana. The woman I followed was too young."

"I bet it was someone who used to work there," Sylvia said. "Like a maid or someone who died there. You didn't even sense her presence or anything, did you?" She looked at Gary. "Who do you think it was?"

Gary took a swig of lager, held up his hand and shook his head as he swallowed it.

Sylvia laughed. "Gary doesn't believe in ghosts. Do you, Gary?"

"Well, with all due respect to Trixie, let's just say I've been around for a while and I've never seen a ghost or anything remotely like it."

Trixie smiled. "Perhaps a spirit has never appeared to you because they're looking for someone a little more *open-minded?*"

Gary smiled back. "You cut me, Trixie. You cut me deep."

"If it wasn't a ghost, then what was it?" Sylvia asked.

"Oh, I don't know. Maybe the product of an overactive imagination?"

There were some oohs and a few people laughed.

"There are more things in heaven and earth, Horatio, than are dreamt of in your philosophy," Trixie said, smiling sweetly.

"Touché," he said and raised the bottle to her. "I love it when you talk Shakespeare to me. You love me really though, don't you, Trix?"

"I do love you, Gary, but sometimes you infuriate me with your lack of imagination and spirituality."

"Well, I'm sorry to infuriate you, but even with a *vivid* imagination, I would still put ghosts and ghoulies in the nonsense box, along with the Easter Bunny and Santa Claus."

Sylvia gave him a dig in the ribs and nodded at a couple of young children over in the corner.

Gary made an 'oops' face, but the kids hadn't heard him.

"Nonsense box?" Trixie said, arching an eyebrow.

Gary shrugged.

"And spirituality?" she asked.

Gary raised the bottle to his lips, pausing a second to consider. "Same thing," he said and took another swig.

Trixie wrinkled her nose. "You're so ignorant, Gary. You're saying *spirituality* is nonsense?"

Gary took a second to swallow his drink before deciding he'd better backtrack a little. "Okay, let's just say that spirituality is there for people who need something to believe in."

"Need?"

"Yeah, some people just need to believe in something beyond the world we can see and feel, something bigger than we are." He shrugged. "I just don't happen to need that."

Trixie regarded him as he tipped the last of his beer. "That is just so patronising," she said.

"What?" Gary asked, genuinely confused.

"You don't believe in God; you don't believe in the afterlife. What do you believe in?"

"I believe in sleeping," Gary replied. He looked at the girl next to him. "Bruce Lee said that."

Trixie sighed and crossed her arms.

"Trix, you already know I don't believe in the big man in the sky, and as we know from previous experience, talking about it can get heated, so let's just not, huh?"

Little pink blushes rose into Trixie's cheeks. She glanced around at the others and made a dismissive gesture. "Whatever you say, Gary."

An awkward silence followed that everyone seemed to feel except Gary.

He abandoned the empty bottle on the table and decided it was time for something a little stronger. He excused himself, oblivious of the daggers in Trixie's eyes, and headed for the study.

He felt good. Loose. The party was going well, he hadn't had a run in with Frank, and Charley was over the moon with Mister Whiskers. Fiona certainly had come up trumps with that one. The smile it had brought to Charley's face made him forget all the reservations he had about having a pet mooching around the house.

He opened the second drawer of his desk and fished out a silver hip flask filled with Old Pulteney twenty-one-year-old single malt. He poured a generous measure into a shot glass and took a hit from the flask. The whisky slipped easily down his throat and he savoured its malty flavour. He thought about taking the flask with him, then changed his mind. The whisky might go down a little too smoothly if he took it with him.

He went outside into the garden and sat on the low curving-wall that encircled the patio, sipping his drink and watching the kids leap around the bouncy castle. Their energy seemed to know no bounds. A mother held her toddler's hand while he did little more than flex his knees on a corner of the castle.

As Gary smiled at the toddler, Trixie sauntered over and sat next to him, pressing down the layers of petticoats that puffed up her dress. Gary glanced at her, but she gazed off across the

36

garden.

After a little while, she said, "I know you think all the stuff I believe in is 'nonsense', but you don't have to try and make me look like a dick in front of people."

Gary looked at her and this time she looked back at him, her mouth straight and tight. "I definitely wasn't trying to make you look a dick," he assured her.

She turned back to the garden. "Well you did."

Gary liked Trixie a lot. She was attractive, intelligent, and could carry a good conversation, but he drew the line at all the supernatural guff. Besides, he thought she did a pretty good job of making herself look foolish by harping on about spirits and auras and the rest of it.

"I'm sorry if I made you feel that way," he said. "I really didn't mean to."

"You know, you're the big successful businessman," Trixie went on. "People look up to you. They listen to you and want to know what you think." She cocked her head and gave a sly half-smile that was incredibly patronising and yet deliciously alluring at the same time. "Doesn't mean you're always right though."

Gary smiled and nodded, conceding the cutting remark, though he couldn't help thinking he hadn't got where he was by being wrong.

"Look, I'm sorry, Trix. I'll try harder next time."

Trixie smiled. "No you won't, because sometimes you just can't help *being* a dick."

Gary laughed and when she leaned against his shoulder he plonked a rough kiss on the top of her head through a mop of wild and fragrant hair.

"Yeah, yeah," she sighed, and the two of them watched the kids on the bouncy castle for a while.

"You have a gold aura," Trixie told him. "Yellow and gold. Did you know that?"

"I don't think so?" She'd talked of auras before, but never directly about his. "Is that good?"

Trixie sat up straight. "Very. People with gold auras often have a soul or a spirit watching over and taking care of them."

Gary raised his whisky. "They sure do."

Trixie smiled, but looked off somewhere.

"I'm sorry," Gary said. "What else?"

She turned back to him. "Enlightened, calm, transcendent even."

"Transcendent?" Gary said, impressed.

"Logical and intelligent. Successful in careers. They tend to lead something of a charmed life."

"A charmed life?" Gary asked. "Or how about they just work really hard to get where they are."

"Maybe," Trixie allowed. "But a lot of people work hard and never get anywhere near where you are in life."

Gary thought about his father. No matter what his father had tried, his life had never seemed to fire on all cylinders. Having said that, a lot of it was his own doing.

Trixie pressed her hands on the wall and leaned forward, ready to get up. "Just don't take it all for granted, Gary," she warned. "God giveth, and he can take it away too."

She pushed herself to her feet, dusted her palms, and set off back toward the house.

"'Giveth'? Really? Is that still a thing?"

Trixie tossed a smiling glance over her shoulder and kept on walking.

As the party wound down, people slowly started saying their good-byes, until only a handful of hardcore family and friends remained. They gathered on the patio as the night drew in, and the air turned from chilly to downright cold. Ladies donned

38

cardigans and shawls, and Gary turned on the tall patio heaters. A few people gave up the alcohol in favour of tea or coffee.

The news of the missing girls had got around and the conversation inevitably turned to that. Gary didn't like talking about it. He felt it was too sombre a topic for Charley's birthday party, but after listening to people air their fears, he couldn't resist joining in. "To be honest though, don't you think this kind of thing gets a bit sensationalised?"

Fiona's father looked aghast. "Sensationalised? There's nothing sensational about these young girls disappearing."

"No, no," Gary said. "I mean the media. They love a good scare: *The Goldilocks Kidnapper*." He hunched his shoulders and wriggled his fingers menacingly as he said it. "I mean, just look at us now, all wide-eyed and afraid for our children."

"As we should be," Frank asserted. "You have to protect your own. You have to take precautions."

"And how do you do that? Wrap our children up in cotton wool and hide them in the attic?"

"Don't be ridiculous."

"Anyway, the question shouldn't be 'how do you protect your family from something like this'? It should be, do we really need to?"

"What on earth are you talking about?" Frank asked, with growing heat in his voice. "Do you want us to deliver our kids right into the hands of these sick paedophiles?"

"Of course not. What I'm saying is, perhaps these stories make us more afraid than we really need to be. People get scared and overreact, then they start smothering the very thing they're trying to protect."

Frank made a dismissive gesture. "I have no idea what you're talking about."

Gary sat up a little. "Bad luck floats around and it has to land on someone, someone who happens to be in the wrong place at the wrong time." They all looked at him as if he were mad.

"You have to put things like this into perspective. The fact is, terrible things like this happen to a very small percentage of people."

"I'm sure the people it happens to don't feel like a small percentage," Frank interrupted, looking to the others for someone to back him up.

"Frank, I'm not trying to make light of anything here, I'm just trying to put a little perspective on it. Of course, it's a terrible thing for the people it happens to. I can't even begin to imagine what the families of those girls are going through right now. What I mean is...well, let me try to illustrate. We went on holiday to Turkey a few years ago. They do a lot of paragliding there from—Fee, what's that mountain called—Baba-something?"

"Babadağ."

"That's the one. They take off from up there, about six and a half thousand feet. We could see them in the sky above our hotel from early in the morning until dark. Hundreds of flights a day. For eighty euros you could fly tandem with a pilot. I'd seen the photos and the videos at the different vendors along the front and I really fancied a go, but at first, I didn't."

"Why not?" Trixie asked.

"Because I was afraid. What if it went wrong? What if the chute fails? What if a freak gust of wind blows us into the mountain?"

"I don't blame you," Lance concurred, munching on peanuts from the bowl on his lap. "Any of those things could have happened. You wouldn't get me up there."

"Yes. They *could* happen, but a few days into the holiday it dawned on me: I was seeing all these people flying up there, every day, *without incident*. So, I Googled it. The year before, there had been sixty-two thousand flights from that mountain. *Sixty-two thousand*. Out of all those flights, you know how many people died? One. Just one pilot who flew on a day with less than ideal weather conditions and was blown into the mountainside by a gust of wind."

"A few people were injured though," Fiona added. "It even happened while we were there. Not necessarily the pilots either. The flights come down on the beach front and sometimes people don't get out of the way in time."

"Yeah, there were some injuries, but hey, sixty-two thousand to one are pretty good odds in my book."

"So, what are you saying?" Frank asked impatiently. "Get to the point."

"The point is, Frank, that the actual chances of me dying were very slim, so I did it."

"You went *paragliding*?" Trixie said.

"Yeah, he did," Fiona laughed. "Shocked me too. Didn't we show you the photos?"

"No," Trixie said. She looked Gary up and down. "Not as wussy as you look then, Mr. Wright."

Gary wrinkled his nose at her. "The photos are on the Mac, Fee," he said. "And there's some GoPro video on there too. If you ever get the chance, you should do it because it's an amazing experience; but the parallel I'm drawing here is that the odds of *your* child being kidnapped are even slimmer than dying in a paragliding accident. But the media and the internet bring these things up so close and personal that we can almost taste them. We begin to think this is right on our doorstep, and it's just not true."

"I see what you're saying," Lisa said. "But this more or less *is* right on our doorstep. I'll be keeping Liz real close until this sicko is caught."

"It's close. I'll give you that. But it's not here in Gableton. And what if he's never caught? Jack the Ripper was never caught. What are you going to do, keep her close until she's old enough to leave home? Fact is, millions of kids went out yesterday, and millions came back home again."

41

"And there are three young lasses who didn't," Frank put in. He turned to Fiona. "What do you think about this cavalier attitude?"

Fiona gave Gary a sideways glance and considered her answer. "Well, what Gary says makes a lot of sense. You can't live in fear all your life. If it's not this, it'll be something else. You'd have to cut yourself off from everything."

Frank shook his head. "That's all well and good, but it doesn't mean we just let our kids go out there and hope for the best."

"But that's just it," Gary stressed. "Everyone is worried now that *their* child is going to be kidnapped. They're going to keep them close, they're going to think twice about letting them go anywhere on their own, when *statistically* they're more likely to get knocked down by a car on the way to school, than being kidnapped. But we don't all wring our hands about that every day, do we?"

"I *always* worry about Liz when she isn't home," Lisa said.

"All I'm saying is: we should just be sensible and not overreact to this."

Trixie shivered and rubbed her arms. "I thought this was a party," she said. "Let's talk about something else."

"Yeah," Lance agreed. "I don't know about the rest of you, but I wanna see this paragliding video."

Once the slideshow was running, Fiona sat by Gary and took his hand. He squeezed it and smiled at her. She smiled back, but her lips were tight, as if something was bothering her.

As usual, Lance was last to leave at around eleven. Gary turned off the patio lights and found Fiona in the kitchen collecting discarded cans and dropping them into a black refuse bag.

"What are you doing?" he asked.

"Just tidying up a bit. Such a mess."

He took a can out of her hand and the bag out of the other. "We can do this tomorrow," he said, putting them to one side. "Let's go to bed."

"Well..." Fiona said, looking around the messy kitchen.

"Never mind, 'well'," Gary insisted.

"Okay, in the morning then, but no shirking."

"Me? A Shirker?"

Fiona just smiled. "It turned out good, huh?"

"Yeah, I think it did."

They climbed the stairs together. Fiona went into the bedroom and when Gary turned off the light, he noticed a strip of white under Charley's door.

He opened it quietly—in case she was already asleep—but there she was, knelt on the bed, playing with Mister Whiskers.

Gary plonked his hands on his hips. "What on earth are you doing still awake?"

"Mister Whiskers wants to play," she giggled.

"I imagine kittens always want to play," Gary told her. "Come on, time to settle down."

"Aw," Charley moaned, but she gathered the kitten into her arms and slid under the covers.

"Shouldn't Mister Whiskers go in his own bed?" Gary asked, nodding to the plush pet bed they had bought for the cat.

"Mister Whiskers wants to sleep with me. He's too scared to sleep on his own tonight."

Gary smiled. "Okay, just for tonight, but he needs to get used to sleeping in his own bed."

Charley nodded, but Gary felt fairly certain that the bed was going to stay looking like it had just come out of the cellophane.

He slid a copy of Sleeping Beauty from the shelf, leaning the book at an angle so Charley could see it. "Bedtime story?"

She rolled her eyes. "I'm twelve, Dad."

Gary replaced the book. "I know," he laughed. "Just teasing." But he felt a tiny pang in his heart just the same.

43

He pulled the quilt up over both of them and sat on the bed. Mister Whiskers seemed content to stay there.

"Did you have a good birthday?" he asked.

"It was the BEST!" Charley said. "Will I be able to go on the bouncy castle tomorrow?"

"I don't think so, kiddo. They're coming to pick it up in the morning. They probably have to take it to another party."

Charley made a face.

"You won't have time anyway. You have all your presents and cards to open."

"I opened all the cards already," she said. "I got a ton of money!"

"Yeah? Did you count it?"

"Yep! Four hundred and twenty-five pounds!"

Gary drew back dramatically. "No way!"

Charley nodded, her smile beaming.

"Four hundred and twenty-five pounds? You have more money than I have!"

Charley laughed. "Yeah right."

"What are you going to spend it on?"

Charley smiled mischievously. "Um, there might be something I want to get."

"Well, it's your money to save for a rainy day or to buy something you really, really want with it."

She nodded.

"Okay, time to get to sleep. Lots to do tomorrow."

When he leaned down to kiss her forehead, Charley wrapped her arms around his neck and kissed his stubbly cheek. "Thanks for Mister Whiskers, Dad. I love you."

"Love you too, Sweet Pea."

He stood in the doorway, holding the handle and said, "Night, night."

Charley said, "Sleep tight."

"Mind the bed bugs don't..."

44

"BITE!"

They both laughed, the old bedtime routine never failing to amuse either of them.

Fiona was already in her nightclothes and brushing her teeth when Gary came in and quietly closed the door. He stripped down to his boxers and slipped into bed. When Fiona was finished, she came in, but sat on the edge of the bed, looking gravely at Gary.

"What?" he asked.

"I know what you said tonight about the odds of something bad happening—and you're probably right—but we *are* going to take some precautions, aren't we, while all this is going on?"

Gary sighed, "Of course we are. I might be a smart arse, but I'm not a complete idiot."

Fiona looked relieved and slid under the covers. "It's frightening to think there's someone like that out there right now."

"Try not to think about it," he said and turned off his bedside lamp.

"I do though. I always feel uneasy these days when Charley isn't with one of us."

Gary plumped up his pillow and eased into it. "Well that doesn't happen very often, so I wouldn't worry. I promise you, nothing's going to happen to her, I'll see to that."

Fiona wanted to say to him, *don't say that! How can you be so sure?* She wasn't superstitious, but she didn't tempt fate either. Gary would laugh at her for such a thought. But that was Gary, always in control, always knowing what to do and how to do it. He was probably right. The abductions had taken place miles away, in other towns, other communities. The other three girls were blonde and curly, while Charley's hair was straight and mousey brown.

She looked at him in the darkness. His eyes were closed, his hands curled and crossed at the wrists in front of his chest. She

45

trusted him, and she loved him. Taking one of his curled hands in hers, she gently kissed it. He opened his eyes briefly and smiled at her.

"Night," he murmured.

Fiona turned off her bedside lamp, and it wasn't long before Gary's breathing settled into a steady rhythm. For a while, she watched the shadow of a moth dancing in the streetlight as it bumped endlessly against the glass, and wondered why it couldn't just move on.

Chapter Four

Gary rose at his usual 7am on Sunday morning. He and Fiona cleared up all the party mess and he ploughed through an hour's work before the clean-up crew arrived at eleven. He called the bouncy castle company and negotiated a discount with them, after finding that the website advertised it as Disney Princess themed, when Walt had nothing to do with it.

He went out to speak with each of the teams, exchanging banter and slipping them a few extra quid to ensure a good job was done. Whether it was necessary or not didn't really occur to him. He just believed people performed better with the right kind of incentive.

As the last van drove off, his mobile phone rang. It was Michelle.

"Hey, Michelle, what's up?"

"Hi Gary, sorry, it's Nigel. Sorry to call you on a Sunday morning, but Michelle insisted I should."

Gary held the phone close to his ear and turned toward the house. "Nigel? Is everything alright?"

"Well, no it isn't, I'm afraid. Michelle had…a miscarriage last night...she...we've lost the baby."

Gary closed his eyes, recalling how radiant she had looked the day before, how pleased they both were. "Oh no. Is she okay?"

"Physically, yes, but it's hit her hard, hit both of us."

"Nigel, I'm so sorry. Is there anything I can do?"

"No, but thank you." His voice trembled, little more than a whisper. "You just, well…you just never expect anything like this is going to happen to you, do you?"

"No, you don't. I'm really sorry. I know how much the two of you were looking forward to this baby. Is Michelle home now, or at the hospital?"

"She's still at the hospital. They just want to keep an eye on her for a while, but I think they're going to let her come home later today. Obviously, she won't be coming into work tomorrow."

"Of course not. You make sure she takes all the time she needs."

"She said for you to pop over when she's home and she'll go over her projects."

"She'll do no such thing. Nigel, tell her to forget about work and concentrate on getting herself back to full-strength. I'm aware of most of the stuff she's working on, the rest we can play by ear."

"Thanks, Gary, I really appreciate that. She needs to rest."

After they said their goodbyes, Gary stood with the phone in his hand and watched a crow, high in the sky above the house, gliding on the wind. He sighed. Sometimes it seemed like the good times were simply stand up targets for the bad times to shoot down. He went inside to break the bad news to Fiona.

Now that the house had been scrubbed and tidied back to its usual shiny-self, they carried the remaining presents into the front room and watched while Charley opened them. The gifts ranged from jewellery to clothes to makeup (of which Gary did not approve) to CDs.

Around three, Lance dropped by to pick up his car, but only

48

stayed long enough for Gary to tell him about Michelle.

In the early evening, Gary noticed some whispering and scheming going on between wife and daughter. He'd tried to catch a hint of what they were up to, but they'd been too secretive for him to uncover what it was. He left them to it, taking time out to sit down and relax with a magazine.

Mister Whiskers wandered over and sat at his feet. Gary paid him no attention until he started making little mewing sounds.

Gary peered over at him and frowned. "Hey, Whiskers," he hissed. "Hasn't anyone told you the rules?"

The kitten looked up at him and meowed even more loudly. If he knew about any rules, it appeared he didn't believe they applied to him. Gary lifted him onto his lap. Mister Whiskers snuggled down and closed his eyes, purring contentedly. Gary stroked the soft fur at the nape of his neck and smiled a little.

He pointed his chin toward the kitchen. "What do you suppose those two are up to?" he asked, but Mister Whiskers didn't appear to have an opinion on the subject.

He held the magazine in one hand while he stroked Mister Whiskers with the other.

"Ah-ha!" Fiona cried. "Got you!" She and Charley stood in the doorway, laughing at him. "'And I don't want it bothering me'," Fiona said, mimicking his previous comments in a deep and grumpy voice.

"All right, all right," Gary conceded.

Charley scooped the cat out of Gary's lap and sat down with him. As much as he hated to admit it, he was sorry to see the little fellow go.

"So, what's going on?" he asked. "What's all the whispering about?"

Charley looked at her mother. "You'll see," she said, with a sparkle in her eye.

Chapter Five

Lance came to dinner on the Thursday following the party. He brought more flowers for Fiona and a bottle of red wine. Gary took him through to the front room where Fiona accepted the flowers, told him he shouldn't have, and gave him a hug.

Gary offered drinks.

"Have you heard anything from Michelle?" Lance asked.

"Yeah, Fiona and I went to see her on Tuesday. She looked...fragile...if you know what I mean?"

Lance nodded.

Gary poured Scotch and added water. "She got a bit teary. I'm usually okay in those kinds of situations, but I was glad Fiona was with me."

"It's hard to know what to say, isn't it?"

"It is. I told her to take as long as she needs before coming back. Knowing Michelle that won't be too long." He handed over the drink.

"Lance!"

Lance turned to see Charley and jumped to attention. "Charley Chan!" he cried.

She ran over to him and gave him a tight hug.

"Thanks for my present! It's awesome! Let me show you what I made." And she was off again like a whirling dervish.

Gary shook his head. "I don't know where she gets her energy. I get worn out just watching her. What did you get her?"

"One of those air-drying clay sculpting sets," Lance told him, as they carried their drinks over to the leather chairs and sat down with Fiona.

"Ah, yeah," Gary said. "She loves art. I think she must get it from her mother because, apparently, I'm *creatively challenged*."

Fiona wrinkled her nose at him.

A moment later Charley returned with a colourful piece of sculpture.

"Wow," Lance marvelled. "Can I hold it?"

"Course you can," Charley said, handing it over.

It was a mythical creature, like a dinosaur with two heads on long necks and a curly tail with a hook on the end. The body was green, the wings red.

"Charley," Lance said. "This is amazing."

Charley beamed with pride.

"This must have taken you ages to make."

"It only took me, like, a couple of hours. I painted it the next day after the clay had hardened."

Lance made to hand it back, but she shook her head. "It's for you."

Lance's mouth dropped open. "For me? Are you sure?"

"Yeah, I made it for you."

"Wow! Well you know where this is going to go, don't you?"

"No?"

"Right on my bedside table, so I can see it before I go to sleep at night and first thing in the morning when I wake up. You know why?" Charley shook her head. "Because he makes me feel all giggly inside."

Charley laughed and looked pleased with herself.

"What about your dad? Have you made one for him too?"

Charley pulled a face. "Nah, he wouldn't appreciate it like

51

you do."

Lance looked at Gary and laughed at the indignant expression on his face.

"Why wouldn't I?" Gary asked.

"You don't take proper notice when I show you stuff," she complained. "You're always doing *work*."

"Well, maybe you shouldn't show me stuff when I'm *doing work* then, huh?"

"She can't show you stuff when you're sleeping, Hon," Fiona joked.

"Funny," he said. "This is what it's like, Lance, they gang up on me." He turned back to Charley. "I accept that I can be distracted at times, *but* I would really like it if you made something for me."

Charley grinned. "Okay, what do you want me to make for you then?"

Gary's reply was so swift and specific that Fiona did a double take. "A dragon," he declared. "With a purple body and yellow wings, and I want him breathing a big plume of orange fire."

Charley's grin widened.

"Oh, and yellow eyes, and maybe curly yellow horns on its head, but I'll leave that for you to decide."

Charley's eyes darted about, brimming with excitement at the thought of creating the amazing creature Gary had described for her. "I'm gonna start it right now!" she cried and sped off, all heels and elbows.

"Dinner in half an hour," Fiona called after her.

Gary watched her go. When he turned to the others, Fiona was looking at him with a puzzled little frown on her face.

"What?" Gary asked.

"Since when did you get such a vivid imagination?"

"See?" Gary said. "You think you know everything about me, but you don't. I can be creative and imaginative when I want to be."

52

Lance was looking at him with much less wonder. "You just described *Spyro the Dragon*, didn't you?"

Gary sighed, "Yeah."

"Spyro the Dragon?" Fiona asked.

"An old video game character," Lance told her.

"You *cheat*!" Fiona laughed and threw a cushion at Gary.

Just before dinner, Gary noticed more conniving going on between mother and daughter and decided something was definitely afoot. As they took their seats at the table, Charley produced a small box, exquisitely wrapped in gold paper and tied with curly red ribbon. Smiling ear-to-ear, she placed the box on Gary's tablemat.

"What's this?" he asked, looking from daughter to wife.

"I got you a present," Charley said.

"A present? Is it my birthday?"

Charley shook her head.

Gary narrowed his eyes. "It isn't *Christma,s* is it?"

Charley pulled a face. "How could it be Christmas?"

"Well, I dunno," Gary said. "But birthdays and Christmas are the only times I ever get presents." He slapped his forehead and pointed at her. "It's Father's Day!"

"Father's Day is in June," Fiona said.

"So how come I have this wonderful looking and completely unexpected present for absolutely no reason what-so-ever?"

"Because Charley wanted to get it for you," Fiona told him.

"Who's a lucky guy then, eh?" Lance said.

"Open it!" Charley cried, bouncing impatiently on her chair.

Gary picked up the gift, putting it near his ear and shaking it. "Is it a puppy?"

Charley giggled, and Fiona told him to stop messing around and just open it.

Gary pulled the ends of the ribbon and stripped away the wrapping paper to reveal an elegant black box. As soon as he saw *Mont Blanc* printed on the top he knew what it was. He looked at Fiona who just smiled at his expression.

He opened the lid, and there was the pen he'd been coveting; a *Montblanc Noblesse Oblige* ballpoint pen, finished in marblesque-green. The last time he'd looked at it on Amazon, the price had been almost two hundred pounds.

He looked at Fiona again. "Have you bought this?"

Fiona shook her head and nodded at Charley.

"I got it for you out of my birthday money," Charley said.

Gary let out a small gasp of surprise. "You shouldn't have spent your birthday money on me, Charley."

"Why shouldn't I?"

"Because, well…it's your money."

"You said I should spend it on something I really, really wanted. Well, I really, really wanted to get that for you."

Gary had to look away from her bright, smiling face while he swallowed back a swell of emotion. He took a deep breath and closely examined the pen with more scrutiny than seemed necessary. "Wow. I don't know what to say," he admitted, his eyes all sparkly.

"Well, there's a first," Fiona laughed.

"Do you like it?" Charley asked.

"Do I like it?" He held out his arms. "Come here you."

Gary hugged her tightly and kissed her cheek. "Thank you, Sweet Pea," he said. "You've been very generous - too generous. I'll treasure this forever."

He closed the box and looked around the table, a slight tremble still on his lips.

Fiona saved him. "Right," she said. "After that nice surprise, it's time to eat." She handed the wine to Lance. "Would you do the honours?"

Gary made to get up, but Fiona stopped him. "No, no. You

keep our guest company. Charley and I have this, don't we, Hon?"

Lance went to work on the seal and Fiona went to get the starter, with Charley in tow. Gary looked at the box and still couldn't believe Charley had spent almost half of her birthday money on him.

Lance gave him a sideways glance as he stripped the foil from the cork. "A very special couple of ladies you have there, Gary."

"Yep," Gary agreed, carefully placing the pen box next to his cutlery, moving it minutely with the tip of his finger to bring it parallel with the knife. "I'll give her the money back though. I don't want her spending her birthday money on me."

Lance eyed him carefully. "I wouldn't. Seemed like she really wanted to do that for you. Seemed important to her."

"I know, but..."

"But nothing. I say leave it. She did something generous for you, let her keep it."

Gary nodded and touched the box with his fingers.

When dinner was over, Lance regaled Fiona with a story about a meeting they'd had that day with a client who was less than satisfied with the service he was receiving.

"I have to admit," Lance said. "I was worried. I mean, we have client meetings all the time, but this is one of our biggest and it seemed, even to me, they had some valid grievances. So, the meeting starts, and they come in with both barrels. I'm like, oh no, this is every bit as bad as I thought it was going to be. Then, while I'm trying to think of a way to salvage the situation, Gary starts talking." Lance reclined in his chair. "And Fiona, it was incredible. I still don't really know what happened. It was like he performed the Jedi mind trick."

Gary laughed, "They don't call me Obi-Wan for nothing."

"It was like…" Lance made a sweeping gesture with his hand. "These aren't the droids you're looking for. There's no problem here. Move along."

They all laughed.

"He took the situation, and not only did he turn it around, but before he'd finished *they* were apologising to *us,* and giving us *more* business. I was like, how the hell did he just do that?"

Fiona looked at Gary with more than a little admiration. "Our Gary can be quite persuasive when he wants to be."

"It was fine," Gary said, dismissively. "They were never going to pull out - they just needed a little massaging, a little T.L.C."

"I don't know," Lance mused. "It was pretty impressive."

"It's just simple psychology. Know your enemy as you know yourself."

"The clients are your enemies?" Charley asked.

"Not quite, but if you know something about them, it makes them easier to deal with." He grinned at Lance. "You didn't think all those business lunches were just jollies, did you?"

Lance chuckled. "Well, I did wonder at times. Do you ever just relax?"

Gary held up his wine glass. "I'm relaxing right now, my friend."

"I'll drink to that," Lance concurred, clinking his glass to Gary's.

"Did he ever tell you about what happened when I went into labour with Charley?" Fiona asked.

Gary rolled his eyes and sat up. "Not relaxing anymore."

"I'm not sure," Lance replied. "Which part?"

"When I called to tell him that I'd gone into labour?"

Lance laughed. "Oh, *that* part? Yeah I was right there when you called."

Fiona made a telephone with her thumb and little finger. "Gary, it's started." She deepened her voice, "Oh, I'm in the middle of something right now, Fee. Can you hang on for an

56

hour?"

"Is that supposed to be me?" Gary asked.

"I told him straight - you'd better have your ass over here in ten minutes!"

"It was a joke," Gary said, trying to laugh it off.

"Yeah, right."

"You should have seen the colour drain out of his face," Lance said.

"I'll bet it did." Fiona went to close the curtains across the patio doors. It had gotten dark outside while they had been eating and chatting.

Lance continued with his side of the story. "I asked him who had called, and he said, 'It was Fee, I think the baby's coming. I'd better go'. He had this proper sheepish look on his face."

"No I didn't," Gary laughed.

"Yeah you did. I remember thinking at the time: 'Ah, now we know who wears the trousers in that house'."

Fiona stuck out her bottom and wiggled it in her tight trousers as she closed the curtains. "Me-e-e-e," she sang.

Gary and Lance laughed, and Charley cried, "*Mum*!"

Beyond the spill of the dining room lights, the man the media called the Goldilocks Kidnapper watched the woman close the curtains. He was standing out on the lawn, but she wouldn't see him from the brightly lit room into the dark night, so he didn't attempt to hide. She probably wouldn't have seen him even if he had been in the light. She was too busy wiggling her ass at the men and acting like a slut.

Once the curtains were drawn, there was nothing more to see, yet still he stood there on the damp grass, watching the shadows move behind the curtains and wondering what they were doing now. It fascinated him to observe *family*.

Seeing her hug the tall guy had disturbed him. He hated to see her being affectionate with other people, especially men. He didn't even like to see her embrace her father. All that *touching*. There was only one place where that would lead.

He stayed for a while longer, just staring at the back of the house until he noticed her bedroom light turn on. He tried to imagine her room, her bed, and the secret things she kept in secret places. When the bedroom light finally went out, and he was sure there was nothing more to be seen, he faded back into the shadows and was gone.

Lance followed Gary into his study and made straight for the desk. He ran his hand over the deep green leather top. "Oh, I'm so envious of this desk!"

Gary grinned. "You say that every time you come in here. It is a beauty though, isn't it?"

Gary had picked up the antique mahogany William IV desk online, about three years ago and had it restored. The panels were finished in beautifully figured flame mahogany; the drawer linings solid oak with gleaming brass locks and escutcheons. The writing leather was a single luxurious sheet of leather with gilt and blind tooling around the edges.

"What did you pay for this? Three thousand?"

"Two and a bit, but the restoration took it to three."

Lance sank into the leather captain's chair and admired the expanse of desk before him. "Man, you feel like a king behind this thing."

"Fiona says I'd live in here if she'd let me," Gary chuckled.

Lance picked up a photo of Charley and looked at it briefly before putting it down again. He hauled himself out of the chair and sauntered around the room, admiring the oak panelling and full bookshelves. He ran a finger along tomes covering business, self-motivation, biographies, psychology, and history. When he turned around again, Gary had sat behind the desk, studying his laptop screen.

"What are you doing?"

"Just checking emails."

"Work emails?"

Gary looked sheepish and grinned. "Yeah."

"You never stop thinking about work, do you? I mean, I'm a bit of a workaholic myself, but you are just insane."

"Have to keep your eye on the ball," Gary advised, distracted by something he was reading.

"What drives you?" Lance asked.

Gary looked up from the screen. "Drives me?"

"Yeah, the way you work sometimes...well, you know, it's like your life depends on it or something."

Gary leaned back in the chair, the leather creaking comfortably. "I've told you about my father, haven't I?"

Lance leaned against the bookshelf and folded his arms. "You told me how he used to move you around a lot, and how money was tight when you were growing up."

Gary let out a little laugh. "Did I tell you why we moved around so much?"

Lance shook his head.

"My dad was a decent enough man, but he was a bit of a fly-by-night. He couldn't hold down a job and he liked a drink. He was never violent or abusive or anything like that, but he was a hard man to live with. He was that guy you see sat on his own at the end of the bar, a beer in one hand and a whisky chaser in the other. He looks fine until you speak to him and then he gazes at you with that thousand-yard stare and you realise the lights are on but there's no one home.

"I remember my mum waking me in the middle of the night—more than once—wrapping me in a blanket and carrying me out, as we did a moonlight flit to avoid the rent and the bills he owed. Sometimes he had a hostel, or something else lined up, other times we just slept in the car. When there wasn't a car it was a bus shelter."

Lance pushed off the shelving and dug his hands in his pockets. "Wow, I didn't know that."

Gary shrugged. "It's not something I like to talk about, but since you asked. My mother did what she could, but we were living off the radar. I'd never known any other way, so I just assumed it was how everyone lived. When I was old enough to understand, I hated it, and I held it against my dad that he'd never been able to sort himself out and support us. I never wanted to put my family in that position."

"Well, you have no worries in that respect," Lance said. "You're pretty far from having to do a moonlight flit."

Gary shrugged. "Who knows? We're all walking a knife-edge, Lance. Even the most successful people manage to lose grip on their business and have to watch it crumble. You never know what's around the corner. I just have to make sure we're safe."

"So, what you're saying is your success is driven by your fear of failure?"

Gary gave an amused snort. He could always rely on Lance to strip things down to their essentials.

"I can understand it," Lance said. "But you need to watch that you don't miss out on things, you know?"

"What do you mean?"

"Money's one thing, but your family? Charley's growing up so fast. If you're not careful, you'll look up from that screen one day and she'll be a young woman."

Gary shifted in the chair a little. "I'm not that bad, am I?"

"I'm exaggerating a bit for effect," Lance said with a grin. "You have a fantastic relationship with Charley, better than I ever did with my dad, but since the new business took off, you're working longer hours. And even when you're not working, it's still on your mind."

Gary gave up the pretence. "I know, I know. You're right. It's like some sort of OCD thing. It gets a hold of me and I find it hard to put it to one side. I feel like if I take my eye off the ball something bad will happen; like the sky will fall or something." He laughed, but there was a steely edge to it.

"But it won't," Lance said, eyeing him carefully.

"I know," Gary said. "*I* know..." He tapped his temple. "But something up here doesn't."

He swivelled the chair to look out of the window. A few stars winked from a bed of deep blue.

"I remember one particular Christmas. I would have been five or six. Christmas was kept low-key with the lack of money and all that, but mum always used to try and do something for me. I usually had at least one present to open; a cheap plastic toy or a Dinky car, but this one year there was only a stocking with an orange, a bruised apple, and a chocolate Father Christmas." He glanced back at Lance. "You know, one of the chocolate ones you hang on the tree? I remember the foil top with the loop was missing and Santa's chocolate hat was showing through. Mum must have pulled it off a Christmas tree somewhere, so I could at least have *something* Christmassy. So, there it was. Christmas morning with no trimmings and no presents. The apartment was dark and cold, and mum was crying. I have no idea where my dad was."

Lance blew a little air between his lips. "That must have been hard. Your mum passed away...how long ago now?"

"Ten years."

"And your dad?"

"Haven't seen him since the funeral. He could be dead for all I know." He rolled the chair away from the window. "Look, fuck this, Lance." He opened the second of the desk drawers, took out the bottle of Old Pulteney and two shot glasses. "You wanna drink of the good stuff?"

Lance said he did.

61

Chapter Six

A few weeks later, Gary spent three days in London, meeting with prospective new clients. He had shaken hands with one, but the other was playing hardball and he'd come away without a deal.

The slip bothered him. He wasn't used to being unsuccessful in striking a deal.

After he'd eaten, he retired to his hotel room and called Fiona.

The phone only rang once before Charley answered. "Dad?"

"Hey, Sweet Pea! What you been up to?"

"Um, school and stuff," Charley said.

"That doesn't sound very exciting."

"I worked on your dragon!"

"You did? It's about time."

Though Charley had started the sculpture on the night Lance had come for dinner, the project had stalled. Gary had teased her about it from time to time, saying she loved Lance more than she loved him, and asking to see the progress. But Charley had refused to let him see it until it was done.

"Is it finished?"

"Um, nearly. It's got a ton of scales. They took ages."

"I can't wait to see it."

"You will...soon."

"How's Mister Whiskers?"

"Ew," Charley said. "He brought a dead bird in today!"

Gary laughed. "What did you do with it?"

"Mum swept it onto the shovel and dumped it outside in the bin. It was so gross, Dad, all its guts were hanging out and everything. Mum put the shovel in a bucket of bleach."

Gary laughed, that was so Fiona.

"Are you coming home tomorrow?"

"Yep."

"Yes!" Charley said. "Mum wants to talk to you. See you tomorrow. Love you, Dad."

"Love you too, Sweet Pea."

"Hey you," Fiona said. Gary could almost see that crooked smile.

"Hey."

"Don't say anything about the bird," she warned.

"Not even, 'I told you so'?"

"Especially not that."

"Is everything okay over there?"

"Everything's fine," she told him. "I've missed you."

"I've missed you too."

"I'm just looking forward to you coming home tomorrow."

"So am I." But there was something in her voice. "Are you sure everything's okay?"

Fiona was quiet for a moment. "Well, I saw Trixie today."

"Yeah?" Gary switched the phone to the other ear. "Is she okay?"

"Well, she was a bit strange."

"Strange?" He hadn't told Fiona about their little tiff at the party. Trixie had seemed okay by the end of the night, but maybe she was still ticked off and was being cool with Fiona too? That wasn't like Trixie, but there's *nowt as fickle as folk*, as his mum used to say.

"Yeah," Fiona continued. "She said...were you talking to her about auras or something the other day?"

63

"Yeah, at the party, she said I had a gold aura which apparently means I have a charmed life. I didn't really take her seriously. Was she annoyed at what I said?"

"No, she just told me to be *careful*."

"Careful? Careful about what?"

"I don't know. She couldn't be specific. She just said she had a feeling something wasn't right."

"Not right? Well that's helpful."

"I know but..."

"Fee, I know she's our friend and all that, but she's as nutty as a fruit cake, you know that, don't you?"

"She's a bit eccentric, but she's a good friend. It bothered me a little, especially with everything that's going on. She's never said anything like that to me before."

Gary sighed. "Look, Fee, you can't take these people seriously."

"These people?"

"You know what I mean: spiritualists, mediums and all that crap. It's all a load of rubbish. And I'm a bit annoyed that she'd say something like that to you and get you all wound up, especially when I'm away. Did she know I'm away?"

"I think so. I'm not wound up though. It just seemed odd, that's all. I know what you think of Trixie's beliefs, but she's had perceptions before that came true."

"Like what?"

"Like when she knew Laura was expecting even before *she* did. And she predicted it would be a boy."

"Well I guess the odds of getting that one right are pretty slim."

"Don't be smart. What about her knowing she was pregnant then?"

"I don't know. Maybe she has a nose for these things; saw the rosy glow in her cheeks or something."

"Hmm," Fiona said, not sounding convinced.

"Fee, seriously, why are you even giving this the time of day? How is it these 'mediums' are only ever able to give generalisations instead of zeroing in on things? How come they can't just tell you to be careful when you're driving home tonight because your late great Aunt Petunia has come through warning that you're going to have an accident?' Now that would be pretty useful, don't you think?"

"Except I don't have a Great Aunt Petunia," Fiona said. Gary hoped she was wearing that smirk when she said it, but it didn't sound like she did.

"You know what I mean."

"It's no big deal," she said, dismissively. "So how was your day? Did you get everything done?"

Gary frowned at Fiona's sidestep, but went with it. "Yeah. Yesterday's meeting went well, they're on board. Today's was tougher, but I'm sure they'll come around."

They chatted about nothing in particular for five minutes, then said their goodbyes. Gary reminded her not to worry about what Trixie had said, and Fiona repeated her brush-off.

After the call, he paced the hotel room, getting more and more agitated that Trixie had set Fiona on edge while he was hundreds of miles away. In retrospect, he should probably have had a quiet drink, watched some TV, and turned in.

He called her instead.

She answered after a couple of rings. "Hi Gary, what's up?"

"Hi Trix. It's about Fee."

"Is she okay?"

"Yeah, she's fine. I believe she saw you today."

"Yes, we had a nice chat."

"You said something about her needing to be careful and that you felt something wasn't right."

"Oh, that," Trixie said, sounding sheepish.

"Yeah, that," Gary said. "I think you spooked her a bit, you know? It wouldn't be so bad if I was there, but I'm stuck here in

65

London until tomorrow. So, can you do me a favour? If you get any more *feelings*, any chance you could keep them to yourself?"

He'd tried to keep it light and jokey, and he probably would have succeeded if he'd waited a while, but with his sour mood, it just came over as harsh. The line went quiet for a moment.

"You want me to *not* warn my friend when I feel something is going wrong?" she asked.

"That's just my point though, Trixie, *nothing's going wrong*."

After another pause, she said, "Okay."

Gary switched the phone to his other ear. "Look, I know you mean well, Trixie, but I just don't want Fee worrying when there's nothing to worry about."

The line stayed quiet.

"We aren't going to fall out or anything over this, are we? I think a lot about you, you know that, right?"

"But obviously not enough to take me seriously when I say I feel something's...*off*."

Gary sighed. "Trix, please, let's not go down this road again. I just don't want Fiona worrying while I'm away."

"If you say so," Trixie conceded, but then her voice pitched up with the shrillness of a frightened child: "*It's...it's in the shape of a zigzag,*" she cried.

Gary moved the phone away from his ear and looked at it. He put it back again. "*What*?"

"I said, if you say so, I won't mention it again."

"No, the other thing you said, when you put that weird voice on. Something about a zigzag."

"When I did *what*?"

"You put a weird voice on and said it's in the shape of a zigzag, or something."

"No, I didn't."

"Yes, you did. I just heard you."

"Gary, I don't know what you're talking about."

Gary sighed and switched the phone back to the other ear

66

again. "Okay, Trixie, whatever. I don't have time for silly games."

"I'm not playing silly games, Gary. And I don't have time for this either."

Before he could say anything more, the line disconnected. He gripped the phone so tightly that the plastic creaked, and he almost slung it across the room. He'd always thought Trixie was playing with a few cards short, but weird voices and *zigzags*— what the hell was that about?

He imagined Trixie sitting alone in her front room and speaking into the phone like a little girl.

It's in the shape of a zigzag.

It creeped him out. Why would she say that right in the middle of their conversation? Then deny that she'd even said it at all! Just another weird Trixie thing.

He rubbed his face with his hands. A headache pressed behind his eyes and he never suffered from headaches. He gathered his papers together, closed his Mac, and crawled into bed, deciding he'd watch some TV for an hour, maybe call Fiona again to reassure her—or at least send her a text—then get some sleep. He wanted to catch the early train and get into Gableton for around eleven.

He nodded off while the news re-ran the footage of Hannah's parents asking their daughter to come home.

Please come home.

Chapter Seven

Because he fell asleep watching TV, Gary failed to call reception to set an early morning alarm call, which meant he overslept and missed the train he'd intended to catch. The train he did board was delayed just outside Birmingham, sitting for forty minutes without moving. Better still, the train's Wi-Fi was down, his phone was flat (again), and he couldn't find the charging cable.

He arrived at the office at two-thirty, his mood as sour as a gooseberry. It didn't improve much when Ed rapped on the doorjamb.

"How was the trip?" he asked

Gary was unloading stuff from his bag and setting up his Mac. "It was okay. ArrowLite is in the bag and they seem like a good crew. Crompton's wanted more than I was willing to give, though. I think they'll come around, but I have the feeling we'll need to keep a tight rein on them or they'll try it on. The manager is a young guy, and a bit of a prick. I'll set up a meeting with Lance and Max and we'll start some planning."

"That's good," Ed acknowledged, and loitered in the doorway.

"I don't have a lot of time, Ed. Was there something else?"

Ed stood back at Gary's tone. "It can wait if it's not convenient."

Gary took a breath and shook his head. "I'm sorry, Ed, come in. This day's just gone to shit. What's up?" He found the mains cable for the Mac and plugged it in.

Ed closed the door. "I've been wondering what we're going to do about Michelle."

"Michelle? Don't worry about it. It's all in hand. We're covering her work between us until she comes back."

Ed took a step closer. "That's not really what I'm talking about," he explained. "I'm more talking about her future here."

Gary stopped what he was doing. "I'm not quite following you."

"Well, to be honest, these are concerns I've had for quite a while, but I've kept them to myself."

"Well spit them out now then," Gary said, with a little more impatience than he intended.

"Michelle's a young woman. Recently married. Ready to start a family. Now, this miscarriage has taken her out for who knows how long. No doubt they'll try for another child and it could all happen again. Some women just aren't made to carry a child."

Gary held up his hands. "Whoa, Ed! She's had one miscarriage. It happens to a lot of women having their first baby. I've no doubt that she'll be fine next time."

"Okay, and what if she is fine next time? Where is that going to leave us? She'll want maternity leave. Six months? A year?" He shook his head. "It's just not good business, Gary."

"What decade do you think we're living in, Ed? Women have careers and families all the time. They're *entitled* to take maternity leave. It's the *law*. Michelle will do whatever's necessary to make both things work. Frankly, I'm shocked that you would even come to me with this. She hasn't even recovered yet. It's bad style, Ed. Bad style."

Ed straightened his back. "I only have the best interests of the business at heart. I simply don't believe that young women

69

make good business partners. I've been in this situation before, and it puts a strain on everyone."

"There's nothing to worry about," Gary assured him, booting up the Mac. "We can take the strain, short term. Everything's in hand."

"But I *am* worried. Michelle is a friend of yours. I would *hope* that you wouldn't allow that friendship to cloud your judgement."

Gary gave him a measured look. "Are you questioning my integrity, Ed?"

"No...I'm just saying there's no room for sentimentality in business."

"How about support and loyalty? Is there any room for that?"

"Not if it has an adverse effect on the business."

"Wow. I really had no idea you held such outdated beliefs."

Ed preened a little. "They may not be 'PC' anymore, but they are just as valid now as they always have been."

Gary gave Ed his full attention. "No, Ed, they aren't. What you're saying here is completely *opposite* to what I believe and the philosophy of this company."

"*Philosophy*?" Ed sneered, openly laughing in Gary's face. "We're running a business here, not a monastery. I'm beginning to wonder if you have the best interests of this company at heart, or your friendship with Michelle."

Gary stared at Ed, his heart pumping. "I always have the company's best interests at heart. And I'm not about to stand here and listen to you plot behind Michelle's back."

"We have forty people working here, we have a responsibility to them."

"And we *are* being responsible to them. Michelle has brought a lot of energy to this business and has been instrumental in its success. Her taking a few weeks off isn't going to bring the walls tumbling down."

"But we need someone *consistent* going forwards, Gary," Ed insisted, emphasising the words by thumping his fingertips on the desktop.

Gary looked from Ed's fingers on the desk, to his face. "Michelle *is* consistent," he told him.

"Well I'm sorry but I don't agree, and I say we need to do something about it."

Gary folded his arms. "Are you talking about *ousting,* Ed?"

"There are certain things that can be done," Ed hinted, unable to meet Gary's eye.

"Jesus Christ, Ed. You're a real snake in the grass, aren't you?"

Ed leaned over the desk. "It's *business,* Gary."

"Yeah, *my* business."

"You hold majority shares, yes, but that isn't all there is to it."

"Been looking into that have you?"

"I haven't just fallen into business you know. I've been around the block a couple of times."

"Michelle stays. If you don't like it, you know where the door is."

"If that's how you feel."

"Yes, that's how I feel. Now if you've finished, I have some work to do." He sat down and pulled the laptop closer. His hands were trembling with anger.

Ed loitered for a moment, as if he had more to say, but turned around and opened the door.

"Oh, and Ed?" Gary said.

Ed stopped and looked back at him.

"Don't ever fucking laugh at me again."

Ed eyed him for a moment, then left.

Gary jumped to his feet and stalked around the desk. "Jesus *Christ!*" he seethed.

That had escalated quickly. Using profanity had been

unprofessional, but *Jesus Christ!*

He got out his mobile phone, but the screen was dark, the battery flat. He cursed and pulled the desk phone over to him. He dialled a number and waited for the connection.

"Hello. Sam? It's Gary. Yeah, I'm good. Sam, I need you to look over the partnership agreement for me. Especially conditions for dissolving or ousting another partner. No, no, nothing serious, but I just want to be prepared. Yeah? Okay, give me a call when you know something."

He put the phone down and tried to get back to work but was so aggravated and unsettled that he packed up and went home early instead.

When he pulled through the gate, Fiona's red Audi was already parked on the drive. He glanced at his watch: four-thirty. Fiona's parents collected Charley from school and she spent a couple of hours with them, until Fiona picked her up on the way home from work around five. Why was she home already? An uneasy feeling crept over him and he couldn't help thinking about Trixie's warning. He grabbed his bags and hurried into the house.

"Fee?" he called, as soon as he entered the hall.

"In here."

Her voice came from the kitchen and sounded calm and even; maybe he was worrying about nothing.

She got up from the breakfast bar and came to him.

"You're home early," he told her.

"I could say the same about you," she countered, embracing and kissing him. "I'm glad you're home."

"Is everything okay?"

"I got a call from school. Charley's been in an 'incident' today."

"An *incident*?" Gary glanced around, wondering where she was. "Is she okay?"

"Yeah, she's fine. Here." She handed him an envelope. On

72

the front, it said 'To the Parent/Guardian of Charlotte Wright'

He fished out the letter and unfolded it.

> *Dear Mr. and Mrs. Wright,*
>
> *I regret to inform you that Charlotte was involved in an incident today, in which another pupil received an injury to her nose. As you should be aware, the school keeps a policy of zero tolerance for physical assault. As such, we request a meeting at 10am tomorrow to discuss Charlotte's behaviour.*
>
> *Yours Faithfully*
>
> *Mrs. R.H. Brennan (Head Teacher)*

"Charley's been *fighting*?"

"It's not quite that simple," Fiona said.

"At least tell me she hit someone who hit her first."

"You could say that, but it's really not that simple."

"Not that simple?" He regarded her suspiciously. "Fiona, you aren't trying to cover for her, are you?"

"No. But it might be better if Charley tells you about it herself."

"Where is she?"

"She's upstairs. She's a bit upset."

"I should hope she is." He started toward the door, letter in hand.

"Gary..."

"No, Fiona," he said. "I don't know what's going on, but I've had a shit day, and now I come home to this."

He took the stairs quickly and marched straight into her room. Charley was on the bed with her legs folded under her.

She looked small and miserable. His instinct was to comfort

her, but he waved the letter instead. "So, what's all this about?"

"It wasn't my fault, Dad! Honest!" she blurted.

"Did you hit someone?"

"Yes but-"

"We've talked about this sort of thing, haven't we?"

Charley hung her head. "Yes."

"And what have we said?"

"You don't settle an argument with your fists," she said glumly.

"So explain to me, how did you end up doing something that you *knew* was wrong?"

Charley spoke into her lap. "There's a girl in my class..." she mumbled.

"There's a what?"

She raised her head. "There's a girl in my class called Tammy Pollard," she said, resentment colouring the tone.

"Is this the girl who you hit?"

"No," Charley said, her lip trembling.

"Gary," Fiona said gently, from the doorway behind him. He hadn't realised she'd followed him up.

"What?" he asked, more sharply than he intended.

She ran a smooth hand from the nape of his neck to his shoulder. "Stop interrupting and just let her tell you."

Gary sighed impatiently and leaned against the wall with his arms crossed.

Fiona sat on the end of the bed. "Go on, tell him what happened."

Charley took a breath that turned into a sigh. "There's a girl in my class called Tammy Pollard. She's kinda shy and doesn't speak much to anyone. Well, last night her dad was in the newspaper. He's been sent to jail for credit card fraud or something. When I came into class, someone had stuck the front page of the paper on the chalkboard. It seemed like all the school was laughing and gossiping about it. I felt sorry for her."

74

Gary shifted and glanced at Fiona, but she wasn't looking at him.

"At break time I went looking for her to see if she was all right. She was hiding away in the corner by the chemistry lab. I asked her if she was okay and she just nodded. I told her not to take any notice of what people were saying. I told her they'd soon find something else to talk about. She said, 'yeah, but sometimes things like this follow you around'. That made me think about Celia Young in junior school. She got accused of stealing even though she hadn't done it. People used to call her names and say she couldn't be trusted after that. So I knew it was true, but I told Tammy it would be okay anyway, just 'cause that's what she needed to hear right then."

Gary uncrossed his arms and wasn't sure quite what to do with them for a second. He didn't so much feel himself getting down from his high horse, as being grabbed by the scruff and unceremoniously yanked from it.

"Then Lauren Chapman came over with her cronies."

"Lauren Chapman?" Gary asked.

"She's a horrible bitch in year eight," Charley said.

"Charley," Fiona said, mildly admonishing.

"Well, she is. She's always in trouble, always bullying younger kids. She's been reported loads of times, but the teachers don't do anything about it."

"I'm sure the school is trying to do something, Charley," Fiona said.

"Well they aren't trying hard enough," Charley insisted. "She started calling Tammy names, saying her dad was a thief and a criminal and that he deserved to be in jail; which is a laugh 'cause I know all her brothers have been in trouble for stealing. Then she said someone had stolen her pencil case last week and that it was probably Tammy who took it. Which is obviously stupid 'cause they aren't even in any of the same lessons. Lauren tried to take Tammy's bag, but Tammy wouldn't let her have it. Lauren got real mad and grabbed Tammy with both hands and shoved her up against the wall."

Gary closed his eyes and nodded. Now he understood. "And that's when you stepped in?"

"I don't know how I did it," Charley said. "There were loads of kids watching but no one was going to help her. I was scared, but I couldn't just stand there and let Tammy get bullied. I grabbed Lauren's wrist and told her to leave her alone."

"Brave," Gary said, and Charley half-shrugged.

"Lauren turned on me then. She asked if I was Tammy's *girlfriend* or something. I said I was just her friend, and didn't she have enough to deal with without this? Lauren said, 'What do you care?' and then she said..." Charley paused and glanced shyly up at her father.

"What?" Gary asked, thinking maybe she was going to have to repeat a swear word.

"Then she said, 'I hear your dad's nothing but a dirty paedo.'"

Gary's back stiffened at such a vile term coming from his daughter's lips. It felt like they'd just crossed a line. "What did you say to that?" he asked.

Charley's gaze fell to her lap. "Nothing," she mumbled.

Gary couldn't help but feel a sweep of disappointment that she hadn't defended him, until she followed it up with a seething, "I just *smacked* her right in the nose."

Gary almost laughed at the way she said it, but Fiona gave him a sharp *don't-you-dare* glare. He covered his mouth to hide his smile.

"Her nose started bleeding, but I didn't care. I grabbed her and made her take back what she'd said about you. I made her say it was a lie. Then Mrs. Williams came and broke it up and took us to see Mrs. Brennan."

Gary sighed, wondering if he should play the straight father role here. With Fiona watching, he guessed he should. "I can

76

understand why you hit her, Charley..."

Fiona angled her head and widened her eyes at him.

"...*but*...you can't go around punching people just because they say something you don't like."

"I don't," Charley sulked. "But I knew I had to do something this time."

"Why?"

"'cause with girls like Lauren, you have to *show* them. They need to *see* that they can't push you around. If I hadn't punched her, she would have thought I was an easy target. Every time she saw me after that she'd start on me."

"That might be true of some people," Gary accepted. "But you could also just as easily have been making it worse for yourself."

Charley shook her head. "No, 'cause when I grabbed her wrist, she looked at me, and I saw in her eyes she was scared. She's bigger than me, and most kids are scared of her, but when I saw that look in her eyes, I knew her reputation was bigger than she was."

Gary glanced at Fiona, both surprised and impressed at Charley's insight. Fiona looked back at him with an expression that said, *I know, right?*

"So I showed her," Charley said. "But not only that..." Her eyes turned up to her father again. "...I had to make her take back what she said about you, 'cause Tammy's right, things like that can end up sticking even when they aren't true, like it did for Celia in junior school."

Gary took in a deep breath and let it out.

Charley looked earnestly up at him. "Are you disappointed in me?"

Gary looked back at her, seeing, for the first time, how her face had lost much of the puppy fat she'd been carrying. She seemed older somehow; wiser too. Lance was right. A tiny piece of her growing up had slipped by without him noticing.

"I'm not disappointed at all," he told her.

"Really? You were mad when you came in."

"I was, but I've had a bad day and I went off at the deep end. I should have known you'd have had reasons to do what you did. I'm not saying punching her was the right thing to do, but at least you were defending someone else when it happened. How could I be disappointed in that?"

"Yeah, but..."

"No buts," Gary said. He sat on the bed and brushed the hair back off her face. "Tell me, is there anyone in your class who's a bit scruffy? Someone who's a bit of a loner and doesn't have many friends?"

"Tammy's quiet," Charley said. "But I guess Danny Linford is a bit scruffy too. He's always late for school and has holes in his shoes."

"Well that kid, Danny Linford? That was me when I was your age."

She gaped at him.

"Yep. My parents didn't have much money and we moved around a lot, so I was always the new kid. I was bullied for it. And I'll tell you something..."

He waited for her to ask, "What?"

"I wish I'd had someone like you to stick up for me then."

She smiled, and he felt her relax.

"I think what you did was brave. It takes something to stand up to a bully. I didn't have it."

"I just did it," she admitted. "I didn't really think about it, or the trouble I might get into. Am I going to get expelled?"

"I don't think so, Honey," Fiona said.

"Nah," Gary said. "You've never been in trouble before, and you were sticking up for someone else. If anyone's in trouble, it'll be that Lauren-the horrible bitch-Chapman."

Charley burst out a laugh.

That assessment felt right to Gary, but he had yet to meet

Mrs. two-wrongs-don't-make-a-right Brennan.

Gary dropped onto the sofa and scrubbed his face with his hands. It had been a long, long day.

"So?" Fiona asked.

"Huh?"

"What do you think?"

"She did her best. Punching the girl out might not have been the greatest idea, but I guess you had to be there."

"I'm glad you didn't tell her it was okay to punch someone - even though I saw that smug look on your face?"

"What do you take me for, Fee?" Gary said.

"A hothead."

Gary smiled. "She's so smart. Smarter than I was at her age."

"She's smarter than you are now," Fiona teased.

Gary gave an amused little huff but didn't come back at her as he usually would.

Fiona eyed him carefully. "Don't worry. We'll work this out with the school."

"Yeah, I'm sure we will," he sighed.

Fiona sat down, nudged him and leaned closer. "Horse walks into a bar... bartender asks, *why the long face?*"

Gary smiled and glanced her way. She could see right through him.

"I had a run-in with Ed at the office today."

"With Ed? About what?"

"He wants to oust Michelle from the business."

Fiona looked incredulous. "*What*? Why?"

"He says young women are bad business partners because of family and babies and all that."

"Are you kidding me?"

"Unfortunately, no. We had a bit of a bust-up."

79

Fiona stood. "Why the arrogant, misogynistic...I was never that keen on him, you know."

Gary rolled his eyes. Fiona had a habit of taking things like this on a personal level.

"I can't believe anyone even *thinks* like that these days."

"It'll probably fizzle out when she comes back, but something he said made me a bit wary. I called Sam and he's going to look over the partnership agreement for me."

"What are you going to do?"

"Nothing, but I need to know where we stand legally. It turned a bit ugly with Ed and I just need to know where I stand if we can't salvage it."

"That serious? You think it could break up the partnership?"

"It got a bit heated, but I hope not. He shocked me though. Those kinds of prehistoric views just don't fit in with my vision of the company and its future." He shook his head. "I can't believe he's not shown this side of himself before."

"You'll work something out," Fiona said encouragingly. "You always do."

"Yeah," Gary said, but he wasn't sure he could.

He thought about his conversation with Trixie and wondered if she really did have a nose for these things. Everything had been going so well, then Michelle, Ed, now this thing with Charley. Their usually-calm waters were really churning.

Chapter Eight

Sam called Gary the next day, shortly before he left for the school meeting, and told him the partnership agreement was tight, but that he suspected Ed was talking more 'shenanigans' rather than 'above board' actions against Michelle.

Gary asked if they had any leverage against Ed if he was to start up with any of those shenanigans. Sam told him that under the 'expulsion' clause, it said a partner could be expelled by the other partners if they were guilty of any conduct that may negatively impact the business. It was thin, but if they could couple it with some other contractual breach, they might have something. Gary hoped it wouldn't come to that, but at least he was a little better prepared.

He met Fiona in the school carpark and they went in together, waiting for five minutes outside the office until Mrs. Brennan was ready to see them. Gary felt like one of the kids in the film 'Kes', waiting to receive the strap.

Mrs. Brennan, a silver-haired woman in her early sixties, came out of her office and invited them in. Gary and Fiona took seats in front of an untidy desk full of papers and folders.

"I'm sorry to have kept you waiting," Mrs. Brennan said as she closed the door. "Always a school emergency happening somewhere." She sat down on the other side of the desk and dragged over a folder. "Thank you for coming on such short

81

notice."

"Not a problem," Gary said, eager to get on with it.

Mrs. Brennan opened the folder but didn't look at the contents. "Charlotte was involved in rather a serious incident with another girl yesterday," she began.

"Yes," Gary replied. "That's why we're here."

Mrs. Brennan offered a pencil-thin smile. "Then I'm sure Charlotte has already given you her version of events?"

"She told us what happened, yes," Gary said.

"That she struck another student in the face?"

"Yes, and about the bullying that led up to that happening."

Mrs. Brennan blinked like an owl at him through her thick spectacles. "May I ask for your stance on what took place, based on Charlotte's version of events?"

"My stance? We're taking stances?" This woman's steely, humourless demeanour was starting to irritate him. "And I'm not quite sure what you mean by Charley's *version* of events?"

"Mrs. Brennan," Fiona quickly cut in. "We accept that Charley could perhaps have handled the incident in a more...mature way, but she was only acting in defence of another pupil who was being bullied."

Unmoved, Mrs. Brennan turned a sheet of paper in the folder. "You are aware of the school's policy on violent behaviour."

"Indeed, we are," Fiona replied. "And we've always tried to firmly impress onto Charlotte that hitting people is not acceptable."

Mrs. Brennan looked up from the folder and offered them another thin smile. Gary wondered if that was as much as she could manage. "Not firmly enough, it would appear."

Gary stiffened and leaned forward, but Fiona patted his knee and spoke quickly again. "But it's so unlike Charlotte to do anything like this," she said. "And we know she's sorry."

"Really? When I asked Charlotte to apologise for what she

did, she refused."

"She did?" Fiona said, and glanced at Gary. "We didn't know that."

Gary didn't glance back, his eyes on the head teacher. "And I hope you asked the other girl to apologise?"

"The other girl was the victim, Mr. Wright."

"The *victim*? Just wait a minute..."

But Mrs. Brennan didn't wait. "Mr. and Mrs. Wright, the school does not tolerate violence among students under *any* circumstances. I'm afraid Charlotte's behaviour was completely unacceptable. The school has no choice but to exclude her for two days."

"*What*?" Gary said.

"Mrs. Brennan," Fiona said. "I'm assuming you have listened to the stories from both girls and any witnesses?"

"I have."

"Then you must know that Charley, Charlotte, was only trying to help another student who was being bullied."

"Yes," Mrs. Brennan replied. "That's the only reason Charlotte's exclusion has been limited to two days."

"This is ridiculous…" Gary started.

"Gary, let me..." Fiona tried to cut in.

"No, hold on, Fee. Let me get this straight; it's the policy of this school to *punish* a child who was trying to help another child who was being bullied?"

"No, Mr. Wright, it's the policy of this school to punish children who behave violently."

Gary's face tightened. "Our daughter is not *violent*," he said through gritted teeth.

Mrs. Brennan turned up the corners of her thin lips. "Mr. Wright, the other girl's nose was bleeding profusely. The bridge of her nose was bruised and swollen. She was lucky not to have received a more serious injury."

"Well let's not talk about what she's lucky *not* to have had.

83

Let's just deal with what actually happened."

"It's my understanding, and you can correct me if I'm wrong, that Charlotte struck the other girl, not in defence of her friend, but in retaliation for a rather unsavoury remark that was made about you."

It was Gary's turn to blink a couple of times. He sat back in his seat. "Mrs. Brennan, you are a piece of work."

"Excuse me?"

"Is it so difficult to understand that if we just backtrack a little, we can see that the whole thing wouldn't have happened in the first place if the other girl hadn't been bullying?"

"I agree, Mr. Wright, and it's at that point that Charlotte should have reported what was happening to a member of staff, instead of escalating the situation."

"*Escalating* the situation? Are you for real? So now you're saying that it was Charley's fault?"

"Not the initial encounter, certainly, but Charlotte went on to turn a simple argument into a physical assault. Whatever the circumstances, I'm afraid two wrongs don't ever make a right."

Gary stood up. "I've heard enough. If you're only going to focus on what Charley did and twist all this around so that it was her fault, then you're an idiot, and I don't have time for idiots."

"Excuse me-"

"No, I don't think I will. Charley got herself involved in a situation. She could have stood by like all the other little shits and watch someone get bullied, but she didn't. She put herself in harm's way for someone else. You don't *punish* that. I'm not saying you should pat her on the back and congratulate her, but I certainly don't expect her to be punished for it either."

Mrs. Brennan closed the folder. "The decision has been made, Mr. Wright. The school can't be seen to be favouring pupils and ignoring bad behaviour."

Gary nodded. "Except for Lauren Chapman, it seems. You

said Charley hit the other girl in *retaliation* for what she said about me, but you're wrong. Charley hit her so that everyone knows she isn't a target. She hit her so that *Lauren Chapman,* and her like, knows that they can't *fuck* with Charley Wright."

Fiona stood up. "Gary! Mrs. Brennan, I'm so sorry."

Mrs. Brennan gripped the arms of her chair, her face white with indignity. "Well, I can see now where-"

"Don't even start with that," Gary warned. "People get pushed into angry situations like this because of the frustrations of dealing with small-minded people like *you*. And then everything gets twisted around so that this conversation doesn't get remembered for your officious injustice, no, it'll be remembered because I said 'fuck' in front of the head teacher."

"Gary, stop," Fiona said.

"But it's okay. You hand out your pathetic little two-day exclusion. I'm sure Charley will enjoy the time off and find something useful to do with it. And don't worry; we'll continue to tell Charley that we shouldn't settle arguments with our fists, even though we all know—even you, Mrs. Brennan—that sometimes we do."

Mrs. Brennan sat rigid, red spots of colour rising in her cheeks. "Have you quite finished, Mr. Wright?"

Gary ran his thumbs under the lapels of his jacket. "You know what? I think I have. Except for one more thing. If Lauren Chapman bothers my daughter again, *under any circumstances*, there will be legal repercussions."

"Is that a threat, Mr. Wright?"

"No, Mrs. Brennan, that's a promise. Now, if you'll excuse me, I have better things to do. Good-day."

Fiona chased Gary all the way back to the carpark. He waited by his car for her to catch up. When she arrived, she stood there, hands on her hips, and stared at him.

"What?" he asked, as if he didn't know.

"*What*?" She tried to find words, then threw her arms up in despair and looked away from him, shaking her head.

Gary took a deep breath and waited. He hadn't dealt with the head teacher in the way Fiona might have, but then again, he wasn't exactly known for his diplomacy in the face of fools.

Then she looked at him from the corner of her eye, her mouth rising reluctantly into that crooked little smile.

Gary was relieved to see it. "One of us had to say it, Fee," he said. "And I knew it wouldn't be you."

Fiona slapped his shoulder. "Stop trying to justify yourself."

"Oh, come on, Fee. She deserved it."

Fiona sighed. "I know she did. She was a bitch. But Gary, did you really have to say *fuck*?"

Gary grinned. "No, I didn't, but I knew it would rattle her cage."

Fiona sighed again and shook her head. She looked at her watch. "I need to get back."

"Me too."

Fiona walked around her car and opened the door, with Gary trailing behind her.

"Hey," he said. She turned, and he slipped his hands around her waist. "*Nobody* fucks with us."

She held his gaze for a moment and he kissed her quickly, intending it to be a peck, but Fiona pushed her head forward and made it longer.

When they parted, she said, "I just hope this doesn't blow back on Charley."

"It won't."

"I'll see you later. And don't you dare breathe a word of this to Charley."

She slid into the driver's seat. Gary slammed the door and watched her drive away.

Gary was right.

They didn't hear another word about the incident or the meeting with Mrs. Brennan. Lauren Chapman didn't so much as glance at Charley, and Charley herself was regarded as something of a hero among her classmates. Whether Lauren's reticence was derived from Charley's fist, or a firm warning from the school, they would likely never know.

Charley took her two-day exclusion and used it to finish Gary's dragon. It was nothing like the cartoony videogame character that Gary had envisioned when he described it for her; and the sculpting, though still rough in many ways, was far more refined and detailed than it was for Lance's creature.

The dragon had its head turned on its long neck so that it was almost looking back on itself. The wings were partially folded backwards, the tail a twisting spiral. Charley had cut hundreds of tiny diamond shapes from thin sheets of clay and painstakingly overlapped them like scales over the entire body. The skin was purple, as he'd asked, but the paint she'd used gave off a kind of shimmering-pearlescence. From its jaws rolled the plume of fire he'd requested, and she'd painted it in hues of dark orange fading through yellow and almost white, depicting the heat perfectly.

Gary was so pleased with it that he bought an acrylic display case, the model finding favour on the bookcase in the study, which made Charley beam with pride.

Michelle returned to work a week and a half after the miscarriage and Ed fell suspiciously quiet on the subject.

Gary was relieved to see the turbulence of the previous few weeks seemed to have settled down again. Busy, yet uneventful spring days rolled into the warmth of the summer holidays.

These tranquil stretches of serenity are often referred to as 'the calm before the storm'.

Chapter Nine

July 20th, 2013

That Saturday started out much as any other. The long school holidays had just begun, and summer had finally arrived, the sun as warm and friendly as the cartoon sun on the plaque on Charley's bedroom door.

Fiona had gone on a shopping trip with friends to pick up holiday clothes for the trip they had booked to Gran Canaria, during the first week in August. The day would consist of shopping, lunch, more shopping, and home around three in the afternoon. Weary and weighed down with bags, she'd flop onto the sofa and beg Gary to make coffee.

Charley, who was usually out of the house in the summer, at a friend's or the park, had been reined in some, mostly by Fiona. Gary had mixed feelings about that, of course. It made sense to be careful, but he didn't like to see her cooped up. While Charley was certainly capable of entertaining herself indoors with drawing or sculpting, she also enjoyed being out with her friends, especially on warm and balmy days, like today.

Gary had tried to heed Lance's advice and attempted to ease back on his working habits, so he could spend more time with his family. The demand for their services was still high though, and inevitably he spent long hours on the phone or in front of his computer.

He was sitting on the sofa with his Mac on his lap, spending time between typing out work emails and watching cute cat videos on YouTube, when the doorbell rang. Before he could move, Charley came thundering down the stairs, as only a twelve-year-old can. He heard her speaking at the door and then she came into the front room.

"Dad, is it okay if I go to the park?"

Gary felt a lurch in his stomach, as if someone had just asked him to put his hand in a basket of vipers.

"Who with?"

"Louise, and Sarah."

Gary hesitated. "Hmm, I'm not sure..."

"Oh, Dad!" Charley cried, obviously prepared for his reply. "It's a really nice day and it's boiling inside! I can't go anywhere anymore!"

"Look, Charley, you know the reasons."

"I know, but Dad, I'm not stupid. I know not to talk to strangers or get into a stranger's car or any of that stuff. And Sarah and Louise's parents have let them go out."

"I know you're not stupid, but you know what your mum's like. If I let you out on your own, I'll have to answer for it when she comes home."

"Well, we won't tell her then," she said, brightly. "I'll be home before mum gets back from shopping."

Gary shook his head. "We can't lie to Mum. You should know better."

"It wouldn't be lying if we just don't tell her. Oh, come on, Dad! *Pleeeease*?"

"It wouldn't be lying, no, but it would be underhanded and not very nice, wouldn't it?"

Charley slumped and sighed. "I guess. Okay, I'll tell them I can't go then." She hooked her thumbs into the waistband of her shorts and walked away with her head hanging.

Gary sighed too. Despite all his posturing at the party, he was still allowing recent events to scare him into boxing her up.

"Hey, how about I come with you?"

Charley looked dubiously back at him. "*You'll* come to the park?"

"Yes, and why not? It's a nice day. I'll bring my work and enjoy the sunshine for a change."

"Seriously?"

"Sure," Gary said and began collecting his things together.

Charley broke into a big grin. "Okay!" And she ran to the door to tell the others.

Gary dropped his laptop and papers into its case. He doubted there'd be any Wi-Fi around the park, but he could get by without the internet for a couple of hours. Slinging the bag over his shoulder, he surprised himself by realising he was quite looking forward to it.

As he headed for the door, his phone rang. It was Fiona. "Hey, what's up?" he asked.

"Stopped off for some lunch." Fiona said. "Just checking in. What you up to?"

"Oh, just a bit of work."

Gary almost heard Fiona roll her eyes. "Well, that's a surprise. What's Charley doing?"

"She's going to the park with Louise and Sarah."

"What?"

"Don't worry, they aren't going on their own, I'm going with them."

Fiona's reaction mirrored their daughter's. "*You're* going to the *park*?"

"Yeah, and?"

Fiona chuckled. "Just wondering why such a momentous occasion hasn't been on the world news."

"Funny," Gary said. "I'm taking my work with me. It'll be nice to sit in the sun for a change."

"Wonders never cease. Okay, well, have fun. I'll be back around-"

"Three," Gary finished for her.

The girls were chatting excitedly when Gary came out onto the drive. The sky was clear blue, the sun picking stars out of every shiny surface.

"Hi Sarah, Louise," Gary said, and the girls returned the greeting. "We'll take the car."

"It's only a short walk," Charley said.

"We'll take the car," Gary repeated. Going to the park was one thing, walking there was another.

Just as he was about to close and lock the door, Charley said, "Wait! Let me get my cap!"

Gary stood by while she ran upstairs, returning, a few moments later wearing her favourite purple cap.

The girls scrambled into the rear seats, laughing and complaining about the stifling heat inside. Gary threw the laptop bag onto the passenger seat and got in, powering down the windows as soon as the engine started. He drove through the gate, looking in the mirror and asking the girls to lower the volume by a few decibels, when a white van sped by, almost clipping the BMW's front end.

"Dick head!" Gary shouted without thought.

The girls laughed in the back and Charley said, "Dad!"

Gary looked in the mirror. "Oh, sorry girls. Pardon my French."

On the way over, a moth fluttered in the windscreen and Gary had the girls laughing when it flew into his face and he panic-flapped it out through the open window. When it was gone, he grinned sheepishly. "I hate moths."

Half a minute later, Gary parked up on the curving road opposite the park. The girls jumped out and ran off across the grass to join a group of other kids. As Gary collected his bag and slammed the door, his phone rang.

"Hi Lance, what's up?" He listened. "Jesus, all of them? Was it a planned outage or...?"

Lance explained that there had been a power cut, and it had taken out the building and their servers. For some reason, the UPS emergency power only partially kicked in and some of the servers had shut down unceremoniously. The power had been restored, but not all the servers were coming back up. It looked like a few of them might be screwed and were going to need restoring; maybe even rebuilding, depending on the state of the backups.

Gary looked across the park at the girls as they talked animatedly with friends by the swings. It was a beautiful day. The sky was pure azure, crisscrossed with airliner vapour trails. Kids raced around, parents nursed babies, mums and dads pushed happy-faced youngsters on the swings or watched nervously while they negotiated the climbing frame.

What could possibly happen on a beautiful day like today?

"I'm coming in," he told Lance. "No, no. I'll be there in fifteen minutes."

He called Charley and waved her over.

"Listen, I've got to go in to work."

Charley took off her cap. "Aww, do you have to?"

"Yeah, it's a big server crash, all hands on-deck." He didn't mention that Lance had told him they already had it covered and that he didn't need to go.

"Aw, okay," Charley said.

He threw the bag back onto the passenger seat and walked around the car to her. "Now listen. I'm not sure how long I'm going to be gone, so you girls *stay together*, okay?"

"Yeah, we will."

"Seriously. *Stay together*." He checked his watch. It was a couple of minutes after one. "If I'm not back before you're finished here, I want you to go home together. Louise and Sarah live close to each other, don't they?" Charley nodded. "Tell

93

them to walk you home first, and then they can go home together. No later than four-thirty, okay?"

"Aw, Dad!"

"Four-thirty, or you can come to the office with me."

"Okay, four-thirty."

Gary walked around to the driver's side of the car and watched Charley heading back to her friends.

"Hey, you got your phone?" he called.

Charley pulled it out of her pocket and waved it in the air without looking back. The Tinkerbelle charm she had attached to it jingled.

"Hey, Charley?" he called.

She turned around and walked backwards.

"How about some Mario Kart tonight?"

She brightened immediately. "Honestly?"

"Sure. Maybe we can get mum to play too. You know how funny that is."

"Yeah! Ha! Thanks, Dad."

Once back in the car, he dialled work via the Bluetooth connection to the radio. He looked across the park. Charley had almost reached the others. "Hey Lance. What's happening?" She turned and waved to him. Smiling and listening to Lance, he waved back. Charley placed a kiss on her palm and blew it to him. Gary snatched it out of the air and blew one back. Charley caught it and pretended to pop it into her mouth and swallow it down. Gary smiled.

He recalled one of the times he'd come down to the park with Fiona when Charley was still a toddler. He'd pushed her on the swings while she laughed and shouted, *Higher, Daddy, higher!* Fiona got all scared and told him to stop.

For a moment he thought about leaving the server problems in Lance's more-than-capable hands, even leaving the work he'd brought with him in the car too, and just go and enjoy the park with his daughter for a few hours.

Then he heard Lance say to someone, "What? You're joking. Gary? Looks like the outage has definitely broken a few of these servers. We'll have to rebuild them."

He glanced at Charley to wave good-bye, but she was already involved with her friends.

He checked his mirror and drove away.

Three hours, and a lot of cursing later, all the servers were back online. Angry clients had called, wanting to know why their websites were offline, but Gary had been able to handle and reassure them.

As things were wrapping up and they were having a well-deserved coffee, Gary's phone rang. He looked at the display and saw it was Fiona. "Hi," he said, glancing at his watch. It was almost four-thirty.

"I can't believe you're still out," Fiona laughed. "Are you coming home soon?"

"Erm, yeah, we're coming now...well, in half an hour or..."

Fiona's voice changed. "Where are you? You don't sound like you're outside?"

Dammit. Did anything get by Fiona?

"Erm, yeah," he said. "I got a call just as we arrived at the park. We had a big problem at the office. A power outage took out the server room and some of them wouldn't come back up. But it's okay now, we have it all under-"

"Where's Charley? Did you take her with you?"

Gary winced a little at the sharp-edged concern in her voice. "No, I left the girls at the park."

"Gary! I thought we'd discussed this."

"Fee, it's okay. There were loads of people around and I told them to stay there until I came back." Not quite true, but he was in damage-control mode now. "I told them to stick together, but

95

if they did need to leave, I told them to see Charley home first and then..." He was over explaining, not only because he wanted to reassure Fiona, but also because he didn't want to appear to have been careless. He wanted her to know that he had covered all bases.

"It's gone four," Fiona said. "Have you called her since you left her?"

Gary dropped the phone away from his ear a moment and cursed under his breath. This was getting worse by the second. "Well, no, I haven't. It's been really busy here, Fee. But look, we're all done now, so I'll swing by the park on the way back and pick them up."

"Just...bring her home, okay? I'll call her and let her know you're coming."

"Okay, see you shortly."

She was pissed at him. Gary blew a lungful of air through his pursed lips and cursed himself for allowing time to get away from him. If he'd made sure he'd got back to the park before now, he wouldn't be in her bad books. But more importantly, she wouldn't be needlessly worrying.

"Lance, guys, good work," he called as he collected his things. "I'm off. I think I might be in the dog-house."

The guys chuckled.

"Don't worry about it," one of them said. "I've been in the dog house since my stag night."

Gary laughed and headed out. As he climbed into the car, Fiona called again. "She's not answering her phone," she said, her voice tense. "I'm just getting voicemail. Does she have it on her?"

"Yeah, definitely. I checked before I left. Maybe she can't hear it? Or maybe..." He searched for inspiration. "...maybe she put it down somewhere. Maybe the volume's down?"

"It vibrates."

"I know. Look, I don't know why she's not answering. I'll be there in fifteen minutes anyway, okay?"

"Okay," she said.

"See you soon."

He reached for the key, fumbling a little before finding and turning the ignition. Damn it! Fiona was giving him the jitters too. The car started smoothly, and he drove quickly away.

On the journey over, he called Charley. After three rings it picked up, but it was her voicemail. "Hiya, it's, Charleeeee! Leave a message and I'll get right back to ya."

Gary looked at her name on the car's display. "Charley, it's Dad. I'm on my way over to pick you up. If you get this, stay put."

When he arrived at the park, it was no longer bustling with activity. The sun was lower, the shadows longer. The clear azure sky had skimmed-over with thin clouds that resembled sheer sheets of chiffon. A thin breeze rustled the trees and bushes.

He got out of the car and scanned the area. A bunch of boys kicked a football about. A man pushed a child on a swing. A group of kids took up another set of swings, some standing, some sitting and letting their feet drag back and forth. All the indications that the park was done for another day.

There was no sign of the girls, or the kids they had joined either.

He looked to his right where a line of trees and bushes separated the park from the canal. He thought about walking down there, then changed his mind. He took out his phone and called Charley. It was engaged. Had Fiona managed to get her? He called it again and this time it rang. Once, twice, three times. "Hiya, it's, Charleeeee! Leave a message and I'll get right back to ya."

He waited for the beep. "Hi, Charley, it's Dad again, where are you? Give me a ring as soon as you get this, will you?"

He put his phone away and scanned the park again. *Where*

could she have gone? If she'd gone somewhere other than home, she would have directly disobeyed the instructions he'd given her. Charley just didn't do that.

Unless she had a good reason.

Abstract feelings of dread began to creep up on him and he had to rein them in.

Maybe they left before Fiona came home, he reasoned, so Charley had gone with the other girls to one of their houses. Maybe she'd lost track of time.

She'll be at Sarah or Louise's house. Stop worrying.

He pushed the uneasy feelings aside and set off for home.

Fiona was waiting at the door when he pulled onto the drive, already looking for Charley.

She rushed to meet him. "Where is she?"

"They must have left already," he said. "She's still not answering the phone?"

"What? No!" She clasped a hand to her forehead. "Left? And gone where?"

"Fee, calm down. They've probably gone to Sarah or Louise's house. She'll have put her phone down in another room or something and that's why we can't reach her." But Fiona's face was alive with worry. "Fee, she'll be okay, there's no need to start panicking."

He almost said 'yet', but stopped himself before the word fell out. Despite all his reassurances, barbs of panic were hooking him now too. He felt a little breathless, like his heart was punching out a few extra beats per minute.

"Where do Sarah and Louise live?" he asked.

"Two streets over on Broad Oak Lane."

"What number?"

"Sarah lives at twenty-eight I think."

"Right, I'll go around there."

"I'm coming."

"No, you wait here in case she turns up while I'm gone."

98

Fiona wrung her hands and thought about it for a moment. "You're right. But call me as soon as you find her."

She looked so small and thin, as if the stress had ravaged her somehow in this short time. He felt guilty that he was responsible for causing her distress. He gave her a quick hug and told her not to worry. Charley would be fine and at one of her friend's houses.

On the way over to Sarah's, Gary's mind started fucking with him, showing little glimpses of arriving at the house to find that the girls weren't there. He tried to drag himself from the sucking quicksand of worry, countering the macabre thoughts with the assurance that he would find them all safe and well. Of course he would. Where else would they be?

But it didn't stop him from driving too fast along the quiet roads.

Twenty-eight, Broad Oak Lane. A nice house with grounds. Gary rang the bell. Despite his churning insides, in his mind's eye he saw Charley opening the door full of smiles and him telling her off for not following his instructions before he hugged her tightly.

A lady answered who he vaguely recognised from Charley's birthday party. The warm smell of cooking drifted into the evening air. "Oh, hello, Gary," she said.

"Hi, Mrs...."

"Chappell."

"That's right. I'm just looking for Charley, is she here?"

Mrs. Chappell's smile slipped. "No, she's not here."

Gary just gaped at her, hardly able to comprehend what she had just said.

Not here? How can she not be here? Louise's then, she must be at Louise's.

Gary was about to ask where Louise lived when Sarah stepped into the hall, followed by Louise.

He just stared at them, his skin shrinking as a flood of

99

frightening scenarios rushed through him. *How could the girls be here, but not Charley?* Panic drove him forward, pushing past Sarah's mother and into the house.

"Girls, where's Charley?"

They glanced at each other, their faces full of guilt.

"Where is she?" The fright in his voice was raw. A tiny corner of his mind tried to rein in the fear, but it was like a dark shadow that was threatening to engulf him.

He grabbed Sarah's shoulders firmly. "Sarah, where's Charley?"

"We had an argument," she blurted. "She left."

"An argument? About what?" Then he realised that the argument was irrelevant. He pulled her closer. "Where did she go?"

Sarah shook her head, her lower lip plumping out and trembling. She was getting upset, but Gary didn't feel he had time to be gentle. It was as if something wild had taken control and was driving him from the inside.

"Where did she go?" He shook her a little and she burst out crying.

"Mr. Wright!" her mother broke in.

Gary ignored her. "Louise, where did she go?"

Louise shied away but still answered, "I don't know. She just went."

"Went where? Toward home? The canal? Which way?"

Louise just shook her head, her lips quivering and her mouth turning down at the corners.

"Mr. Wright!"

Gary rose to full height and felt unsteady. "Oh my God," he said, running a hand through his hair. "Where is she?"

"Mr. Wright, you're scaring the girls."

"I told them to stick together," he said to her. "I *told* them..." He turned back to the girls, speaking rapidly, almost babbling. "Is there anywhere else she might have gone? Another friend

100

maybe, or, or another place you like to go?"

Sarah wiped her eyes. Both girls shook their heads.

"Girls you have to *think!* Where did she go?"

"Mr. Wright, you need to calm down."

Gary turned on her. "Calm down? You stupid woman! My daughter's missing!"

Mrs. Chappell blustered, but Gary was already on his way out. As he strode swiftly down the path, he took out his phone and dialled Charley's number again. "Hiya, it's, Charleeeee! Leave a message and I'll get right back to ya."

"Charley, it's Dad again, we really need you to call. Please call."

He rang Fiona. "Is she there?" she asked before he had chance to speak. It broke his heart to have to tell her that she wasn't. "They had an argument and she left on her own. She might have been upset. Fiona, is there anywhere else she might have gone? Any other school friends she might have gone to?" He heard quick panicky breaths in the phone's speaker as she thought about it.

"She has other friends, but no one who she really sees outside of school. Oh my God, Gary, where is she?"

"Fee, hold on, I'm coming back."

Minutes later, he dashed into the house, hoping that Charley had turned up in the few minutes it had taken him to drive home. Fiona's face was tear streaked and frantic. "She's still not answering. We should call the police."

"Not yet."

"Not yet? Why not? *Charley's missing!*"

"I know she is!" Gary shouted back at her. He took a couple of breaths. "I know she is. But she's only been missing a couple of hours, I don't know if the police would even get involved at this stage."

"Well call them and find out!"

"Does Charley have an address book? Maybe we can find

101

something in there, someone we don't know about."

"She keeps all that kind of stuff in her phone now."

"But maybe there's someone else. The girls had argued, maybe she was upset and didn't want to come home. Maybe she wanted someone to talk to."

"Gary, we need to call the police. *Right now*!"

The shriek in Fiona's voice scared him. "Okay, okay. We'll call the police. But let me call her one more time before I do."

"What's the point? If she's found her phone, she would have seen all the missed calls and voice messages. She would have called us."

"Just once more, for luck," Gary said.

He called the number, his hands shaking. It rang once, twice, then halfway through the third ring he heard the click of a connection. He shot an excited look at Fiona and held up his hand. "Hello? Charley?" No reply, but over the line came a kind of rustling sound, as if the phone was being moved or handled. Was it in her pocket? Was she walking? Maybe she was on her way home. "Hello? Charley, it's Dad, can you hear me?"

Then he heard a deep, slightly quivering breath. Not Charley's breath. Not even a child's breath.

An icy shadow passed over him and time seemed to slow.

"Charley?" he whispered.

A man's cold hard voice replied, "Forget her, she's dead."

The colour drained out of Gary's world, blood shrinking away from his skin like the tide sucked from the shore by a Tsunami.

Forget her, she's dead.

"WHAT? Who is this? *WHO THE FUCK IS THIS*?"

But the phone was dead. He groped for the stair rail, missed and grabbed onto a spindle. Spots exploded before his eyes and he thought he was about to pass out. He saw Charley's beautiful young face, saw her laughing, saw her blowing him a kiss in the moments before he drove away. *Forget her, she's dead.* Was that really what he'd just heard? *Was that even possible?*

Fiona's frightened voice brought him back. She clawed at him, her eyes pleading. "Gary! What is it? Who was on the phone?"

Her terrified face filled his vision. How could he reply? How could he repeat the murderous words he'd just had spoken to him?

"Wait, wait," he said and dialled Charley's number again. The call went straight to voice mail without ringing first, a sure sign that the phone was turned off now.

"Gary! Tell me what's happened!" Fiona screamed. "Who was on the phone? What did they say?"

Gary gave a bewildered shake of his head, as if he'd been punched senseless and all his communication skills were rolling around his skull.

Fiona grabbed at his clothes and shook him. "*TELL ME!*"

"It was a man," Gary managed, his eyes wide and frightened. "He said... he said..."

Fiona searched his eyes. "He said *what*?"

"He said...Charley's dead."

Fiona threw back her head, her fists clenched to her throat, and uttered such an animalistic cry of anguish that Gary shrank back in terror. He'd never heard such a sound from her before, didn't even know she was capable of such a cry.

"*Noooooooo! Nooooooooo! Noooooooooo!*" she screamed over and over.

Gary grabbed her wrists. "Fiona! Fiona!" he shouted, but he didn't know why. It was like they had stepped aboard an insane rollercoaster ride, rushing headlong and out of control into a nightmare. She fought him, her hands and head thrashing. He clawed her to him and held on to her tightly.

She struggled for a few more moments more, then slumped against him, crying, "No, no, no," into his shoulder

Gary held her, his face ashen and bewildered. Reality had

103

lost its substance, like a dream floating at the edge of consciousness.

Was this really happening? Was it? Was Charley really dead? Was she?

He held Fiona away from him and searched her face. "We need to call the police. It might not be true, Fee, he might be lying."

Fiona just gazed at him in a daze; her face white, her eyes dull.

"Fee, he might be lying, she might still be alive. We have to find her!"

Fiona found his eyes and searched them. She nodded, uncertainly at first, then more determinedly, as if drawing strength from his words.

"I'll call the police and you call everyone else. Everyone. Friends, your parents, everyone."

Fiona wiped her face and took out her phone while Gary rang the police.

Immediately after he'd placed the call, he wanted to go out searching for Charley, but Fiona insisted he stay with her until the police arrived.

He rang Lance a couple of times but couldn't get him, so he paced the house while Fiona called everyone they knew. Even with the police on the way, he kept returning to the window and expecting to see her walking up the path with a sheepish explanation of where she'd been.

He wouldn't care. He'd just hold her and never let her go.

Fiona's parents arrived within minutes, followed by friends. The house bustled with people talking and asking questions. The police officers arrived; their bulky blue uniforms, squawking radios and equipment feeling surrealistically alien in their home. To Gary, the officers seemed all too calm as they asked questions and requested a recent photo of Charley that could be copied and circulated.

In between the questions, he tried to comfort Fiona, taking her hand or placing his arm around her shoulder while she clutched a handkerchief to her eyes when the tears came time and again.

When the officer asked what Charley was wearing, it was Fiona who shakily answered, "A purple tee shirt with a...a picture of a butterfly on the front...denim shorts, a pink belt...and...and..."

She broke down in tears.

"She had her cap on," Gary added. "Sort of purple with dark blue piping. She wrote 'Charley' on the visor with one of those glitter gel pens."

The officer took all the details down and looked up again. "Footwear?"

"What?" Gary said. He had drifted away for a moment, picturing her again at the park in those clothes as she tipped her hand and blew a kiss off the palm.

"What kind of shoes was she wearing?"

"Probably her Nikes," Fiona said, her voice trembling. "I'll have to check. White socks with pink hearts on them."

The police asked all the same questions they had asked the parents of the other missing girls. Had they argued? Did she have any money with her? Were all her clothes and the things important to her still here? Was there any reason why she might not want to come back home?

Gary began to grow angry and frustrated at what he perceived as pointless talking and a lack of action.

"Why are we just standing around talking!" he shouted. "She hasn't run away! We should be organising search parties, talking to people, find who was at the park this afternoon. Someone must have seen something."

"Mr. Wright," the detective said. "We have to get a full picture of what's happened—"

"I'll tell you what's happened! Someone has fucking taken

my daughter!"

"We don't know that yet. She left the park upset with her friends, she may have gone somewhere to—"

"There isn't anywhere!" Gary yelled. "We've spoken to everyone she might have gone to."

"She may have just gone off to be by herself for a while."

"*She wouldn't do that!*" Gary bellowed in his face. "Can't I get it through to you?"

"Mr. Wright, I need you to calm down."

"What about the call? The man on the other end and what he said. *He had her phone for Christ's sake!*"

"She might have lost her phone or had it stolen. There are some sick individuals out there who'd get a kick out of saying something like that to you."

"But he said 'she'."

"Sorry?"

"If someone had found it, how would he know it was a she? He said, '*she's* dead'."

"You would have called her by her name, wouldn't you, when you thought she had answered?"

"Yes, I did say her name," Gary replied. "Her name's Charlotte, but we call her *Charley*. I called her Charley on the phone. If I called someone you didn't know, 'Charley', would you think I was talking about a girl, or a boy?"

The detective considered this for a moment. "Even so, there is still the possibility that the phone was stolen from her, and the person who has it knows who she is."

Gary wasn't interested in theories. "Someone's taken her," he insisted. "And we aren't about to find her by fucking sitting around here just talking about it!"

"Mr. Wright, I know this is a distressing time, but you just need to take a breath and calm down."

"Fuck calming down!" Gary shouted. "I'm through talking."

Gary stormed off into the kitchen and tried Lance again. This

106

time he answered.

"Hi Gary, sorry, I went to the gym. What's up?"

"Lance, can you come to the house, something's happened."

"I'll be there in ten," Lance said and hung up.

Gary looked at his phone, he hadn't even had to explain what the problem was, and Lance was on his way.

Gary met him at the door. Lance had seen the police cars and the activity. He looked worried, and more than a little scared. "What the hell's going on?"

Gary grabbed his arm. "Lance, Charley's missing."

Lance shook his head. "Missing? What do you mean?"

"She went to the park with a couple of friends today. I didn't want them to go alone so I was going with them, but then I got that call from you about the power outage and..."

"Jesus, Gary," Lance breathed. "I knew I shouldn't have called you. I told you, you didn't need to come."

Gary glanced around anxiously to see who might have heard him say that. Fiona wasn't too far away, but she wasn't looking over and seemed to be engaging with her mother, her face pale and drained with worry.

He drew Lance to one side. "Listen, I'm feeling pretty crap about myself right now. Any chance you can keep that to yourself for the time being?"

"What?"

"That you told me I didn't need to go to the office." He looked across at Fiona's parents and Lance understood immediately.

"Oh God, I'm sorry," Lance said. "I didn't think."

"It's fine, it's fine," Gary replied, wanting to quickly brush the matter aside with minimum fuss.

"What can I do?"

"The police are screwing around, going through their standard book of missing child questions. They think she's run away, or some shit, but something's happened to her, Lance, I

107

know it."

"You don't know that for sure," Lance argued, but Gary cut him off.

"Lance, there's something more." The two old friends looked at each other and Gary saw dread in Lance's eyes. "We'd been ringing her and just kept getting her voice mail all the time. Then just before I called the police, I tried her one more time and... and..." He had to stop because an intense rush of emotion seized him in a powerful grasp and shook him like a ragdoll. He covered his mouth, his lips quivering.

"Gary, what is it? Tell me!"

"A man answered her phone, Lance. He said... he said, Charley's dead."

Lance swayed, his face white and his eyes wide. "Oh my God, Gary! No! Have you told the police?"

Gary shook his head in frustration. "They know, but they're saying we shouldn't give it much weight. I don't know if they really believe that or if they're just trying to ease our worry. They're saying Charley might have lost her phone or had it stolen, and someone is playing a sick joke."

"They could be right?"

"You didn't hear him, Lance. He was cold. Whoever he is, he wasn't playing a prank. He has Charley. I'm just hoping he's lying, that he still has her and he's just saying that to throw us off."

"What do you want to do?" Lance asked, his voice solid and determined. "Whatever it is, I'm right with you."

Gary gave the busy room a quick glance. "I'm not hanging around here kicking my heels. Let's go out and look for her, maybe she's somewhere close. We can ask if anyone's seen her."

"Sure," Lance agreed. "Let's do it."

Gary went to Fiona. "Fee." The unbridled worry and anguish in her eyes broke his heart. "I'm going out with Lance to look for her." They just looked at each other for a moment, his fear reflected in her eyes, then he took her in his arms and hugged her tight.

"Find her, Gary," she whispered in his ear. "Please find her and bring her home."

"I'll try," Gary whispered back to her.

He took a school photo of Charley with them. It had been taken late last year, but she hadn't changed a great deal. Her face had slimmed a little, but her hair was still straight and mousey, with that little dusting of freckles across her nose. They took Lance's car and set off for the park.

The day was still bright, but hazy. The smell of barbeque drifted from somewhere nearby. High above them, the buzz of a light aircraft droned. It should have been just another lazy Saturday evening, but it was far from it.

The park was mostly deserted. Gary turned toward the swings where he'd seen her blow that final kiss. His jaw clenched. *Not final*, he told himself. Not final. There was still hope, still a chance. What did they say about the first twenty-four hours and how crucial they were? She could still be alive somewhere, if only they knew where to look.

"Any idea which way she went?" Lance asked.

"No. The girls didn't take notice of which way she went, but..." He walked toward the swings, wanting to be near the place where he'd last seen her, as if he might draw the inspiration needed to set him off in the right direction. He stood in the spot and looked around the park.

Lance did likewise, not quite understanding what Gary was looking for.

"This is the place I saw her last," Gary said. "Right here."

He thought about how he had driven away and left her here. Messing about with fucking servers while something bad was happening to his daughter. Tears blurred his vision. He didn't seem to be able to move away from this spot. He felt as if he was standing at the epicentre of a nuclear blast that had laid

109

waste to everything for miles around.

"Gary?"

Gary turned, his expression filled with indecision and agony.

"Where should we look?" Lance asked.

He didn't know. He didn't want to move. Didn't want to lose this delicate, ephemeral link with his beautiful daughter.

"Gary?" Lance placed a hand on Gary's shoulder.

Gary swallowed hard and looked back across the park to the tree line. "I...I have a feeling about the canal. I did earlier, but let's just speak to the people here first. Maybe someone has seen her."

After a fruitless round of questions with the few kids still hanging around the park, he and Lance headed down to the canal. Light still clung to the sky, but the heat of the day was cooling fast. They stood on the stony canal path, looking left and right. Gary tried to think where she might have gone if she'd come this way.

A cold, darkness crept over him. He slowly turned to look behind him where a wide embankment sloped gently up to the trees and bushes enclosing the park grounds. It was gloomy there beneath the trees and the earth was black. He didn't know why, but it made him shiver.

"What's up?" Lance asked.

"I don't know," Gary replied.

He took a few steps up the embankment, scanning the trees and the ground, not sure what he was looking for, but feeling something about this place. The earth had fallen away from around the base of a tall oak tree, exposing a tangle of knotted roots that you wouldn't normally see. They twisted together like tortured souls, trying to find a way into the black earth.

"You see something?" Lance asked.

"Not really," Gary said quietly. *It's just that this place and that tree is creeping me out and I don't know why.*

He gazed up through the branches of the tall oak, right up

110

into its leafy-green canopy, then followed its craggy lines of mossy bark back down to the tangled roots. Finally, he glanced at the earth at the base, sprinkled with dead foliage.

There was nothing to see here.

He tried to shake the weird feeling and returned to the path. "Come on, we'll head down this way a bit, if we don't see anything, we'll head the other way."

A half hour later they were back where they started. They'd seen a few people walking the path, a group of teenage lads coasting on bikes, the gears clicking agreeably, and a couple of fishermen done for the day and packing away their tackle. But none of them had seen Charley.

As they walked back to the car, Gary noticed a new group of boys hanging around the swings. Lance pulled out his keys, but Gary stopped. "Hang on, Lance, let's just have a word with these lads before we go. They weren't here when we arrived."

The boys eyed them suspiciously as he and Lance approached them. One young lad held a well-kicked football under his arm, the stitching busted, the hexagonal leather patches coming apart at the seams.

"Hey, guys," Gary said. He held up the photo. "Have any of you seen this girl today?"

The boys leaned in for a closer look in the fading light, most of them shaking their heads right away.

"That's Charlotte Wright," the lad with the ball said.

Gary's heart back-flipped. He stooped a little to bring himself more to the boy's height. The lad looked a little younger than the others, more Charley's age.

"You saw her today?" he asked.

"I saw her, yeah."

"Was she with two other girls?"

"Nah, she was walking off that way." He pointed toward the road she would have taken if she had been heading home.

"You're sure?" Gary asked. "You're sure it was her?"

"Yeah," the boy replied. "I know her, she's in my class."

"Was she with anyone?"

"Nah, she was on her own. She looked like she was mad at somethin', kinda stomping along and swinging her arms."

Gary looked at Lance. Charley had left because the girls had argued. He imagined her marching away, legs and arms swinging stiffly. That was Charley alright. The boy was sharp to have picked that up.

"Is there anything else you can tell me? Did you see anything more?"

The boy shrugged. "Not really. We were in the middle of a game, losing 3-1, so I only saw her for a second before I got back into the game."

It wasn't much, but at least they had a positive sighting, the direction she was heading, and that she hadn't left with anyone.

"What's up then?" the boy asked. "Is she missing or somethin'?"

"Yes," Gary replied, and it felt so unreal to admit that. "She's missing. I'm her dad. Would you mind giving me your name and address?"

"Sure," the boy replied. "I'm Kevin."

Gary wrote down his details, in case the police wanted to interview the boy further. As he put away the pen, he noticed its lustrous green barrel and shining gold plate. He recalled Charley's happy expression when she'd handed him the box with its red bow. He caressed the pen with his finger, the intimate touch seeming to split the moment and highlight the fact that Charley was missing. Not just missing, but *taken*. Someone had taken her. It was surreal. It was a scene from a movie.

"I hope you find her," Kevin called. "She's nice."

The boy's words brought tears pricking into Gary's eyes. "Yes she is," he agreed huskily, and they headed back to the car.

The house was an ant's nest of activity. As well as the police, more friends had arrived. He looked around for Fiona but couldn't see her anywhere. Someone touched his arm and he turned to find it was Trixie.

"Gary, I can't believe this." Her eyes were wide and frightened. "We've been trying to organise search parties, but the police don't seem to know what they're doing yet."

Gary took her arm and moved her to the side of the room. "Did you know something like this was going to happen?"

She shook her head and looked shocked. "No I didn't, Gary, honestly."

"But what you said..."

"I just felt something wasn't right."

"Trixie, I know I've always made fun of these flashes of yours, these perceptions, but can you help us now? Do you have any idea where she might be?"

Trixie's eyes filled with tears and she shook her head. "I'm sorry, Gary, I can't do that, I only wish I could. I'm not a medium. I'm just sensitive to some things."

Gary nodded and touched her shoulder with affection.

"I'm sorry," she said again, wiping away tears.

"It's okay." He looked around again. "Have you seen Fiona?"

"She's in the dining room with her mother."

"Is Frank there?"

"Not last I saw."

He found her sitting at the dining table with Audrey at her side. She looked wrung out, but when she noticed him, she raised her head hopefully. Gary crouched beside her and took her hands.

"A boy from her class saw her leaving the park this afternoon, heading toward home. He said she was on her own."

Fiona explored his eyes, hoping for more, as if trying to fathom some hidden secret in his words, some further clue to where Charley was now.

"It's not much, I know, but at least we know she was alone and which direction she was heading. I'm going to tell the police."

He squeezed her hands and she nodded.

Gary found a detective and gave him the information about the boy. The detective wrote down the name and address and said that they'd get an officer over there to interview him. He went on to tell Gary that they were preparing to release a statement and a public appeal for information on TV and radio. Gary was thankful to hear some sort of positive action, but he still didn't believe that Charley was with someone, unless it was against her will. At least an appeal might bring people forward who had seen her somewhere on her way home, maybe even saw what happened to her.

"We're going to escalate this to the Missing Persons Bureau. It's normally seventy-two hours, but with Charlotte being so young we can expedite it."

"Missing Persons Bureau? What can they do?"

"They have a database of missing persons. They can sometimes help us find someone based on previous cases."

Gary didn't understand how they could do that, but he nodded all the same. It was another step in the right direction.

"If we don't get much from the appeal, we'd like to arrange a press conference for tomorrow. Would you be willing to go in front of the media?"

Gary nodded numbly. Panicky dread crawled up inside him as it dawned that night was falling and, inconceivable as it was, Charley might not be coming home tonight.

The detective seemed to see these thoughts in Gary's stricken face. "Missing children usually turn up within twenty-four hours. Try not to worry too much."

Tell that to my wife, Gary thought.

He tried to focus on the faint glimmer that she could just be with someone, somewhere, maybe a friend who they didn't know about. An appeal might make them realise what was going on.

And if she was being held against her will...then perhaps seeing it on the news would frighten her captor into releasing her.

Now they knew which direction she had taken, the detective told Gary they would send out officers to look for CCTV cameras along the route. Maybe she'd been picked up on one or more of them.

"In the meantime," the detective said, "allow me to introduce you to Chloe Taylor."

A young woman stepped forward, late twenties, blonde bobbed hair. She wore little makeup and was smartly dressed, but not in police uniform. She smiled and took his hand, shaking it firmly.

"Chloe is a Family Liaison Officer, or a FLO, as we like to call them. She's here to work closely with you and help you through this. She will also relay information from you to us and vice-versa. I think Chloe has some questions for you, so I'll leave you to it."

Chloe drew him to one side and took out her note pad and pen. There wasn't anywhere to sit.

"Chlo the FLO, huh?" Gary said.

She smiled. "I know, unfortunate, right? Is it okay if I call you, Gary?"

He nodded.

"Gary, I understand how distressing this must be for you, but most missing children are back home in twenty-four to forty-eight hours, so try not to worry too much."

Gary offered a tight smile.

"Charlotte is twelve, is that right?"

115

"Yeah, she just turned twelve a few months ago. We call her Charley."

"Oh," Chloe said. "I like those boy/girl type names. So how has Charley been lately?"

"Been? She's been fine. We had a big birthday party for her in March, lots of guests, we got her a kitten...she loves animals...she..." He caught the hitch in his voice and controlled it.

Chloe gave him a moment to recompose. "Has Charley been in trouble for anything lately? Anything that would make her reluctant to come home?"

Gary closed his eyes and touched his brow with his fingers. "Look, she hasn't run away," he said patiently. "You can forget that, right now."

"Gary, I understand how this-"

"No, you don't seem to understand at all. Charley doesn't wander off without telling anyone. She doesn't stay out beyond the time we've told her to come home. She doesn't ignore the instructions we've given her. Something has *happened* to her! *That's* what *you* to need understand."

"I know it might seem that way, but you need to just take a step back and think carefully for a moment..."

"I don't need to think carefully," Gary said evenly. "I don't need to think at all. She was perfectly happy. There wasn't anything wrong, there wasn't anything bothering her, we hadn't argued! We were going to play Mario Kart, for Christ's sake!" His voice broke and he rubbed his skull with the knuckles of his fist. "There is absolutely no reason *at all* why she wouldn't want to come home. What else do I need to say to get that through to you?"

Chloe said nothing while she waited for Gary to regain his composure.

"I'm sorry," he said, his anger dropping off the boil.

"That's okay," Chloe said softly.

"Look, I get it, I understand you have a process that you're supposed to follow, but in this case, it doesn't apply. We're just wasting time."

"Gary..."

"You know about the phone call, don't you?"

"Yes, I know about the phone call."

"Then why are you asking all these pointless questions?"

"Because we have to be thorough."

Gary made a dismissive gesture.

"Gary, just think for one minute. Because of the phone call, it could be easy to assume that she's been abducted, but the fact is we don't know who has her phone. She could have lost it, or it could have been stolen, or she could have given it to someone."

Gary closed his eyes and sighed at the same old line being strung out again. No one was listening to him.

"Let us do our job."

"And while you're doing your 'job', my daughter's... *somewhere*, with God knows who."

Someone grabbed his shoulder and spun him around. It was Frank. Audrey was right behind him trying to pull him back. Frank shrugged her off, but she kept grabbing at him.

"I warned you about this, didn't I?" Frank shouted. "What did I say? I told you to keep her close, didn't I? And what do you do? You abandoned her on the park!"

"I didn't *abandon* her!" Gary shouted back. "She was with her friends."

Audrey pawed at her husband. "Frank, come back. Come back, please."

"You left her there," Frank said. "I warned you to look after her, but you are so cocky with your clever words and your clever ideas. Think you know better than everyone else. Now look where we are!"

Fiona came over and tried to push between them. "Dad, stop it! We all need to calm down! This isn't helping anything!"

117

Frank aggressively stepped closer, his face just inches from Gary's. "Calm? Some people around here have been too calm."

Gary thrust his fist into Frank's chest. "Back off, Frank."

"This is all your fault! If you'd taken notice of what I said, our granddaughter would be home and safe now."

The accusation stabbed Gary hard. "I'm warning you, Frank!"

Frank turned his body and limbered his shoulders. "Think you're good enough to have a go? I might be an old man, but I'll still put you on your arse."

"It's always a fight with you, isn't it, Frank?" Gary yelled. "You can't solve *everything* by putting someone on their arse."

Frank half punched, half shoved Gary in the face. Gary retaliated, grabbing at him.

"MY GOD!" Fiona screamed. "STOP IT! Just stop it! Stop it! *STOP IT!*"

The distress in Fiona's face and voice dropped the wind right out of Gary's sails. Frank stopped struggling, but still jutted out his chin out in defiance.

Fiona looked from one to the other. "Charley's missing and all you want to do is *fight each other*?" Gary touched his mouth and checked his fingers for blood. "What are you thinking? What are you...?" She shook her head and walked away.

"Fiona!" Frank called. He tried to follow her, but Audrey held him back.

"Let me," she said firmly.

Frank began to protest but something in his wife's face told him now wasn't the time. He gave one last smouldering look at Gary, straightened his shirt, and walked away.

Audrey held Gary's gaze for a moment, then went in search of Fiona.

Gary turned to Chloe. "I'm sorry. I can't do this now."

"I can give you a moment, but we really need to get through this, it's very important."

118

"Important to you maybe," Gary muttered, and walked away.

He couldn't face the crowded rooms, the looks and the questions, so he took himself upstairs, to the study where it was dark and quiet.

That look Audrey had given him. Did she blame him too? Of course she did. It *was* his fault. More than any of them even knew.

It was all his fault.

He sat at the desk and thought briefly about the bottle of Old Pulteney in the second drawer. He wasn't a praying man, he wasn't even a believer, but he leaned his elbows on the desk and clasped his hands together, whispering tearfully against them. "Please, God, if you're real and you're listening, please let her come back safely. I'll take care of her better, I promise. Just…just don't let anything happen to her, please."

Someone knocked on the study door. Gary unclasped his hands and quickly wiped his face. "Yeah?"

Lance came in and quietly closed the door behind him. "Hey. You keeping it together, Buddy?"

"It's all my fault, Lance," Gary said.

"Take no notice of what Frank says. He doesn't mean it. He's just angry and scared and needs someone to blame. He'll be fine when he calms down."

Gary shook his head. "I shouldn't have left her. There was this one moment when I almost didn't. But it was such a nice day. There were kids playing in the sand. I thought about this one time we went to the park when Charley was little. I pushed her on the swings…" His fists clenched on the desk. "Why did I leave her, Lance, why?"

"You weren't to know. You need to stop beating yourself up. You aren't the bad guy."

Gary wiped his eyes.

"Let's go out again. It's got to be better than sitting around

119

here doing nothing."

Gary gazed at him. "Thanks, Lance."

Lance nodded. "Come on then. Let's go." He turned to leave.
"Lance?"

He looked back. Gary's mouth and lips quivered but he couldn't speak the words of gratitude he wanted to say.

Lance went around the desk and placed a comforting hand on Gary's shoulder. "I know, Buddy," he said. "I know."

Gary clasped his friend's hand and the tears flowed.

Chloe was busy speaking to Fiona as they made their way out, so he was able to avoid another confrontation about the pointless questions.

The sun was swimming on the horizon when they set out to look for Charley again, orange spears of light spiking through the treetops. As darkness fell, and the cold of night descended, they searched sheds and out-houses, peered into the windows of empty houses, checked the backs of properties, and called out her name across dark, misty fields.

In the dead hours, as they drove the streets around and around, neither of them willing to admit the search was fruitless, Gary grew silent and sullen, his insides churning with fear. Charley was out there somewhere. He didn't know where. He didn't know who with. He didn't know what was happening to her. He clenched his fists and gritted his teeth, trying to block out the mind torturing possibilities.

With the red glow of dawn tinting the belly of the clouds, they returned to the house, tired and dejected. Lance got out of the car to come in, but Gary told him to go home and get some rest. In the daylight they could go out searching again.

The house was still packed, but much quieter than before. Bleary eyes rose expectantly when he walked into the house, but he could only shake his head, and they went back to waiting.

He didn't see Fiona and didn't feel he could face her. What could he say? He went to the bathroom and washed his face. Charley was everywhere, from her toothbrush, to her bathrobe, to her plastic Snow White shampoo bottle.

He walked down the landing to her room, pausing at the door to run his finger lightly over her name on the ceramic plaque, the swirls of his fingerprint sensing the tiny ridges in the artist's deft brush strokes.

When he opened the door, he was instantly consumed by her presence. The bed covers thrown back as she had left them, her shape still imprinted on the sheet. Her iPod discarded on the dresser, the earphone cable tangled with her hairbrush. The faces of Deville and the rest of the boyband cast their pretentiously sultry looks down on him from the poster on the wall.

A shroud of absolute misery covered him. Tears wanted to come, but he refused to give in to them this time. He sat on the edge of her bed, careful not to disturb where she had lain, and looked around at all her things.

At one end of the room sat piles of old toys that were too young for her now, but she wasn't quite ready to give up yet. A chalkboard easel with a little multi-coloured clock in the corner. A stack of games in battered boxes: *Hungry Hippo* and *Operation.*

He covered his face with his hands and asked how this could be happening? How could one simple stupid thing lead to all this?

The door creaked. For a moment Gary thought Fiona had come looking for him, but it was only Mister Whiskers sliding his lithe body through the small gap. He saw Gary and froze, just staring at him as if wondering what he was doing there instead of Charley.

Gary leaned forward, rubbing his fingers together and

121

making that soft *ch-ch-ch* sound that cats seem to like so much. "Come on, Whiskers, come on then."

The cat regarded him for a few more moments, then padded into the room as if it was his own personal space. He came over to the bed and rubbed himself against Gary's legs, his tail straight up in the air with a little curl at the end.

Gary scooped him off the floor and onto his lap. "Hey fella," he whispered. "You looking for Charley?" Mister Whiskers purred. "Me too. But don't worry, she'll be back soon, you'll see."

Gary laid back across the bed with Mister Whiskers in his arms, his head and shoulders propped against the wall. A heavy blanket of exhaustion descended on him all at once. He closed his eyes, his fingers stroking the soft fur on the nape of Mister Whisker's neck. In seconds he drifted into a fitful sleep.

At some point he dreamed of that day he and Fiona took Charley to the park. She was just a toddler and he was pushing her on the swings. She was laughing, and there was no more beautiful sound in the world than his daughter's laugh.

Higher, Daddy! Higher!

He awoke to someone shaking him gently. He opened his eyes and saw it was Fiona. With the dream fresh in his mind, he glanced about him, confused, and then the reality came crashing in. He sat up, his neck cricked and stiff.

"What is it? Has something happened? What time is it?" As he glanced at his watch, Fiona told him it was eight o'clock.

"Nothing's happened," she said. "The police are putting out another appeal this morning. They're going to arrange a media conference for two o'clock this afternoon. They want to go over what's going to happen."

"Who's here?" he asked.

"My mum and dad are still here. I told everyone to go home and get some rest, but Trixie and a few others refused to leave."

"Lance?"

"Not yet."

Gary rubbed his face with his hands and ran them through his hair. "Okay, just let me wash my face and brush my teeth. My mouth tastes like shit."

Lance arrived an hour later, looking tired and disappointed when he heard there had been no developments.

The appeal went out midmorning. They all gathered in the sitting room to watch it. When Charley's photo appeared, there were small moans and sighs from everyone present.

Gary wasn't happy with it. The police were still making it sound like Charley might have run away, rather than had been abducted. Everyone who knew Charley didn't believe she had run away.

After the broadcast, he and Lance went out again. The sun poured from the sky and everything appeared different than it had yesterday. How could a new day dawn and the world just carry on while Charley was still missing?

This time, they walked the route from the house to the park instead of taking the car. They showed the photo to everyone they met and asked if they had seen her. Always the same vacant look and a 'no sorry' reply.

When they reached the park, Gary cast his gaze across the houses that curved around the length of the boulevard. He could see ten or fifteen almost identical dwellings right there in front of him. She could be held in any one of them, or in any one of the tens of thousands of houses in Gableton. And what if she'd been taken out of town? She could be anywhere.

The near-impossible odds of finding her by wandering the streets crushed his hopes. They were searching for the proverbial needle in a haystack. The only way she was going to be found was either through someone who knew she had been abducted, or through the person responsible for abducting her.

Or, perhaps, someone who had noticed something unusual.

He decided that he urgently wanted to get to that press

123

conference and appeal directly to whoever had her, to release her unharmed.

He looked at his watch. Eleven-thirty-five. The conference was arranged for two in the afternoon. It seemed like an age away. Everything was outside of his control and he didn't like it. He felt as if it was all slipping through his fingers and there wasn't a thing he could do about it.

They walked back to the house in silence. Lance stopped to talk to one or two people and show the photo, but Gary didn't even slow down.

At the house, Lance tried to talk to him, but he just excused himself and went upstairs, intending to go to the study, but ending up in Charley's bedroom again instead.

He thought about the night of her birthday, finding her still playing with Mister Whiskers. She'd counted her money and had already decided she was going to buy him the pen he'd liked so much.

He put his finger on the copy of Sleeping Beauty, taking it down from the shelf but not looking at it. He sat on the bed and just glanced despairingly around him. Would she ever see this room again?

Fiona came in.

"Lance said you'd come up here."

He couldn't look at her.

Fiona tilted her head to read the title of the book he held on his knee. "Sleeping Beauty," she said. "Charley's favourite."

Gary glanced at it. "Yeah." He turned the book over to look at the colourfully illustrated cover. "One time, when she was little, she asked me to read it to her at bedtime. I was busy as usual. I didn't want to have to read it and tried to talk her out of it. But she looked at me with those big brown eyes and I couldn't disappoint her."

Fiona tried to smile a little.

"So, I read it and did all the voices the way she liked it. She

124

always loved the part where the prince rides his horse to save Beauty and chops through the thorn bushes to get to her. The second I read, 'the end', she wanted me to read it again, but I had other stuff to do. I told her I'd read it again the next night." He hung his head. "Obviously I didn't. I tucked her in and she asked: if she was ever locked away in a secret castle, would I come and save her like the prince did?' I told her I'd find her no matter where she was."

"Gary..."

"It's funny how you just make promises like that without even thinking about them. You just never believe something like this could happen to you." His voice broke and the tears came fast. "And now she's out there somewhere, Fee, and I can't find her. I can't be her prince and find her like I promised I would. I don't even know where to start looking."

Fiona knelt in front of him, hooking her hands behind his neck and pulling his forehead to hers.

"Come on," she said softly. "This isn't you. You're the fighter, the one who never gives up."

It was true, but right now he was in despair.

"The police said the press conference will bring in information, some clues."

Gary turned his head against hers, unable to look into her eyes. "Fiona...I'm so sorry."

"Don't," Fiona whispered. "We're going to find her, okay?"

She held his face in her hands and lifted it to look into his eyes. "Okay?"

He nodded and wiped away the hot tears, and then together, they went to face the music.

The press conference had been set up in the assembly hall of Charley's junior school, Saint Maria Gorettis. The police drove them over, with Chloe, who gave them some final preparation of what would happen starting with the lead detective who would read a statement and appeal for information. Then Gary and Fiona would say something. The conference would not be open to questions.

Not all stories of missing children are big news, but Charley's was that much bigger since the link between the three blonde girls had been established. *The Goldilocks Kidnappings*. People were obviously thinking Charley might be a fourth victim, but Gary couldn't understand why. She was the right age, but she didn't have curly blonde hair like the others. Why would the proclaimed *Goldilocks Kidnapper* take a girl without blonde hair?

Photographers jostled each other across the street from the school as they were ushered in through the main entrance. Police officers manned the doors and a low murmur drifted from the school's main hall.

While they waited outside the assembly hall doors, Gary clasped Fiona's hand. It was ice cold and trembling. He squeezed it and tried to give her a look of solidarity. She smiled, but it was tight and strained.

Chloe gave them a nod, and the doors opened to the staring eye of the media. The room exploded with clicking cameras and flashing bulbs that threw crazy lurching shadows in every direction.

A backdrop had been set up behind the conference tables, hung with *Lancashire Constabulary* posters and Charley's school photo printed on boards with MISSING PERSON in large, red text.

They took chairs behind tables bristling with microphones. In the semicircle of reporters, photographers and cameramen before them, he saw signs for BBC and ITV, Channel 4, Channel 5 and Sky News. Everything had a surreal dream-like quality to it. Despite his experience, Gary felt uncomfortable and exposed.

He checked on Fiona, taking her hand again. The gesture prompted a frenzy of picture taking as the photographers tried to capture the moment.

The detective prepared to read the statement and the large hall filled with a strange hush, interrupted only by the odd click of a camera and flash of a bulb.

The police statement outlined the approximate time Charley went missing, where she was last seen and what she was wearing. The detective asked that if she was watching this, she should come home, or even call to let them know she was safe. There was no reason for her to be afraid. He also stressed concern for her safety and appealed for anyone who might have any information, no matter how small, to come forward.

Then it was Gary's turn to speak and the media attention focused on him. He tried to moisten his lips, but his mouth was dry as a moth's wing. He hadn't really prepared what he was going to say, just speaking from the heart and hoping someone heard him and felt their pain.

"Our daughter's name is Charlotte, but we call her Charley. She's just twelve years old. At home, she has a cat she called Mister Whiskers. She's a loving, caring child who wouldn't hurt anyone for the world. She..." He paused and swallowed, glancing at the lead detective as he did so. "The police think she's run away, but I firmly believe she's been kidnapped and is being held against her will."

The camera flashes almost blinded him. Reporters, ignoring the 'no questions' instruction, started shouting his name, trying to draw his attention, while others simply threw questions at him, one asking clearly if Gary thought Charley was a victim of the Goldilocks Kidnapper.

The detective stood up and attempted to calm everyone down. "There will be no questions at this time," he insisted. When it all quietened down again, he continued. "Mr. Wright obviously has strong feelings about what has happened to his daughter, but we must follow all lines of enquiry."

Gary stood up too. "And while you're wasting time doing that, someone is holding Charley against her will!"

"Mr. Wright…" the lead detective said, but Gary ignored him and looked directly into the nearest TV camera.

"To the person who's holding my daughter…," he said, then corrected himself. "To the *man* who has my daughter…please don't hurt her…you can let her go. You have that power. You can just take her somewhere and drop her off. You can let our daughter come home to us where she belongs. Please, just stop and let her come home."

Fiona was weeping freely.

He leaned across the table, his face strained and desperate.

"I'm asking for everyone's help here. He's holding her somewhere. In a house, or a flat, or an outbuilding. Please look to your neighbours, look to your families, no matter how unlikely that might seem. This man is someone's son, someone's uncle, maybe even someone's husband or father. Just take a look and see if there's anything unusual happening. Are curtains closed all day and night? Have windows suddenly been boarded up? Have you noticed any unusual behaviour? If you've seen *anything* suspicious, anything at all, please call the police and let them know about it."

He scanned the faces of the reporters and the photographers. He didn't feel he had said enough; didn't feel that his plea had gone deep enough. He wanted to say more, yet there was nothing more he could say.

The detective took over again, inviting everyone to rise and leave the conference. Gary took Fiona's hand and helped her to her feet. She was so pale and weak. As she stood, her legs gave way and she fainted back into her seat. The room exploded again.

Gary held his wife tightly while the cameras clicked and flashed and clicked and flashed.

After the broadcast had finished, and in such spectacular fashion too, the man the media called the *Goldilocks Kidnapper* stopped the video recorder from capturing to the hard disk and sat staring at the screen. Later he'd transfer the recording to DVD for permanency.

He crawled from his spot in front of the TV, to the cupboard in the alcove. The rectangle of threadbare carpet wasn't fitted all the way to the edges of the room, the bare boards grinding at his bony kneecaps.

He opened the door and dragged a cardboard box into the open and onto the floor. The box contained a collection of clothes and belongings. They weren't in any kind of order, or neatly folded, just a jumble-sale-like box of shirts and skirts and socks and underwear. He ran his hand over the folds, his fingertips caressing the fabrics lightly. Touching their clothes thrilled him, as it always did.

He picked up the latest additions to his collection. A pair of denim shorts with a pink plastic belt, a butterfly printed tee-shirt, a pair of white socks with pink hearts all over them. A purple cap with 'Charley' written across the visor in glitter pen. He dropped each item into the box, pausing at the tee-shirt to hold it up to the light. The shirt was bloodstained. It was unfortunate. He hadn't meant for that to happen.

He glanced into the dark hall. In the kitchen was a gnarled and pitted door that opened to a short wooden staircase leading down to his father's annexed workshop.

The body was down there. He'd bathed and dried her carefully, then wrapped her in black plastic bags, tightly wrapping it with duct tape. It was cooler in the workshop, but realistically he needed to dispose of her before she started stinking up the place. It didn't take long for a body to start

129

stinking, as he knew well, and it was summer after all.

He'd already picked out a place in the countryside. It appeared to be well off the beaten track, but the land would belong to someone, so he'd have to be meticulous in burying the body and hiding the evidence.

He pushed the box back into the cupboard and was about to close the door when he remembered something. He dug in the front pocket of his jeans, bringing out a mobile phone with the back missing. Further exploration produced the phone's back casing and the battery. He flicked the phone from side to side, the colourful Tinkerbelle charm jingling, then threw the pieces into the box with the rest of the things and closed the door.

Chapter Ten

After the media conference went out, people turned up in their hundreds to help look for her. They formed search parties to comb woods and fields. Divers dredged the canal. Police made door-to-door enquiries. Local businesses came together and raised a one hundred and fifty-thousand-pound reward for anyone with information that led police to Charley's whereabouts.

They were only a few days into the investigation when an officer dragged a large sack into the hall.

"What's this?" Gary asked.

"It's mail sent to you by the public," the officer informed him.

Gary stared at the heavy looking sack. It was full to the top with mail. He was lost for words.

The officer dusted his hands. "I should warn you; while there'll be a lot of goodwill in those letters, you're also going to find some poisonous crap from the crazies out there too."

"Really?" Gary said. "How do you know?"

The officer gave him a long look. "Because there always is."

Gary had hundreds of posters and flyers printed with Charley's photo and description, and with the help of friends and family, pasted them to walls and billboards and lamp posts. They left them in supermarkets, shops, foyers, libraries, garages, and handed them to anyone who would take one.

He and Fiona appeared on *This Morning* to talk about Charley and the nightmare they had endured since her disappearance. BBC's *Crime Watch* TV series reconstructed and aired Charley's last known movements. The programs generated thousands of calls.

But none of them led to Charley.

About a month after that officer had dragged in that first bag of mail, Gary sat down in the spare room with it, and six more just like it. The corner of the room was piled high with packages and gifts, soft toys and more. So many flowers had been delivered that they'd had to ask that they be redirected to Gableton Hospital, just keeping any cards or tags that came with them.

He loosened the ties on the first sack and tore open the first envelope his hand fell upon. It contained a religious card, the front embossed with silver praying hands. Inside, the sender had printed an inscription saying that she was praying for Charley's safe return and had signed it simply, *Elizabeth*.

Gary looked at the card for a long time, emotions swirling around inside him. A woman called Elizabeth, someone he didn't even know, had felt their plight and had taken time to write to them. He slid the card back into its envelope and placed it to one side.

The next one he chose was a handwritten letter that went on for several pages. It started off with prayers for Charley's safe return, and continued to explain how the writer had also lost someone close to them. In some ways, it seemed more like the writer was reaching out to him with their pain, rather than trying to console him with his.

He picked out another and was reading it: *Stay strong. God is watching,* when Fiona came in and asked what he was doing.

He gestured to the bags. "I just thought I'd take a look at a few of these letters."

Fiona placed her hands on her hips and viewed all the sacks and parcels. "We need to sort these," she said. She took a letter off the top and sat down. Gary watched her read it, her eyes scanning quickly from side to side. "This is from a lady who lost their daughter. Oh my God. She was *murdered*...by her boyfriend."

Gary picked up another letter. It was addressed to him personally and felt flimsy.

"This is so awful," Fiona said. "I think I remember this in the news when it happened."

Gary opened his envelope and took out a single sheet of paper. He unfolded it and what he saw written there took his breath away.

Fiona glanced up from her letter and noticed his expression. "What is it?"

For a moment he didn't want to tell her. Didn't even want her to see it. He just wanted to screw the filth into a tight ball and throw it on the back of a fire where it belonged.

With a look of resignation, he handed it over.

Did you fuck her in the ass
before you killed her u
murdering pedo fuck!

"Oh my God! Who sent this?"

"I doubt they signed it," Gary said.

Fiona ripped it to shreds and crushed the pieces into her fist.

133

"You didn't need to see that," she told him. "I can't believe anyone would be sick enough to send something like that."

"I can. There's probably a lot more like that in these sacks."

"Isn't what's already happening to us bad enough, without that?"

"People think it was me. They think I killed her."

"No, they don't," Fiona insisted. "Not the people who matter anyway. Look, maybe you shouldn't read any more of these until they've been sorted. Reading stuff like that isn't going to be good for you." She spread the letters on top of the bag. "We don't have time to look at them all anyway." She stooped over the bag and tightened the laces. "I'll get something organised with family and friends. We'll take shifts at going through them and sort them out. What do you...?"

She looked to where Gary had been sitting but he wasn't there anymore. She turned to see him walking out of the room and closing the door behind him.

He didn't read any more letters.

Gary went wherever anyone was willing to give him air time, retelling the story and trying his utmost to keep Charley in the public eye. He believed there was still a chance that someone might notice something unusual, think of the missing girl they'd seen on the news, and call the police.

More appeals went out, but two months after Charley had disappeared, they were no closer to knowing what happened to her. No fresh clues had been uncovered, or any new lines of enquiry formed. The investigation was scaled back to a core team, and the police regretfully had to admit that the chance of Charley being found alive was unlikely.

On TV and radio he was strong and positive, but alone in the evenings, he took to his study and drank through his tears, asking himself why. Everyone saw the change—the downward spiral of his spirits—but there wasn't anything anyone could do. His enthusiasm had all but disappeared, his ambitions and zest for life extinguished.

He hadn't been into work since Charley went missing; citing that he was far too busy trying to keep Charley's name in the public consciousness to work. But when it was all over, he still didn't return.

One day, about four months after Charley disappeared, Fiona asked if he'd like to go out for lunch.

"What?" Gary asked. He heard her, but was thinking, *lunch? Who gives a fuck about lunch?*

"We've been cooped up in here for too long, we should go out for lunch. Nowhere fancy, just the shopper's restaurant at the supermarket. Anything to get us out of the house for a while."

Why is she asking me this? Gary thought. *Why does she even want to go out for lunch? What's the point?*

Outside felt like a huge scary place now, full of strangers who would recognise and judge them.

That's the guy who abandoned his daughter on the park and got her kidnapped.

"I don't want to," he said.

Fiona knelt beside him. "Come on, Gary. Please? Just for me?"

He looked at her. She'd lost so much weight, but she was still as beautiful as the day he met her. How could he explain to her that his heart lurched at the very thought of going out somewhere public? Why couldn't he just stay here and have a drink or two?

Fiona's face slipped from hopeful to disappointed. He hated that look because it reminded him that all this was his fault.

She started to get up, but he grabbed her hand. "Okay then, but I'm not really hungry."

Fiona drove, while Gary watched the world go by, a world he didn't really feel a part of anymore. He realised that he was rubbing the palm of his hand with his thumb, and the palm was sweaty. He stopped himself, made fists with his hands and tucked them by his sides, but his heart and stomach still churned with anxiety.

What's going on with me?

Fiona backed the car into an empty slot and opened her door. Halfway out of the car, she noticed Gary wasn't moving.

"Are you all right?"

He looked around the carpark, seeing people going about their business, loading cars with shopping, strolling around without a care in the world. For some reason they bothered him. Being around these people bothered him.

"I don't know," he replied. "I just feel weird."

Fiona settled back into her seat and pulled the door to, but not closed. "We can sit a little while if you like."

Ignoring the feel of Fiona's eyes on him, he watched a woman passing items of shopping to her husband, who was packing them into the boot of their car. The couple probably weren't much older than he and Fiona. Two children were playing in the back seat. He looked at the parents again and an uncharitable thought darkened his mind.

Why us?

Why me and not you?

You have two kids, now we have none. Why couldn't this have happened to you instead of us?

The woman glanced in his direction, saw him watching her and smiled. Gary felt bad for wishing misfortune on them, and yet he couldn't help the bitter thoughts crawling in the cracks of his mind.

"Gary?"

He turned to Fiona.

"Look, we can go back home if you want..."

Gary glanced around again. His heart felt like a swooping bird. *What am I afraid of?* They were just people getting on with their lives.

"No. I can't let this get a hold of me. If it gets hold of me..." He left the rest unsaid and got out of the car.

The busy scene inside the supermarket assaulted his senses, as if he had walked into a wall of sound and vision. The harsh lighting made his eyes ache. Rows of shelving threatened him. The vivid shapes and colours of the packaging intimidated him. And through it all, people scurried around like ants.

Fiona linked his arm. "Are you okay?"

"I don't know," he replied.

His eyes darted around, never resting, as if this mundane life tableau was something he had never witnessed before. He had always been an active participant, another ant moving through the maze, rather than an observer, watching from the sidelines.

He had to reassure that unreasonable part of himself that this was nothing threatening or frightening. They were just ordinary people going about their ordinary business.

He cupped his hand over Fiona's fingers and forced a smile. Fiona set off, but still he hesitated. She felt it and looked at him again, waiting to see what he wanted to do. He took a deep breath, nodded, and let her guide him.

As they approached the restaurant, he was relieved to move away from the clamour of shoppers and beeping cash registers. The restaurant was busy, but there were empty tables here and there. Fiona had to coax every choice out of him: what do you want? Do you want cake with it? Tea? Coffee? A cold drink? Sugar? Milk?

It made him want to scream.

In the end she ordered him a baked potato with cheese and beans. It was Fiona's choice, Gary didn't care. He didn't think he could eat it anyway. He wished he was back at home, with a glass of whisky.

Fiona carried the tray to an empty table and sat down. Once she'd arranged the drinks and set the tray to one side, she looked across the table at Gary and smiled.

"So," she said. "This is okay, isn't it?"

He nodded, but it wasn't okay. It was far from okay. It all felt like a charade, like they were on a movie set with the director just off camera, calling out instructions. *Okay, now look at your wife. Smile at her, that's it. Just smile at her like everything's okay.*

But it wasn't okay, and all the smiles and baked potatoes in the world couldn't make it so. Charley was missing, and he was pretending that it was all right that she was missing because it was four months ago? Like he could come out and eat a fucking baked potato and drink a plastic cup of crap tea, as if none of it mattered.

Why did Fiona even want to do this?

He needed to get out of there. He saw himself thrusting back the chair and rushing out, another scene from the same fucking movie. People standing around in shock. People knocked to the floor as he crashed through the oppressive crowds.

He braced his foot against the tiles, pushing back on his chair, ready to just walk out, just get up and get the fuck out.

And then their food arrived.

The waitress smiled as she set down their plates.

"Would you like any sauces?" she asked

Gary looked at the steaming potato with its oily yellow lava flow of cheese and shook his head. Sauces? Just the look and smell of it was enough to turn his stomach.

The waitress invited them to enjoy their meal and left.

Fiona unfolded her paper napkin.

"This looks good," she said.

Good? Gary thought.

A woman arrived at the table next to theirs, wrestling with a couple of heavy shopping bags. She sat down with a sigh and

138

looked at Gary. She did a double take and smiled a little too brightly. "Oh, hello," she greeted.

Gary nodded at her, but didn't meet her eyes.

He coaxed some cheese and a little potato onto his fork and put it in his mouth. The cheese was scalding hot and greasy, the potato powdery dry. His stomach clenched at the feel of it on his tongue. He wanted a drink, but not the crap tea in front of him.

The woman at the next table kept glancing his way, then a younger woman arrived with a tray of drinks and set them down. "Food'll be here in a minute, Mum," she said.

Her mother leaned toward Gary with a puzzled smile and said, "I know you, don't I?"

Gary looked at Fiona, his eyes full of panic. This was why he had been afraid to come out. She'd probably seen him in the newspapers or on the television and thought she knew him. He felt as if he was going to throw up the little bit of cheese and potato he'd just swallowed.

Fiona spoke for him, "No, we haven't met."

"Really?" the woman persisted. "But I'm sure I know you from somewhere." She swivelled around in her seat to look properly at Fiona. "You too."

The daughter, who was studying Gary intently, said, "Mum?"

Gary wanted to slide under the table and crawl out of there on his hands and knees.

The woman touched her forehead. "Well I'm sure I know you from somewhere."

"*Mum*?" the daughter pushed.

The mother finally paid her attention. "What?"

The daughter leaned in and whispered words that really weren't whispers at all because Gary heard every one of them.

"They're the parents of that *girl*...you know, the one who left his daughter on the park a while ago and she got kidnapped."

139

The mother looked at Gary again, suddenly horrified. "Oh my goodness! Oh, I'm so sorry!"

"That's okay," Fiona said.

"No, no, I'm so sorry." She turned to her daughter. "Let's move and let these people have some privacy."

Privacy? Gary thought. *We're in a café.*

The commotion the woman was creating, while hastily collecting her bags, was attracting the attention of other diners.

"Really," Fiona said. "There's no need to move."

"No, no," the woman insisted. "We're intruding. We'll just...oh, there's a table over there. Amy...just...yes...you get the drinks. I'll get these bags." She looked apologetically at them both. "I'm so sorry."

Gary stared at the congealing cheese on his plate while mother and daughter indiscreetly moved their things to another table. A few moments later the mother returned to get the purse one of them had hurriedly left behind, apologising all the while.

The restaurant filled with muttered conversation, whispers, and movements around them. Chairs shifted and carrier bags rustled as people moved tables or cut their stay early.

When the noise had abated, Gary raised his head from the cooling food and looked directly at Fiona. He didn't have to glance around to know they were now sitting in their own little void of empty tables.

Fiona stared back into his eyes and nodded. "Okay," she accepted. "Let's go home."

Chapter Eleven

Gary fell deeper into drink and despair. There were no answers. No happy reunion. Not even a funeral or a place to lay flowers. Nothing but an empty bedroom and even emptier hearts.

Sometimes he'd go out in the evening and return in the early hours of the morning. When Fiona asked where he'd been, he'd just tell her he'd been driving around, looking for Charley.

It was heart-breaking for Fiona to see her strong, confident husband scratched away by depression and remorse. He was hanging by his fingertips, hoping against hope that Charley might still be found safe and well.

For Fiona, that time had just about passed. She'd read books and watched television shows about abduction, even before any of it had happened to them. She knew all about the first twenty-four hours and how the likelihood of finding them alive after that grew more remote by the minute. In the early days, she'd found courage and strength in Gary's unwavering belief that Charley was still alive, but as weeks stacked into months, she had forced herself to face the terrible reality that Charley was probably never coming home. Three other girls had gone missing before Charley, and not one of them had been found.

Charley wasn't officially being counted as another victim of the Goldilocks Kidnapper; and Gary certainly refused to even entertain the idea that she had been taken by the same person.

But did that really matter? *Someone* had stolen Charley from them. That was all they really needed to know.

She'd tried to help Gary in his grief. Losing their precious daughter had hit him harder than she thought anything ever could. It had knocked his planet so far out of orbit that she was afraid he might never come back.

But he made it so difficult for her to find him. When he wasn't out looking for Charley, he was in the study with a bottle, getting quietly smashed. Those evenings inevitably ended with Fiona helping him to bed and listening to his drunken weeping while he told her yet again how sorry he was.

Yes, it was difficult to watch him come apart, but it was even more difficult to see him make no attempt to do anything about it.

She was trying her best, she really was. She sympathised with him and she talked to him. She assured him time and time again, that it wasn't his fault. But nothing worked. Nothing she said got through to him. It was like the clock reset every day and they were back to square one.

Anyone would think that he was the only one who missed Charley, and that he was the only one entitled to grieve for her.

And eventually, she began to resent him for it.

Chapter Twelve

The wheel of time never pauses, never waits for anyone to catch up. If you miss that crucial boat then chances are, it's gone for good.

As autumn painted the lush summer greens with brown and gold, Gary knew he had let it all slip through his fingers. He'd fumbled the ball. All of his attempts to find Charley had amounted to nothing. Not a single lead or clue. He'd lost control of the search and the investigation, of himself and his life. He'd failed her in every way possible.

With the shifting seasons came the feeling that the day Charley disappeared was from another time. A time that was now fading into the distance and from memory; a hazy ship far, far away on the rim of the horizon. He began to feel like Charley had been a beautiful dream that had ended far too soon.

Then at the beginning of November, another girl disappeared. Her name was Angela Mears. She had been with friends to the cinema where they had met some older boys. The friends wanted to go for coffee with them after the movie, but Angela didn't feel comfortable with it, and she had promised her parents she would be back by ten. Her friends told her not to be a pussy, but she insisted that if she didn't arrive home when she had promised, her parents would ground her for a week. She left them outside the cinema, telling them she was going to take the bus home.

That was the last anyone had seen of her.

She was thirteen years old, with long, blonde, curly hair.

With the chill of December came the equally chilling promise of Christmas. The season of goodwill descended like a dark wraith on the Wright house. Gary would have snipped it out if he could, like the unwanted frames of a movie, and burned the entire painful scene. But there was nowhere to hide from it, no way to avoid it, and when it arrived it was every bit as terrible as he had feared.

The previous year, they had spent Christmas Eve watching *Polar Express* and eating mince pies topped with squirty cream. When Charley was finally in bed, he and Fiona had wrapped a few remaining presents and Fiona had made up their Christmas stockings from the usual collection of silly gifts (he got a set of *Emergency Moustaches*) and enough sweets to see them clear through to Easter.

Charley had excitedly woken them at six in the morning and demanded that they get up, pulling at Gary's arm until he reluctantly agreed to get out of bed. They opened their presents, ate breakfast and cooked dinner. Lance came later, and they played board games and laughed and drank mulled wine, and it was perfect.

Just perfect.

This Christmas Eve saw him sat alone behind his desk, getting smashed, while he recalled every second of that last Christmas together. He hadn't realised at the time, that each of those moments with Charley was like a precious stone to be treasured.

On Christmas morning he awoke a little after eleven, fully dressed and spread out on top of the single bed in the guest

144

room. He didn't know how he had gotten there. His head throbbed, and he had a tremendous thirst. He checked their bedroom, but Fiona wasn't there, the bed neat and made. He went downstairs and into the kitchen where he gulped down half a carton of juice.

Other homes were filled with excited children, Christmas decorations and a twinkling tree. Families together for Christmas lunch. Families just *together*. In Gary's house, there were no gifts or Christmas cheer. The house was especially quiet and sombre.

When he walked into the front room, the sound of Fiona's tears transported him back to that Christmas when he was eight years old, only this time he didn't even have a bruised apple or a stolen chocolate Santa.

Fiona was sitting on the edge of the sofa, clutching a photo of Charley to her breast and quietly weeping. Her eyes were red and swollen. He walked over to her, but she didn't look at him.

He couldn't remember the last time they'd shown each other any affection. He didn't feel capable of affection anymore. He gently took the picture away from her and set it aside. Fiona looked up at him as he held out his hands, unsure of what he wanted. She placed her cold hands in his and he pulled her to her feet, gazing into her eyes. His head and mouth moved as if trying to articulate something that had no words to describe it. Then his face crumpled, and he snatched her to him, clawed her to him, and held her in a crushing embrace while they both wept against each other.

They stood in that dark, cold room, crying and clinging together for what seemed like an eternity, their faces hot and wet, their agony spilling out in floods of tears.

When the great wracking sobs had subsided, Gary stepped back and wiped the back of his wrist across his eyes.

Then he walked away and left her alone again.

Chapter Thirteen

January 18th, 2014 was a Saturday. The Lester family had been out shopping, picking up bargains in the January sales. At four in the afternoon, they stopped at McDonald's for some food, before setting off back to get the car from the multi-story carpark in the middle of town.

As they entered the carpark, their daughter, Vicky, shouted to her older brother, "Last one there stinks!" and ran off towards the car, which was one floor down, her blonde hair bouncing behind her. Her brother, however, wasn't in the mood for a race and let her go. Her mother called for her to wait, but she either didn't hear her, or didn't think it mattered.

When they arrived at the car less than a minute and a half later, Vicky was nowhere to be seen. They called out her name, thinking she was hiding somewhere, but her mother sensed something was wrong from the start.

They searched the carpark but couldn't find her.

She was just twelve-years-old.

Chapter Fourteen

Gableton sparkled with frost on that February morning when the doorbell rang. Gary was up and dressed for a change, and reasonably sober. He stayed seated. He wasn't going to answer it. Fiona would do that. She was better at seeing people than he.

After a muffled exchange, he heard Fiona invite them in. He stood up, his heart picking up pace. Who was it? Why hadn't she just turned them away? Whoever it was, he didn't want to see them. He didn't want to see anyone.

The choice was taken from him when Fiona came into the room and looked at him with intense, frightened eyes. "It's Chloe," she said. "She has some...news."

Chlo the FLO.

Fiona stood at Gary's side, the two of them watching like small frightened animals, as Chloe closed the door.

"Shall we take a seat?" she asked.

"I'm okay here," Gary said, but his voice felt like it came from a distance; like he was disembodied and watching this from somewhere far away.

"Please?"

Reluctantly, he sat down on the sofa with Fiona. Chloe took the armchair.

"This is going to hit the news pretty soon," she began. "So, I wanted to let you know before it did."

Gary found it difficult to catch his breath. He waited, his heart clenched, his muscles tensed for the bad news he knew was about to come.

Charley's body has been found. I'm so sorry.

"Some remains have been found in woodland," Chloe said.

"Remains?" Gary repeated. "What do you mean, *remains*?"

"A body."

"Is it Charley?" Fiona asked, tears in her eyes.

"I'm afraid I can't say for sure right now. The remains have been buried for a while." She paused, and Gary could see her choosing her words with care. "Visual identification isn't possible. Identification will have to be done forensically, probably with dental records, or if that's not possible, you may be called upon to give a DNA sample."

"But it is a young girl?" Fiona said.

Shut up! Gary thought. *Why are you pushing this? Why do you fucking want to know all these things?*

"Yes, I'm afraid it is."

Gary covered his face with his hand. The blackness he was so afraid of was drawing closer, threatening to devour him.

"Could it be Charley?" Fiona asked.

"In all honesty, Fiona, I don't know. But I'm afraid it might be."

Fiona nodded silently. "When will you know for sure?"

"The remains have been taken to the mortuary and will be examined there. If the dental records are conclusive, I would expect to hear something in the next couple of hours."

Gary's mind pushed back the blackness. There was still a chance it wasn't Charley…but what if it was? Their beautiful daughter discarded in woodland and left to rot like discarded rubbish. He crushed his fist against his face, his knuckles pressing hard into his lip. Jaw clenched, chest heaving with stress and anger. He wanted to lash out at something.

"Are you okay, Gary?" Chloe asked.

He swallowed hard and nodded, but it was a moment or two before he could find his voice. "Yes. It's just...so hard..."

Chloe nodded. "I know," she said. "I wish I could have brought something more definite."

"You'll come back to tell us?" Fiona asked. "When you know? It doesn't matter what the time is."

Chloe nodded. "Of course I will."

She looked at Gary again and he saw something in her eyes, something that said although this had never happened to her personally, she did understand what he was going through. She had lived through this nightmare with them at a very intimate level, and at the height of the investigation, she and Fiona had grown close. He hadn't allowed her to get close to him though. He wasn't sure why.

"Thank you for coming to tell us, Chloe," Fiona said. "And for your honesty."

Chloe stood. "I'll come back as soon as I know anything."

While Fiona saw Chloe to the door, Gary got up and paced the room. After the months of waiting it was all suddenly moving too fast for him. Charley's decomposed body could be lying on a mortuary slab. His hopes of finding her alive might soon be crushed.

What happens then? asked a tiny, frightened part of his mind. *What happens when even that tiny light is snuffed out?*

He turned one way, then after two paces turned back, and back again, like a caged animal.

He noticed Fiona standing in the doorway watching him. He stopped pacing, embarrassed that she had seen him so tormented.

"It just goes on and on, doesn't it," she said.

"It's not her," Gary said.

"What?"

"It's not her."

Fiona looked toward the window. The naked winter trees

149

stood starkly out against the smokey grey sky. "We'll just have to wait and see, won't we," she said and left him there.

Gary took to the study. He wanted a drink but resisted the urge. He opened his Mac and continuously refreshed the BBC news website, until about thirty minutes after Chloe left, the 'breaking news' bar reported that human remains had been found in woodland. The story appeared on other news websites, but it must have been a press release, because they all carried the exact same report.

The wait after that initial announcement was almost unbearable, like a condemned man waiting for the touch of the executioner's cold hand on his shoulder. He wanted to know, and yet he didn't want to know at all. What he really wanted, what he desperately needed, was to be told that it wasn't Charley.

An agonizing two hours and thirty-two minutes later, Chloe returned. Gary came down from the study as Fiona opened the door.

They moved silently through to the living room as if in slow motion, and took the same seats as they had earlier. Fiona clasped Gary's hand in hers, but he barely noticed. He couldn't think. It was as if all his mental processes had been cleared away to receive this one single piece of news.

Please don't let it be Charley, he silently begged. *Please don't let it be Charley.*

Yet he knew it was. He knew she was going to say Charley's name. He clenched his teeth, his body rigid, ready to take the devastating news.

"It's not Charley," Chloe told them.

Fiona covered her face with her hands and began sobbing.

Gary felt lightheaded. "It's not Charley?" he breathed.

Chloe shook her head and let the news sink in.

"It's not Charley," he said again. "Is that one hundred percent certain?"

"The remains have been positively identified," Chloe told him. "It's definitely not Charley."

"Oh my God," Gary whispered, his hands trembling as relief washed over him.

Then the sobering thought struck him. "Who is it?"

"I can't tell you that right now, Gary. I can only tell you that it isn't Charley."

"Of course," Gary replied. "Sorry. Thank you, Chloe. Thank you so much."

"It's nice to not be giving bad news for once," she said, and got to her feet. "I can't linger. It's busy at the station, as you can imagine. Don't get up, I'll see myself out."

Fiona wiped her eyes and nodded.

"Take care," Chloe said and left.

Gary turned to Fiona, so elated that he could have punched the air, but she was still sobbing.

"It's okay, Fee," he soothed. "This is good news. It means Charley could still be out there somewhere. She could still be alive."

Fiona shook her head and turned away from him, her face full of pain.

"Fee, what is it? What's wrong?"

Fiona gave him such a pitiful look, but there was resentment in her eyes. "What's wrong with you?" she asked.

"What's wrong with *me*?"

"How do you keep this up?

"Keep what up? What are you talking about?"

"How can you keep believing she's alive after all this time? After all that's happened."

"Because we have to keep hope, Fee. What else do we have if we don't have hope?"

Fiona closed her eyes, fresh tears streaming down her cheeks. "I can't, Gary...I just can't..."

"Can't what? Can't believe in your own daughter?"

Fiona opened her eyes again, anger now simmering behind the tears.

"Don't you try and turn this into something it's not! This isn't about believing in Charley. Of course, I believe in her!"

"Then can't you just be grateful it's not Charley's body they've found?"

"But that's just it, Gary!" Fiona spat. "*That's just it!* I wish it *had* been Charley they found!"

Gary stared at her, shocked into silence by her words.

Fiona stared back at him, her eyes wide and wild. "There. I've said it."

Gary shook his head, nostrils flaring. "You don't mean that."

"I only wish I didn't."

"You don't mean that!" he shouted.

Fiona clasped a hand to her forehead, her face lined with agony.

Gary grabbed her wrist and tore her hand away from her face. "Why would you say that?" he demanded. "Why would you even *think* that?"

She yanked her wrist out of his grasp. "Because then we could have her home! We could have her home and we could cry and we could grieve. And then maybe these constant knots I feel in my stomach would go away…this endless *emptiness* would go away. I could stop torturing myself, imagining what's happening to her every minute of every day. I'd rather have her back to bury her than a lifetime of not knowing."

Gary understood that. The not knowing ate into you like a cancer. It tortured and tormented you. But he couldn't go where Fiona had.

"You realise what you're saying, don't you? You're *wishing* our daughter *dead*! *How could you do that*?"

"I'm not wishing her dead!" Fiona cried. "Because she's already de-"

Gary leapt to his feet and she flinched. "Don't you say it!

152

Don't you *dare* fucking say it!" He faced her, challenging her, his hands balled into tight fists.

Fiona glanced at those fists. "He told us right at the start," she said quietly. "He told us, but you just refused to believe it."

Gary stared at her, lost and bewildered. He shook his head and she had to cast her gaze to one side, unable to bear the hurt in his eyes.

"I'm sorry, Gary, but it's true and I had to say it."

"It's not true!" he insisted. "We have to have hope. Until we know any different, we have to keep hoping she's alive, no matter what."

She shook her head in despair.

"Fiona, we *owe* it to her–we *owe* it to Charley–not to give up on her."

Fiona hung her head. She was so thin and weary, like she'd just walked a thousand miles, and had been asked to walk a thousand more.

"I'll try," she said. "I'll try, but I don't know how much I have left."

That night Gary had a nightmare. He opened his eyes wide in the darkness, confused and frightened, his breath short. He threw back the quilt and hauled himself out of bed, relieved to be out from beneath its stifling cover. The dream's darkness clung to him, crowding his mind like black, beady-eyed crows. He leaned on the window sill to steady himself and his nerves. "My God," he whispered.

He'd dreamed he'd killed someone, but it had been so long ago that he no longer remembered who it was. He'd hidden the body, and no one had ever discovered his hideous crime. He had gotten away with murder and it had happened so long ago that he had somehow been able to put it out of his mind and

153

forget about it.

But now the memories had been awoken, and the terrible crime he had committed crashed over him.

He'd killed someone.

The dream shifted.

He was part of a police search party. Someone had put a rifle in his hands. He didn't know why he'd been handed a rifle, or what they were looking for, but somehow, he knew all this was a ruse. The police were leading him into a trap designed to expose his guilt and shame. He was trapped, and the walls were closing in.

He followed the tail of the search party as they traversed a decrepit old cinema. Red velvet curtains hung, torn and dusty; the white screen vandalised with a long tear that looked like a jagged bolt of lightning. The seat cushions were split and rotten. Mould grew everywhere. It was like The Picture of Dorian Gray made real.

Worst of all, were the rows of dead children sitting in the cinema seats; their lifeless eyes staring at the blank screen, their doll-like heads cocked this way and that. White moths crawled over their eyes and faces, and into their open mouths.

The police officers walked steadfastly by this parade of dead children, without so much as a glance, as if they couldn't even see them.

They gathered at a door at the back of the theatre. The door terrified Gary because he was certain that the damning evidence was concealed behind it. No, he *knew* it was there. Once opened, the evidence would be exposed, and all eyes would turn to him. He would be arrested. Charged. Sent to trial and imprisoned for the rest of his life. His family and friends would be cursed and shamed by his crime.

As the officers opened the door and went inside, Gary hung back.

What's the point of this charade? he thought. *They have me, the evidence is right there. Why don't they just kill me and have done with it?*

And then he remembered the rifle in his hands and realised, almost with regret, that he had the means to end it right now.

He upended the rifle, pressed the barrel beneath his chin, and closed his eyes. Alone in his darkness, he felt a deeply emotional sweep of despair and loneliness that it had finally come to this; that this was how his life was going to end.

He curled his thumb around the steely curve of the trigger, the metal like an icy sliver, and pressed down on it.

Nothing seemed to happen. No explosion of gunpowder or the stunning impact of a bullet. He had a moment to wonder if the weapon had misfired, or maybe it was empty, another ploy to expose his guilt.

But then, he was tumbling backwards into the void, the darkness behind his eyelids folding beneath waves of yet deeper blackness.

This is it, he thought. *This is what it feels like to die.*

And in those fleeting moments between life and death, he had a terrible revelation: *We all die alone.*

That was when he'd awoken, breathless and slick with sweat.

"You okay?" Fiona's drowsy voice asked from beside him.

"Yeah," he lied. "I'm fine."

He returned to bed, but he couldn't sleep. The nightmare seeped through his mind, saturating him with its vivid bleakness.

Pulling the trigger hadn't happened as he might have imagined. No flash, no explosion, no impact of the slug tearing through the tissues and cavities of his head. All he felt and heard was the silent implosion of his life, of his *soul*.

Though it had only been a dream, those simple secret details made it feel so real to him. As he'd tumbled into that silent abyss, he had experienced all the despair, regret and loneliness he imagined he would feel if it were real.

Suddenly he was crying, though he didn't quite know why, stifling his sobs so as not to wake Fiona and have to explain why he was weeping like a baby. The covert crying stuffed a headache into the front of his skull. He needed painkillers, or he'd never get back to sleep. He slipped quietly out of bed again to get some tablets from downstairs.

At the door, he hesitated. He could *feel* the darkness on the other side of the door and was chilled by the certainty that something was waiting for him out on the landing. A person? A presence? He didn't know exactly what it was.

It's nothing, he told himself. *It's just the early hour and the lingering influence of the dream.*

He gripped the handle tightly, but still had to force himself to open the door.

There was nothing there.

Of course there wasn't.

He stepped out onto the landing and looked down the hall at Charley's room. Through the grainy gloom, he could make out the door and the white smudge of the nameplate.

He went downstairs, and five minutes later he was back in bed, feeling lost and sorry for himself, and wondering where all this was going to end.

Fiona was already up and dressed when he woke the next morning. He brushed his teeth but couldn't be bothered taking a shower. The thought of breakfast made him want to throw up.

Fiona was in the living room with the newspapers. She raised her head with a strange look on her face.

"What is it?" he asked.

She offered him one of the newspapers.

Gary shook out the creases and read the headline - the body

156

found was that of thirteen-year-old Angela Mears, the girl who went missing on her way home from the cinema.

Gary shook his head sadly. "So that's who it was. It must be terrible for her parents."

"Don't you get it, Gary? Don't you understand now?"

"Understand what?" Gary asked, glancing again at the paper for something he had missed.

"Angela went missing *after* Charley."

"And?"

Fiona threw up her hands. "Okay," she said, "I can't... I just can't..."

"Fiona, I don't know what you mean. Tell me what you mean."

She looked about her, as if searching for the right words. "This girl went missing *after* Charley."

"So?"

"If she's dead, doesn't it stand to reason that Charley is too?"

"It doesn't mean that!" Gary snapped.

Fiona sighed. "Why doesn't it?"

"Because for one, we don't even know for certain that Charley was taken by this...this Goldilocks...*killer*."

Fiona shook her head, seemingly too exhausted to even try to argue anymore.

Gary tossed the paper onto the chair. "Fee, listen to me. Charley doesn't fit this guy's...what do they call it? His MO, his profile. She isn't blonde or curly-haired."

"But she's the right age."

"That's one thing out of three, Fee. Kids go missing all the time. This one guy can't be taking them all."

"So, Charley going missing when all this is happening is just a coincidence then?"

"Coincidences happen all the time," Gary told her. "Some far more unlikely than this."

Fiona folded her arms across her lap, her gaze going off

157

somewhere while she thought about it. Gary gave her space, hoping she would come around to his way of thinking at last.

"When we were sorting through all that mail," she said. "There was one letter in particular that I remember."

Gary listened, wondering where this new train of thought was taking them.

"It was from a seventy-five-year-old woman. Her son had gone missing forty years ago. She'd never heard from him again, doesn't know what happened to him. Doesn't know if he's alive or dead. She said that every day she waits for him to call. Every day she expects him to come walking through the door. *Every day for forty years*. Is that how we're going to spend the rest of our lives, Gary? Just waiting for her to never come home?"

Gary hadn't dared allow himself to think that far ahead. He took it day by day, sometimes minute by minute. He'd endured seven months of not knowing what happened, what could be *happening* to Charley. He couldn't even begin to contemplate decades of not knowing. He'd rather be dead.

"So this old lady," Gary said. "She's kept hoping her son is still alive for forty years?"

Fiona nodded. "Forty years."

He looked her hard in the eyes. "And *you* want to give up on our daughter after seven months."

Fiona's face drained of emotion and turned to stone. "You absolute bastard," she seethed. "Fuck you!"

It was the first time Fiona had ever spoken to him that way. And so they faced each other. Intimate strangers. Changed in ways neither of them could ever have imagined possible.

Fiona got up. "After forty years, does it really matter if he's dead or alive? He's still gone."

She headed toward the door.

"Well, I'm not giving up on Charley!" Gary shouted after her. "And neither should you!"

She didn't look back.

He got to his feet. "She's out there somewhere! I know she is!"

Fiona slammed the door behind her.

Chapter Fifteen

In the annexed workshop, his long-fingered hands worked with slow and careful precision on the sculpture he was honing from a solid block of lime wood he'd purchased from a local timber merchant. With a small curved gouge, he scooped out tiny wood shavings, which floated away like blossom petals freed by the wind. Occasionally he swept off the loose shavings and blew away the dust; drawing back to get a better critical overview of the work.

In the background, an old portable CRT TV played, the sound low but discernible. A couple of words broke through his concentration. 'Discovered' and 'body'. He paused and turned towards the screen. A news program reported that a walker had found the body of Angela Mears in woodland.

He dropped the chisel and hurried to the TV, turning up the volume, his face so close to the screen that he could feel the tube's heat and its static crackle.

The report cut to a helicopter shot of the woods where they'd found her. A yellow forensic tent had been erected over the site, preserving evidence and hiding it from the prying eye of the media.

His eyes darted about the screen. He had chosen these woods for her body. The tent covered the spot where he had carefully buried her.

He grabbed his forehead and gritted his teeth.

How had they found her?

How?

He was meticulous in choosing his burial sites, careful in hiding the evidence.

Anger crawled around his guts.

Nosey, interfering FUCKS!

He had taken her out there. *He* had dug the hole. *He* had carried her from the car and decided how she should lay.

He pressed his clenched fists into his eye sockets.

They had found her! Found her and ruined everything.

They would remove her from the spot he had chosen, touching her, examining her for clues. Tears of anger squeezed from his eyes. But their efforts would be wasted. They may have found the body, but he was far too careful to leave clues. He'd washed her, just like he used to wash Christina when she was a baby. She used to laugh and play with the bubbles. But *they* didn't laugh. That was when he was finally sure he'd made a mistake. When they just lay in the water, cold and still, while he washed them.

He heard a sound from somewhere deeper in the house and tilted his head to listen. Christina. She didn't know what he did down here, she was innocent, but his father knew. His father knew everything, his father was why he was here.

William!

His father's voice. Always loud. Always demanding. He would have been drinking. He'd always been drinking. Laying there in the dark, waiting for the creak of the door. His father's shadow crawling across the ceiling. Even now the smell of alcohol made him sick to his stomach. If he smelled it on the breath, it made him want to throw punches.

William!

"No, no, no," he whispered, rocking back and forth. "I'm not ready. I'm not ready for that now."

161

William!

He slammed his head with the heel of his palm and grasped his skull with his long, bony fingers. Mother used to say he had the fingers of a pianist and father always used to laugh and ask, 'which one?' She often played the old piano in the back room on Sunday afternoons; and schooled him in piano playing. He quickly learned how to play his favourite hymn, *All Things Bright and Beautiful,* and discovered that playing was a beautiful thing, like sculpting, stroking the keys with his long fingertips, taking the notes and shaping them into music.

He heard the hymn in his head, but it crawled and writhed and slithered around like slimy brown worms. The corners of his mouth pulled down in a grimace, his jaw trembling, teeth clicking together.

All things bright and beautiful.
All creatures great and small.
All things wise and wonderful.
The Lord God made them all.
WILLIAM!

He jumped at the voice. "*I know! I know!*" he shouted, slamming the palm of his hand into his skull again. There was no way to avoid it. He'd tried before. Once his father had decided it was time, he had to do what needed to be done. He wiped his face with his sleeve and stood there crying, a string of spit hanging from his wet lips.

All things bright and beautiful.

He walked to the back of the room and hauled open the door in the floor.

All creatures great and small.

Beneath it lay the cage door of steel bars his father had installed all those years ago.

All things wise and wonderful.

She cowered on the mattress, huddled beneath the thin quilt he allowed her. She dragged it over her face to block out the

162

painful light.

"The Lord God made them all," he sang, his voice small.

The girl whimpered.

Hush, hush. I'm not going to hurt you.

Had he said that out loud? He wasn't sure. Should he offer words of comfort? Was that the right thing to do?

Was it Mother?

It didn't matter anyway, because it was all a lie. This time he *was* going to hurt her. He was going to hurt her bad. *It was time.* No matter how it started out, eventually his father told him it was time.

In his mind's eye, he saw the hammer fall, and jumped at the splat of splitting flesh and the crack of splintering bone. The uplifting melody of All Things Bright and Beautiful playing in the back room, while the hammer turned the face into a mask of red. Hands clawing, blood splashing, gurgling, gurgling.

Why did you let him do it, Mummy, why?

He removed the key from the chain hanging around his neck and unlocked the cage.

Chapter Sixteen

Fiona sat alone in the front room. Gary was upstairs in the study. No doubt slouched behind his desk, glass of whisky in his hand, staring blankly into the night.

He used to work up there sometimes. But not anymore.

So many things didn't happen anymore.

She hadn't told Gary yet, but she had taken a trip to the hospital last week and met with her manager. She'd explained that she was ready to return to work, that she *needed* to return to work. Under the circumstances, the hospital had been more than understanding and accommodating to her extended leave, and what's more, they were happy that she was ready to take up her post again.

She looked up at the ceiling and sighed. Since the argument, everything had worsened. He kept to himself even more now, and when he was around, he was sullen, the atmosphere unbearable.

Yet she believed the man she loved was still in there somewhere. A changed man, yes, but still the man with whom she'd shared deliriously happy times and quiet, intimate moments. She was sure that somewhere, deep down inside, he loved her too. But he was lost. More than that, he was hiding.

If only he'd let her help him.

If only he'd help himself.

He needed something to occupy him instead of just sitting and waiting. She didn't know how he was able to keep it up, waiting and waiting for something that was never going to happen.

She felt so weary, but she had to try to talk to him again. With a sigh, she dragged herself from the chair and climbed the stairs.

Standing quietly in the doorway, she surveyed the scene. The bottle. The glass. His demeanour. She knew he'd seen her reflection in the window, but he acted like he hadn't.

"What are you doing?" she asked.

"Nothing," Gary replied and took a drink.

Fiona entered the study and rubbed her arms. "It's cold in here."

"I've had the window open."

She sat down, and for a while, neither of them spoke. Gary continued to look out of the window and sip his whisky. He didn't want her there, she could see that. It made it difficult for her to broach the subject she'd come to speak to him about, but she must.

"I've decided to go back to work," she said at last.

His gaze fell to his glass for a moment, then returned to the window. "If that's what you feel you have to do."

"What about you?" she asked.

"What about me?"

"Have you thought about going back to work?"

"No."

"I really think you should. It might help you cope better, take your mind off things."

"It won't."

"How do you know if you-"

"It won't," he said, firmly cutting her off. Then his voice softened, "I'm not the same as I was anymore."

"Yes, you are," Fiona assured him.

165

"I'm not," he insisted. "I'm...I'm *broken*."

"You're not broken," she told him gently. "You're just broken-hearted."

He closed his eyes, his jaw clenching, heat rising into his face.

"You spend so much time alone now," Fiona pressed. "Just thinking about it all, going over and over it."

"Look," Gary said, his tone verging on aggressive. "If you want to go back to work, then fine, you do that. Good for you. But we can't all go around pretending Charley doesn't exist anymore."

He knocked back the last of the Scotch.

"That's not fair," Fiona said.

"Fair? Nothing's fair."

She watched him pour another. "You think that's going to help?"

"It's about the only thing keeping me sane," he said, and deliberately took a drink.

"Is it?" Fiona asked, her voice cut with pity. "All I know is, since you started drinking so heavily, your mood has just gotten darker."

"Oh, it's dark alright, but it's not because of the booze."

"You aren't going to find any answers in a bottle, Gary."

He sprang up, seizing the neck of the bottle, and hurled it across the room. It exploded against the wood panelling, splitting the grain and showering the wall with glass and liquor.

Fiona let out a startled scream.

Gary looked at her, his face tight and angry. "Are you happy now?"

Fiona caught her breath, her lips trembling, her eyes glassy.

Gary turned away from the hurt in her eyes. "Just leave me alone."

Fiona looked at the big wet splash and the deep crescent shaped gash in the panel. Little rivers of whisky glistened in the

166

lamplight. She stood up. "You need to get help, Gary," she said and walked out.

Gary sat in the dim light, his mouth curled in a sneer. He reached into the bottom drawer of his desk, took out another bottle, and cracked the seal.

Chapter Seventeen

Gary had left the house some time ago. He didn't tell Fiona he was going out, she just heard the door slam when he left.

She took a pack of cigarettes from her bag and shook out the last one. She lit it and inhaled deeply, holding in the smoke and relishing the burn.

Gary didn't know she'd started smoking again, or maybe he did but just didn't care.

Living with him tied her stomach in knots most of the time. When he was around, she was angry and frustrated, but when he wasn't, she felt so lost and missed him so much.

Sometimes it was almost as if he didn't really exist anymore, like he had died.

She tapped ash into the empty packet.

She understood his pain. She could see it. It pinched his features, as if everything had been concentrated into a needlepoint that was lodged under a fingernail, a constant reminder of the agony that consumed him. She understood it. She did! She must have worn that same expression for months after Charley went missing. But there came a point where something had to change, didn't there? A turning point?

For her, it had been the day they found the body of Angela Mears.

Did it make her a bad person to want to try and move

forward with her life? To try and put things back in some sort of order, even if that order didn't make much sense right now?

Gary seemed to think it did.

He reminded her of the clock in the living room, when its battery didn't have juice enough to drive the motor anymore, the second hand stuck in the up-sweep, twitching at twenty to the hour but not getting anywhere.

That was Gary, still stuck on July 20th, 2013, the day Charley vanished from their lives, twitching as if he was still alive but unable, or unwilling to move forward.

She took another drag on the cigarette. The nicotine sent a swirl of light-headedness through her.

Charley's gone.

She said it in her head, saw the words, examined them.

Charley's gone.

Like a whisper in the deepest, darkest corridors of her mind.

"Charley's gone," she whispered.

She'd never said it out loud before. She almost said it that day she and Gary had argued, but he had stopped her. It gave her a strange, cold comfort to voice it now, like a long-kept secret that had festered away in her mind. A secret that she had wanted to tell someone, anyone—even this empty room—but was too ashamed to admit that she was even capable of such a thought.

She sucked in a breath and squeezed her eyes shut. *"CHARLEY'S GONE!"* she screamed, tears springing into her eyes. "SHE'S GONE! SHE'S GONE! *SHE'S FUCKING GONE!"* The words tore violently at her throat and set her ears ringing.

She hoped Gary could hear it, wherever he was. She hoped the world could hear it.

It was what she felt.

It was what she *knew* inside.

Charley was gone. Forever.

The old woman who had written to tell them about her

missing son had spent a lifetime waiting for him to return; was that what Gary expected her to do too?

Curdling anger and resentment rose inside her.

Charley wasn't ever coming home, so what was the use in waiting? She wasn't going to let it ruin her life as Gary was letting it ruin his.

Does that make me a bad person? Does it?

They could start again if they really wanted. They could put all this behind them. She wasn't too old to have another child...if only Gary would...if only Gary...

She hung her head, the cigarette forgotten and dangling from her slender fingers. The thoughts chased each other around and around, and her tears fell, cold as winter rainfall.

They had been so happy. Why did this have to happen to them?

"Oh Charley," she whispered. "I miss you so much."

She'd never stop loving her beautiful daughter, but in her heart, she knew that she was never coming home. Surely a mother has an instinct about such things?

But how could she make Gary see?

Maybe she couldn't. Gary might never recover. He would never let go, never stop hoping, even if that hope destroyed everything else in his life. He would be like that old woman, his life still twitching but not moving while he waited for a knock at the door. A knock that Fiona knew would never come.

Maybe she was clinging to their marriage the way Gary was clinging onto the hope that Charley was still alive.

But she had to try.

She crushed out the cigarette on the empty packet and decided what she was going to do. Gary wouldn't like it, but she had to try. God help her, she had to try.

She went to the kitchen and collected some black refuse bags from the cupboard under the sink, then climbed the stairs.

Gary let himself into the house, hung up his jacket, and stood gazing at the watercolour paintings Fiona had bought and hung in the hall, a lifetime ago when such things seemed to matter. A ladybird delicately climbed a blade of grass, the painting fringed with flower petals. It was Charley's favourite.

He'd been to the park again, standing on the grass verge and gazing at the spot where he last saw her waving and blowing him a kiss. That ghost of a memory haunted him. That one moment where he could have made the choice to stay with her and none of this would have happened.

A noise from upstairs brought him back.

"Fiona?"

He climbed the stairs and glanced into their bedroom. It was empty, the bed made. At the end of the landing, the door to Charley's room was open. Someone moved inside.

For a second, he was unable to breathe.

He rushed down the landing, a million impossible thoughts crashing through his mind. But when he burst into the room, it was only Fiona he found inside.

She stopped what she was doing and stared defiantly at him. He saw the open drawers and the black refuse bags on the floor, a stack of Charley's pastel coloured tops in Fiona's hands.

"What are you doing?"

"What does it look like I'm doing?" Fiona replied. She tried to brush past him, but he blocked her path.

"Put them back. Put them all back."

His eyes flashed around the room, searching for what else she might have moved. Thankfully, she hadn't touched the bed, he could still see her outline in the sheet.

She tried to pass him, but he blocked her again. "I said, 'put them back'!"

She closed her eyes, her features drenched in frustration and

171

agony. "No Gary, it has to stop. This has to stop now!"

Gary snatched the clothes out of her hands. "This room stays exactly how it is," he warned her. He carefully laid the clothes back in the drawer.

"It's over, Gary."

"It's not over."

"It is!" Fiona wailed. "Charley's gone."

Gary whirled around and grabbed her by the arms. "Don't say that!" he shouted in her face. "Don't you ever fucking say that again! Do you hear me?" He shook her hard, his fingers digging deep into the flesh of her upper arms before he realised what he was doing. He released her and stepped back, shaken by the intensity of his anger.

Fiona massaged her arms where bluish circles were already forming beneath the skin. Her eyes brimmed with tears.

"Why did you do it?" she asked so quietly that Gary missed it.

"What?"

Fiona looked at him, the tears spilling down her cheeks. "Why did you leave her?"

A chill wriggled deep inside him and settled in his core. It was the first time she had ever asked him this simple question.

"It was work," Gary said, "I had to-"

"Work! Work! It's always fucking work!"

Gary flinched.

"You didn't need to go in that day," she told him. "I heard Lance say it in the hall. You didn't need to go in, but you went anyway."

Gary's breath went out of him. She knew. All this time she had known it was his fault. His throat dried. He struggled to swallow.

Fiona pinned him with accusing eyes full of hurt and longing. "Why did you leave her, Gary? Why did you leave her when you didn't need to?"

172

Gary just looked at her, snared by her eyes and her question, like an animal in a trap.

"We talked about it," she said. "We agreed to be careful with everything that was going on. *But you just left her there.* Why did you leave her, Gary?"

His mouth moved but no words came out. He shook his head, his face crumpling with pain and emotion. He couldn't answer because there wasn't an answer that made any sense now.

Why did I leave her? Why? Why? FUCKING WHY!

"You said you'd keep her safe!" she cried. "You promised me! *You fucking promised me!*"

She blindly struck at him, wild slaps and punches at his face and body. He made no attempt to shield himself, just standing there and accepting all of her anger and grief. One blow glanced off his mouth, drawing blood from his lip. He tipped back his head and released a cry of agony as Fiona struck him over and over and asked *Why? Why? Why?*

Eventually she fell against him, weeping. Gary stood with his arms at his sides, unable to hold and comfort her. He had no right to comfort her. All he could say was, "I'm sorry, Fiona. I'm so, so sorry."

She pushed away from him. "I can't go on like this anymore. I can't go on living that day over and over. I have to move on, *we* have to move on."

Gary shook his head. "I can't," he wept, and it was true. "I just can't. Not until we find her."

"Not even for us? Not even for me?"

He couldn't reply.

"And how long will you wait, Gary? Forty years? A lifetime?"

"Until the day I die."

Fiona tilted her head, and even managed to smile a little through the tears. "I know you will," she said, "but I just can't

173

wait with you."

Gary stood there and wept.

She looked hopelessly around Charley's room. It was like something abandoned, like a relic uncovered by archaeologists and preserved for the rest of time.

"I can't live like this anymore," she said. "I'm sorry but I can't. I'm going to move back with my parents."

Gary looked at her and felt as if he had his eye to the wrong end of a telescope. Fiona was tiny and distant, and not the woman he had loved anymore. Or perhaps it was that he wasn't the man she loved anymore.

"Please don't," was all he could say.

Fiona couldn't look at him. "I'm sorry, Gary. I just... I just can't..." She hid her face with her hand and fled.

"Please don't," Gary whispered to the empty room.

The front door slammed, and she was gone.

He stood for a while, then hitched a sigh and wiped a sleeve across his hot, wet face. A line of blood from his lip smeared across the back of his hand, like the jagged blip of a heart monitor. His head ached and his heart ached.

He delved into a refuse bag and began returning Charley's things back to their drawers.

Chapter Eighteen

With the house empty now, Gary didn't need to hide and drink in the study anymore. He brought his bottle of Old Pulteney down to the front room and sat staring at the blank TV screen, a glass of Scotch in his hand, the open bottle on the table.

His mind crawled around all that had happened, viewing it from every angle as if it was some kind of morbid curiosity. Every way he examined it, the result was always the same. It was all his fault.

The doorbell rang.

He took a drink.

So he'd finally managed to drive Fiona away. So selfishly wrapped in guilt and misery, as he was, he'd failed to see or, more likely, not cared how she was coping. Even Chlo the FLO had offered her more support than he had.

The doorbell stopped ringing and Gary's mobile started vibrating instead. He pinched it between his finger and thumb and sent it in a flat spin across the room. It struck the wall and exploded into meaningless pieces of plastic and electronics. The ringing stopped.

How did people do it? How did they recover from the death of someone they dearly loved? Gone from your life forever. How was it possible to recover from that loss?

But people did it every day. They mourned, they cried, they

remembered, and they missed them, but then came the day when they were able to move on with their lives. He'd done that when his mother died, why couldn't he do the same for Charley? Why couldn't he just accept that she was gone and that her body might never be found?

And that was the crux of it, wasn't it? While she was only missing, there was still hope. It might only be the tiniest wisp of a hope, a single spark in the black of night, but it was there, glowing weakly in the darkness. He couldn't just ignore it. He wouldn't abandon her again.

The house phone rang, the answer machine eventually picking up. "Gary, it's Lance, I'm at the front door. Let me in."

Gary sighed.

"I know you're in there and I'm not going away, so you might as well come to the door."

Gary sighed again and dragged himself to his feet. When he opened the door, Lance still had his phone to his ear. He looked Gary up and down, as if he hadn't known what to expect. Gary left the door open, for Lance to come in, and went back into the house. He got another glass from the cabinet.

Lance came into the lounge and looked around as if expecting to find something hugely out of place.

"I'm glad you dropped by, Lance," Gary said. "I've had to drink alone far too many times recently."

"Fiona called me," Lance explained. "What's happened?"

Gary filled the second glass. "I went to the pub one night, you know, thought I'd stand at the bar and get wasted. Maybe talk some shit to someone and get into a fight. But everyone around here knows who I am. That poor dumb fuck who left his daughter at the park." He turned, drink in hand. "Pretty soon I was standing alone at the bar. Can you believe that? Happens all the time. Like I'm bad news, or bad luck, or both. And they're probably right. Now I know how Typhoid Mary must have felt." He set down the drink for Lance and sat on the sofa.

"Funny thing that. People I mean."

Lance looked at him as if he had grown another head. "I don't know what you're talking about. Gary, tell me what's happened. Why is there blood on your lip?"

Gary waved his hand. "Sit down," he said. "Take a drink with me. We can drink to the good times, can't we? The late, lamented good times we spent together here in this house."

Lance only looked at him. "Gary?"

"Oh, for fuck's sake, Lance! She's gone. Okay? Fiona's gone. She couldn't stand to be around me any longer, so she's gone to her parents."

Lance looked stunned. "Oh man. I'm sorry. She wouldn't tell me...not even when I asked. She just asked if I'd come around and see if you were okay."

Gary sneered. "How very big of her."

Lance perched on the armchair, his hands clasped before him. "Hey, look, no matter how it all seems right now, Fiona still loves you."

"Yeah right," Gary said and rested his head on the sofa back. "That's what she said when she slammed the door and left." He closed his eyes and let out a slow, shaky sigh.

"Give me that," Lance said and took the glass out of Gary's hand. "What the hell are you doing, Gary? All this is bullshit and you know it. We *all* loved Charley, you know? We all miss her. And as much as it hurts me, I know it's nothing compared to how it feels to you. But you've got to stop this. You have to find a way around it."

Gary kept his eyes closed.

"Whatever's happened between you and Fiona, it'll pass. You two are the strongest couple I know."

"Not anymore."

"Bullshit."

"She blamed me today," Gary muttered.

"What?" Lance asked.

177

Gary swallowed hard. "She blamed me. She must have heard us the day Charley went missing, when you said I didn't need to come to the office."

"Oh Christ," Lance said.

"Can you believe it? She's kept it to herself all this time. If that'd been me, I'd have packed that fucker into a spike and stabbed her through the heart with it."

"No, you wouldn't."

"Yes I would!" Gary shouted. "Because I'm a cunt!"

"No, you're not."

"I am." He settled back down. "It must have been festering away all this time, eating at her, until I forced her to let it loose."

"Look, whatever she said, it was in the heat of the moment. She didn't mean it."

"Oh, she meant it alright," Gary replied. "And what's more, she's right. She's absolutely one hundred fucking percent right."

"She's not," Lance insisted. "And she didn't mean it. You know as well as I do that we've all said and done things that we wish we could take back."

"Yeah we do," Gary said. "But I can't take my 'thing' back, Lance. My thing caused us to lose Charley."

That stopped Lance in his tracks, the voice of reason halted for a moment. "You didn't know that was going to happen."

"No, but I should have. Fiona talked about it right after the party, when I came out with all that bullshit about odds and chances. I promised her nothing bad would ever happen to Charley. I *promised* her, Lance. Can you believe that? How fucking arrogant is that? How can *anyone* promise something like that?" He fell silent for a moment. "But I *believed* it, Lance. I really did. I really believed we were invincible, that nothing bad could happen to us. Bad things only happen to other people. And now it's all gone, everything washed up and gone."

"But it doesn't have to be. You can stop this thing you're doing to yourself, this *self-punishment*. I know it's hard, but if you could just get yourself over this...this..."

"This what? This hitch? This bump in the road?"

Lance gave him a look. "That's not what I was going to say, and you know it. But when you lose someone, after the grief, eventually there comes a time of healing. I'm not saying you ever forget them or miss them any less, but just somehow the pain becomes bearable enough that you can function and get on with your life again."

"But that's the problem. I'm not healing. The pain isn't getting any less and nothing is getting any better. This isn't the same as somebody dying. I lost my mum, I know how that feels and this isn't the same. Charley's out there somewhere...I know she is, I *feel* she is."

"I understand that," Lance said gently. "But even if she is out there somewhere...what if she's still gone for good?"

Gary's face changed, slamming on Lance like a heavy oak door. "Now you sound like Fiona." He stood up, the action taking Lance by surprise, and he got to his feet too, not sure of what was happening.

"Anyway, thanks for checking up on me, but as you can see, the razor blades are still in the bathroom and the pills are still in the medicine cabinet. There's the booze, but that's a slow death, so you can stop worrying about me."

Lance looked wounded. "That's not why I'm here. I'm here to look out for you."

Gary sighed. "You're a good friend, Lance. You always have been, but this isn't helping me or you right now. I want to be on my own."

"Gary, I'm sorry, I didn't mean to-"

"It's fine," Gary said. "Don't worry about me."

He placed his hand on Lance's shoulder and though he didn't exactly frog-march him to the front door, it was near enough.

Lance stopped in the hall and turned deliberately, as if to

make a final stand. "I'm sorry if I upset you."

"You didn't. Don't worry about it."

"You know where I am if you need me."

"Of course I do."

"Okay if I call you?"

"Stay on suicide watch for as long as you like."

Lance sighed. "Will you stop saying that? I just want to know you're okay."

"I am okay."

He reached past Lance and opened the front door. The rejection on Lance's face made Gary hate himself even more, but he really wanted to be alone again.

Lance touched Gary's shoulder briefly and left. Gary closed the door without watching him go. He leaned against it, closed his eyes and inhaled deeply.

Mister Whiskers padded into the hall. Gary scooped him up and carried him to the living room window where he watched Lance get into his car and drive away. "Just you and me now, pal," he said. "Just you and me."

Chapter Nineteen

A couple of days later, Fiona called to collect some clothes and personal items. She wanted to take Mister Whiskers too, but Gary wouldn't allow it. She expressed concern about his ability to look after the cat in his perpetual state of drunkenness, but Gary assured her that he was taking care of Mister Whiskers just fine - even if he wasn't doing a good job of caring for himself. Fiona didn't believe him, but when she took a sneaky look into the kitchen, she found fresh food and water in his dishes.

Gary stayed in the living room while she packed her things into the car.

She stood in the doorway. "Okay, I'm done."

Gary nodded, but didn't look at her, staring stubbornly straight ahead.

Fiona took in the bottle and the glass in his hand. His unshaven, dishevelled appearance. For a moment it seemed as if she might say something, but then she gave a little shake of her head, with a look of pity and regret that cut Gary deeper than words ever could.

Gary opened his mouth to call out, ask her to stay, beg her to stay, but it would be a waste of air. Even though she'd called ahead to let him know she was coming, he'd made no attempt to impress her. He was unkempt, unshaven, and already inebriated. What the fuck was wrong with him?

He sat alone in the house and drank.

And despised himself for it.

Dark thoughts with beady eyes and sharp yellow beaks pecked at him, chipping away, chipping away.

Several glasses later, there came a knock at the front door. Gary's heart skipped. Maybe Fiona had forgotten something and had come back for it. Maybe this time he could spit out the bitter resentment and find the words to ask her to stay.

But it wasn't Fiona, it was Ed, along with Sam - the company lawyer. Seeing the two of them together on his doorstep confused his intoxicated mind and he simply stood staring at them.

In the end it was Ed who spoke up. "Hello, Gary."

"Ed. What do you want?" Gary asked, swaying back on his heels.

Sam glanced at Ed, his eyes edgy, his hands restless.

"Just thought we'd drop by," Ed said. "See how you are and have a little chat."

"And since when do you need a lawyer to do that?"

Ed smiled, and Gary thought about sharks smelling blood. "It's not like that, Gary."

"No? What is it like?"

"We're just concerned, Gary," Sam said. "That's all."

Gary opened the door wide and walked off down the hall. He was already seated by the time they came into the lounge.

He raised his glass to them. "Can I offer you one?"

Ed laughed. "Little bit early for me."

Sam shook his head, looking like he'd rather be anywhere but here.

Gary dragged the bottle over. "Never too early to get smashed."

Ed laughed again, but this time there was a nervous edge to it.

182

While Gary poured the whisky, the two men hovered. When the offer of a seat wasn't forthcoming, they sat down anyway.

"It's just been a while since anyone's heard from you," Ed offered. "So, we just thought we'd come and see you, see how you are keeping."

Gary's empty gaze slid over them and he sipped his drink.

Sam shifted nervously, wringing his hands.

Ed smiled, as if all this was normal. "So, how have you been keeping?"

"How do you think I've been keeping?" Gary asked, his voice low and gravelly.

Ed nodded, his expression grave and oh so fucking understanding. "Yes, I'm sorry. It's been a nasty business."

"*Nasty business*," Gary whispered.

The alcohol made it feel like the room was slowly shifting around him, like they were riding the slowest carousel in the world.

"Ed?" Gary said.

Ed stopped nodding and raised his eyebrows expectantly.

"What the fuck are you doing here?"

Sam writhed like a worm on a hook and adjusted the knot of his plaid tie. "Ed, I think we should..." he started to say, but Gary cut him off.

"You want to know when I'm coming back to work, is that it? After all, it's been what?" He glanced at his watch. "*Eight fucking months!* I mean *Jesus Christ*! How long does it take for someone to get over the loss of their child?"

Sam held up his hands and shook his head. "No, Gary, no, you have it all wrong."

"Have I? Have I really? Then what the fuck are you doing here? You want to know how I've been *keeping*? Let me fucking tell you how I've been keeping. *My twelve-year-old daughter's missing, and I don't know where she is!* Can you imagine that, Ed? Can you even grasp the concept of it? Does that tiny fucking

183

little closed mind of yours even have a clue? Is she dead? Is she alive? Is she buried in some woods, or lying in a ditch? This is all I can think about all the time and it drives me fucking crazy. There's hardly a minute of the day goes by that I don't think about her, and every time I do, it hits me: she's *missing.* Charley's missing and I don't know where she is."

He leaned back in his seat, his hands trembling, his breathing short and shaky. "And that's just the days. At night I lie in bed, thinking how all this wouldn't have happened if I *hadn't* done this or *had* done that. And my mind torments me with these little...*vignettes,* let's call them. These nightmarish little scenarios where I imagine the most *horrible things,* Ed, things that I can't even begin to describe to you. Things that are being *done to my little girl.*" He clenched his teeth and his fists and tears rolled down his face. "And I hear her crying, and I hear her begging him not to hurt her; and I hear her calling for me, calling for me to come save her." He shook his head, his eyes full of pain. "But I don't know how to find her; I don't know how to save her." He took a few deep breaths and wiped his face. "And that's how it is, Ed, every fucking day. *That's* how I'm keeping."

A long, awkward silence passed.

"I'm really sorry, Gary," Sam said. "I told Ed we shouldn't be intruding on you, but he insisted."

Instead of taking that as a cue to excuse themselves and leave, Ed said, "I know it's been a difficult time for you, Gary, but life goes on."

Sam twisted in his seat. "For God's sake, Ed! Are you kidding me?"

"What? You know as well as I do that there are certain business matters that need attention. We need Gary to-"

"Didn't you hear any of what he just said?"

"Of course I did. I can appreciate the emotional stress of something like this, but-"

184

"Ed?" Gary said.

Ed turned from Sam to Gary. "Yes?"

"Get the fuck out of my house."

"Excuse me?"

"You heard me. Get the fuck out of my house before I fucking throw you out."

"Okay," Sam said, his hands making a *let's all calm down* gesture. "Let's just leave, Ed."

Gary's eyes burned, his lips tight and hard, nostrils flaring. "Don't think I don't know what you've been up to, you fucking snake."

"Don't you threaten me," Ed blustered.

"He didn't threaten you, Ed," Sam said. He got quickly to his feet, watching Gary carefully, as if he'd just realised the family dog was rabid.

"Sam's right," Gary said. "I haven't threatened you, but if you aren't out of here in five seconds flat, I'll do more than threaten you."

Ed and Gary both got up together and faced each other.

Sam inserted himself between them. "Calm down, Gary. I know you're upset, but this isn't going to do anyone any good."

"Upset? I'm somewhere between drinking myself to death and a jar of fucking pills, and this prick is telling me *life goes on*?"

"Oh, poor me, poor me, pour me another," Ed mocked.

Gary launched at him, a white-hot flare of rage sending him forward. He clawed past Sam and crashed into Ed, the two of them careening across the room and slamming into the wall. Ed's back bashed an oval concave in the plasterboard.

The heel of Ed's palm jammed into Gary's eye socket, but he shook his face around it and seized Ed by the lapels, dragging him along the wall and knocking pictures askew as they went.

Ed struggled to defend himself but was no match for Gary in his drunken rage. All Gary wanted to do was punch this rat-

185

faced little man until his knuckles bled. His fist smacking over and over, splitting Ed's lips and shattering his perfect white veneers.

He drew back his arm, but Sam intervened, grabbing both of Gary's arms and yanking them behind him. They stumbled backwards into the sofa, almost toppling over it. Sam leaned way back, but kept his arms firmly hooked around Gary's.

Gary struggled against him, all reason gone, screaming for Sam to let go, and frenziedly trying to get back at Ed.

Sam threw him forcibly to one side, so he could quickly get between him and Ed again. He held up his hands. "Gary! Calm down! Calm down! We're leaving, okay? We're leaving!"

Gary stood with his hands in fists, chest heaving, pumped with adrenalin and anger.

Panting, Sam shook his head as if he couldn't believe this was happening.

Ed pulled his crumpled shirt down but didn't tuck it back into his pants. "You maniac!" he yelled.

"Ed, just shut the fuck up and leave!" Sam said.

"He assaulted me!" Ed shouted. "I told you he was-"

"GET THE FUCK OUT OF MY HOUSE!" Gary screamed in a voice that silenced Ed and sounded like it should have ruptured his vocal cords.

Sam manhandled Ed toward the exit, almost tripping over his feet in his haste.

"You've not heard the last of this!" Ed blustered over Sam's shoulder.

Gary stalked after them.

Sam jostled Ed out through the door and part-way down the path, with Ed protesting every step of the way. Sam shouted something and pointed his finger in Ed's face before starting back toward the house.

Gary slammed the door hard enough to shake the foundations.

186

He slapped his hands high on the door, his whole-body heaving with a raging fury like he had never experienced before. It was more than just Ed. It was a rolling snowball of rage that had gathered up all that had gone wrong over the last eight months. He squeezed his eyes tightly shut, his lips peeling back from his gritted teeth.

"FUUUUUCK!" he shouted, the word stretching out in a helpless scream of frustration. "FUCK IT! *FUCK IT ALL!*"

He lashed out at the half-round table, where Fiona used to display a vase of hand-cut flowers from the garden. The table somersaulted with force and smashed into the living room door. Gary didn't see what happened to it because he was attacking the prints on the wall, sweeping two of them off their hooks. They dropped to the floor, the glass shattering, and the frames breaking apart. Only the middle of the three survived, swinging on its hook at a crazy angle.

In his blind anger, he overreached and lost his balance, stumbling and sliding down the wall, crashing to the floor with his arms raised high.

He couldn't get up. He didn't want to get up. Getting up was something living people did, not dead people like him. He rolled onto his back among the broken frames and the shattered glass. "Help me!" he shouted. "*God help me!*"

He folded his arms across his face and broke into huge wracking sobs that went on and on. The phone started ringing at some point, but he didn't even hear it.

When he was all cried out, he wiped his face and got wearily to his feet. The table lay on its side, one leg sheared off. The door had sustained a deep gash in the lower centre panel. Two broken pictures lay on the floor, glass fragments scattered across the boards. The one picture still hanging on the wall was the print of the ladybird climbing the grass stalk.

He straightened it.

He recalled the Saturday afternoon Fiona had excitedly

brought the prints back from her shopping trip. She'd taken forever to hang them, changing the order, testing the height. She'd shouted for him to come and look at them. He'd liked them a lot. Charley had liked the ladybird one the best.

What would Fiona think of me if she saw this? he thought miserably. Destroying the home they had so lovingly built together.

He picked the prints out of the broken glass and shook them off, leaning each of them against the wall. He'd get them reframed. He stood the table on its three good legs and gathered all the paraphernalia that had sat atop it, including his car keys. Then he went to the kitchen to collect the dust pan and brush.

Chapter Twenty

Gary shrugged into his coat and stepped out into the damp afternoon. He'd stumbled blindly through the last two weeks, mostly in a drunken stupor. Lance called. Fiona didn't. He ate little, and drank throughout the day and night, but no amount of alcohol could drown his pain.

In even his most drunken of states, he still somehow managed to put out fresh food and water for Mister Whiskers. The cat seemed to be the only creature that could stand to be around him anymore.

At least when he was out he couldn't drink, unless he took his flask with him—which he sometimes did—and hated himself for that too. He had intended to just walk, to get out of the house that felt more and more like his prison, and just walk.

But he ended up sitting on a bench at the park.

Apart from four or five boys playing football, the park was pretty much empty. His heavy, bloodshot eyes stared at the place where he last saw her blowing him a kiss. He'd promised her they'd play Mario Kart.

The events churned over and over in his mind, questioning his thinking, asking why, marking the places where a different decision might have led to another outcome. An outcome where Charley and Fiona were both safe and sound at home waiting for him.

A muddy football rolled to Gary's feet. He tapped it with the side of his shoe, rolling it to the young lad who was running over to retrieve it. The boy picked it up, but instead of returning to the game, he walked over.

"Hi, Mr. Wright," the boy said.

Gary looked more closely and realised it was the young lad who he had spoken to on the day Charley disappeared, the one who had seen her leaving. He was taller now and had filled out some.

"Hello," Gary said. He searched his alcohol-befuddled mind and somehow dredged up his name. "Kevin, isn't it?"

"Yeah." He seemed to take in Gary's dishevelled appearance and his bloodshot eyes, perhaps comparing the way he looked now to the way he looked then. "I'm sorry you didn't manage to find Charley."

Gary's mouth widened a little, but it didn't really pass for a smile. "Me too."

"I miss her at school. She was always kind. I remember one time I'd forgotten to bring some sugar for the Home Ec class and she gave me some of hers. I think it left her a bit short, but she gave it to me anyway."

Gary nodded. "Yeah, that sounds like Charley."

The boy turned the muddy ball in his hands, glanced at his football mates, then back at the ball again. "My mum died last year," he said.

Gary watched him turn the ball. "I'm sorry to hear that."

The boy nodded. "Sucks to lose someone you love, don't it?"

"Yes, it does. Had she been ill?" Gary was thinking about his own mother and her long battle with cancer.

Kevin's friends began calling for him to return to the game, but he ignored them.

"No, it wasn't anything like that. My mum always had troubles up here." He pointed to his temple. "Mental problems. Depression and all that. My dad looked after her. Last summer,

190

not long after Charley went missing, we were having a barbeque in the garden. My dad went to get the sausages and burgers from the fridge, and while he was gone, my mum took the bottle of lighter fluid and sprayed it all over her face and down her front."

Gary listened with growing horror.

"I shouted for my dad, but we had music playing on the stereo and he couldn't hear me. I tried to stop her, but she got the clicky-lighter thing and set fire to herself."

He looked briefly toward his mates again, but his eyes were far away.

"She started screaming and running around like she'd suddenly realised setting yourself on fire isn't such a good idea. My dad came running out and got her on the ground. He tried to put the fire out with his hands, but then his hands were on fire too. I remembered a video we watched at school one time about smothering a fire, so I grabbed the cover for the barbeque and my dad managed to put the fire out with it." He paused, eyes full of the painful memory. "She was burned pretty bad by then though. All her hair was gone and her face was...bad. Dad called for the ambulance and they took her to the hospital, but she died a few days later. My Gran said it was a blessing."

"I'm sorry," Gary said. "That must have been a horrible thing for you to see."

Kevin silently turned the ball. "I have nightmares about it sometimes, but not as much as I used to."

"That was quick thinking, about the cover."

"Yeah. If I'd been quicker though, maybe she wouldn't have died."

"Maybe," Gary agreed. "But thinking about what you could've done can drive you crazy."

Couldn't it just.

The other boys were shouting and impatiently gesturing for him to return to the game.

191

"Anyway, I'd better get back before they throw me off the team." He smiled a little, showing goofy front teeth. "I hope you feel better soon, Mr. Wright. You can't stay like this all the time."

"Like what?"

"Sad," the boy said simply.

They locked eyes, and something passed between them. A common pain. The pain of loss.

He turned then, drop-kicking the ball to the others. One of the lads bounced it off his chest and deftly took control of it.

"See you later, Mister Wright," he said, jogging off to re-join the game.

Gary watched him wave and shout and vie for position. He thought again about how resilient people could be, how they were able to recover from the most horrible of things. Kevin had lost his mother in such traumatic circumstances, and yet there he was, playing football as if he hadn't a care in the world.

It's easier for a child than an adult, Gary reasoned.

Kevin dribbled the ball past the older boys and shot for the goal. It was a good try from that distance, but it went wide. The others called 'bad luck'. One of the older boys ruffled his hair as he trotted downfield to take his position.

Gary headed back home.

Chapter Twenty-One

Kevin's words stayed with Gary for the rest of the day. He kept off the booze that night for the first time in many weeks. He fed Mister Whiskers, and when he'd eaten a little something himself, he pottered around the house; punching cushions and tidying up. He fell asleep watching TV, eventually crawling into bed around twelve thirty, pretty much sober for the first time in weeks.

In the morning, he felt as if something had changed, though everything was exactly the same. The two most important people in his life were still gone, but he felt their absence even more powerfully than before.

Yet, he couldn't deny this new feeling of positivity and possibility that had settled over him.

He showered, shaved, and ate a bowl of cereal at the breakfast bar, all the while thinking about Kevin and his mum. He'd been wrong yesterday when he'd told himself that overcoming loss was easier for a child. The problem was that he'd *made* it harder for himself, surrounding himself with anger and bitterness, refusing to allow himself to grieve and start the hard road back to normality. He just had to get on with his life. It was what Fiona had been telling him, but it had taken the strength of a twelve-year-old boy to knock it into his thick skull.

He decided to do something real about it. He'd take the

pictures for re-framing and hire some people to fix the damage to the house, so the next time Fiona called, everything would be back in order. Not only that, he would go to the office to look at taking up the reigns again.

Thinking about a plan made him feel good. It made him feel positive and in control again.

But there was one final obstacle standing in the way of making a true recovery, something he needed to do.

Standing at the door to Charley's room, he gazed at the white, ceramic rectangle with her name written across the face. His mind cast back to Greece and the street artist painting the details, while Charley excitedly told him how she wanted it to look. She'd laughed as he painted her name with a flourish, and turned to look back at them, her eyes sparkling, her smile lighting up the night.

Charley.

He placed his hand gently over the plaque, his fingers hooking over the top edge. He sucked in a small breath, his stomach tightening in nervous knots, then prised the plaque from the door. It wasn't difficult. The plate made a ripping sound, leaving two sticky foam squares behind on the paintwork.

He took a moment to gauge how what he'd done made him feel, and was surprised to find he didn't feel much of anything.

He turned the plaque over and stroked his thumb affectionately over her name. Next to the door was another of the half-circle console tables that Fiona liked so much. This one had all of its legs. He placed the plaque gently into a small wicker basket on the table top.

Steeling himself, he went into the room.

The air was stale, the light stifled by the half-drawn curtains. He looked from her old toys and chalkboard, to the posters she'd stuck up on the wall, her keyboard, bed, the dresser cluttered with her things. A few colourful sculptures sat on the

194

windowsill, gathering dust.

All of it just as Charley had left it that day.

Seeing her things again weighed heavily on him, dragging on his new positive attitude like dead weights.

He sat on the edge of the bed and placed his hand on the sheets, his fingers lightly touching the place where she had lain.

"I'm sorry, Charley," he said, "but I think it's time now. I need your mum back..." And saying those words brought forth unexpected tears. "I need her. And it seems the only way for me to get her back...is to let you go." He shook with emotion, holding on as best he could. "I'm sorry for leaving you on the park that day. I'm sorry I wasn't a better dad. Wherever you are, Charley, I promise I won't stop hoping. I'll never stop hoping, even if everyone else has. But for now—just for now—I have to try to move on without you." He bowed his head. "I love you, Sweet Pea. I miss you so much."

He wiped away the tears and picked up one of the black bags that still lay discarded on the floor. He opened one of the drawers and looked at Charley's clothes. The pastel colours were laid out, all neat and ready to be worn.

He closed the drawer.

"Maybe tomorrow," he whispered and left, feeling the soft click of the door as it closed quietly behind him.

Kate was seated at the front desk, as usual, when he walked into the office reception. When she saw him, she smiled and rose to meet him. "Gary. It's so good to see you."

Kate was a middle-aged lady with a gentle way of speaking, which was somehow soothing. One of the guys in the office once joked that if his parents died in a plane crash, Kate was the one he'd want to break the bad news to him. Gary had a great deal of respect for her and felt heartened by the warmness of her welcome. It wasn't the awkward, can't look you in the eye, don't know what to say, mutterings he had encountered before, but a warm-hearted greeting from a woman he had known for a long time.

"Thank you, Kate," he said. "It's good to see you too."

"I'm so sorry for what happened. Would you give my love and prayers to Fiona?"

"I will," Gary replied. "Thank you."

He excused himself and entered the main office. Each developer had his own workstation with an assortment of photos, models, and bobbleheads from Star Wars to Iron Man.

Bob Jameson saw him first and was immediately on his feet to greet him. Rounds of handshakes and commiserations followed, but through it all, Gary was aware of the ones holding back. The ones who didn't know what to say to him. One guy was so mortified by his presence that he kept his eyes glued to his monitor the whole time.

"Where's Lance?" Gary asked.

"Where do you think?" Bob said with a grin and hooked a thumb over his shoulder.

Gary felt the chill as he let himself into the server room. The air conditioning unit and server fans droned out a constant hum that could easily drive you crazy if you thought about it too much.

Lance looked up from the console he was working at, the concentration on his face lifting and turning to delight when he saw who'd just walked in.

He clasped Gary's hand and shook it warmly. "Good to see you here, Buddy. What brings you to the cave today?"

"I dunno," Gary replied. "I guess I've started thinking about coming back...wanted to try it on, see how it feels."

Lance smiled and nodded. "That's good to hear. And how does it feel?"

Gary glanced about the familiar surroundings. Being back in

196

the office made him think of the old days when they were trying to get WebTech off the ground. Vying for clients. Bidding for contracts. It had been an exciting and extremely satisfying time.

"It feels good," he decided, though that wasn't entirely truthful. It also reminded him of the long hours he'd spent doing what he thought was important to secure his family's future. Working beyond what was necessary and refusing to gear down, even when the business had soared even higher than any of them had ever dreamed it could.

What he wouldn't give to have spent those hours with Charley and Fiona.

Lance must have seen his melancholy expression. "You okay?" he asked.

Gary swallowed thickly. "Yeah, I'm good. I'm getting myself back together. I need to show Fiona that I'm ready and she can come back. I need her to come home."

Lance nodded. "She wants to come back, you know?"

Gary raised his eyebrows. "You've spoken to her?"

"A little. She misses you."

Gary wanted to say, *so why doesn't she come home then?* But he knew the answer to that, it was standing right here in this server room.

He nodded. "I suppose I should speak to Ed…but I'm not going too."

Lance made an awkward face. "Yeah, I heard about that. Ed's tried gunning for you, but Michelle, Sam, and I have kept him in check."

"Gunning how?"

"Just bitching about how long you've been off and how it's affecting the business."

Gary frowned. The situation with Ed was something he would have to deal with, but not yet. "And *is* my time off affecting the business?"

197

"Nah, why would it?" Lance said and laughed, but then he sobered a little. "Seriously though, it could be better. Ed and Michelle are good, but a ship without its captain can end up in dangerous waters, if you know what I mean?"

"Point taken," Gary said. "We'll sort it out once I get back on my feet. I'm going to check my office and stop by Michelle. Is she in today?"

Lance said she was.

Gary leaned in the doorway and knocked on the frame. She glanced up from the monitor, and for a moment it was as if she didn't recognise him. Then she smiled, but it was a smile weighed with sadness.

"Hey," Gary said. "Hard at it as usual."

Michelle came around the desk and gave him a warm embrace, but it had been such a long time since he had been close to anyone that it made him feel uncomfortable. He wasn't sorry when she broke away.

"It's good to see you," she said. "How are you doing?"

"Oh, day to day, you know?"

Michelle nodded. "What are you doing here?"

"Just checking things out. I'm thinking of coming back. It's been long enough."

"Oh, that would be wonderful," she said, then her smile faltered. "Lance told me about Fiona."

"Yeah," Gary replied, but he didn't want to get into that.

"I'm sorry I haven't been to see you, especially with how good you were after the miscarriage. It's difficult to know what to say with everything that's happened."

"That's okay, Michelle. Who does know what to say? It's not something any of us have had to deal with before."

"I know," Michelle said, suddenly teary. "I still should have called you though. It's just that, with losing the baby, and then this happening to Charley...it all kind of got on top of me."

Gary placed a hand on her shoulder, it was all he could

198

manage, and wondered how it was that he seemed to end up comforting others about Charley, rather than the other way around.

She composed herself, wiping her eyes and sniffling a few times. "I'm sorry," she said. "You're a lovely man, Gary. This shouldn't have happened to you. It makes you wonder what God is thinking."

Gary wanted to get away. His previously buoyant mood was sinking fast. "I believe he works in *mysterious ways*," he said, without any attempt to hide the sarcasm.

He said a hasty good-bye and headed to his office. Some things had been moved around in his absence. He angled the phone and straightened the desk pad.

After saying a brief farewell to the others and promising to be back soon, he returned to the car, pulling his coat lapels in against the cold. The flat grey slab of sky extended right to the edge of the horizon.

The visit to the office had not been as bad as he had feared. At least the initial awkwardness of getting reacquainted with his colleagues was over. He could finally start the business of putting his life back together.

It wasn't a great idea, considering the new path he was trying to take, but he drove the route home that took him past the park.

His intention had been to simply drive slowly by, as a sort of final nod and acknowledgement that he was putting what happened here behind him. But he eased on the brake, stopping in almost the exact spot as he had when he dropped the girls on that far away afternoon. School was in, so the park was absolutely deserted, almost desolate. Even if this had been a Saturday, it was far too cold and grey for slides and swings, probably even too cold for Kevin and a game of football.

He recalled Charley backing away from him and blowing him a kiss.

Drive away now, just drive away.

He opened the door and got out.

This is the last time you do this, he promised himself. *The very last time.*

He stood at the edge of the park, melancholy thoughts of what was and what might have been, juggling for position in his mind. Despite his earlier strength and what he had said at the office, he felt as if he might collapse right there on the wet grass and never get up.

What are you doing? he asked himself as he swept rainwater off a bench with the edge of his hand and sat down. *For Godsake, go home.*

He rested his elbows on his thighs, his hands dangling between his knees.

Empty swings swayed minutely, the roundabout still. The buffed stainless steel of the slide glittered and shivered with the silver drops of the morning's cold rainfall.

A vacant playground is such a lonely place; like a once-loved toy that had become outgrown and abandoned. Like the old toys in Charley's empty bedroom. No laughing children, bikes, or riotous boys kicking a football around. No toddlers patting the sand and discovering its grittiness in the mouth.

The only voices were the lonely cawing of the crows in the trees beyond the canal. The only movement the acrobatic tumble of wind-blown leaves.

Sometimes he dreamed of pushing her on the swings.

Higher, Daddy, higher!

Other times he'd dream he came to the park and found her standing by the swings. She'd look up and smile, as if it had been a while since she'd last seen him. The dream was so vivid, so lucid, that he sometimes felt it may really happen one day.

It was the foolish reason that drew him here time after time.

He hung his head. At his feet lay an autumn leaf, as dry and dead as his soul.

200

He shouldn't have come. He closed his eyes. *Go home*, he told himself. *Go home, out of the cold. Go home before the memories drag you back down, sinking all those good intentions beneath waves of drink and self-pity.*

When he opened his eyes to do just that, he found a young girl standing a little way off on the wet grass, staring at him in that slightly unsettling way that small children sometimes do. She wore a buttoned-up navy blue coat, with white socks pulled up to the knee. Her hair was long and blonde.

He smiled at her, but she only stared back at him, her eyes so intense that he began to feel uncomfortable.

She seemed too young to be out on her own. Maybe five years old. He glanced around for her parents, but the park was deserted, apart from the two of them.

"Hello," he said. "Are you lost?"

Her eyes softened and drifted away, her head turning, her hand slowly rising to point off toward the canal. Gary followed her gaze and finger, expecting to see her mother somewhere over there, perhaps sitting on a bench, maybe attending to a younger child so she hadn't noticed how far the little one had wandered.

But there wasn't anyone else around.

Of course there wasn't, he thought.

An icy wind rustled the trees and shook the bushes.

He looked back at the girl. There were patches of dirt on her coat, mud and dead leaves caught in her hair.

Had they been there a moment ago?

She pressed her rosebud lips together, her smooth brows drawing into a soft frown, her arm stretching minutely out, subtly emphasising urgency.

Dark wings of dread spread over him. It was as if everything had shifted into slow-motion. Something was wrong here. Very wrong. His gaze shot back toward the bushes, looking harder for something untoward, something he had missed. But all he

201

could see were leafy evergreen bushes, and dense knots of black in the naked trees where the crows had built their homes.

He and Lance had searched for Charley down by the canal. That ancient oak with its exposed roots that had spooked him so. If he had the geography right, the tree was right on the other side of those bushes.

What was it about that tree?

It all felt surreal, like he was under water. For a fleeting moment, he felt the cold barrel of the gun under his chin and that long backwards tumble into the devouring darkness.

We all die alone.

When he turned back to the little girl, she was staring at him again, her arms by her sides, her eyes piercing and darkly hostile.

The hair rose on his arms and the back of his neck in swathes of gooseflesh.

What was happening?

The little girl's face transformed into a terrible visage, her eyes bulging, head violently shaking, face flushed purple, tongue squeezed out between her small white teeth.

Gary shrank back, crushing the back of his fist across his lips.

I'm in the middle of a horrible nightmare, he told himself. *This isn't happening. It isn't happening.*

She unleashed a terrible piercing shriek that startled the crows from the trees.

Gary cried out, his attention drawn to the dark mass of birds launching skyward. When he looked back again, the little girl was gone.

He stood up and looked around for her. His skin crawled. His scalp felt as if it was about to shrink off his skull.

What the fuck just happened?

He set off across the wet grass toward the big oak with its tangled roots, picking up pace until he was in a sprint bordering on panic. He skidded to a halt, slipping a little on the muddy ground. He looked back toward the bench, but the little girl was still nowhere to be seen.

He leaned into the bushes, pressing down on the leaves, and peering through snarls of crisscrossing twigs and branches. The land beyond sloped down to the path, where he and Lance had stood by the canal, wondering which way to go. Through the hazy-grey gloom, he saw the oak and followed the trunk down to where the ground had fallen away, exposing its naked roots.

Someone was down there among those roots.

A dark, hunched shape.

Gary pressed deeper into the foliage and the earthy scent of wet bark and leaves. Glittering spider webs stretched and tore. Water trickled from veiny green leaves and spilled off his jacket like streaming quicksilver.

For a moment, Gary was unable to comprehend what he was seeing, and then it all became horrifyingly clear.

A man had his hands around the throat of a small child lying on the ground, leaning in and grunting with effort, using his weight to choke and strangle.

Gary tore into the bushes, clawing at the branches and shouting something outraged and hideously incomprehensible.

The man's head shot up in surprise and fear, but before Gary could tear free of the clinging branches, the man scrambled to his feet and sprinted off toward the canal.

Gary finally broke through bushes and started after the man, but he only made it a few paces before switching his attention to the child lying on the ground. She wore a blue coat and white knee socks. There were mud and dead leaves caught in her blonde hair.

No, no. It wasn't possible.

He pushed the denial aside and knelt beside her. Her eyes were slitted, fixed and staring, her pupils open and black, her lips blue. Mucus bubbled from her nose and tears pooled in the corners of her eyes. Her tongue protruded horribly from between her small white teeth.

She looked in a bad way-

No, she looked dead.

-but perhaps he could still revive her.

It's not too late. Please don't let it be too late.

"ABC," he panted, trying to calm the raging panic, so he could recall the steps of the first aid course he'd attended years ago.

CALL FOR HELP.

But he didn't have a phone and there wasn't anyone around.

"*HELP!*" he shouted, just in case someone was near enough to hear him. "*SOMEBODY HELP ME! CALL AN AMBULANCE!*"

He turned his attention to the little girl, stroking back her hair, focusing on what he had to do, running on adrenaline.

'A' is for…

"Airway, airway."

He lifted her chin and gently pressed down on her forehead, tilting her head back and opening her throat. He tried to look inside her mouth for debris, but it was too dark to see. He hooked a finger into her mouth, sweeping her tongue.

'B' is for BREATHING

Check for breathing and signs of life.

She stared blankly up at him like a doll, her cherub face flushed with pinprick-haemorrhages, throat scuffed and bruised. The whites of her eyes were full of blood.

Can't you see she's dead already! Fuck the steps and start CPR!

He scooped away the slick of snot with his thumb and wiped it off on his trousers; then pinched her nostrils and blew into her mouth, watching her chest rise. After five Rescue Breaths, he turned his ear to her mouth. No breathing or signs of life. He pressed two fingers to the carotid artery in her neck, but was unable to detect even the faintest pulse.

Compressions.

The instructor advised compressions for a child was one-third the depth of the chest.

"Couldn't that break the ribs?" a doubtful woman had asked.

"Possibly," the instructor had replied, "but you can recover from broken ribs, you can't recover from death."

The class had all laughed, but right now the possibility of breaking this little girl's ribs wasn't in the slightest bit funny.

He nestled the heel of his left palm in the centre of her chest, locking his arm straight and covering his left hand with his right. He leaned sharply on her, feeling the sapling-like spring of her young ribcage.

Please don't break.

He counted off the compressions.

Oneandtwoandthreeandfourandfive

What had the instructor said? Thirty compressions to the rhythm of *Staying Alive.* In the clean, controlled classroom environment, they had all laughed at that too, but the instructor hadn't gone on to explain how your heart would be beating so hard you feel like you are going to faint, or that you might have to wipe the snot from a child's dead face.

...eightandnineandtenandeleven...

He imagined her heart inside her chest, squeezing like a tennis ball, blood forcing through her lungs, where the cells sucked in the life-giving oxygen to nourish her brain and keeping it from dying.

...twentyseventwentyeighttwentynineTHIRTY.

He raised himself high on his knees and shouted into the treetops. "SOMEBODY HELP ME!"

No reply but the thump of his heart and the heavy rasp of his breath.

He wasted no time. Two breaths followed by thirty more compressions.

He paused again to shout for help. But he knew the park had been deserted. There wasn't anyone to hear him. How long could he keep this up? Already the deep breathing and exertion had made him nauseous and light-headed.

Yet he had to keep going. Just keep going until something happened, until someone heard his cries and came to help. There was nothing else he could do.

Just as he was beginning to despair, a cautious voice called, "Hello?" from beyond the bushes.

Gary stopped the CPR. A man peered through the bushes, and somewhere on the other side of the scrub, a dog chuffed and growled.

"Call for an ambulance!" Gary shouted. "There's a little girl here and she's not breathing!"

"Oh my God! I'll do it now!"

Gary leaned back on his knees for a second, the small of his back aching, dizziness and nausea swirling around him. He wiped sweat from his brow, the ends of his fingers tingling. The paramedics needed to hurry because he couldn't keep this up much longer.

Then he saw her, standing a little way off, her mouth pulled down at the corners. The girl lying dead on the black earth, and the one standing before him, one and the same.

She gazed down at her body with those sad, blue eyes, and silently shook her head.

"NO!" Gary shouted.

It wasn't over. He could keep going. He could keep the blood flowing and the tissues alive until help arrived.

He pumped the little girl's chest with new found strength and vigour.

Oneandtwoandthreeandfour...

He felt a rib crack and eased off slightly.

Tears blurred his vision. A string of saliva hung from his lip.

He stopped at twelve and held her small, soft round face in his hands. "Please," he wept. "*Please.*"

But there were no signs of life.

He leaned over and blew into her mouth again, but the breaths were weak and broken by sobs. Bolts of pain shot through his shoulders when he tried to apply more compressions.

Oneandtwoandthreeand...

The song whirled around his head like the insane backing-track to an out of control situation.

By the time the green-garbed paramedics burst through the trees with their cases of equipment, Gary was half insane. When they tried to take over, he fought them, desperately trying to keep working on her even though he had no strength left to do so. They had to physically drag him away from her.

The world spun around him, the colour washing from his vision. He lurched forward and heaved a thin stream of yellow bile onto the dark ground.

Exhaustion settled over him and he slumped on his knees, breathing hard, sweat trickling down his face and back,

The paramedics worked on her.

He'd done his best, but it hadn't been good enough.

I did everything I could, he thought. *It's out of my hands now.*

Only it wasn't.

It was only just beginning.

Chapter Twenty-Two

She was dead.

Despite all his efforts. She was dead. He had failed her.

The paramedics laid her small, inert body on a stretcher, covered her with a blanket, and put an oxygen mask on her face, but Gary knew she was dead. She was dead before he laid eyes on her, let alone his hands. The man in the black woollen hat had seen to that.

But he had seen her *before* he'd found her body. She'd pointed him to the place where she was being murdered, just meters from the bench where he had been thinking about Charley.

It wasn't possible.

Yet how could he deny it? He had seen her with his own eyes. *Twice.* Had she already been dead when she appeared before him on the park bench? Or had she still been alive and needing his help?

She had been a what? A ghost? A spirit?

His mind wrestled with the concept. All those times Trixie had tried to convince him of a spirit world and all the times he had virtually laughed in her face.

She'd come to you for help. She needed you to help her.

He hadn't been quick enough. He hadn't understood.

He had failed her.

Just as he'd failed his own little girl.

When the police arrived, Gary couldn't think coherently. It was like he was shell-shocked. As if some big circuit breakers in his mind had tripped, shutting off all but the little girl and how he had tried to save her.

It replayed over and over in his mind; wiping her face, blood in her eyes, her chest rising, the crack of her ribs. The CPR going on and on, as if it would never end.

"I tried," he told the police officer, who was attempting to uncover what had happened. "I tried to bring her back. But it was too late."

His face was grey and shiny with perspiration, his eyes wide and crazy. He needed someone to tell him he'd done all he could, that there wasn't anything anyone could have done to save her.

But no one did.

Maybe because you didn't do everything you could. If you had heeded her, then maybe you could have gotten to her quicker and saved her life.

He was taken to the police station where he gave a written statement. They were suspicious of him. And why wouldn't they be? His own daughter had gone missing and, less than a year later, he's a witness to the murder of another child?

Damned right they were suspicious of him.

It didn't help that he couldn't tell them the whole truth. When they asked what had drawn his attention to the trees, he'd had to lie. How could he explain that the girl herself had shown him? They'd think him crazy. More than that, they'd think him guilty.

When he came out of the interview room, Fiona and Lance were waiting for him. The sight of Fiona reduced him to tears and he stumbled into her arms.

"I tried, Fiona," he wept. "I tried my best to save her, but I was too late."

209

Fiona looked at Lance, confused and alarmed at how fragile he was.

Lance put his arm around Gary's shoulder. "It's okay, Buddy," he told him. "It's okay."

Once home and back in his own surroundings, he managed to recover a little. After a couple of stiff drinks, he was able to recount all that had happened, all except the part about seeing the little girl's... *ghost.* Yes, he was able to say it to himself, but he couldn't face explaining it to anyone else yet...or maybe ever.

"Jesus," Lance said.

"To be honest," Gary said, staring into space, "I don't think Jesus had much to do with it."

Fiona held a hand to her face, distressed and tearful. "It's horrible," she said, and Gary knew she was thinking about Charley, because he was too.

"What did the police say?" Lance asked.

"Not much, but they're suspicious."

"Suspicious of what?"

"What do you think? My own daughter goes missing, and then I'm witness to another girl's murder." He smiled bitterly, thinking of what he'd said at the party. "What are the odds?"

Fiona stood up. "It's so horrible. How could anyone do that to a child?" She looked at the two men, but they had no answer. "It's so unfair."

Yes it is, Gary thought. *When one stupid decision can tear down your entire world, then yes, it's all un-fucking-fair.*

"I just wish I could have saved her," he said.

"You did what you could," Lance told him.

"Did I?" Gary asked, thinking of the precious moments he wasted.

"I don't see what else you could have done."

Gary looked at the clock. It was approaching midnight. "You know what," he said, "I can't think about this anymore." He put down his glass. "Do you mind if I turn in?"

"Not at all," Lance said. "Get some sleep."

He wearily massaged the tight knots in the small of his back, where the overstressed muscles had begun to stiffen and clench. His neck and the area between his shoulder blades ached like a bad tooth.

"Gary," Fiona said gently, moving closer to him and placing her hand on his arm. "You did everything you could."

He looked deeply into her eyes; wanting to hold her and kiss her, wanting to see her crooked smile again. He missed her so much. But there was a gulf of distance and sadness between them.

"She still died though, didn't she," he said.

"Sometimes it's just too late for anyone to do anything."

Maybe she was right. Too late for that little girl, maybe too late for him and Fiona. Maybe too late for everything.

He broke away from her. "You okay to see yourselves out?" he asked, not waiting for a reply. He trudged out the door, leaving them in the living room.

Fiona stood quietly watching the empty space where he'd been. "I don't know what to do," she said. "He looks so thin. What should I do?"

"You could stay?" Lance suggested. "Keep an eye on him?"

She crossed her arms and looked around the cold, untidy room. She'd seen the broken pictures stacked against the wall in the hall, and the damage to the door, but she hadn't asked how they had happened. She only had to think of him hurling the whisky bottle to work it out.

"I can't," she said.

"He came in the office today," Lance told her.

Fiona raised her eyebrows. "He did? What for?"

"He said he wanted to get his life back together. He said he wanted...no, he said he *needed* for you to come home."

Fiona thought about it for a second, then shook her head. "I can't stay, Lance. Not yet. Not until I can be sure."

Lance didn't try to persuade her otherwise.

"This thing has knocked him for a six though," she said. "I'm worried for him. Will *you* stay, Lance?"

"Of course I will."

Fiona hugged him close.

"Thank you," she said. "It's all such a mess."

"We'll get through it," Lance assured her.

Fiona tried to smile, and nodded, but she wasn't convinced it was true.

Gary had all but forgotten about Lance and Fiona by the time he had wearily climbed the stairs. He paused to look down the landing at Charley's room. The first thing he noticed was that the nameplate was gone, and it took him a moment to remember that he'd taken it off himself.

My God, was that only this morning?

The second thing was that the door was slightly ajar. That was curious, because he kept her door closed. Always closed. When he came out of there this morning, he must have failed to close it properly.

He trudged along the landing and pulled the door to, listening for the click of the latch. He heard it, but pushed on it to confirm that it had shut properly.

As he turned, he saw Charley's name plaque in the basket on the little half table and picked it out, turning it thoughtfully over in his hand. After a moment, he pressed it back onto the torn foam sticker pads. It didn't want to stay, so he pressed it hard until it stayed put. It wasn't straight, but it would do.

He collapsed, belly first and fully clothed, onto the bed, and lay there for a minute or two, his face buried in the quilt. He kicked off his shoes and rolled onto his back, his head on the cool pillow.

212

He'd hoped that exhaustion would let his mind drift quickly to sleep, but instead he lay there staring with aching eyes at the dark ceiling, images of the little girl flashing like a strobe light in his mind.

Head turning. Finger pointing.

Her name was Emma.

She'd gone missing just a half hour earlier, from the back garden of her grandparent's house where she'd been playing.

Lifeless blue lips, slitted eyes, the whites full of blood.

He curled into a ball, hands gripped tightly between his knees. The more he tried to clear his mind, the more vivid the images became.

His finger sweeping her tongue.

Airway. Breathing. CPR.

Can't you see she's dead!

Oneandtwoandthreeand...

He thought about how he'd wiped the mucus from her face, and that one small intimate gesture released his dammed emotions in a terrifying rush. He grabbed his mouth and tried to stifle the horrific scream that tore from his throat.

Time had stretched out before him like an endless highway on a dark night, while he had tried to save her.

In the end, it had all been for nothing. All his efforts had made no difference.

He had made no difference.

The barrel of the rifle slid beneath his chin, the circular touch of steel, cold and uncompromising. His thumb hooked over the reversed trigger and pressed down on it before he could change his mind.

And then he was falling, falling, while darkness folded over him like layers of black silk. Only this time, something shone in the void. Emma's tiny white face. 'We all die alone,' she whispered, her voice

Gary awoke gasping for breath. He scrambled up and gathered himself against the headboard like a frightened mouse. His shoulders were stiff and aching, his back muscles clenched in pain. He peered through the shadows, fumbling with the lamp and finding the switch. The room lit briefly before the bulb blew with a flash and a pop.

He settled back into the darkness, feeling small and afraid. Blobs of white floated before his eyes, obscuring his sight.

The dream again. Only this time he knew who he had murdered. *He* had strangled the little girl among the roots of the old oak tree. *He* had squeezed her throat until her tongue bloated from her mouth and blood haemorrhaged into the whites of her eyes.

He rested his head against the wall, hoping for the chilly winds of the nightmare to blow away, but his gaze was drawn to the door. The first time he'd had the dream he'd felt that something was lurking out on the landing. That same feeling prickled his senses now, scuttling through his mind like a fat spider.

Something's waiting out there, listening to your nightmare.

That was something Trixie might say. Where had it come from?

Open the door and find out.

He didn't want to open it. Opening the door made him feel the way he did that day Fiona asked him to go out for lunch. He was afraid of...*something*...something unsubstantial. An irrational fear that he must strive to overcome.

He got off the bed and winced, bracing his aching back with the heel of his palm. The room felt so cold. Half-walking, half-hobbling, he reached for the door handle, hesitating as Emma's

214

tiny face slipped into his mind, stuck in the dark void between life and death.

We all die alone.

Stop it!

He yanked the door open to a dark and silent landing.

There was no monster lurking there.

Did you really expect there would be?

"Yes," he whispered at the darkness. "Yes, I did."

He looked down the landing at Charley's room.

The door was open. Just a crack.

Gary stared at it for a long time. He'd closed it and tested it. He'd stuck the plaque back on the door. The plaque was still there, a little slanted, but it was just where he had left it. He'd had to press on it firmly to make it stick. How could he have done that if the door hadn't been properly closed?

He walked along the landing—the moon casting everything in soft, blue hues— and wondered if this might be another dream.

The door was a couple of inches ajar, a long slice of darkness revealing nothing of the inside. He touched the panelling with the backs of his fingers and gently pushed.

He scanned the room slowly, his eyes straining to penetrate the deepest shadows. Nothing appeared to be out of place.

He reached around the door frame and flicked on the light, flinching and squinting at the sudden painful glare. As his eyes adjusted, it seemed that everything was exactly as he had left it that morning.

And yet it wasn't. Something wasn't right.

I don't want to go in there.

That was stupid, he'd been in many times since Charley disappeared.

But not since Emma.

No, not since Emma.

He reached for the light-switch, glancing toward the dresser as he did so.

And that was when he saw it in the reflection.

He lowered his hand, his neck creaking as he slowly turned to look at all the old toys at the other end of the room. In the middle of the chalkboard, in red chalk, was a shakily drawn zigzag.

He glanced nervously left and right.

Nothing else seemed out of place.

Nothing but the red zigzag, that hadn't been there yesterday morning.

He moved closer, noting that there didn't appear to be a red chalk stick among the dusty colours on the chalkboard's narrow wooden shelf. He crouched before the easel and closely examined the marking.

A zigzag.

Its sharp saw-teeth and diagonal lines disturbed him.

He rubbed it out with his fingers, the drawing reduced to a smear of red dust.

He backed slowly away from the red smudge, glancing side to side, as if something might be hiding, lying in wait. He switched off the light and closed the door, pressing one hand on the doorframe to ensure the latch caught.

In the en suite, he washed his face and leaned on the porcelain, gripping it tightly and gazing in the mirror at the skull-like apparition staring back at him with hollow, haunted eyes.

216

An image of the man strangling Emma dropped into his mind; leaning hard, putting all his weight onto her delicate, slender neck.

"Is that what happened to you, Charley?" he whispered. "Am I hoping for the impossible? Am I chasing ghosts?"

Forget her, she's dead.

He heard a soft sound from behind him. Like a sigh. He looked over his shoulder into the shadowy bedroom and thought he heard faint whispering. Hairs rose on the nape of his neck. He turned fully around and stood in the doorway, his heart picking up the pace a little.

Nothing.

He imagined Emma standing silently in the shadows, only she wasn't pointing away now, she was pointing *at* him.

Accusing him.

He shivered and asked himself again how he could have seen her when she was being strangled to death at the roots of the tree.

It had been her ghost.

He didn't believe in ghosts.

There are more things in heaven and earth, Horatio, than are dreamt of in your philosophy.

Maybe, he thought, *but I still don't believe in ghosts.*

Perhaps a mental link had been forged, connecting him to her dying body, because he was the only person near enough to help her.

Mental link? Seriously? Was that any better an explanation than ghosts?

Yet he couldn't deny he had seen her. She had guided him to the place of her murder. He had to accept that, somehow, she had come to him for help.

And he had blown it by wasting precious seconds puzzling over a little girl out on her own.

He thought about Charley backing away from him, her hand

217

rising to place a kiss on her palm.

Tears blurred his vision. "Charley," he whispered, and wept into his hands.

Chapter Twenty-Three

He awoke to the phone ringing. It was a reporter asking for a statement about what had happened yesterday. Gary told him to fuck off and put the phone down. A second later it rang again. Gary let it. After a few rings the answer machine picked up. Two minutes later it started ringing again, so he snatched it off the cradle, slammed it back down, and knocked it off the hook.

He pulled the cover over his shoulders and grasped it tightly to his chest. Maybe he wouldn't get up at all today. Maybe he'd just stay in bed and sleep and that sleep would be dreamless.

And maybe it wouldn't.

Maybe he'd dream of beady-eyed crows and moth's wings and zigzags.

He opened his eyes. The zigzag.

Had that been real?

He checked his fingers for chalk dust, but then remembered he had washed his face; or had that been part of the dream too.

Slipping out of bed in his boxer shorts, he went onto the landing. The doorbell rang but he ignored it.

To his relief, Charley's door was closed. He let himself in and looked directly at the chalkboard.

There was no zigzag.

But he could see the smudge of red dust where he had

erased it with his fingers.

So it hadn't been a dream...

"Morning."

Gary almost screamed.

It was Lance.

"Jesus Christ, Lance!" Gary cried. "You nearly gave me a fucking heart attack!"

"Sorry," Lance said, an amused little grin on his face.

"What the hell are you doing here?"

"Nice to see you too," he said. "I stayed, just to make sure you were okay. Slept on the sofa."

"I'm fine," Gary said gruffly.

Lance looked around the door. "What are you doing?"

Gary stepped between him and the chalkboard. "I don't need a babysitter."

Lance shrugged and stepped aside to let him out.

Gary closed the door carefully, placing his hand on the frame and pulling until he heard and felt the click. He pushed and pulled on the handle a few times to make sure the latch had engaged.

Lance watched him quizzically. "You okay?" he asked.

"I'm fine."

"We were just a bit worried about you, that's all."

"You don't need to be," Gary lied.

He returned to the bedroom, stepped into his discarded trousers and pulled on a crumpled shirt.

"Press are outside," Lance advised.

Gary peeped through the curtains at the mass of people and vans congregated on the street in front of the house.

"Oh my God," he moaned.

The doorbell rang again.

"Want me to get rid of them?" Lance asked.

Gary sighed and ran a hand through his tousled hair. "No, leave them. They never go away, not really."

"You want some breakfast then?"

"Look, Lance..."

Lance held up his hands. "I know, I know."

"It's not that I don't appreciate what you are trying to do, it's just..."

"I know," Lance repeated. "Don't sweat it. I have to go anyway...work and all that."

He turned to leave.

"Lance?"

Lance looked back.

"Thanks."

The two men regarded each other for a moment, then Lance nodded and left.

The press hung around all day, and Gary left them to it. He kept the downstairs curtains closed, his time spent in an unsettling semi-darkness.

Fiona called him. She asked why he'd gone into work, but he ruined it by becoming defensive and dismissive, trying, for reasons he didn't understand, to make out that it didn't matter.

He took his first drink shortly after the lunch he didn't eat.

The one time he ventured out was into the garden looking for Mister Whiskers. He hadn't seen the cat since the day before, and that wasn't like him. He called out his name and shook his food bag, but the cat was nowhere to be seen. Gary hoped he was okay.

In the early evening, when he was under the influence but not totally out of it, the mystery of the zigzag trickled into his thoughts. He didn't know how it had got there, but knew it had been real; the red-chalk smudge in the middle of the board had convinced him of that. But what was the significance of a red zigzag? He felt sure there was something more to it, but he

221

couldn't quite recall what it was.

Drink in hand, he climbed the stairs to the study, checking Charley's room as he did so. The door was still closed.

He sat down behind his desk and wiped off the grey film of dust that had settled on the aluminium casing of his Mac. He opened the lid and powered it up, turning on the small desk lamp while it completed its boot-up routine.

A scribbled reminder on his deskpad said, *Call local radio station. Set up meeting.* That had been just after the search for Charley had been scaled back and he was trying to keep her story alive. Charley's case was still open, but the Goldilocks investigation had put an immense strain on the police. Charley hadn't been discounted as a victim, but the fact that she didn't fit the MO put her in the 'maybe' file. Would Emma go in the 'maybe' file too? She had blonde hair but was much younger than the other girls. He tore off the top sheet and threw it into the wastepaper basket.

He started up a browser session and typed 'zigzag' into the search field. Google came back with thirty-two million results. Topping the list was a production company, an education facility, and a hairdresser. Not very encouraging. He scrolled down a little and found *Wikipedia*, which offered a brief explanation of what a zigzag is and that the origin of the word was unclear.

Amending the search to 'zigzag meaning' brought up a list of dictionary definitions, so he changed 'meaning' to 'symbolism' and one hundred and twenty-three thousand results came back.

Some talked about the zigzag in relation to Greek mythology, or Native Americans, or religious uses. He clicked through each one that looked interesting, but none of them seemed to fit, until he found something about the meaning of zigzags in dreams. He hadn't dreamed about zigzags, but he had certainly just awoken from a disturbing dream when he saw it. The text suggested that seeing a zigzag in dreams indicated potential disaster and growth through suffering.

His gaze fell away from the screen. Growth through suffering? Was that some kind of cosmic joke? Charley had been taken away so that he could grow into a better person? And potential disaster? His daughter was gone, and so was his wife, what more was there left to be destroyed beside himself?

Could that be it?

Suicidal thoughts came and went, but up to now they had only been thoughts. If he took his own life, how could there be growth?

He swivelled the chair to look out of the window and into the garden. He could see his face reflected in the glass but pulled focus on something moving on the lawn.

Mister Whiskers.

He hurried downstairs to the kitchen, flicked on the outside lights, and opened the back door. Mister Whiskers eyed him from across the garden, his head bobbing.

"Hey, Whiskers," Gary called. "Come on, puss-puss."

The cat regarded him curiously, his eyes catching the patio lights and shining like turquoise marbles. He looked away and began licking a paw.

"Here, puss-puss," Gary sang. Usually that brought him trotting over, but he remained disinterested.

Gary grabbed his food bag and shook it. That always worked. "Here, puss-puss. You must be hungry. Come on, Whiskers."

The rattle of the bag caught the cat's attention and he stalked a little closer, walking with that high-shouldered swagger of which only felines seem capable. When he was a few yards away he slowed and stopped again, his head low and cautious.

Gary signed. "Come on, Buddy, I haven't got all night. Where've you been hiding all this time?"

He snatched the bowl from just inside the kitchen door and

shook some food into it. Mister Whiskers raised his head, sniffing the meaty aroma on the air. He seemed interested, but steadfastly refused to come any closer.

"Come on," Gary urged. He stepped out of the kitchen and onto the patio in his bare feet.

The cat's head darted quickly, warily, and then he slowly began to ease back, his eyes staring intently at Gary, a low growl in his throat.

"For God's sake, Whiskers, what's the matter with you? Come and get-"

The last word dried in his throat as he realised that Mister Whiskers wasn't staring at him at all.

He was staring past him.

He was staring at something *behind* him in the kitchen.

Gary's breath became short, as icy shards of fear slipped down his spine. He pressed his lips together and swallowed hard.

The cat growled lowly in his throat.

Gary wanted to turn, but sheer terror rendered him immobile. Every hair on his body rose to attention.

Mister Whiskers hissed, his spine arched, his ears flat against his skull. Fur bristled over his back.

"Oh shit," Gary whispered.

With a nerve-shredding feline shriek, Mister Whiskers leapt into the air, his legs stiff, his claws extended, his back curved like a horseshoe. He twisted as he landed and bolted off down the garden.

Gary whirled around as the door slammed in his face.

He screamed, high and feminine, and stumbled away in fright. His legs twisted together and tripped him, the metal bowl clattering from his grasp as the patio lights flickered and died.

Gary winced at his grazed palm, but the sting of it instantly evaporated when he looked up and saw someone standing on

224

the other side of the door, their face pressed to the frosted glass, a single eye staring at him.

Someone was in the house!

He screamed again, but this time it was edged with outrage.

He scrambled to his feet. The face was still against the glass when he rammed the door open with his shoulder. He expected to feel the weight of a body against it, but the door flew wide.

What the fuck?

He dived inside and yanked the door away from the wall to look behind it, though it would be impossible for someone to hide there.

He hunted through the kitchen. Checked behind the island. Stuck his head into the hall.

Nothing.

No one.

The house was quiet and empty.

"Oh fuck," he whispered.

Was this it? The start of madness? Seeing things that weren't there? Starting with that little girl, Emma. Could it all be hallucinations? His disturbed mind, the tablets and the alcohol conspiring to drive him insane.

But you saw Emma. You know you did. You saw her before you even knew she existed.

The patio lights stuttered and came back on.

He went outside and stood with his hands on his hips, breathing deeply, feeling his pounding heart slowing.

He glanced back at the house.

Did you really see someone with their face pressed to the glass?

Yes.

Did you really?

YES!

He had seen it and he didn't give a fuck.

He picked up the bag and the bowl, angrily kicking the spilled Kitty Morsels to the edges of the patio as he did so.

Mister Whiskers had retreated way down to the bottom of the garden.

Gary set off to try and tempt him again.

While he could argue that these...*visions*...could be hallucinations, the zigzag had been there. He'd seen it and he'd rubbed it out. The physical evidence that it had existed was still smeared on the board in the morning.

Maybe you put it there yourself.

The thought that he may have staggered into Charley's room in the middle of the night and drawn a zigzag was a disturbing one. That would explain why the door was open too.

But why a zigzag?

The article said zigzags could appear in your dreams. Maybe he had been dreaming about them and his subconscious mind had made him draw one in the one place, besides the park that just about defined his torment.

Mister Whiskers lowered his head suspiciously as Gary approached, and eyed him warily, muscles tensed and ready to dart.

"Whiskers, come on fella, stop messing me about."

The cat darted off, scrambling easily up the fence and dropping over the other side.

Gary sighed, the Kitty Morsels bag hanging from his fist.

"Fuck you then, Whiskers. Be a dick."

That made him think about Trixie at the party.

Sometimes you just can't help being a dick.

On the heels of that, came the awkward phone call he'd made to her from the hotel room in London, just before Charley went missing.

It's in the shape of a zigzag, she'd said in the voice of a little girl.

Gary dropped the bag of food in the garden and raced back to the house.

He dialled her number and it rang only once before she picked up.

"Gary," she said simply, almost as if she had been expecting his call.

"Trixie, do you remember that night I called you about worrying Fiona?"

"Yes," she said, almost before he had finished speaking.

"Why did you say that about a zigzag?"

"I didn't."

"I heard you."

"I didn't say it, Gary."

Why was she denying that she'd said it when he'd plainly heard her say it?

"I heard about the little girl at the park," Trixie said.

"You did?"

"It's all over the news."

"I haven't been looking."

The line went quiet, but he could hear her breathing.

"Trixie, what's happening?"

"I don't know." Her breathing became shaky, frightened.

"You know something though, don't you? You can *sense* something?"

"I..."

"Please, help me Trixie. I feel like I'm losing my mind."

"There's something around you."

"What?"

"Something...a presence...not bad exactly, but something dark, something *angry*."

"I'm angry," Gary said.

"It's not you."

"What then? The little girl? Is it Emma?"

"Maybe..."

227

"Maybe? Trixie, for God's sake, help me!"

"I'm not a medium!" she said, her voice distressed. "I can't speak to the dead."

"Well, what can you do?"

"Nothing really. I'm just sensitive to some things. Sometimes I feel like I can see something in the distance, something that I can't quite make out. This is like a darkness around you Gary, and it scares me."

He saw Emma's white face in the void. *We all die alone.*

"Let me come and see you."

"No!" Then more gently, "No. I can't be near you. It's almost too much for me now even, just talking on the phone."

"What is it, Trixie? Tell me what you know."

"I don't know anything."

"Please, Trixie, I need your help."

"I'm sorry."

"What does the zigzag mean?"

"I don't know... I'm sorry."

"Trixie, please."

She was crying. "I can't help you, Gary. I'm…I'm so afraid."

"Trixie, please."

The line disconnected. Gary listened to the dial tone until it broke into a long continuous drone. He dropped the phone back onto its cradle.

Trixie gripped the phone tightly, her hand trembling, knuckles white. Her breathing was shallow and shaky. She felt awful. She felt guilty. But she'd also never felt so terrified in her life. She lived across town from Gary and Fiona, but she could *feel* that house, she could see it, like a silhouette cut from black card. And there were people at the windows.

There were people at the windows!

228

The house was marked, like a drop of blood on a wedding veil.

She couldn't help him. She didn't know anything. All she knew was that whatever was happening, it was happening to him and him alone, and there wasn't anything anyone could do to help him.

She set her phone down and leaned back in the chair. Around the room, scrawled on pieces of paper discarded on the floor, pinned to the walls, in the margins of books, drawn on the mirror in lipstick, on every blank space she could find, she had drawn zigzags. Black and blue and green and purple, but predominately they were red.

Red zigzags.

Red zigzags.

Red zigzags.

She felt compelled to draw them, was obsessed with drawing them. Every time she drew one, she felt as if it would reveal something to her, as if the shape held some secret that she could decipher.

If only she could see what was behind those jagged, pointy lines.

See the meaning.

As she mulled it over, her hand rested on her thigh, her forefinger lightly describing the zigzag over and over. It was like a tick burrowed under her skin, like an incessant itch that wouldn't go away, no matter how much she scratched it.

She picked up a pen and a notebook and drew another zigzag, followed by another, and another, scribbling them faster and harder, tears flowing and blurring her vision, until the pen began tearing through the paper.

Chapter Twenty-Four

Though media interest in Gary remained high, he'd returned the phone to the hook, choosing to screen the calls through the answer machine instead of cutting himself off completely. Sometimes the press left a message, other times the call disconnected as soon as the message started to play. It was a nuisance, but with his mobile phone smashed, it was the only way Fiona could contact him, though she never did.

On the morning of the third day following Emma's murder, the phone rang. The machine picked up and invited the caller to leave a message. Gary expected to hear the click of disconnection, but instead, a man began to speak.

"I'm sorry to bother you, but this is Steve Fletcher, Emma's father." Gary sat up. "I was wondering...well, *we* were wondering, Nola and I...if you could spare us some time to talk about what happened to Emma?" The line went quiet for a moment. "It's been difficult for us...as I'm sure you must know with what you've been through yourself. If you could just speak to us, maybe...I don't know...could you just call me on..."

Gary jumped to his feet and snatched up the phone.

"I'm here."

"Oh," Steve said. "I'm sorry. I didn't think you were there."

"Reporters," Gary said.

"Ah, yeah," Steve replied, obviously under similar strain.

"I'm sorry to bother you like this, but could we come over and talk?"

"I'm not sure there's much I can offer you," Gary said.

"I don't either, but, Nola...if you could just talk to her? There are some things bothering her, things that you might be able to put her mind at rest about."

Gary thought about Emma's tiny strangled face and the blood in her eyes. Was there anything he could say to ease their pain?

"Please," Steve said.

Reluctantly, Gary agreed.

The police brought them over, and Gary was heartened to see Cloe driving the unmarked car. Gary nodded to her as he invited the Fletchers in, and she acknowledged, concern in her eyes.

Beyond the gates, cameras clicked, recording the moment. Tomorrow's headlines in the making.

He took them through to the living room where they sat together on the sofa. He wondered if he should offer tea, or something stronger? Fiona had always been the perfect host. He'd managed to lay off the drink when he knew they were coming, but he could have used a stiff one to calm his nerves.

Looking at Nola, he already regretted agreeing to have them over. The agony set deep in her eyes mirrored Fiona's in the days following Charley's disappearance. It transported him back to that time like it was fresh, and the nightmare of Charley's kidnapping was relentlessly unfolding before his eyes.

Watching the two of them clinging to each other, doing their best to comfort one another, he wondered if their fractured world would break, as it had for him and Fiona.

Nola held a crumpled tissue to her nose, her eyes red and tired. Now they were here, they seemed overwhelmed, struggling to find words for the questions they felt compelled to ask.

"I'm sorry," Steve began. "It's just so difficult..."

"I know," Gary sympathised.

"We wanted to talk to you about Emma...about her last moments."

The little girl's dead face flashed in Gary's mind's eye.

Did they really want to know about that?

"I'm not sure there's anything I can tell you really," Gary admitted. "She was already...gone when I got there."

"You saw *him* though," Steve said, his face staunch, body rigid.

"I saw someone, a figure, it was dark under the trees. He ran, I was going to chase him, but I tried to resuscitate Emma instead. Maybe I should have just chased him down...you know, if I'd known."

"No, no," Steve said. "You did the right thing. You tried to save our little girl."

"Did she say anything?" Nola asked. Her voice was soft and timid, with what sounded like an Irish lilt to it.

Gary wished he had something to give her, some small gesture, a word of comfort, but he had nothing, and he wasn't about to lie to a grieving mother.

He shook his head. "I'm sorry. I just did what I could until the paramedics arrived."

"Did she seem like she'd been..." Nola looked to her husband, her expression lost and frightened.

Steve took his wife's hand, his eyes scarily intense. "What Nola means is, the police aren't telling us much yet, so we want to know...what we *need* to know is...had she been...*interfered* with?" His lips quivered around the question. Gary could see it had taken every bit of strength he had to ask it, and knew how

232

afraid he was to hear the answer.

"She was fully dressed," Gary said. "I don't think he'd touched her like that."

Nola burst into fresh tears. It was hard to tell if it was with relief or renewed agony.

Steve nodded, silent tears running down his cheeks. "Thank you," he said. "Thank you."

Gary touched his fingers to his lips, both were trembling.

Nola opened her bag and took out a photograph. She gazed longingly at it for a moment, then handed it to Gary. It was a picture of Emma, sitting between her two brothers. She was smiling, cute dimples in her cheeks. Despite her blonde locks, her eyes were dark and sparkled with mischief. She looked so different in life. It was difficult for him to reconcile this happy family photo with the harrowing images he harboured of her in death.

"I just wanted you to see her," Nola said. "See her as she was."

Gary nodded and was glad to have seen her alive. It seemed to put it into a better perspective. Before seeing the photo, it was as if Emma had always been a dead little girl. He handed the photo back and Nola cradled it to her breast.

"Emma was our baby," Steve said. "We have two sons, her older brothers. For the second one we'd wanted a daughter, but it hadn't worked out that way. Life, huh? Then it just happened. Nola was expecting again and before we knew it, we had the little girl we'd always wanted."

Nola leaned into her husband and dabbed her eyes with the tissue.

"She was such a good little girl," Steve continued. "Never any trouble. She was always happy, always smiling. She didn't like the dark much though. What kid does? But as long as we left her bedroom door open a little, she was happy."

"She liked the door open?" Gary asked.

233

"Yeah, not wide open, just a crack, just enough to reassure her."

The skin shrank over Gary's arms as he recalled Charley's bedroom door standing open a crack after he was sure he'd closed it.

He listened as Steve lovingly told him sweet stories of his lost daughter, and it reminded him of so many things about Charley. Things he'd forgotten.

Nola put Gary on the spot by asking him if he would attend the funeral the following week. A funeral was the last thing he wanted to go to, but the plea in Nola's eyes made him unable to decline.

As they were about to leave, Nola turned to him. "Are you a good man, Mr. Wright?" she asked, her voice soft and musical with her southern Irish accent.

The question took Gary by surprise, and for a second, he wasn't sure how to reply. Good, bad, could anyone be truly defined in terms of black or white?

"I do my best," was all he could offer.

Nola nodded, then she surprised him by gently cupping his face with her palm. Her hand was so icy cold against his cheek that he had to resist the urge to draw away.

"So much pain," Nola whispered. "I hope you get your daughter back one day, Mr. Wright. Have faith. God can do wonderful things."

Steve offered their telephone number to write down. Gary reached for the pen Charley bought for him, but it wasn't in his pocket where he usually kept it. Nola produced a ballpoint and wrote down the number on an old receipt.

Gary watched the tortured couple walk down the drive while the photographers clamoured for the best shot. He touched the place where Nola had placed her hand and thought about Fiona's cool fingers on his lips on the night he met her.

Closing the door, he silently wished them luck.

234

Gary turned the house upside down looking for his pen. Sofa cushions lay askew, drawers hung open, cupboards ransacked. He usually kept the pen on him, but sometimes he left it on his desk or in its original box in the drawer. He'd searched the house twice, but he couldn't find it.

Angry and frustrated, he fell into the leather captain's chair behind his desk and took out the bottle of Scotch. He felt weepy as he poured one. *Crying over a stupid pen*, he thought. How pathetic was he now? It was little wonder Fiona had left him.

But it wasn't just a pen and he knew it. It was the special gift that Charley had bought for him with her birthday money. Sometimes, he just liked to hold it, turning it in his fingers so the light flashed off the gold plate. And for a little while, he'd lose himself in the warm memory of the night Charley gave it to him.

It had been special. And now he had lost it.

Misplaced it, he corrected. It had to be somewhere in the house, he just didn't know where.

He drank and brooded on the pen and Steve and Nola's visit. Nola's eyes haunted him, and he still fancied he felt iciness in his cheek where she touched it.

He dropped into bed a few hours later, falling into a troubled and fretful sleep.

When the phone rang Gary didn't know if he was awake or still dreaming. He reached out a fumbling hand and picked up the receiver.

"Hello?"

No one replied.

"Hello?"

Someone sobbed on the phone, soft and distant.

"Hello?"

More weeping sounds, small and hollow.

"Who is this?"

A girl's voice, young, gently weeping.

"Who is this?"

The phone went dead.

Gary continued to hold the receiver to his ear, listening to the monotonous tone and thinking. He broke the connection and dialled call-return. The recorded voice gave him a number that sounded like a mobile.

Gary's finger hovered over the redial button, his heart beating fast, then he pressed it. The phone went through the beeps of the number and the line connected. He listened to it ring three times and was about to put it down when a sleepy, male voice answered on the fourth.

"Hello, Marsden."

Gary didn't know what to say.

"Hello?" the voice asked. Then more quietly, "Dad?"

Gary jumped in. "Hello...no...no...I'm sorry to bother you at this late hour, but-"

"What time is it?" A rustling sound. "It's twenty to four. Who is this?"

"I'm sorry...my phone rang just now and when I redialled it came back with your number."

"My number?"

"Yes, someone called me from your number."

"That's not possible," the voice said. "There's only me here."

"Well-" Gary began.

"*Who are you?*" the voice asked, in a way that made Gary feel like he was guilty of something.

"It doesn't matter," Gary said. "I'm sorry. It's a mistake."

The line went quiet for a moment. Gary could hear him breathing. "Don't call here again."

The connection broke and Gary was left with that long tone again. He fitted the receiver into its cradle and wriggled back down under the covers.

The room was cold.

It was always cold now.

Chapter Twenty-Five

Gary sat slumped on the sofa, his black suit soaked through with rainwater, his white shirt transparent and pasted to his skin. A smudge of dirt on his lapel had melted into a long muddy brown streak down the front of his jacket.

He had known attending Emma's funeral was a mistake. The day before, he had found himself with the phone in his hand, ready to call with some excuse for why he couldn't make it. He considered just not showing up at all, but he didn't know how to face Steve and Nola if he ever saw him again.

Against his better judgement, he set aside all his reservations, his gut feelings, and went to the funeral.

The media presence was immense. The police had created a cordon to keep back the press and onlookers. Representatives from all the major TV stations were there, reporters looking into cameras and speaking authoritatively into microphones. A battlement of cameras all pointed toward the church, their eyes all poised to capture every nuance of emotion.

Once through the cordon, he found a place near the sandstone wall of the church building and waited alone. The congregation was sizable, standing in groups, talking quietly, consoling each other and sharing their grief. Their black garb reminded Gary of the crows that took to the air when Emma screamed, when Emma *shrieked*.

He closed his eyes and touched his brow, his hand trembling.

When he looked up again, people were casting curious glances his way, some furtive, others pinning him with uncomfortably long stares.

Leave now while you have the chance.

One man broke away from a group and wandered over. His hair was black and curly. On his neck, he wore a tattoo that may once have been a small bird, but was now little more than a blue blur. More crude homemade tattoos adorned his hands and knuckles.

"I'm Aedan," he said, his accent thick and Irish. He offered his hand, his shake firm and cold. "I'm Emma's uncle on Nola's side."

"I'm Gary."

The guy who tried and failed to pump the life back into Nola's dead daughter.

Aedan nodded and turned to watch the other mourners for a time. Gary wondered if Aedan knew who he was, or if he just saw him as a lonely stranger in the crowd. He soon discovered which it was.

"I just wanted to thank you for what you did for little Emma." His eyes flicked briefly to Gary and then back to the crowd.

Gary felt exposed somehow, vulnerable. "I didn't do much," he said. "I couldn't save her."

Aedan moved quickly in front of him, almost as if he was squaring up for a fight. "No, no," he said. "You *tried*." His eyes were dark and unnerving. He looked away and wiped a tattooed hand across his lips. He leaned in, his mouth so close to Gary's ear that he could feel the warm breath of his words. "And at least she wasn't in the hands of that filthy fucking paedo bastard when she died."

Aedan eased back enough to look into Gary's eyes. They

239

were just inches apart. Gary held the gaze.

Technically, it wasn't the truth, but then he thought about the 'other' Emma, the one who had stood over him and sadly shook her head when she knew that his attempts to revive her had failed. At least, he supposed, that part of her wasn't alone with her killer in the end.

Aedan glanced about him, as if checking whether anyone was watching them. He leaned in again. "If only I could get my hands on that cunt...you know?" He spoke through gritted teeth and Gary heard the crack of the knuckles in his tightened fists.

He stepped back, upset and agitated. With hard tears in his eyes, he took Gary's hand again and squeezed it firmly. His mouth writhed as he struggled with his raging emotions. Finally, he nodded, as if they shared a common bond. The powerful grip released, and Aedan walked away.

Gary relaxed and blew out a shaky, thin stream of air between his lips. This was almost more intense than he could stand.

The crowd stirred, all heads turning to the funeral procession driving slowly along the road. Mourners stood aside as the hearse pulled onto the church forecourt and stopped. The little coffin was barely visible beneath the mountain of flowers on and around it. Set prominently on the lid, lay a floral tribute spelling out EMMA in carnations and chrysanthemums.

The sight of the coffin sent many of the mourners into fits of grief, handkerchiefs pressed to eyes and mouths.

Distantly, the photographer's cameras clicked.

Steve, Nola, and their parents climbed out of the cars. The footmen removed the flowers and after a brief discussion, Steve, both grandfathers, and Aedan conveyed the small casket into the church and set it before the altar.

Gary allowed the rest of the congregation to enter behind the pallbearers, before quietly slipping into a pew at the rear of the church.

240

The priest spoke of love and anger for a life cruelly taken away, but Gary barely heard the words. Grief consumed him. Grief for the daughter he could not, and probably never would, lay to rest. There was no closure for him. No place to lay flowers. He was forced along a never-ending river of pain that flowed into a black void of despair.

It was all too much.

He made to slide along the pew, intending to escape the smothering atmosphere, when he saw her standing atop the altar's marble stairs.

He blinked, trying to tell himself that it was just a little girl who had escaped her mother's hand, the mother too embarrassed to try and get her back while the priest spoke.

But she was dressed in the same blue coat and white socks as she was on the day he tried to bring her back from that other place.

It was Emma.

He let go of the breath he'd been holding and glanced around. The congregation quietly mourned, as though they couldn't see her.

No one can see her.

No one but you.

Emma's dark eyes pierced him from all the way across the church's cavernous interior.

What does she want?

The priest stood down and Steve got up, walking right by his daughter without even knowing she was there. He unfolded a piece of paper and cleared his throat, his breath buffeting the microphone and echoing around the church.

Gary tried to focus on him, on his words, but his eyes kept shifting back to Emma and her intense stare.

She's blaming me, he thought. *She's blaming me for letting her life slip through my fingers.* The accusation blazed in her eyes.

Gary tensed as Emma took a few steps toward her father.

241

She looked up at him and raised her hand, almost—but not quite—touching his. Steve hesitated, his expression full of confusion and distress. He glanced down, his fingers stroking the empty air. For a moment, Gary thought he could see her too. Their fingers almost touched, but then she moved away and the moment passed. Steve cleared his throat, found his place, and continued with his eulogy.

Emma skipped down the altar steps into the aisle, walking slowly by her casket. She trailed her fingers lazily along the polished veneer side wall, her eyes shifting back to Gary. Her small hand dropped away from the coffin, her eyes focused on Gary as she stalked toward him.

Gary wedged his foot against the kneeler rail, forcing himself up against the wooden back of the pew. With rising panic, he glanced around, unable to believe that among all these people, he was the only one who could see her.

Is she really there?

When he looked back at her, she had somehow cleared the distance in a moment and was stood right beside him. Gary stiffened with fright, turning his face away and bowing his head; too ashamed to look into the child's eyes, too afraid of what he might see there.

A small, waxy hand reached into his field of vision. Gary squeezed his eyes tightly shut and asked God for forgiveness, asked Emma for forgiveness.

"Please," he whispered. "*Please.*"

"Are you all right?" someone asked.

Gary opened his eyes. The lady sitting in front peered over her shoulder, raising an eyebrow at his odd behaviour.

The hand had vanished, and so had Emma.

"Yes," he whispered. "Thank you."

The woman returned her attention to Steve. Gary let out a long shaky breath and hung his head. Something on the old polished oak beside him caught his attention and he eased away

242

from it.

Roughly scratched into the dark varnish, was a zigzag line.

The rain drizzled miserably, and the wind had grown icy teeth as they carried the coffin back to the hearse for its final journey to the graveyard. Gary stood at one side, his collar turned up and his hands tucked into his pockets.

He'd decided he wasn't going to the cemetery when Aedan approached him.

"You're coming to the cemetery, yeah?" he asked, in a way that didn't feel like a question.

Gary gave him a nod and trudged back to his car. Grateful to be out of the wind, he started up the engine and turned on the heater.

The hearse pulled onto the road, the three limousines following suit. Gary waited while all the family and friends joined the funeral procession, before he tagged onto the end for the short drive to the graveyard.

At the cemetery, he pulled in behind the cars already parked along the narrow paths. People disembarked—pausing to put up umbrellas—before making their way to the graveside. Gary had to make do with turning up the collar of his already damp jacket. The wind took advantage of the openness of the cemetery, gusting sheets of rain at him and compounding the misery.

The undertakers conveyed the coffin to the grave and laid it beside its final resting place.

As the priest recited the final rites of the committal service, Gary noticed one of the grandparents staring at him from the other side of the grave with a scornful, almost hateful, expression.

Gary diverted his gaze across the cemetery. A crow swooped

243

low over the graves and landed on a mossy headstone. It shook its ebony head, ruffling its feathers, its sleek black body shining with rain. Then it took flight again, crossing the grey sky toward the taller trees. As he followed its path, he saw a lonely figure in a blue coat and white socks, just standing there beneath the trees, watching the funeral party.

The priest offered a small, wooden casket filled with grave earth to Steve and Nola - ashes to ashes, dust to dust. Nola grasped a hand full of dirt but didn't throw it into the grave. Instead, she stood there, helplessly weeping with her hand hanging by her side.

The priest moved around the mourners, offering dirt to anyone who wished to partake in the ritual. Gary managed to tear his gaze away from Emma long enough to draw a little earth into his palm, but as he approached the grave to throw it in, the grandfather pointed an accusing finger at him.

"Why's he here?" he shouted. "Keep him away from her."

Steve looked miserably at Gary and put his hand on the old man's shoulder. "Dad, don't."

But the old man was agitated. "He knows more about what happened than he's telling! He was *there*...how could he not know who it was?"

Dozens of eyes turned on Gary, some full of apology, others etched with suspicion.

In the distance, Emma turned and began to walk away.

Gary's gaze flicked to watch her, and the old man mistook it for something else. "He knows more!" he insisted. "Look at him...look at his face! He knows more than he's telling about all this."

"Dad, please stop."

All those accusing eyes.

Gary opened his fist and let the dirt fall from his hand.

Nola strode up to him and grabbed at his shoulders, her hands sliding down and catching his lapels. The earth in her palm smeared into the soaked wool of his suit. Her face turned up into the rain, her expression a mask of agony. "Please," was all she could say. "*Please.*"

Her agonised features streamed with rain and tears; Gary saw Emma's strangled visage in her mother's expression.

Friends and family tried to take her away. For some reason, none of them looked at him. Nola clung on, unable to let go, as if he was the final link with her daughter.

And perhaps he was.

Gary was dragged by the jacket, heaved and jostled as they tried to pull her off him. Finally, they prised her fingers open and she was led away, weeping hysterically.

Steve limply stared into the grave at his daughter's coffin.

Gary fled the scene. It was more than he could stand.

He let himself into the house and collapsed onto the sofa, his arms and legs askew, like a Guy Fawkes dummy hurled atop the bonfire. A numbness spread through his body that seemed to paralyse him. He stared at the bloom of window light reflected in the dark television screen. It seemed to pulse in time with the throb of his heart.

The coffin had been so small. He didn't remember her being that tiny when he was knelt over her body, trying to force life back into her.

His hand, the one he had wiped her face with, was palm up on the cushion, curled like a dead spider. He tried to move it but couldn't, even his fingers refusing to bend to his command.

Tears streamed down his face. He wanted it all to end. He had the pills and the alcohol. He could just let them lead him down that long, painless tunnel into what he hoped would be permanent darkness.

The dream came back to him. That cold circle of steel

pressed beneath his chin, that desolate feeling of loneliness as he squeezed the trigger.

We all die alone, he thought morosely. *Even in a room full of people, when the time comes, we all die alone.*

A breathy sigh came from nowhere and everywhere.

Gary shifted. "Huh?"

A white moth fluttered against the TV screen. More bumped at the window.

Another sound, barely a whisper, but he heard the word this time.

Daddy.

The atmosphere slowed, the room falling quiet and still, like a sleepy village after a heavy snowfall. All he could hear was the slip of his breath and the pace of his heart.

Something moved through the bloom of light on the TV screen, as if someone had walked by the window. He deciphered his own blurred reflection in the dark glass, and there beside him, sat the wispy thin shape of a child.

Daddy.

He cried out, shocked from his stupor, and instinctively pushed himself away from the place where she was sitting

She wasn't there. He looked around him, behind him.

He was alone.

When he looked back to the TV screen, she wasn't beside him anymore, her pale shape was standing way back, almost lost in the bloom. He looked behind him, but she wasn't there, only existing as a blurry reflection in the screen.

"What do you want from me, Emma?" he asked.

The fuzzy image appeared to stare at him.

Daddy

The whisper touched his ear, like a gentle breath.

"You want your daddy?" he asked.

Daddy

Help

Please help

The outside light seemed to change, like a shadow had passed over the house, and then he couldn't see her in the glass any more. The moths were gone. He shivered, yet felt strangely serene.

He hooked a finger over the knot in his tie and dragged it loose.

She was haunting him.

But why?

She wanted her daddy. Okay, he could understand that. But why was he involved in this? Just because he was there when she died? If she wanted her father why the fuck couldn't she just go to him?

He thought about calling Trixie, but after last time he doubted if she would help him, wasn't even sure if she could.

You're on your own with this.

But he didn't want to be involved at all. What did she want him to do? Go tell her heartbroken parents that their dead daughter was haunting him?

No way. If she needed her father, she'd have to find another way.

He was done with it.

Emma lay dead before him, her throat bruised and her eyes full of blood. Dead and dying moths lay around her head, and writhed, tangled in her golden locks. Not far away, a crow watched him with its beady eye, its claw curled around a branch like an old man's fist.

He found that spot on her breast bone where he could flex her ribcage and pump her heart.

He leaned on the heel of his palm.

Oneandtwoandthreeandfour...

After the compressions, he turned his face to listen for signs of life.

There were none.

He pushed back on her forehead, raising her chin to open her airway, but as he leaned down to cover her mouth with his, her eyes snapped wide. She grabbed his collar and dragged his face down to hers, her grip far stronger than any little girl could possibly be. The inside of her mouth was black, and her breath stank of death.

"It's in the shape of a zigzag!" she screamed.

Gary woke gasping and grasping at his throat where she'd held him. The room was frigid, his breath rolling out in wispy vapour clouds. The air felt cold enough to crack.

The sound of a child sobbing filtered through the night.

Whispering, like icy slivers, floated through the darkness.

Something fluttered against his face, and he screamed, sure it was one of the moths that had been tangled in Emma's hair.

But that had only been a dream.

He wondered if he was still dreaming, but this felt solidly real. He dragged the quilt close to his face, controlling his breathing so he could listen.

Small sobs broke through the whispering.

Emma?

He'd left the curtains open, the streetlight casting slanted shadows across the walls and ceiling. Moths touched and bumped against the net curtains.

The room looked like a charcoal drawing, all black lines and deep pits of darkness. The door was open, just an inch, just a crack. He scanned the wardrobe, the dressing table, back to the window...

Oh my God! There was something in the window!

His fists clenched around the quilt, his knuckles white, his eyes pinned wide in the darkness.

She was twisted in the net curtain, around and around like

248

an insect entombed in a spider's web. He could just make out her shape, her small hands folded across her chest.

A passing car illuminated her pale, doll face, her coldly glinting eyes staring at him through the layers of net. The curtain was wrapped tightly around her waxen features like a death-shroud. Her mouth stretched wide against it in a silent scream.

I'm cold, she whispered. *So cold.*

Gary broke free of the paralysing terror and clawed across the bed, tumbling off the mattress and onto the floor.

Help me! she shrieked after him. *Help me, Daddy! Help me! Help me!*

He scrambled away from that thing, that wraith.

Daddy! Help me! HELP ME!

He crawled to the open door, throwing it open so savagely that it bounced back. He wriggled onto the landing, rolling onto his side and kicking himself away with his bare heels, only stopping when his shoulder pressed up against the banister and he could go no further.

He turned, fearfully, to see if she was still on the windowsill, but she wasn't, she was rushing toward him like some tiny demon, the white veil rippling across her face and billowing out behind her.

She hunched over him, her arms rigid at her sides, her hands curled into claws. Beneath the net, her tiny face screamed grotesquely.

HELP ME! HELP ME! HELP ME!

Gary threw the crook of his arm across his face and squeezed his eyes tightly shut. The shrieking went on and on, piercing his eardrums and slicing through his brain, until it abruptly stopped. The house fell eerily still and quiet.

He lay there on the carpet, panting and whispering, "Oh God. Oh God."

He risked a peek over his elbow. She was no longer lurched

over him. The bedroom door stood wide, the room beyond dark and empty. The net curtain hung straight and undisturbed.

He slumped flat on the floor, panting with relief, oblivious to the wooden spindles digging into his head and shoulders.

"Oh Jesus Christ," he whispered, wiping tears of fright from his eyes.

At the end of the landing, Charley's door stood ajar.

Chapter Twenty-Six

Steve answered the door, the surprise at seeing Gary standing there fully evident on his face. "Gary," he said.

"Hello, Steve."

"It's a bit early," Steve said.

"I know, I'm sorry," Gary replied. "But I need to talk to you."

Steve glanced up and down the empty road, then back at Gary, his eyes dwelling on his dishevelled appearance and the dark circles beneath his eyes.

"You'd better come in then," he said and stood aside. "Nola and the boys are still asleep. We'll head through to the kitchen."

He guided Gary down a narrow hall lined with family photos. One of them was the one Nola had given him to look at when they came to see him.

The kitchen was small and cluttered with knickknacks. Once the door was closed, Steve seemed to relax some. The room was cold. Dirty pots soaked in the sink. A tea towel lay in a pile on the tiles in front of the cooker. Steve picked it up.

"She sleeps a lot," he said, wrapping the towel around his hands, "but I think it's helping her. I read once that the best way to recover from physical injury is to sleep. The body can concentrate on getting better. I'm hoping it can help her mentally as well."

"I think I've heard that too," Gary agreed. "They sometimes induce comas in badly injured people."

Steve nodded and put the towel to one side. "I'm sorry about what happened at the funeral," he said. "I don't know what got into Dad. I've never seen him act like that before. And then with Nola..."

Gary dismissed it with a shake of his head. "It's okay, I understand."

"Well, still, I'm sorry it happened. Can I get you something to drink?"

"No," Gary replied. "I need to talk to you about...well…something."

Steve gestured for Gary to take a seat at the small circular dining table. Two pink pig-shaped condiments sat in the middle, the nostril holes in their snouts to let out the salt and pepper stored in their bellies. On the wall, another pig looked out of its pen, the text beside it read: 'Bless this Mess'.

"What is it?" Steve asked. "Is it Emma? Have you remembered something?"

"No, nothing like that, but it is about Emma."

A wariness came into Steve's eyes that made Gary uncomfortable and unsure how to proceed. Perhaps trying to talk to Steve about this wasn't such a good idea.

"You look troubled, Gary," Steve said. "You look...*blown*."

"I haven't been sleeping well," Gary admitted.

"Yeah," Steve said, like he knew. "What's going on?"

"Well, it's difficult...I don't really know how to say this without sounding crazy."

"Spit it out. Whatever it is, just tell me."

"It's Emma. I don't think her..."

Don't say soul. Don't say spirit.

"...I don't think she's at rest." Even with the words adjusted, it still came out sounding foolish.

"Not at rest? What are you talking about?"

252

Gary took a deep breath. "I know this is going to sound crazy, Steve, but Emma, she's…" There was no other way to say it. "…well, she's haunting me."

Steve narrowed his eyes. "Haunting you as in the memory of what happened?"

Gary shook his head. "No, I mean *really* haunting me."

Steve was silent.

"I know how it sounds, but I've seen her."

"You've *seen* her?"

"In my house."

Steve leaned back and folded his arms, carefully studying Gary's face. "You're telling me Emma's *ghost* is haunting you?"

Gary winced inside. There it was, the elephant in the room: *ghost*. It sounded childish and silly, and conjured the episodes of Scooby Doo he'd watched as a child. But how else could it be said? Emma was dead, and he had seen her walking around. She was a spirit, a ghost, no matter how ridiculous it felt for him to say it out loud.

Reluctantly, he nodded.

"When have you seen her?"

"At first it was only a presence. I always keep the door to Charley's room closed, but it started opening of its own accord. You said Emma liked the door open a crack? Our cat felt it too…it spooked him. He doesn't stay around the house anymore. But last night…last night I saw her in my house, in my bedroom."

"You were dreaming," Steve insisted.

Gary shook his head, worried at Steve's tone, and that things could turn bad at any moment. "I wasn't dreaming, Steve. I've seen her, and more than once."

Steve studied him carefully. "What does she look like? Does she speak to you?"

Gary wasn't sure how much he should tell. Describing her standing in the window, wrapped in the net curtain and shrieking for her father wasn't likely to help. "She looks much like she did on that day I saw her. She cries..." He paused. "She asks for you, she asks for her daddy."

Steve clenched both his jaw, and the fists laying on the table top.

"I'm sorry, Steve. I know this is difficult, especially with everything you've already been through, but I didn't know what else to do."

"What are you on?" Steve asked, barely suppressing anger. "Are you taking something?"

"Steve, I swear..."

"You come here, looking like shit, reeking of whisky, and telling me my daughter is *haunting* you? What are you trying to do? I don't know what you are trying to do here."

"I'm not trying to do anything..."

Steve leaned threateningly over the table, the veins thick in his throat. "*Then what are you doing here*?"

Gary sat back, distancing himself from the accusing stare. "I don't know," he admitted. "I just can't stand it, Steve. Whatever's happening, I can't deal with it. I can't bear to live it over and over. First Charley and now Emma, I just can't take it. I just need someone to help me."

The stoniness in Steve's features softened a little. He eased himself back and sat looking at Gary for a while, turning it all over in his mind.

"Nola says she's seen ghosts in the old country when she was a kiddie. But she's Irish, and the Irish have a lot of belief in that kind of thing. She says ghosts are the spirits of people who have unfinished business here, and can't cross over."

Gary remained quiet, giving Steve space to reason it out with himself.

"So, let's say, for just one second, that I believe what you're telling me, that Emma's spirit's not at rest, and she has 'unfinished business'. Why would she come to you, a stranger,

254

and not to her own father?"

"I don't know," Gary admitted. "All I can think is maybe it's because I was near to her when she died. Or that I tried to save her? Or maybe it's because of what happened to Charley. Maybe it's because of that."

Steve considered for a moment, then he shook his head. "No," he said, with a sweep of his hand. "This is bullshit. It's bullshit and I think you should leave."

He stood up.

Gary remained seated. "She was at the funeral."

Steve froze.

"When you were speaking, she was standing right next to you."

Steve took a step back and Gary knew he'd hit on something.

"You felt her presence, didn't you? I saw you pause and look down. You seemed uncertain. For a moment I thought you could see her too."

Steve's eyes grew distant. "I did feel something...like, I don't know, like for a moment she was right there, holding my hand like she used to."

Gary leaned forward. "She *was* right there, Steve. She was standing right next to you, looking up at you."

Steve covered his mouth while a shuddering rush of emotion swept through him. From behind his hand and through the tears, came a husky whisper, "*She was there?*"

Gary nodded, the emotion reaching him too. "She was there, Steve. She was almost touching your hand."

Steve moved the hand from his mouth and looked at it, upset and bewildered. After he'd given it some thought, he said, "You think maybe, she has...unfinished business?"

"Maybe," Gary replied.

"Maybe she just wants...to say goodbye?" He looked at Gary.

"I guess it could be that simple," Gary said, although her screaming 'help me help me' didn't seem to quite fit that scenario.

"What can we do? How can we help her?"

"Come to my house," Gary suggested. "Maybe that would be enough. Maybe you could make contact with her and then all this would stop."

"This is crazy," Steve said, still resisting. "I don't believe in this kind of thing."

"I don't believe in it either. I never have...until now. Now, I have to believe it, because I'm living with it."

Steve went over to the window and looked out of it for a while.

"Nola can't know about this," he decided. "It would kill her." He looked suspiciously toward the door as if she might be up and listening.

"She doesn't need to know," Gary agreed.

"Nola's sister's coming later. I'll make some excuse to go out and I'll come around then."

Gary stood up. "Thank you, Steve. I don't know if it will do any good, but at least we can try." He extended his hand. Steve gripped it, painfully tight, and Gary saw a threat flash in his eyes. A warning that if this was a sick joke, he was going to pay for it.

They arranged a time, and when Gary left, he felt empowered. He had set something in motion. If he could sort this thing out, then maybe he could get back to straightening his life out and having Fiona come home. He felt that he was taking steps to regain control.

But he wasn't.

Far from it.

Steve arrived at quarter past eight. The night had already fully spread its dark wings. He glanced around the hall, taking in the

256

three-legged table, the gashed door panel, and the broken pictures leaning against the wall.

"Did Emma do that?" Steve asked.

"No, I did," Gary replied.

Steve nodded as if that was normal, or maybe he just understood.

"Is Nola okay?"

"Maggie's with her. They're nagging. Maggie's been really supportive...a God-send. I told them I was going for a drive, so I haven't got too long."

"Okay," Gary said. "We'd better get on then."

Steve looked wary. "What do you want me to do?"

"Things seem to happen upstairs mostly, in and around Charley's bedroom. Maybe if you just go in there and speak to her?"

Steve peered nervously into the darkness at the top of the stairs, his eyes wide and restless.

Gary flicked on the light. "It's okay. It's only Emma. It's just your little girl." But as he said it, he remembered her swathed in net and screaming, 'Help me!'

Steve nodded and took a couple of deep breaths. "You're right. Okay, where is it?"

"Up the stairs at the end of the landing, the door with the little nameplate on it. I'm going to wait down here if that's okay with you?"

Steve's eyes shone with fear for a moment, and then he checked himself. "Yeah, yeah...like you say, it's only Emma."

"It'll be okay."

Steve nodded and started up the stairs, while Gary went through to the lounge.

He told himself he hadn't wanted to go up there with Steve because his presence might adversely affect things. She was asking for her father, so best it was only him. But that was a lie. He was simply afraid to go up there. Afraid of how Emma

257

might appear, assuming she did at all. His shredded nerves just couldn't take it.

The floorboards creaked above him. Gary glanced from the ceiling to the bottle of Scotch in the cabinet. He could use a stiff drink right about now, but he'd held off the whisky after Steve's comment about the alcohol on his breath this morning. He'd held off all day. If this thing with Emma got sorted, maybe he could hold off tomorrow too, and if he could hold off tomorrow maybe he could hold off for good. It was a wistful thought, as tangible as highland mist, but it offered him some comfort.

He stood at the patio window and gazed out across the darkened garden, remembering Charley's birthday party, the marquees and the guests; her face when they gave Mister Whiskers to her, and how she had kissed him and thanked him. Fiona's smug look and crooked grin from across the room.

God, he missed them both so much.

Everything had crumbled so quickly after that. Michelle's miscarriage, falling out with Ed, and then Charley's disappearance. Eventtually, everything came around to that dark summer's day.

Gary flinched as a powerfully loud crash rushed overhead, as if something heavy had been dragged violently across the floor. The whole house seemed to shudder.

A scream followed, so shrill that he wasn't sure if it was male or female. He heard the fast thunder of feet on the stairs, and a moment later the front door slammed.

Gary rushed into the hall, grabbed the bannister post and looked up the stairs. "Steve!"

No answer.

He continued to the front door. Steve was already halfway down the drive.

"Steve!"

But Steve wasn't stopping.

"Steve!" Gary shouted and gave chase. He was right on his

heels, but Steve wouldn't slow. Gary snagged his arm and Steve spun on him, shrugging off the hand and staring back with genuine terror in his eyes. He held his hand and arm in an unnatural, stiff fashion and when Gary glanced at it, he hid it behind his back.

"What happened?"

Steve's face was white in the darkness.

"Steve? Tell me what happened?"

Steve looked toward the street, as if longing to escape down there.

"Did you see Emma?" Gary pressed

Steve looked back at him. "No, I didn't see her, but I saw the others."

"Others?"

"The other children."

"What other children?"

"The murdered girls!" Steve blurted. "They're in your house, Gary! They're in your daughter's bedroom."

Gary took a step back, his skin shrinking.

"You need to get out of there. You need to get out now."

Steve turned and began to stride away.

Gary stood there for a second, his breath gone. Not just Emma, but all of them? He ran after him, taking him by the shoulder and turning him around again.

"Don't touch me!" Steve shouted.

Gary held up his hands. "Just tell me what happened. At least tell me that."

Steve hesitated. His eyes crawled all over the house and then he glanced behind him as if to ensure the exit was still clear.

"I went up to the room like you said. I didn't know what to do, what to expect. It felt stupid, but I just called out her name, told her I was here. Then there was *something*, I don't know what it was, just something in the air, but it didn't feel like Emma. The room went really cold. I could see my breath. There

259

were sounds all around me, giggles, whispers, sobbing. I asked if it was Emma and then I heard another sound, like a squeak."

"The chalkboard," Gary whispered.

Steve looked at him. "Yes, it was."

"A zigzag."

"How do you know?"

"Because I've seen it too."

"It was just appearing on the board in red chalk. I went over and reached out to touch it. There was a sudden blast, like an explosion, and a sound that I can't even describe. Then something bit me." He raised his arm and showed Gary a deep and savage bite in the meat between his forefinger and thumb. It looked like a human bite, the teeth penetrating the skin, each leaf-shaped puncture-hole a deep well of dark red.

"Oh my God," Gary said.

Steve's gaze fell fearfully on the house again. "They were all around me, just standing there and staring at me...and their faces; oh my God, their faces!"

"Who was standing there?"

"The dead girls. They're in your house. They wanted me out of there. You need to get out too." His face darkened. "Those girls...they're angry."

Trixie's words came clearly back to him.

Something...a presence...not bad exactly, but something dark, something angry.

Steve backed away, shaking his head. "This doesn't have anything to do with Emma. Don't ever call me again."

Gary watched him leave through the gate. A moment later a car started and sped away.

A biting wind blew in. Slowly, Gary became aware of the house behind him, and was consumed by the eerie feeling that it was watching him. He turned to face it. Light spilled from the hall and landing. A bulb still burned behind the half-closed curtains of Charley's bedroom. As he looked away, a flicker drew his attention back to it.

A shadow? A bat?

Bats tended to swoop around the house at night. He watched for another glimpse of their small darting bodies, but the night remained quiet and still.

Dead children were haunting the home he'd built for his family. It was difficult to accept, but he didn't doubt it. Any of it. Steve had seen the zigzag. And that bite mark was certainly no hallucination.

But why him? What did they want?

Why had Emma not shown herself to her father when she had the chance?

But he knew the answer. He had known it all along.

Despite her calling for her daddy, it wasn't really her father she wanted, it was him. For some reason, it was him.

He walked back to the house, closed the front door and looked around. The house didn't seem any different for the revelation that a bunch of dead girls had taken up residence. Perhaps he should go up there and try to make contact with them, see if he could find out what it was they wanted.

He gripped the bannister rail and peered up the stairs. Even lifted a foot onto the first riser before he lost his nerve.

He went to the lounge and poured that whisky he'd been denying himself. He knocked it back and poured another, casting furtive glances toward the door, as if he might see one of them standing there all... all what? Dead? Strangled? Stabbed?

Emma had just looked like a little girl when he saw her. Well, at first she had. But last night she had been desperate, terrified.

Those girls...they are angry.

Angry at him? Angry that their young lives had been cruelly taken away? Even if that was true, what did it have to do with him? There was only one life he might have saved, and he'd blown it. If Emma was angry at him then that was fair enough.

261

But the rest?

Another thought hit him. If they were all victims of the Goldilocks Killer, and if Fiona was right, did that mean Charley was with them?

But…what if she *wasn't* with them…?

He knocked back the second whisky and took a couple of deep breaths before returning to the foot of the stairs.

"Charley?" he called.

Silence.

He climbed the steps, certain risers creaking as they always had, his hand sliding over the bannister's polished surface. At the top, he hesitated. The door to Charley's room was open and the light was on, probably left that way when Steve fled.

Except it's only open a little bit.

Just a crack.

The way Emma likes it.

Gary walked the length of the landing. The nameplate was still slanted. He pushed the door, letting it swing wide. The room was quiet. He stepped over the threshold. A red zigzag was emblazoned on the chalkboard, right where Steve said it was.

"Charley?" he whispered. "Are you here, Sweet Pea?"

He scanned the room, every wall, every corner, every shadow.

"Charley? It's Dad. Are you here?"

The temperature plummeted so rapidly that his skin stiffened with goosebumps. Something shifted. He spun around but was unable to see what had made the sound.

A sob came from behind him and he whirled the other way.

I'm cold, so cold.

"Emma, is that you?"

Soft whispering floated around the room, too low to discern the words.

Gary turned slowly on the spot, trying to keep up with the

whispering as it drifted around him. His heart raced. His breath left his lips in short, steamy clouds.

Tendrils of frost crept from the corners of the dressing table mirror, spreading like jagged, white lightning. The light dulled. The atmosphere became so oppressive that he almost felt crushed by it.

This wasn't Charley, and it wasn't Emma either.

This presence was much darker.

Those girls...they're angry.

"Why are you here?" Gary asked.

The whispering stopped.

"What do you want from me?"

He heard the unmistakable click and scrape of chalk on the board. Yet there was no chalk, no ghostly hand, just a red zigzag line appearing on the black surface. Before the zigzag was finished, a second started, then a third, then yet another and another, until zigzags were being drawn all over the board at once. They over-lapped, growing bigger, faster and more violent until the chalk lines had merged into a solid mass of red.

The board suddenly spun off the easel and flew directly at Gary. He threw up his arms and the board smashed into him. He staggered as floorboards seemed to bow and bulge beneath his feet. Charley's dressing table shifted away from the wall. The pile of games tumbled. The bed jumped and rattled.

Something zipped past Gary's head, bounced off the icy mirror and landed on the dressing table. A magazine spun around in the air, as if flung by an unseen hand. A CD case flew by and smashed against the wall. The head of Charley's bed rose and crashed down again.

Gary bolted for the door, but it slammed shut. He grabbed the handle and pulled but it wouldn't budge.

All around him, the room erupted into chaos.

He pressed himself up against the door as the light flickered and game boxes flipped into the air, the colourful contents spilling. The dressing table cleared of all Charley's belongings. Drawers flew open and slammed shut again. Something heavy hit the frosted mirror, cracking the glass.

The room was in a rage, as if something was venting its anger and frustration.

"*STOP IT!*" Gary shouted, but the chaos just seemed to grow more frenzied. "*WHAT DO YOU WANT FROM ME?*" he screamed, into the swirling debris.

Instantly, it all stopped, and everything fell to the floor.

The overhead light swung lazily, shadows stretching and warping.

A red line slowly drew downward on the mirror, through the crack. The line stopped and drew upward, then down, up, down.

The red zigzag.

"I don't know what it means," Gary said. "I don't know what you want from me."

Behind him, the door clicked and slowly swung wide.

"Why can't you just leave me alone?" he asked wearily.

He turned off the light and closed the door carefully, feeling the click of the latch and pushing on it to ensure it was closed, even though that didn't seem to matter anymore.

As he walked away, he heard a soft click. He turned to find the door had opened. He pulled it closed again, but as soon as he started to walk away, he heard the soft click of it opening.

He sighed, but was determined they weren't going to wear him down.

With gritted teeth, he grasped the handle firmly, but as he pulled the door closed, a young girl's deathly white face drifted into the dark space between the door and the jamb. He cried out and jumped back in fright as the door violently slammed shut. The plaque with Charley's name on it tumbled to the floor.

Gary waited for his racing heart to calm before picking up the plaque and pressing it back onto its stickers. It took a few more attempts this time, but eventually it held.

As he walked away, he heard the soft click of the door opening again.

He didn't look back.

Chapter Twenty-Seven

Anyone in their right mind would have gotten the hell out of that house there and then. But Gary wasn't in his right mind, he was drunk, and he wasn't about to be chased out of his own house by a bunch of tantrum-throwing kids. They might have good reasons for being pissed, but fuck them! What did any of it have to do with him?

He took to the study instead, stubbornly sitting behind his antique desk in his captain's chair and drinking steadily, until the clock struck midnight. At some point, rain started tapping at the window like brittle fingernails, and thunder rumbled disagreeably somewhere distant.

The Mac's hi-res screen cast a soft glow on Gary's face. He had the browser open at the BBC News website, on Charley's story. He'd had to search for her because she'd been indexed and archived beneath the terabytes of news and bullshit that had been reported since she disappeared. He'd typed in her name and up popped her story, old news that everyone—except him—seemed to have forgotten about.

That wasn't a fair thought, but alcohol and fair-thinking don't usually go hand in hand.

At the top of the story was the photo of Charley that he'd taken out with him on the day she disappeared. Inserted into the text lower down were photos of him and Fiona at the media

266

conference, the police combing fields, and frogmen dredging the canal. Under all of that, was a graphic showing the route she had probably taken from the park, and a timeline of events that led to her disappearance.

Out of the whole sequence, there was only one that really mattered: 1.05pm: Mr. Wright leaves park to attend office emergency.

Fucking office emergency.

He pushed the Mac to one side and took out the bottle of antidepressant pills from the desk's top drawer. He set them on the green leather, next to the whisky, then picked up the phone and speed dialled Fiona's number.

"Hello?" Her voice was sleepy.

Gary didn't speak. Tears pricked his eyes.

"Hello?"

He listened to her voice, imagining her soft features, her fragrance, the laughter once bright in her eyes.

Tears brimmed and streamed down his face.

"Gary?"

He dropped the phone onto the cradle and broke into wracking sobs, rocking back and forth in his misery. He angrily opened the pills and threw the cap. As he reached for the Scotch, he saw Charley's framed photo and hesitated.

That incessant thought crept around the back of his mind: what if she was still alive? What if, by some miracle, she was still alive and managed to escape from where ever it was she was being held? What if she was found, or set free? She'd come home to find her family broken and her father gone. He'd told her when she was a little girl that he'd find her, no matter where she was. He had failed to do that, and then he'd fail her again by not even being here for her when she returned.

He hurled the pill bottle away from him, the tablets scattering and tick-tacking on the hardwood floor.

He grasped his face in his hands, sliding them up his cheeks and grabbing fistfuls of hair. There was no escape, no way out. He would probably be trapped this way until the day he died, like that old woman, waiting for a knock on the door that would never come.

Charley smiled up at him from the Mac's screen. The side bar contained links to the other missing girls, the girls who had taken residence in the room down the hall. He clicked the link to the story on the Goldilocks Killer. A line of photos followed the heading, images of all the girls thought to be his victims. Gary hadn't really looked at them before. Samantha Redman, Linda Wade, Hannah Reid, Angela Mears, and the last one, Vicky Lester. All fresh-faced young girls, smiling at the camera. Out of the five, only Angela had been found. She had been pretty; just a young girl with a whole life ahead of her.

He'd never really given any of them much thought. Never considered what might have happened to them, because he'd refused to believe that Charley was a part of it.

He reached out and first touched Angela's face through the screen, his finger sliding from one to the other. He saw all of them, each sweet, innocent face, and acknowledged that they were all probably dead and buried somewhere.

He covered his mouth and started crying for them and their families. As he sobbed, he realised he wasn't crying alone. He could hear them, their ghostly voices weeping from every corner of the house, slipping in and out, becoming louder and louder, until Gary was forced to cover his ears.

And then abruptly, it stopped.

He touched his fingers to his temple. His head ached.

"I'm sorry," he said. "I'm sorry for what happened to you all. But there's nothing I can do to change that."

Gary winced as a girl's high-pitched screech, like a shriek of feedback, cut through the house. Charley's picture fell flat, slid off the edge of the table, and fell onto the floor. He heard the glass smash.

He covered his eyes and sighed. Why couldn't they just leave him alone?

He rolled the chair back from the desk, intending to get up and retrieve the picture, but in his drunken state, the chair slipped out from under him, pitching him head-first onto the floor. He ended up face down in the leg space under the desk, his cheek pushed up into his eye, mouth puckered like a plunger.

"Fuck," he said, slurring even that single word.

As he lay there, too drunk to get up, his eyes followed the boards to something laying among the dust bunnies beneath the drawer section of the desk. Something long and slender. He raised his head a little. Green and gold. It was his pen!

He rescued the pen from its hiding place and rolled onto his back. His treasured pen! Right there under the desk all this time!

He wiped off the dust and pressed it to his lips, the kiss freezing as his focus shifted to something on the underside of the desk. A small, rectangular sticker with printing on it. The writing was too miniscule to read from his position, but it wasn't the writing he was staring at.

It was the red zigzag.

The sight of those vivid red lines hit him like a splash of cold water. He struggled out from under the desk, banging his head as he did so.

Clearing the leather top of all its clutter, he tipped the antique onto its back, the drawer contents tumbling and clattering. He heaved it over again so that it was lying flat on its green leather top with its legs in the air.

He examine the sticker more closely. It wasn't really a zigzag at all.

It was a name.

Marsden, initial 'W'. The 'W' and the 'M' of Marsden were joined together, the final up sweep of the W being the first up sweep of the M, making the first two letters look like a zigzag.

The first time he'd seen the zigzag, it was drawn on the chalkboard in Charley's room. Then scratched into the Church pew. They'd drawn one for Steve and then scrawled hundreds of zigzags on the chalkboard for him. Plus the one on the mirror.

All of them a facsimile of the one hidden under his desk for all this time.

Now he knew what it meant.

After he'd purchased the desk, he'd had it restored. He re-read the old yellowed sticker. This was the company he'd called to do the restoration work for him. He'd used a small, local firm he'd found in the business pages or online somewhere.

WMarsden & Son.
Carpentry and Furniture Restoration.

Marsden had come to the house to collect the desk himself. A tall man with a thin, pale face, aged perhaps sixty or so. His white hair was crewcut, the fringes tinged with the yellowy-brown stains of a chain-smoker. He was an earthy type, with a broad northern accent. and had been accompanied by a younger lad, who Gary had assumed was the 'son'. The lad was pale and gangly like his father, but quiet. Gary didn't remember him speaking at all. Marsden had ordered him about with a sharpness of the tongue that made it clear he didn't have much patience with him.

The two of them had carried the desk from the garage and loaded it into the back of a white van. A couple of weeks later,

Marsden called to tell him the desk was ready and looked beautiful, if he did say so himself. They'd brought it back at the weekend because it was the only day Gary could spare to supervise the delivery, and inspect the work, before paying for it.

Gary had been more than satisfied. Marsden had done a masterly job and the desk was indeed beautifully restored and finished.

For a few extra quid's worth of enticement, Marsden had agreed to carry the heavy desk up to the study,

Charley must have been eight or nine at the time and had been running in and out of the bedrooms and along the landing; laughing and giggling with some friends who were over. Gary had told them to calm down and stay in Charley's room until they'd finished moving the desk.

"Kid's," Gary had laughed in that good-humoured parental-tone.

Marsden had just smiled and nodded. "They're doing no harm."

The son never uttered a word and constantly avoided eye contact. Gary got the idea Marsden was the overbearing kind of father who could stifle a child, who *would* stifle a child. Maybe quick to criticise and slow to praise. Maybe the type who believed that to spare the rod was to spoil the child.

The boy had been no child though. Probably in his late teens or early twenties. He had moved with a slowness, but jumped to his father's instructions.

When the desk was in position, Marsden sent his son to bring up the drawers and fit them onto their sliders. Gary had paid the man and been given a handwritten invoice for the work. Marsden voiced his thanks, folding the money and slipping it into the breast pocket of his work shirt. When the lad had a bit of trouble fitting the drawers, Marsden had told him to get out of the way and did it himself.

271

Gary had never thought about them again. Until now.

The zigzags were clearly a reference to Marsden. There was no way it could be a coincidence. But what did it mean? Why had the girls shown this to him? What did they want him to know? That Marsden was their kidnapper? Could the man who restored this desk be the Goldilocks Killer? Could it all be that closely interlocked?

Then he remembered the night the phone had rung in the early hours and he'd heard that faint sobbing on the line. He'd called back through the redial service and when the other party had picked up, he'd answered, "Hello, Marsden?"

Gary shivered, and his stomach lurched.

Hello, Marsden.

WMarsden.

WM

Zigzag.

He'd spoken to the Goldilocks Killer that night and he hadn't even known it.

His stomach rolled again and he had to grab the wastepaper basket so he could puke up old whisky and bile. He wiped his mouth with the back of his hand, the vomit sour and burning his throat. The call of more alcohol was difficult to resist, but he needed a clear head. He needed to think.

He went to the bathroom, washed his face and swilled the sourness from his mouth. The reflection staring back at him from the mirror was shocking. Sallow complexion, dark rings under his eyes.

What have I done to myself?

He fell back against the wall and slid into a sitting position on the cold tile floor as the enormity of it all settled on him.

Did he actually have the name of the Goldilocks Killer?

The man who had kidnapped and killed at least one young girl and probably five more?

The man who had murdered Charley?

272

You don't know that!

That stubborn part of his mind still protested.

"You don't know that," he whispered in agreement.

But the corridor was narrowing, the possibilities diminishing.

This isn't about Charley, he insisted to himself. This was about something else, something that he didn't fully understand.

It all stemmed back to Emma and the day she was murdered. Emma *must* have been killed by the same man who had kidnapped the other girls, or it didn't make any sense.

Sense? There was sense to be made of this?

Nevertheless, it was likely that they were all murdered by the same man, and that Emma had somehow brought his other poor victims with her. They wanted justice for their murders. They wanted Marsden caught.

No, they don't, a small voice spoke up from the back of his mind. *They want more than that...they want* revenge.

Why did he think that? He had no basis for it...except...

Those girls...they're angry.

But that didn't mean they wanted him to...

He shook the rest away and considered what he could realistically do with this information. He could take it to the police, though explaining how he came by it might be difficult.

The ghosts of the dead girls in my house told me.

Would they take him seriously? Or would they think him crazy and waste more time investigating him?

The idea of finding where Marsden lived, and going there himself surfaced for a moment, floated briefly and turned over in the moonlight like the pale belly of a whale. It was a crazy idea. The kind of thing that happened in movies.

But you're considering it.

At the height of the investigation, Chloe had asked him for a list of people or companies who had worked for them in the last three years. Gary kept records in perpetuity, and so had found

273

the invoices for jobs he'd had done. There had been a new boiler, retiling of the bathroom, some landscaping, replacement of two blown double-glazing units, and obviously all the people he'd hired for Charley's birthday party.

Marsden's restoration work had not been among the companies he'd given to the police. That meant it must have been further back than three years since he'd hired them.

He returned to the study and opened the filing cabinet drawer where he stored all his old invoices. He kept them in green suspension folders, each folder neatly labelled with the year. He found the one from 2010 and searched through it. He spotted it almost immediately, the W and the M masquerading as a red zigzag. A printed invoice with handwritten details:

Restoration and finishing of one
William IV Mahogany desk - £500.

The handwriting was a childish, half-print, half-script and the address was scrawled along the bottom of the page.

Gary retrieved his Mac from the floor and set it atop the filing cabinet. He loaded up Google Maps and typed 'Riverside Gableton' into the search field. The site immediately honed into the area and displayed it as a coloured gradient map. Riverside was a flat piece of land sitting inside a loop of the River Ribble. He moved the pointer to the 'Satellite' button, changing the map to aerial photographs of green fields, trees and bushes. A thin, brown string of a road, not much more than a dirt path, wound through the greenery and led to a cluster of structures that resembled farm buildings. He hovered the pointer over the central building, hoping for a popup giving more information, but nothing appeared. He dragged the little man who gave you a street level view of the area and dropped him onto the dirt road, but no street level views were available. That probably meant it was a private road.

He sat back and viewed the overall area again. The buildings were on their own, with just that single road leading in and out.

Private. Isolated.

He moved the zoom slider toward the plus sign, enlarging, but blurring the image a little as it lost some resolution. Set at angles to the main building, were a couple of large outbuildings—barns maybe—or storage. There were also two small vehicles parked out front, along with a large, white Transit van.

Gary pressed the ball of his thumb against his teeth and gnawed at the skin. Then something caught his eye. He stopped gnawing and leaned forward. Between the farmhouse and the van was a blurry little smudge that was most certainly a person.

Was that him? Was it Marsden?

The blurry image chilled him.

He moved the slider toward the minus sign again, widening the view. His eyes skipped around the image, following the roads until he found his own house. He zoomed in some, centring the image so that the house fitted in the top left of the screen, the farmhouse in the bottom right.

He checked the scale line and estimated the Marsden farm was around seven kilometres away.

So close.

Maybe he could fabricate a story for the police. He could tell them how Marsden had looked at his eight-year-old daughter like a sex-starved mongrel, and how he must have waited a further four years before returning to kidnap her. It sounded unlikely. Would the police believe him enough to send a couple of officers out to question him? Hadn't the Yorkshire Ripper been questioned multiple times, yet remained free to murder more women?

He looked at the map, and the idea of going to the farmhouse himself surfaced again.

Seven kilometres.

He could be driving down that dirt path in twenty minutes.

Maybe less, at that time of night.

And what would you do when you got there?

Maybe snoop around and find evidence to tie Marsden to the missing girls. Compelling evidence that would convince the police that Marsden was the man they were looking for. For a second, he imagined himself at the house, creeping around outside, peering through windows and searching the out houses.

Maybe he could even get inside.

Stop it!

It was ridiculous.

And yet it wasn't.

The more he thought about it, the more he wanted to take control. He'd been out of control for such a long time.

He could knock at the door and if Marsden answered he could claim he had furniture he needed restoring and thought he'd drop by to discuss it. *Not a good time? No problem, I'll come back when it's more convenient.*

But when he envisioned the scenario and the exchange, it was far more chilling. What if Marsden knew who he was? Maybe he'd be attacked. The farmhouse appeared to be in the middle of nowhere, there'd be no one to see or hear.

The better choice, the safer choice, would be to hand this over to the police. No matter how it sounded, they would still have to investigate it.

His head was starting to hurt from overthinking.

He walked out onto the landing and looked at Charley's room. Were they in there now, watching him from that vertical slash of darkness between the door and the jamb? Were they listening to him?

He leaned against the wall.

"Okay. What do you want me to do?" he asked.

The room stood silent and still.

276

"I don't know what you want me to do. Tell me what you want me to do."

The door slowly opened wider, the hinges creaking.

"I'm sorry for what happened to you, but what can I do?"

The door slammed hard, making Gary jump. He stood in the middle of the landing, facing Charley's room.

"What do you want me to do with this?" he asked angrily. "You want me to call the police?"

The door wrenched open and slammed shut, opened and slammed, opened and slammed, as if by a kid having a tantrum. In fact, *exactly* like a kid having a tantrum.

Gary's heart thumped in his ears and his face grew hot.

"You want me to go then, is that it?"

The door clicked softly and opened, just a crack.

"You want me to go alone?"

The house was silent.

Gary closed his eyes.

Chapter Twenty-Eight

Though he went to bed at a little after three, Gary woke early, from what seemed like the best night's sleep he'd had in months. The sleep had been uninterrupted and dreamless, sliding through his mind like a silky black ribbon.

After showering, he went out on the patio, shaking a bag of cat food and calling for Mister Whiskers. The cat was nowhere in sight, so he washed out his dishes and filled them with fresh food and water, setting them out at the edge of the patio. He tried to eat a little breakfast, but his stomach was turning itself inside out at the thought of what he was going to do. A shot of Scotch would have gone down well, but alcohol was out of the question. He drank coffee instead.

He needed to keep his wits about him. Things could go bad today.

You don't know anything, he told himself. You don't know what might happen.

What if it was true though?

He would be walking into the lion's den. Putting himself in harm's way. There was no escaping that simple truth.

You're just going to scope it out. That's all. Maybe the evidence will be right there in plain sight. These girls want you to help them, would they really put you in danger?

Maybe.

After all, those girls…they are angry.

Children could be incredibly selfish. And these were dead children, angry at being snatched violently from life. Who knew how their minds worked?

They'd made it clear that they wanted him to go, and go alone, but he was still considering taking someone with him, and there was only one person he could trust.

Lance.

Friends come and go, but Lance had been there almost from the start. At every milestone. Through good and bad; thick and thin. Gary remembered how he'd called Lance on the day Charley went missing and how he had said 'I'm on my way' without even knowing what was wrong.

Gary could easily spin Lance a yarn if he wanted to. Hell, he could probably tell him the truth about the ghosts and the hauntings and Lance would still go with him.

Lance would put himself in harm's way.

And that was why he couldn't ask. He couldn't ask because Lance would go with him, no matter what.

And what if it went really bad?

Gary couldn't be responsible for putting his friend at risk. If anything happened to Lance, he'd never forgive himself.

Perhaps he should leave a note then, or send an email in case it all went wrong? There was every chance it could go wrong.

His attention was drawn to the knife block. He walked over and drew the chef's knife almost all the way out, resting the point in the slot. The steel blade gleamed.

He tried to imagine what it might feel like to stab a man in the chest with it, and found he couldn't.

The phone rang.

Gary removed the knife from the block and took it with him to the phone.

"Hello, Gary? It's Trixie." Her voice was quick and breathy.

"Glad you could join the party," Gary said.

"What?"

"Nothing...bad joke."

"What's happened?"

"Happened?

"You know what the zigzag means."

Gary closed his eyes and laughed. He didn't mean to, it just came naturally, unexpectedly. He thought about all the times he'd made fun of Trixie, both to her face and behind her back. He'd always been so positive, so one hundred percent sure she was full of shit. At dinner parties he used to cringe whenever she started on about spirits and auras.

All the time he had been wrong about her.

There are more things in heaven and earth, Horatio, than are dreamt of in your philosophy.

"I thought you didn't know anything about any zigzags," he said.

"I didn't," she said. "Well, I did, but it's complicated."

"Yes, it is," he agreed.

"I have to know what the zigzag means, Gary. I *need* to know. It's driving me insane."

"It's not a zigzag." He could feel her holding her breath for the answer. "It's a set of initials."

She gasped, the sort of sound you make when seized by the answer to the question that has eluded you for the longest time.

"Of course it is," she said. "A W and an M joined at the hip. A zigzag. I can't believe I didn't see it." Then came the obvious question. "Whose initials are they?"

Gary thought about sharing the details with her. She was, after all, probably the only other person in the world he *could* share them with, without them thinking he'd lost his mind.

This wasn't for her though. This was for him. The angry squatters in Charley's bedroom had made that clear. It was time to wrap this up and see it through.

"Trixie, I just want you to know I'm sorry for all the times I

280

made fun of you, all the times I tried to make you look small."

"All the times you were a dick, you mean?"

Gary smiled and tried to imagine that patronizing, yet alluring, look at the other end of the phone. "Yeah," he said. "For all the times I was a dick. I'm sorry."

"Never thought I'd hear you say that."

"Neither did I, but a lot has happened in a very short space of time."

Trixie seemed to understand he was getting ready to hang up on her. "Whose initials are they, Gary?" she asked again.

"I can't tell you."

"Why?"

"Because…" he began, but didn't really know how to reply.

"Is it the man who took Charley?"

Gary gripped the phone tightly, the earpiece pressed hard against his ear.

Is it the man who took Charley?

Is it?

The reality of what he was going to do slid across the surface of his mind like a razorblade. He'd thought that going to the farm might be dangerous, but realistically there was no 'might' about it. Marsden was a murderer. A serial killer. If he had the slightest hint of why Gary was there, he would be in serious trouble.

He raised the knife and looked along the blade.

"Trixie, there's something I have to do, and…it may not turn out well for me. If it does go bad, I want you to do something for me. Will you tell Fiona I'm sorry for everything? Tell her I love her. Despite everything, I've always loved her, and I always will."

Trixie's voice was small and scared. "My God…Gary? What are you going to do?"

"Whatever I have to," Gary said. "Goodbye, Trixie, and thanks."

281

"Gary..." he heard her say, but he pressed the disconnect button and set the phone down in its cradle.

A few seconds later, the phone began ringing again, and it was still ringing when he left for the Marsden Farm.

Chapter Twenty-Nine

There are key moments in everyone's lives when the decisions we make, both good and bad, shape our destinies.

If Gary had taken a phone with him that day, maybe he could have called for help when he needed it. If he'd told Trixie what he was going to do, perhaps she would have called the police and things wouldn't have turned out the way they did. If he'd told Lance of his intentions, maybe his friend would have talked him into contacting the police instead, and none of it would have happened.

But he didn't do any of those things.

He went alone, and without telling a soul where he was going. If anyone had asked him why, he wouldn't have been able to explain, because sometimes the things we do don't necessarily come with reasons we can understand. Gary rolled the dice that day and took his choice. Sometimes fate rewards the brave, other times it destroys them. We can never know, for sure, which it will be.

Gary's stomach rolled like a ship in a storm on the journey across town to Riversway. By the time he stopped the car outside the ungated road that led to the Marsden farm, his heart was racing and he was on the edge of vomiting.

Even the entrance to the property was secluded. He'd passed the last of the housing estates a good five minutes ago. There were no residences nearby, only fields and empty roads. He couldn't even see the farmhouse because a copse of trees blocked the view.

He took a deep breath, reversed a little, and eased the car onto the property, driving slowly as the suspension attempted to smooth out the rutted, potholed dirt track. He followed the path around the copse of trees and the farmhouse finally came into view; a stark, white building with a grey roof. It was surrounded by outbuildings and a few dilapidated sheds. There were no animals around or even in the nearby fields, so it wasn't a working farm. But why would it be a working farm? Marsden's business was restoration and carpentry, among other, more unsavoury pastimes.

As he drove closer, he could see the once picturesque farmhouse had fallen into disrepair. Chunks of the rendering had crumbled and fallen away, leaving the underlying brickwork exposed, 'like deep red wounds in the tired whitewash. Roof tiles had slipped, much of the purple-grey slate devoured by an expanding carpet of moss. Grass stood tall in the gutters, while Honeysuckle grew thick and wild around the big picture windows.

A single-storey extension had been tagged onto the original building, sitting a little lower than the rest of the house. The frontage was occupied by a big double door with rows of small square windows along the top. Gary guessed it might be Marsden's carpentry workshop.

A car and smaller van were parked out front, but there was no sign of the Transit.

He wondered about the Google Maps images and how old they were. Maybe Marsden no longer owned the van. But then again, if he still ran the restoration business, they would need it for larger items of furniture. It was the middle of the day, so he was probably out, possibly with his son, on a pick-up or delivery.

Gary brought the car to a stop and pretended to look for something on the seat next to him, while his eyes watched the house and outbuildings for signs of life. Nothing moved. The clouds hung, low and grey. The farmhouse looked like it might have been a derelict, had it not been for the vehicles out front.

He took the knife out of the glovebox. It was big and broad and long. On reflection, he should have selected something shorter and thinner; how was he going to conceal a knife this size? His pockets weren't deep enough, and he ruled out the waist band of his trousers, opting instead to slide it—blade first—into his left jacket sleeve, where he cupped the handle in his palm. If he needed it quickly, he could take it out with his right hand and hope he didn't slice open his arm in the process.

He took a deep breath, blood thumping in his throat, and got out of the car. He straightened his clothes, trying to look as ordinary as possible to anyone watching from the house. Adrenaline pumped through his veins as he walked toward the house.

A sign in the corner of the window read: "NO CALLERS".

He hesitated for a moment, then knocked on the door anyway.

"Hi," he rehearsed under his breath. "I was just in the area and I..."

No.

"Hi, I saw your ad and was wondering if you might...if you'd be interested..."

Damn it!

"Hi, you did some work for me a while ago and..."

Don't make him think back to who you are, you idiot!

He took a step back and looked up at the house, at the bay window. Nothing moved.

He glanced left and right, then dropped to his haunches and pressed his thumb to the flap of the letterbox. The spring squealed. He paused and licked his lips.

What if he opened it to another pair of eyes looking back at him?

The rusty spring creaked and twanged as he pushed the letterbox open. Peering through the slot, he saw an empty hallway, stairs to the left, and a door at the end of a narrow hall. No movement, no shadows.

He eased the flap closed again and went to the window. The room was sparsely furnished, containing a sofa, cluttered coffee table, gas fire, and large flat screen TV.

Not only did the house look empty, it looked unlived in.

It looked dead.

He turned away.

The entrance to the path was hidden by the same trees that concealed the house from the road. He waited for half a minute, convinced that the white van would come into view at any moment.

When it didn't, he returned to the car and drove around to the rear of the house. If he was going to follow through with his plan, and the van rolled up, he didn't want to alert them to his presence.

He slammed the door and viewed the empty fields at the back of the house that rolled right up to the river's edge. The property was about as stark and isolated as it could be, like one of those lonely frontier homesteads you sometimes saw in western movies. Yet, here it was, right on the fringes of Gableton.

He turned his attention to the house. The kitchen window was fogged with a milky-film and shrouded with fine, white spider webs. Gary cupped his hand and pressed his face to the glass. An old kitchen, with old cupboards and an equally old wooden table in the middle.

He stepped back and stood like a man at a crossroads. Did

286

he get back in the car and leave? Go home and no doubt face the wrath of the angry girls in his house, or did he do what he set out to do?

He used an elbow to punch through one of the small window panes in the back door, wincing at the impossibly bright sound of shattering glass in the still afternoon. He waited, expecting to hear a shout of alarm.

When none was forthcoming, he carefully reached through the jagged opening and turned the key that was already engaged in the lock. It was stiff, suggesting it hadn't been unlocked in some time; the handle too. When he pushed on the door, it didn't open, so he shouldered it a couple of times until it came unstuck.

A rotten mop toppled out of the corner, and as he pushed, something slid along the floor. He put his head around the door and saw a box full of old newspapers. He threaded himself through the gap and crept inside, glass fragments crunching beneath the soles of his shoes.

He closed the door quietly and returned the mop and box to their original places.

A few days' worth of dirty pots cluttered the sink, and on a stained wooden chopping board, lay a piece of steak, partially diced, but left to dry out. It smelled musty and unpleasant in there.

A mechanical chugging sound started up somewhere close by. It sounded like a compressor running, like the one that had inflated Charley's Disney Princesses castle. He listened, trying to fathom where it was coming from, when it stopped.

He went over to the door and peeped into the hall. The unpleasant smell was more distinct here. He crept along the hall, deeper into the gloomy house.

Stairs on his right, living room to the left.

Living room first.

The central part of the floor was covered by a thin,

threadbare carpet, exposing a broad border of varnished, but heavily scuffed boards all around the outside. Beneath a flat screen television sat a DVD player/recorder. On the coffee table lay a spread of recordable DVDs. The childishly hand-printed titles read, *The Simpsons Season 8 episodes 5-8, Family Guy Season 3 episodes 17-20.*

He passed a glance over the crowd of cheap ornaments and trinkets on the sideboard, but his attention was drawn to an old cupboard built into the alcove by the window.

He removed the knife from his sleeve and placed it on top of the cupboard, then opened the double-doors. Inside, he found the electric meter, black spider-webs, and an old cardboard box full of discarded clothes. He was about to close the doors when he realised the box was full of children's clothes. Girl's clothes.

He dragged it out of the cubby hole and onto the floor, a sick feeling curling around the pit of his stomach like a glistening wet slug.

He moved aside pastel shaded t-shirts and skirts, a school jumper, underwear and socks. Though he tried not to think about it, he knew these were souvenirs.

The trophies of a serial killer.

His hand froze on an upturned cap. With trembling fingers, he pinched the visor and slowly pulled the cap from beneath a lilac blouse. He turned it over and suddenly his breath was gone.

No. No. Please God, no!

Written in glittery gel-pen across the visor, was her name.

Charley.

His head swirled, and his skin shrank. Blood thundered in his ears. For a moment, he thought he might pass out, as he almost had when he heard those evil words spoken to him.

Forget her, she's dead.

He squeezed his eyes shut, gripping the cap tightly, his knuckles bloodless.

This can't be happening! Please, don't let this be true!

He dug deeper into the box, turning the clothes over until he found what he was looking for; her purple t-shirt with its colourful butterfly printed on the front. He lifted the shirt, his mind wandering back to the last time he had seen her wearing it, when she'd caught his kiss and swallowed it.

One side of the shirt was darkly stained. It was blood. Charley's shirt was stained with blood.

CHARLEY'S SHIRT WAS STAINED WITH BLOOD!

His whole body began to shake. "No no no," he whispered.

That tiny flame of hope that had burned for so long had finally been extinguished. Charley was gone. Forever. He'd let his life be savagely ripped limb from limb. He'd lost Fiona. He'd lost everything. And it had all been for nothing.

Marsden had probably killed her the day he took her. When he said on the phone she was dead, he had likely been telling the truth. And as Fiona had said, he just refused to believe it.

He began shaking his head. "No no no NO NOOOOOOOOOOOOOOOO!" He screamed it, the word ripping from his throat like a raw and bloody thing.

He slammed the cupboard doors in rage, and kicked in the panelling, tore one door from its hinges and hurled it across the room.

He pounded his fists into the wooden top, screaming "NO! NO!" with each torturous crash of his hands. He struck with such force that the top's overhang split and splintered away.

He turned on the room, kicking the coffee table and sending DVDs flying, before he grabbed the sofa and upended it as if it was made of nothing.

He looked for something to hurl through the TV, but when he couldn't immediately find anything, he collapsed to his knees. He clasped his face in his hands and cried, his chest and shoulders heaving, until all his breath was gone and it seemed he might suffocate. With his next gasp came a frightening, animalistic scream of emotional agony. The pain was crushingly physical, like the heel of a giant's boot, grinding him into the earth.

It was real.

She was gone.

Charley was gone.

His beautiful daughter was never coming home. She would never play Mario Kart again. Or make him a mythical dragon. Or pretend to catch his kiss and swallow it down. She would never know what it was like to be a teenager, or a young woman, or a mother.

She was gone.

Forever.

For a while, he was lost, swept up in the current of a bitter river that clashed him against jagged rocks until he was raw and bloody.

Sometime later, he raised his aching head and wiped the saliva stringing from his lips. His hands were bleeding; the left one painful enough that something might be broken.

It didn't matter.

Nothing mattered.

He understood now why they had brought him here. He'd had to see for himself. He had to know that Charley was gone so the anger would bloat up inside him like it had for those murdered girls. Marsden had taken their precious young lives and Gary had to see for himself that his beautiful daughter was gone too.

Someone had to make Marsden pay. Someone had to take revenge for them. Gary was more than willing to assume that role and see it through. When Marsden came back, he'd kill him and burn this fucking place to the ground.

To hell with the consequences.

He found the knife and staggered into the hall, his mouth a downward curve of hate, his teeth gritted, jaw muscles bulging.

All he could think about was making Marsden pay for what he'd done. He'd use the knife on him and make him suffer as Charley and all those poor innocent girls had suffered.

He thought about the son again, with his thick arms and his shifty looks. Could Marsden really be bringing kidnapped girls here and murdering them without his son's knowledge? What if father and son were in this sick thing together?

He looked at the knife and wondered about tackling two strong, able-bodied men with it. He was no fighter; could he do that?

Could I?

Yes, he could.

But he had to be prepared to deal with two murderers, and he couldn't mess it up, as he had everything else.

Would they come into the house through the front door? If they had some furniture with them, perhaps they might enter through the big doors of the extension. They never used the back door, he was certain of that at least.

It didn't matter which way they came, he would surprise them and take them both out. One couldn't be doing this without the other's knowledge.

They were in it together.

The mystery compressor started up again. He turned his ear to the sound and followed it into the kitchen. There was another door in the corner.

He opened it quietly, half expecting a cubby-hole full of old brooms and dusters, but instead discovered a short flight of wooden steps leading down into the semi-darkness of the extension.

He flicked on a switch at the top of the stairs and the place illuminated with cold fluorescent light. Holding the knife before him, he quietly descended the steps into a gritty smell of concrete and wood shavings.

It was the workshop where Marsden did his restoration and

carpentry. Against one wall stood a thick, timber workbench, complete with vice and tool rack, and a well-used wood lathe swathed in shavings and sawdust. Two Queen Anne style chairs leaned against the wall, the wood partially stripped of the varnish. A fine layer of sawdust covered everything.

As he moved deeper into the workshop, he noticed a heavy wooden tripod covered with a filthy, paint spattered drop cloth. A shape sat beneath the cloth, but it was the compressor rattling away at the other end of the workshop that held his interest. Beside it, was a weird looking wooden door that was built into the concrete floor.

The compressor's reservoir tank reached capacity and the motor shut down with a loud hiss and shudder. The air smelled of hot engine oil. The stillness that followed was broken only by the steady hiss of air bleeding slowly from the reservoir tank and into the rubber hose that fed into the concrete.

But where did the hose go?

Gary eyed the door. It looked like the compressor was feeding air into the space beneath it. He frowned.

Why would Marsden be feeding air into a space in the ground?

The hairs on Gary's body rose, as realisation dawned.

Feverishly, he slapped back the bolt and heaved the timber door up and over, letting it fall wide and flat. Underneath, lay a second door, constructed from steel bars.

The rectangular space below was hollowed out like a shallow grave, about six feet, by four feet, by three or four feet deep. Huddled beneath a filthy quilt, on a bare mattress, a figure moved. The quilt shifted, and a few locks of blonde hair poked out. Gary recalled the photos of the missing girls from the BBC website. Last on the row had been that of Vicky Lester.

With reeling shock, Gary realised he had found her, *he had found Vicky Lester*.

And she was alive!

He fell to his knees and tried to yank the door open. When it refused, he looked around the frame and saw it was secured with a welded hasp and padlock.

"Hey!" Gary shouted. "Vicky! I'm gonna get you out of here."

Her slender fingers drew the grimy cotton aside and the dirty face of the young girl peered up at him from her cold, lonely prison-pit.

Gary stared in horror at her thin, wasted face. Her left eye was bruised black and puffed tightly shut, her cheek swollen and distorted.

"Oh my God," he uttered, anger rising inside him and flaring white like burning magnesium. How could anyone do this to a child? He had to get her out right now. He couldn't leave her locked in that fucking place for another second.

As he glanced around for something to prise the door, Vicky whispered, "Daddy?" in a small and hopeful voice.

Gary reeled. *Daddy.* A name he never thought he would hear directed at him again. Emotion swelled, but he had to keep it together.

"No," he told her, fighting back tears. "I'm not your daddy, but I'm going to get you out of here. I'm going to get you back to your daddy."

"Daddy, it's me...it's Charley."

Gary froze and the whole world stopped turning on its axis.

Had he really heard what he thought he'd heard?

He leaned on the bars and looked hard. Her face was different, the swelling distorting her features, and her hair was blonde. But the roots were dark! Her hair was dyed?

"Charley?" He whispered her name, almost too afraid to say it aloud in case she said 'no', and he had only misheard her after all.

"Dad," she wept. "It's me, it's Charley."

It was like someone had applied an electric shock to his brain. His vision bleached out briefly, like he'd looked directly into the sun. Blood thundered in his ears. It was as if the whole universe had folded over on itself and things that were impossible were now real. Things that he believed long dead had somehow returned to life!

"Charley!" he cried. "Oh my God! Charley!" He fell onto the cage door, crawled onto it, reaching through the bars to touch her. "Is it really you?"

Charley raised her arm weakly, their fingers touching.

"It's really me. I knew you'd come," she said, her voice thin and weak. "I always knew you'd come and find me. You promised me you'd find me."

Gary grasped her hand and wept, tortured by the pain in her eyes and words. "Oh my God, Charley! I can't believe it! I can't believe it's you. My Sweet Pea, my poor baby!"

He wanted to take her into his arms, to kiss her, to hug her, to protect her, but with the bars between them, he could only touch her poor bruised face, hold it gently in his hand for fear of hurting her.

It all seemed like a surreal dream, but he could see and touch her. The impossible had happened, the thing it seemed only he had believed. Just minutes ago, he was certain she was dead, and now... now *she was alive!*

"Charley," he wept, "Oh Charley."

She pressed her cheek to his palm, holding his hand lightly in hers. For a moment, they stayed that way, both crying tears of joy and pain. Gary gently touched her face, her hair, as if he was afraid she was nothing more than a wisp of a dream that might evaporate into wakefulness at any moment.

The swelling and the angry purple bruising looked so painful.

"How did this happen?" he asked.

"I tried to get away," she said. "He hurt me."

Gary burst into tears. "I'm so sorry, Charley, I'm so sorry."

"It's okay, Dad," Charley said. "Don't cry. You're here now.

294

I'm okay now you're here."

"I kept hoping you were out there somewhere, but sometimes even I doubted it was true."

"I know," Charley said. "Emma told me."

"What?"

"Emma...she told me to hang on. She told me you were coming for me... I thought it was just a dream, but now I know it was real."

Gary was speechless. He had thought Emma and the others had only wanted revenge against the man who murdered them, but perhaps it wasn't that after all.

He wished with all his heart that Fiona was with them, and knew Charley was alive. It was like a miracle. It *was* a miracle. He remembered what Nola had said to him.

God can do wonderful things.

"Okay," he said, and had to force himself to let go of her. He wiped his face. "How many of them are there keeping you here?"

"Just one."

"One?"

"I don't think anyone else lives here."

"Not two? A father and son?"

"No," Charley said. "I've never seen anyone else."

"Are you sure?"

"I've never seen anyone else. Only him."

Gary didn't know if he could trust that to be true.

"Is he old?"

"Um..."

"Old like me? Older?"

"Um, no, younger."

Younger? The son?

If Marsden junior was the Goldilocks Killer, where did Marsden Senior come into it?

"Do you know where he is right now?"

"He went out a while ago...to get some stuff."

"What stuff?"

Charley sobbed, "He said he needed black bags to wrap me in after he'd killed me. He said he was going to do it when he came back."

"Oh Charley." She'd been through so much. How much emotional damage had this monster caused? What other abuse might she have endured? He pushed it aside. He couldn't dwell on it right now. He had to get her out.

"Okay," he said. "I'm going to get you out of here."

He was breathing hard, adrenaline pumping. He grasped the hefty padlock and pulled on it as if, by some miracle, it might not be locked. "Do you know where the key is?"

"He keeps it with him," Charley said. "On a chain around his neck."

"Okay. I'll have to break it then."

He began to get up off the cage door.

"Don't leave me!" Charley cried.

Gary fell back on the bars. "I'm not leaving you, Sweet Pea. I'm just going to have a look for something to break the lock."

Charley nodded uncertainly, her eyes wide and terrified.

He rummaged through the tools on the workbench and brought back a hacksaw. He tried sawing at the padlock, but it didn't take long for him to realise he was getting nowhere with a worn blade and the hardened steel. He switched to the bars, and although the saw was cutting these a little easier, the blade was too worn, the going too slow. He threw the hacksaw aside in frustration.

"Okay," he said. "I'm going to go look in the other rooms, maybe there's a spare key somewhere, or a phone."

"No, no, don't do that! Don't leave me!"

"Just for a minute, Sweetheart. I'll just have a quick look around and if I can't find anything right away, I'll come straight back."

Charley shook her head, tears cutting the dirt on her cheeks.

Gary reached for her. "I've found you, Charley. There's no way I'm letting you go again."

Charley looked helplessly up at him through the bars, her eyes full of hope and fear.

"I'll be gone for just a few minutes. I promise."

Reluctantly, she nodded. "Okay."

He gazed at her, still not quite able to believe it really was Charley. "Just hang on," he said. "It's over now, you're safe."

He squeezed her hand and then made his way back up the narrow wooden stair case and into the kitchen.

Chapter Thirty

Charley watched her father disappear up the steps and felt more afraid than in all the months she'd been held prisoner. She wasn't sure exactly how long that had been, maybe less than a year, because she only remembered one winter, but it felt much longer than that. The time before she was kidnapped was a hazy memory. An innocent time when all she had to think about was art and school and music and having fun with her friends, instead of how she was going to survive another day.

On that long-ago summer afternoon, she'd gotten into an argument with Louise and Sarah over something she couldn't even remember anymore, and had been so angry that her father's instructions about not leaving the others had been the furthest thing from her mind.

She'd pulled her cap low on her head and stomped away from the park, aware that a young lad from her class had paused his game of football to watch her strop, but too angry to care. She ended up walking along the highway toward home, her mind preoccupied with the argument, what had been said, and how she could have better responded.

She hardly noticed the van parked by the side of the road until she was almost on top of it. A man had the side door open and was doing something inside. The road was quiet, with high privet hedges running alongside the narrow pavement. The van was up on the kerb too, creating an even tighter space between it and the hedges.

Just as she was about to veer off and cross over, the man looked up and smiled at her. He was tall and gangly, dressed in scruffy jeans and a hooded grey top. On his head he wore a black, woollen hat.

"Excuse me?" he asked. "Do you have the time?"

She glanced at his wrist and saw the watch he was wearing.

He raised his arm a little and wriggled his hand. "It's stopped. I forgot to wind it last night." He grinned, but was subtly moving toward her.

Charley wasn't sure what she should do. He was making eye contact with her and had asked a question. It would be rude to ignore him and cross over. She'd been warned relentlessly not to speak to strangers, but he had only asked for the time, was giving him the time the same as speaking to him?

She reached into her back pocket to get her phone, stepping into the shadow between the van and the hedge and realised she was now hidden from the road. She picked up her pace, planning to call out the time as she quickly strode by, but when she looked down at the display, he lunged at her.

It happened so fast. One moment she was standing on the pavement, and the next, the world was blurring around her as he threw her effortlessly into the van.

Her dad's warning about sticking with her friends, and the faces of all those missing girls, flashed through her mind.

As the man climbed in after her, she scrambled to the back of the van and yanked on the door handle, screaming for help.

He slammed the side door, the inside of the van darkening, the outside sounds muting. He dragged her back and slammed her up against the side of the van. Holding up a pale, bony fist, he warned her to stop shouting.

Charley could hardly breathe. She was closed in, cut off from the outside; staring at him, confused and terrified of what he

299

was going to do.

"Give me that!"

For a moment, she didn't know what he meant, until he snatched the forgotten phone from her hand and slid it into the floor space between the seats. Tinkerbell tingled with alarm.

He found a roll of tape on the floor and pulled out a strip. "Put your hands together in front of you."

Charley felt a rush of panic, tears pricking her eyes. "Please!" she said. "Why are you doing this? What do you want?"

"I want you to put your hands together," he said, his voice low and threatening.

"Why?" she asked, even though she knew the reason.

"Put your hands together."

"Please, just let me-"

He grabbed her wrists and dragged her towards him, trapping her arms under his, and the wall of his chest. There was little she could do to fight his strength. He wound the tape around her wrists until she was tightly bound. When that was done, he pushed her flat and did the same with her ankles.

Once she was secure, he relaxed, panting a little, and wiped spittle from his mouth.

"You aren't going to scream, are you?" he said, "If you scream, I'll have to tape your mouth too, and then you'll find it hard to breathe. You aren't going to scream, are you?"

Charley shook her head, tears brimming.

He leaned over her, removing her cap and touching her hair affectionately. "I've waited so long to be with you, Christina," he said. "All those others...they could never be you, not really." He stroked her cheek with the backs of his fingers and gazed at her, his eyes becoming fluid. "You look so much like her," he whispered. "You *are* her. Except for your hair. Your hair's all wrong. But we'll change that, and then you'll be perfect. Just perfect."

Charley stared at him, her eyes wide and terrified, unable to comprehend what he was saying to her.

"Don't be afraid," he said gently. "I'm not going to hurt you. I love you." He smiled then, but it was an unattractive, liver-lipped smile, his teeth all stained and grey. "We'll soon be home."

He squeezed through the seats into the cab, started the engine, eased the van off the kerb, and drove along the quiet road.

Charley lay on her back, bound and afraid, so intensely afraid. She knew what was happening to her. She was being kidnapped by a paedophile who was probably going to rape and murder her.

Rape and murder.

Just a few minutes ago they were only words. Words that had nothing to do with her. But now they were at the forefront of her mind. These things were likely going to happen to her. Murder she knew. To kill someone. Rape was more insubstantial. She knew men did it to women and that it was very bad. It was sex. Forced sex. But she didn't fully understand what that meant.

They talked about sex in school sometimes. The other girls seemed to know more about it than she did. Sarah claimed that sex is when a man puts his *thing* into a woman's vagina. It all sounded gross and unlikely to Charley. She once saw James Vernon's thing when he pulled out the front of his gym shorts, and it had been all limp and floppy, so Charley didn't really see how that was possible.

But the man would know.

He'd know, and he'd make her do it.

She wondered if he was the man who had taken those girls she'd seen on TV. Those pretty, young girls with blonde hair. They all kinda looked a little bit like her, except she didn't have blonde hair.

Your hair's all wrong, he'd said, *but we'll change that, and then*

301

you'll be perfect. Just perfect."

It was him.

She wasn't like the others, so he was going to change her, change her hair, colour it blonde and curl it.

Charley's breath started coming in little gasps as she felt the hopeless urge to cry. She bit down on her lower lip and pushed it back. Crying wasn't going to get her anywhere.

She felt vulnerable, lying helpless and submissive, so she struggled to sit up, raising her legs to counterbalance her upper body and see-sawing herself into a sitting position. Once up, she shuffled back until her spine rested against the side panel.

A little breathless at the exertion, she checked on her captor. He was concentrating on driving. She twisted her hands and pulled against the tape, but it was hopeless. She looked around the van floor, but there wasn't anything lying around with which she could cut her bindings.

But even if she could cut the tape, what then? Jump out of a moving van? She looked at him again. Maybe she could grab his face, gouge his eyes and blind him. Crashing and getting injured was better than what might lay ahead of her.

But she couldn't get free so what was the point of thinking about it?

Despairing for a moment, she thought about her dad. As soon as he found out she was missing he would come looking for her. Maybe someone had seen her being kidnapped and called the police.

A tiny glow of hope kindled inside her, offering a little comfort. The urge to cry came again. She breathed deeply, fighting the tears blurring her vision.

Charley tried her best to keep track of the route they took, but there were simply too many twists and turns to remember. The last part of the trip seemed to be over rough ground that bounced her around.

The van stopped, and the man climbed into the rear with

302

her. When he saw she was sitting up and looking directly at him, he hesitated. Almost half-heartedly, he produced a white cloth bag that might have been a pillowcase. "I'm going to put this over your head, okay?"

"Why?" Charley asked. She didn't want a bag over her head. She wanted to see where she was going and know what was happening to her.

"Because I don't want you to see where I live."

"Why?"

He sighed, his mouth becoming a hard line. She was annoying him, but she didn't care. "Because I don't, okay?"

He was irritated and threatening, but Charley disregarded the intimidation. "Why does it matter if I know where you live?" she asked. "There's nothing I can do about it, is there?"

He looked at the bag, his hands running over it, thinking for a moment.

"No, it doesn't matter," he agreed, and tossed the bag to one side. But then he lunged at her, his hands slamming on either side of her head with a hollow boom. "But you have to do as I say," he warned, his breath like rotten meat and onions. Charley turned away, but he followed her, his face in hers, noses almost touching. "You do *everything* I say. Understand? *Everything.*"

Charley refused to nod or make any kind of acknowledgement, but he seemed satisfied that he had made his point just the same. He unlatched the side door and slid it open. Right outside the van was a front door set in the stone of a white building.

The man jumped down and unlocked the front door, pushing it wide. He took Charley by the feet and dragged her to the opening as if she was a bundle of cargo. Tucking his shoulder into her midriff, he tried to lift her, but she leaned back, making it difficult for him to do so. She wasn't sure why she was doing it, only that she wasn't going to make anything easy for him.

"Lean forward," he said. "I want to pick you up."

"Why can't I just walk?" Charley asked.

The man drew back and stared at her, his expression pissed. Charley looked fearfully, yet defiantly, back at him. He grabbed her in a powerful grasp and hauled her up over his shoulder, lifting her easily and shrugging her around a couple of times until he found a good balance. He carried her inside and kicked the door shut behind him.

The house interior smelled bad; a revolting, musty stench that caught at the back of Charley's throat. He carried her past stairs and along a narrow hall with doors on either side. Charley saw all this moving away from her. Then she was in a kitchen, passing by an ancient ceramic sink, with spider web cracks over its yellowed surface. To her right was a table with chopping board and knives.

She imagined grabbing one and stabbing him with it. But that was a stupid thought.

She was a child. She couldn't do something like that.

Could she?

He swung open another door and snapped on the light, before descending a few stairs, his shoulder driving a breathy little *huff* out of her with each step.

It was a woodwork shop. Old furniture and lengths of timber lay all over the place. The air smelled of wood shavings, dust, and polish.

He set her back on her feet and spun her around to face a big set of doors at the end of the shop. Eight small square windows across the top, four on each door. They let in some light, but not enough, hence the need for artificial light, even in the day. The achingly pure sky gave the square windows the appearance of blue tiles.

The man walked over to a door set into the floor and opened it up.

Panic gripped her. *He's going to put me in there!*

304

She pulled and twisted her bindings.

The man moved her closer. "Get in," he ordered.

"Why?" Charley asked. She was afraid, so afraid, but she was angry too.

"Because I said so."

"But why do you-"

He stepped up to her and shook his fists in her face. "Stop fucking questioning everything I say and get in!"

Charley's heart raced. She looked from the man to the pit and back again, desperately trying to think of something she could say to stop him from putting her down there.

The man let out an impatient sigh and made to grab her.

"But you said you love me!" she blurted at him.

He froze as if he'd been slapped. Charley saw the look on his face and pressed on. "You said you love me. Why would you put me down there if you love me?"

He stepped back, unsure and unsteady, his confidence stripped away. He slapped a hand to his brow and grasped the ball of his forehead with his long, spindly fingers, squeezing it hard.

"Please," Charley said. "You don't hurt the people you love, do you?"

His hand slid slowly down his face until he was looking at her through the spread of his fingers. "No," he whispered, with a tiny shake of his head.

He stood that way for a long time, his hand feeling the bones of his face. Every so often, he'd make a soft sound, like a little whine of indecision.

"Please let me go," Charley begged.

"I can't," he whispered.

"Why can't you?"

His eyes darted all around him, as if someone might be listening. He dropped his hand. "I just can't, alright? You have to get in the pit now."

305

"No, please."

"Now."

"Please, let me go," Charley begged.

"I don't want to hurt you," he said. "I *never* wanted to hurt you. It was *him*. It was always *him*."

"Who?" Charley asked.

He closed his eyes tightly, his face screwing into a twisted mask of pain. He held his breath, letting it out in a hideous low screech from his throat.

Charley was transfixed, frightened, yet fascinated by his bizarre behaviour. He began singing through tears, his voice strained and high. Charley knew the song; it was a hymn she'd sung many times in the school assembly hall.

"All things bright and beautiful. All creatures great and small. All things wise and wonderful, the Lord God made...them all."

He cocked his head slightly, staring into space, tears streaming, his nose and lips wet. He sniffed once and swallowed it down.

"Get in the pit," he said, his voice wrung of emotion.

"But you said-" Charley began.

"Get in the pit."

Charley's heart hammered but she stood her ground. She wasn't willingly getting into the pit, no matter what.

He seized her by the shoulders. "*GET IN!*" he screamed. "*Get in get in get in!*"

He shoved her, hard. Her hands and feet were taped, there was nothing she could do to help herself. The hole was only three-feet deep, but the fall seemed to go on forever, as if she was tumbling into the deepest, darkest crevice on earth.

Though she landed on an old flattened mattress, the impact still knocked every bit of wind out of her. Her right elbow struck the concrete floor, a jarring knife of pain shooting into her hand and shoulder.

She stared up in horror, her eyes bulging, chest heaving, unable to draw breath. The man didn't seem to care; angrily hurled the cage door over, the bars clanging and ringing like tuning forks. He snapped on the padlock, then raised the wooden door so it stood up straight.

"*I told you to do as I said, didn't I?*" he shouted and slammed down the door, plunging Charley into darkness.

Dirt and dust sifted onto her face and into her eyes. Not only couldn't she breathe, she was also blinded too. She tried to blink out the dirt, but her eyes only pricked and welled up with tears.

She lay in the lonely blackness, thinking she was going to die, just suffocate right there on the floor of this horrible, cold pit, without ever seeing her mum and dad again.

But then she felt cool hands on her, helping her to sit up. "It's okay," a girl's voice soothed. "You're just winded. Your diaphragm's spazzed out, but you'll be okay again in a minute."

The girl gently rubbed her back, and although it didn't seem to help her breathing much, it felt good to be touched so tenderly.

Just when Charley thought the end was coming, she managed to catch her breath. She rubbed her eyes with her bound hands until the tears washed out the grit, and after a few minutes, she felt a little better.

"What's your name?" the girl asked.

Charley took a few more grateful breaths before she answered. "It's Charley."

"Charley's a boy's name," the girl said.

"It's Charlotte, but everyone calls me Charley."

"Oh yeah," the girl said, as if it was something she had once known but had forgotten. "I'm Hannah."

Charley turned quickly to look back at the girl. Her eyes had partly adjusted to the dim light slitting through the cracks around the door, and she could just make out the shape of her.

"Hannah Reid?" she asked.

307

"Yeah," the girl said, surprised. "How did you know?"

"You've been on the news. Everyone's been looking for you."

Hannah let out a small gasp. "They are?"

"Yeah," Charley said. "Everyone: the police, your family, your neighbours. People came from all over to help look for you."

Hannah covered her face and started crying. Charley shuffled around and hooked her bound hands around Hannah's neck and hugged her. She couldn't help but cry a little herself, but it was okay to cry since *he* wasn't there.

Hannah wiped her eyes and face. "I didn't think anyone was looking for me."

Charley was aghast. She removed her arms from around Hannah's neck. "Why would you think that?"

"Because he told me no one was looking for me. He told me no one cares about me anymore, no one but him."

"Well he's a liar," Charley sneered. "Your mum and dad were on TV and everything."

"Were they?"

Charley nodded. "I saw them."

"How...how were they?"

"Um, well, they were upset. Your mum was crying and that."

Hannah was quiet for a while, and then Charley realised she was silently crying again.

"Listen, Hannah, we have to find a way to get out of here. We have to work together to find a way."

"He won't allow it."

"He won't allow it? We aren't going to ask his permission."

"He keeps you locked in here most of the time. But then sometimes he takes you upstairs."

Fear wriggled through Charley's core. "And what happens then?"

"He makes you do things."

"Things?" Charley asked.

Hannah nodded. "Yes," she whispered. "Disgusting things."

Charley wanted to ask about the *things*, but was too afraid to hear the answers.

"Is there anyone else here?" she asked instead.

Hannah shook her head.

"Any other girls? Like us?"

"There was. When he first brought me here there was another girl...her name was Linda, but he called her Christina. Later he came and took the chain off her and put it on me. Then he started calling me Christina and he took Linda away. She never came back. I don't know what happened to her, but I think maybe he, I think he..."

Murdered her, Charley silently finished.

Hannah started crying again. "Now you're here, he'll come and take me soon."

Charley tried to comfort her. "Maybe he won't," she said encouragingly. "Maybe he'll let us stay together and then we can find a way to get out of here."

"Do you think?" Hannah asked, hopefully.

Charley nodded. "We can talk to him. If we talk to him, we can make him see sense and he'll let both of us stay here."

They heard a noise from the workshop above and they both fell silent, listening. When the noises stopped, Hannah said, "At first he was nice to me. He seemed to think I was his sister."

"His sister?"

"Christina. She must have been his sister. It was weird, but at least he didn't do anything to me. He kinda just wanted me around. We watched cartoons on the TV, stuff like The Simpsons, and just kinda hung out. He talked about things he'd done with his sister, but like it had been me, like how he used to put me in the bath when I was a baby and changed my nappy. When he thinks you're Christina, it's okay...well, kinda."

"That *is* weird," Charley agreed. "Was there no way you could have got away when he took you upstairs?"

Hannah moved her leg, and Charley heard the clink of chain links.

"He keeps me chained around the ankle. When he takes me upstairs, he fastens the other end to his belt, or padlocks it to these links he has screwed into the walls."

"But he hasn't chained me up," Charley said.

"He will though."

There came a loud bang and some shouting. They waited, but that was all.

"Do you know his name?" Charley asked.

"William, I think, but I don't know if that's really his name." After a moment Hannah asked, "Did you really see my mum and dad on the telly?"

"Yeah," Charley replied. "They were asking for you to come home. Then it showed loads of police and people out looking for you." Charley sucked in a sharp breath. "My elbow's really hurting. I banged it when he pushed me in here."

"Let me see."

In the darkness, Hannah could do little more than carefully feel around her elbow. Charley winced.

"It's kind of sticky and gooey," Hannah said. "It must be cut and bleeding."

"It stings. Do you think you can get this tape off my wrists?"

"Um, I dunno. He left it on. He'll get angry if you take it off."

"I don't care!" Charley said. "I want it off. We have to fight him, Hannah. We can't make everything easy for him."

Hannah thought about it for a moment. "Okay, give me your hands."

She picked around the tape until she found the end. "Got it," she said, and unwound it from Charley's wrists. When the tape came free, Charley uttered a gasp of relief and rubbed the numbed skin. She probed gingerly at her elbow with the tips of her fingers, drawing in little sucks of air through her clenched teeth. The skin was split and sticky with blood.

"Yeah, it's cut," she said. "Is there anything I can cover it with?"

"Only toilet roll."

Hannah tore off a wad of tissue and gave it to Charley, who held it firmly over the bleeding.

"Where do you live?" Hannah asked.

"Here in Gableton."

"Gableton," Hannah said thoughtfully. "I didn't know that's where we are. My uncle lives in Gableton."

Charley thought about her own mum and dad.

Did they even know she was missing yet?

If only someone had seen her being thrown into the van. They might have taken the registration and the police would rescue her. Maybe it would be over before anything really bad happened.

But what if no one saw, she thought with dread. *What if no one knows where you are, and no one ever comes?*

No one had come to save Hannah or any of the other missing girls. The terrifying possibility of being held here for more than a few days crossed her mind. She couldn't just sit back and hope someone would come and save her. She had to *do* something. She remembered what her dad had said one time.

Know your enemy as you know yourself.

"Hannah, I need you to tell me everything you know about him. What he wants, what he does, and why he does it."

Hannah nodded and gathered her thoughts while Charley listened.

Time passed slowly in the dark. The girls talked a lot at first, about the way they were kidnapped, about their families, about school. They cried too, and comforted each other. Charley kept turning the conversation back to their captor and asking more questions as they occurred to her. But eventually conversation dwindled, and they could only sit huddled together in the darkness, listening to the hiss of air blowing into the pit and anticipating the abrupt rattle of the compressor.

Nightfall filled their prison to the brim with inky blackness. They lay together under the quilt, keeping each other warm.

Charley lost sense of space, the hole in the ground seeming like it might have been an open desert plain, stretching away on all sides, until she reached out and felt those claustrophobic concrete walls with her fingertips.

"Do you think we'll ever get out of here?" Hannah whispered, her voice sleepy.

"Of course we will," Charley whispered back as she drifted off to sleep.

She dreamed of home and Mister Whiskers.

It was still utterly dark in the pit when Charley woke to the sounds of movement from somewhere above. She roused Hannah and they listened together. Hannah found Charley's hand in the darkness and held it tightly.

The fluorescents came on, knife-edges of light filling the small gaps in the frame above them. They heard him come down the steps, and then the wooden door opened, flooding the pit with an eye-watering glare. The girls shielded their faces and squinted up in fear as he unlocked the gate. He stood high above them, a blurry silhouette against the fluorescent brilliance.

"You took the tape off," he said.

"It was hurting me," Charley replied.

He seemed to consider it for a moment, playing with the

padlock in his hands.

"If you'd done as I said, I would've taken it off for you." He put the padlock to one side and pointed at Hannah. "You, come out of there."

Hannah turned to Charley, an expression of utter terror on her face. Charley looked helplessly back at her, suddenly gripped by the reality of it all. She had to try to do something to work this out. Hannah was relying on her.

"I don't want her to come out," Charley said. "She's my friend."

"You be quiet!" he shouted. Then to Hannah, "Come out now!"

The girls only stared up at him.

He sighed impatiently and jumped down into the pit. The girls cowered away from him, but he grabbed the chain and dragged Hannah toward him. She whimpered as the metal cuff dug into her ankle. He held her bare foot and unlocked the padlock, releasing the steel manacle.

Charley panted in fear, her mind racing. It was all happening too quickly. Why couldn't he just stop and talk to them for a moment? She tried to think what her dad would do, how he would control the situation. But he was so much older and smarter than she was.

"What...what...?" Charley started, but he immediately swung around on her, his finger in her face.

"I told you to be quiet, *Christina*."

Charley and Hannah shot frightened looks at each other, their eyes wide. Hannah gave out a tearful gasp.

He grabbed Charley's foot and fitted the steel shackle around her ankle. The metal halves pinched her skin and Charley yelped, but he just ignored her and snapped on the lock.

Charley couldn't catch her breath. She looked at the lock and chain on her ankle, at Hannah, at the man as he rose to full height.

"Come on you," he said, to Hannah.

Hannah stared up at him, her mouth open, her breath stolen by the rapid pump of her heart.

"Please don't take her away," Charley pleaded. "Just leave her here with me and we'll be okay. We'll be good."

"Can't do that," he said impassively. "It's time. Come on."

Hannah stared up at him, unable to move.

He tried to pull her up by the arm, but Hannah resisted, letting her legs stay floppy and refusing to support herself.

"Stand up!" the man demanded. "Stand up now!"

Hannah was crying and refusing to stand up by herself. He got around behind her, raising her up under the arms and dragging her to the bottom end of the pit.

"NO! NO!" Hannah screamed, her hands reaching out in panic. "CHARLEY! HELP ME! HELP ME!"

Charley started to get up, but he pointed a threatening finger at her and said, "Christina! Stay where you are!"

"Please," Charley begged. "You don't have to take her away. She's my friend. Leave her here. We'll be good, we promise we will!"

He ignored her and hoisted the terrified girl up onto the floor of the workshop, pinning her there while he climbed out himself.

Charley scrambled to her feet, despite his warning, her head swirling with dizziness after being sat for so long. "Stop! Please don't take her away!" she cried. It was all moving too fast, like the last grains of sand trickling through an hourglass. "Don't take her away! Please don't take her away!"

The man heaved the barred door closed, forcing Charley to crouch.

Hannah stared at Charley through the bars with wild and terrified eyes while the man fumbled with the lock.

She could run. Charley thought. *Why doesn't she run?*

Run, Charley mouthed at her. *Run!*

But she didn't run, she just sat there holding herself and crying. She was just a terrified young girl after all.

Once he'd secured the cage door, he turned back to Hannah.

"No, no!" she screamed, pushing herself away from him.

He wrapped his big arms around her, but as he lifted her, she grabbed a loop of chain from the floor. He carried her toward the stairs, the slack quickly taken up, the chain yanking Charley's foot into the air.

"*Charley! Charley!*" Hannah was shrieking now. *"Don't let him take me! DON'T LET HIM TAKE ME!"*

He pulled harder, trying to break Hannah's grip on the links. The steel cuff bit into Charley's flesh, dragging her forward.

Charley didn't know what to do. She'd said they could talk to him and Hannah had believed her. Why wouldn't he listen?

"*Please,*" Charley cried through her tears. But it was useless, he'd decided he was taking her and nothing was going to stop him.

He yanked harder, his mouth a grim curve of anger and determination. The chain dragged Charley another couple of inches before it tore from Hannah's white fingers.

"*NO! NO!*"

The shrillness of Hannah's screams slashed at Charley like knives.

As he climbed the stairs, Hannah reached out, no words now, only her terrible, terrible screams.

Charley grabbed the bars. "Hannah!" she cried. She caught a final glimpse of Hannah's terror-stricken face, and then they were gone. The door slammed and the cries grew muffled. She heard him shouting. Hannah begging.

It all went quiet.

Charley drew her knees to her chest and hugged them. She sat there shivering, seeing Hannah's pleading, terrified face over and over. It was too horrible. He'd taken Hannah away

315

and he was going to *kill* her.

He was going to kill her!

It was unreal. It was impossible.

Charley burst into wild sobbing tears and buried her face in her hands. "Hannah," she cried. "Hannah."

Charley cried until she had no more tears.

He'd left the wooden outer door open so at least she didn't have to endure that pitch black world. She had no clue what time it was, except that the windows above the door were like eight tiles of black onyx.

She laid her head on her knees for a while. Her eyes were so tired and yet she was afraid to sleep. She kept wondering about Hannah, kept hoping that he might bring her back.

She dozed, in and out, jumping awake from weird dreams or when the compressor fired up.

The next time she raised her head, he was looking down at her through the bars with something in his hands.

"What have you done with Hannah?" she demanded. The sound of her voice surprised her. It was different somehow. Calmer and more mature.

"Never mind her," the man said.

"What have you done with her?"

"I told you to never mind her! Where did you get those clothes?"

Charley didn't understand what he was asking. They were her clothes.

"Christina, where did you get those clothes?"

"I'm not..." Charley began, but then stopped, remembering what Hannah had told her.

When he thinks you're Christina, it's okay...well, kinda.

"They're...someone else's clothes," Charley said.

316

"Well, I can see that. They don't suit you. Here, I've brought one of your nice dresses."

He threw a bundle of cloth onto the bars. It hung above her for a moment before sliding through and falling onto her legs. It was the faded, flowery summer dress Hannah had been wearing.

"Put it on," he ordered.

"I don't want to," Charley replied. "It's cold."

"I said, put it on." His voice was even, but mildly threatening.

Again, Charley didn't know where she got the courage to defy him, but she did. "It's too cold in here for a dress like this."

He sighed. "If you don't put it on, I'll come down there and put it on you myself."

Charley looked despairingly at the thin cotton dress. She didn't want to put it on, but she didn't want him to do it for her either.

"Turn around then," she said.

He seemed amused. "Oh? Since when did you get all shy? I've seen you naked hundreds of times. I used to bath you when you were a baby."

"Well I'm not a baby anymore," Charley said. "Girls need privacy when they get older, even from..." she hesitated and licked her lips. "Even from their *big brothers*." She held her breath and stared at him, fully expecting him to laugh at her and say 'what are you talking about? I'm not your brother.' But instead, his livery-lips split into a wide grin and he turned his back.

Working quickly, she stripped off her t-shirt, a swath of goose-bumps rising over her back and shoulders. Gathering the dress into a cloth loop, she dropped it over her head and wriggled out of her shorts, pushing them down and onto the chain where they hung from one leg hole, as if on a washing line to dry.

317

When it was all done she said, "Okay."

He turned, his face lighting up with his creepy smile. "Ah, that's so much better. Much more like the Christina I know. Once your hair is back to how it used to be, you'll be perfect again. Just perfect."

Charley had to hold back tears as she watched him collect her things. In one deft swoop, he had stripped away her identity. He had taken her clothes, and he intended to dye her hair too, so she looked like those other girls. Like Hannah had looked. Like his sister must have looked.

That was his plan. The same as he'd done with Hannah. Take everything away from her and try to make her think no one cared about her but him.

But it wouldn't work. She wouldn't let it.

"What have you done with Hannah?" she asked again.

"Hannah?" he said harshly, and then his voice softened. "Hannah...won't be coming back."

Charley was filled with outrage. "What have you done with her?"

He winced a little, but continued carefully folding her clothes, paying them every bit of his attention. As he folded the tee shirt, he noticed a blood stain on the side and along the hem.

"How did this happen?" he asked angrily.

"I cut my elbow," Charley said. "When you pushed me down here."

"If you'd done as I told you to, it wouldn't have happened!" he spat. Then he softened again. "But don't worry, I'm going to take care of you now, just like I used to before..." He stopped and lowered his eyes, his features darkening. He placed the tee shirt on top of the shorts and then his face brightened again. "You must be hungry."

"No, I'm not," Charley said, her voice smouldering. She was hungry, she hadn't eaten since breakfast the day before, and her stomach growled even as she spoke.

318

"I'll make you a sandwich," he said, as if he hadn't heard her. "Peanut butter, your favourite."

"I don't want it."

"Come now, you have to eat. I'll make you one, and a nice glass of milk."

"I don't want it!"

He frowned, but went off to make it anyway.

Charley remembered what Hannah had told her.

He's nice to you at first, wants to please you. Then he changes, and he starts doing stuff to you.

She had to find a way to escape before that happened.

The milk sat untouched and the sandwiches curled when he opened the doors the next morning. She'd slept fitfully. The cold seemed to permeate everything, and the compressor startled her every time it fired up.

He frowned at the untouched food, but didn't utter a word as he unfastened the chain from the bars. He looped the chain through his belt and padlocked it so she was tethered to him.

"Come on."

"Where are we going?" Charley asked.

He raised his fists. "Stop fucking questioning everything I say!" he shouted. Charley flinched. "Just get up and come with me!" He yanked hard on the chain, the steel cuff painfully scraping at her ankle bone.

His instant anger and impatience frightened her, so she decided it might not be a good idea to push him. Reluctantly, she climbed out of the pit.

"Well, that's better," he said.

As they moved toward the steps, she was filled with dread. Hannah said he took her upstairs to do disgusting stuff to her.

Was this it? Was it going to start so soon?

319

He led her through the kitchen, like an animal on a leash. She hardly noticed that musty old stench at the back of her throat, or the blackened spider webs hanging from the ceiling. Her mind raced around in panic, terrified of what was going to happen to her.

In the hall, he began to climb the stairs. Charley's chest tightened and she halted.

"Where are you taking me?"

"Just come on," he ordered, continuing up the stairs.

No, no, she thought, *not now, not already!*

Tears welled up and she started sobbing, her breath coming in sharp panicky snatches.

The chain slack ran out before he reached the top of the stairs. He turned and cast his eyes over her. "Stop crying. Just do everything I tell you to do and I won't have to hurt you. Do you understand?"

Charley felt faint and unreal. Her heart fluttered like a small bird, her eyes wet and full of fear.

He jerked on the chain, making her yelp when her toes painfully struck the bottom step.

Still, she didn't start up the stairs.

He pulled the chain taut, his eyes full of threat. "Don't make me have to come back down there for you."

There was no escape. She was in his power. Reluctantly, she climbed the stairs.

He opened a door to the right and stood aside so she could go in before him. Her mind scrambled in panic for something she could say to avoid having to go into that room, but her imagination was crammed too full of fear and dread for things she was still too young to understand.

He tilted his head impatiently. "Go in!"

If she didn't go in there, he would force her. He would hurt her. She just had to do as he said and pray that it wouldn't be as horrible as the insubstantial and surreal thoughts swirling

320

around in her head.

She trudged the few steps, the chain clinking as it dragged behind her, and looked inside. She'd expected a bedroom with the bed all laid out and threatening. But it wasn't a bedroom, it was a bathroom.

For a moment she was confused, and then she saw plastic bottles containing bleach powder and developer set out on the toilet seat, alongside a mixing bowl and clear plastic gloves. He'd brought her up to dye her hair!

Relief rushed over her.

"Go on," he said.

The bathroom was small and grotty and smelled of mildew and soap scum. She caught her reflection in the rust-flecked mirror over the sink. Her face was stark and sickly and strangely unsymmetrical; her eyes too large, hair tangled and in need of brushing. The tired, worn dress hung shapelessly over her collar bones.

How am I here? she asked herself. *How am I going to get out of this?*

"Put this towel over your shoulders," he ordered, and pushed her down over the bath.

He was gentle, and that alone set her nerves on edge. But his hands worked deftly, from coconut oil—to protect her hair, he said—to the bleach. He brushed, stroked and treated her hair as if it was precious.

After thirty minutes, he washed out the solution.

He rubbed her head with a smelly towel, and when he took it away, he smiled. "Christina," he said, as if this was the first time he'd seen her in a long while. "That's better. That's so much better."

Charley looked over his shoulder at the mirror and barely recognised herself. The bleached hair made her look so different.

She didn't like it, she didn't like it one bit.

321

I'm Charley, she told herself as he led her back downstairs to the pit. *I'm Charley Wright, and I always will be, no matter what he does to me.*

Boredom and loneliness were the most difficult aspects of being held captive in those first few weeks. She spent many long hours wrapped in the old quilt to keep out the cold, alone in the dark with nothing to do.

Sometimes she'd dream about being back home in her room with all her things. She'd imagine the simple pleasures, like lying on her bed and listening to music, or reading a book. She'd think about her mum and dad and Mister Whiskers. How big would he be now? Would he still know her with blonde hair? What would her mum and dad be doing and how would they be coping with her disappearance? They'd still be looking for her; she knew it. Her face would have been in the newspapers and on TV, just as Hannah's had. Her mum and dad would never stop looking for her unless...unless they thought she was dead. How long would she have to be missing before everyone thought she was dead?

Maybe they thought that already.

Sometimes she'd imagine escaping and being reunited with them all. What they'd say and the fuss they'd make. Walking into her home, seeing and touching everything to ensure it was real.

Eventually, though, the dreams wore thin, like the summer dress he'd made her wear, and there was nothing but endless darkness.

The loneliness became so unbearable that she even began to look forward to his visits. She knew when he went out because she'd feel the ground vibrate and hear the dull rumble of the van moving off. He came to see her at various times of the day and night, usually bringing food to share with her. She'd given up the hunger strike on the second day when he'd brought stew, and the aroma of it was just too mouth-watering to resist. He'd sit on the rim of the pit with his legs dangling and talk about things they used to do together when she was a toddler, as if she really was his sister.

Charley watched him carefully while they ate, looking for cracks in the pretence, but he always spoke as if he genuinely believed that she was his sister.

Sometimes he'd halt in the middle of a sentence and become sullen for a while, as if he'd remembered something that he didn't want to talk about, something that darkened his bright recollections of the perfect times he claimed they'd spent together.

Charley played along, pretending that she remembered it all. If she could gain his trust, maybe he'd loosen the tight grip he had on her, but for the moment he was forever wary.

She'd tried to talk to him about her loneliness and boredom, but he didn't listen, or maybe he just didn't care, until one day she'd worked herself up so much that she was already crying and angry when he opened the pit.

"You can't just keep me in here like this!" she shouted at him.

He looked guiltily down at her.

"I'm a person! I'm a human being. *I'm your sister*! I can't stand it down here all the time without anything to do or anyone to talk to."

"I do everything for you!" he shouted back at her. "I cook for you. I bring you food. I empty your shit! You need to be more grateful, or maybe I'll just leave you down there for a few days with nothing to eat or drink...then we'd see how grateful you'd be!"

I'm only down here because of you! Charley wanted to scream back at him, but his threat to leave her for days was far too real and frightening to even contemplate.

"I'm sorry," she said. "I am grateful. It's just that I get so lonely when you aren't here."

He calmed down a little. "Well, I should think so," he said.

They ate in silence.

When he closed the pit that night, she wondered if that was the last light she would see for a while.

The next morning, however, he opened up as usual.

"I'm going to let you have breakfast in the kitchen," he announced. "And then I'm going to let you stay in your bedroom, like you used to. Would you like that?"

Charley could barely contain herself. The promise of getting out of the cold pit, even for a few minutes, brought tears of joy. "Oh yes!" she said. "Thank you. Thank you for being so kind to me."

He nodded. "But I'm warning you, Christina, this is only a trial. If you try anything like you have in the past, then I'll have to hurt you and put you back in the pit."

Charley shook her head. "I won't, I promise."

He unfastened the chain from the bars and looped it through his belt, securing it as usual with the padlock, then took her upstairs.

She blinked at the sunlight streaming in through the kitchen windows. After the grey of the pit, the grass was so lushly green that it almost hurt her eyes to look at it. The low clouds were blown from subtle shades of blue and grey and purple. The trees were shedding their foliage for winter, the falling leaves made from wonderful reds and browns and golds. The world had never seemed as beautiful as it did in that moment.

After they'd eaten cereal in the kitchen, he took her upstairs. Like everything else in the house, the bedroom was shabby. No carpet, not even a rug. The mattress was tired and sagging, the covers stained and threadbare.

He detached the chain from his belt and padlocked it to a

324

steel loop screwed into the wall by the bed.

"This is nicer than down there, isn't it?" he said.

Charley nodded. It was still cold and dirty and miserable, there were dead moths and insects on the window sill, but it was a million times better than the pit.

But more importantly, allowing her to stay there meant that he might be starting to trust her.

For a while, the days passed by slowly. He kept her in the bedroom all the time and she still had to use a bucket for a toilet. She spent long hours gazing out of the window and across the river at the distant houses, dreaming of seeing someone and raising the alarm.

Help, I'm being held prisoner!

But no one ever came by, and the houses were far too distant to make a difference.

Eventually he allowed her downstairs too, but continued to keep her tethered to him. He especially liked for them to sit on the sofa together and watch the recordings he'd made of The Simpsons and other cartoons, as Hannah said he had with her. He liked for her to lean on him while he curled her hair around his fingers.

Sometimes she felt like she was nothing more than a human doll for him to play with.

One day she asked if he would bring her some art materials. He said he never knew she was artistic, but a few days later brought a sketchbook, poster paints and colouring pencils, brushes, and mixing trays.

It was like heaven; like the door to a world long-closed had suddenly been reopened. A world full of bright and vibrant colours. She painted anything she could think of to brighten the room, birds, intensely colourful butterflies, caterpillars, the sky

325

she could see through the window.

One time she painted a big ladybird climbing a stalk, bright red with huge black spots. She even managed a smile when she finished that one.

She sketched her bedroom back home as best she could remember it, with her untidy dressing table at one end and all her old toys at the other. She tried to sketch her mum and dad but got frustrated when she couldn't capture their likenesses. She painted Mister Whiskers as she remembered him, but with his mouth turned up at the corner in a cheeky smile.

She missed them all so much.

She hid those pictures under the mattress, so he wouldn't see them. No doubt he would be angry if he realised she was painting things from her old life. But it wasn't only that. She didn't want to share that part of herself with him. He owned her so completely, that at least she had this one small thing that belonged to her and her alone.

Another time, she painted a purple dragon with yellow horns and wings, a big plume of fire rolling from its gaping jaws. When she'd finished, she thought about her dad and tried to picture all the little things about him that she loved. The creases he got between his brows when he was working, or his smile when she told him a joke, or the gentle way he cuddled her when they watched TV together. She remembered his face when she'd given him the special pen she bought and how he'd hugged her for it. Most of all she remembered that last day on the park; blowing him a kiss and him catching it and blowing it back. He'd promised they'd play Mario Kart when they got back home.

Her face grew hot, tears blurring her vision, and she had to put the painting aside while she cried.

One night, screaming brought Charley into an unsettling wakefulness. She'd been dozing, and the light had faded from the sky, the room taking on a shadowy eeriness that frightened her. Even her paintings seemed dark and ominous. She sat up on the bed, her eyes darting, heart thumping as she listened to the cries and the clamour of a struggle.

"Get off me! Get the fuck off me!"

A girl's voice.

Charley listened as the struggle moved through the house. Something smashed. Banging sounds like someone kicking the wall. Whoever it was, she was putting up a heck of a fight.

Why didn't I fight like that? she wondered.

She heard him shout. The girl's voice changed from angry to crying, to begging.

"Let go of me! Please let me go!"

A door slammed and then silence.

He's taken her to the workshop, Charley realised. *He's putting her in the pit like he did with me and Hannah and all the others.*

A cold shiver slithered through her. She felt sick. Did this mean he'd grown tired of her and had found a 'new' Christina? Would he take back the dress and put it on this other girl and start calling her Christina? Would he drag her screaming from the pit and kill her as he had Hannah?

Is this my last night?

It was fully dark when she heard the familiar creak of the stairs. She slid off the bed and stood up, her body rigid with fear.

He entered the bedroom carrying a plate of sandwiches and a glass of milk, seeming to be surprised at her standing there. "I'm sorry to have left you all day," he said. "I've had things to do."

Charley had no breath to speak. She watched him, looking

for signs of his intentions.

"I haven't had time to cook anything, so I've made some sandwiches instead." He offered them, but she was too afraid to take them. "Not hungry? Okay, I'll put them over here then."

He picked up her paintings and leafed through them. "Oh, I see you've been keeping yourself busy. Christina, some of these are really quite good. I never knew you were so artistic."

The only thing Charley heard in all that was that he still was calling her 'Christina'.

He looked up from the sketches. "Have you ever tried wood carving?"

She shook her head.

He put the pictures to one side and smiled. "Maybe I'll teach you one day."

Charley swallowed down her fear. "Who was that I heard before?"

"Heard?"

"Someone screaming...a girl..."

He ran his hand over the bed linen. "Oh, I think you must have been dreaming, Christina. You know what a vivid imagination you have."

Charley didn't push it. He wanted to act like it never happened, but she knew it had. What she couldn't understand was, if he hadn't taken this other girl to swap them, what had he taken her for?

A few days later, when she knew he'd gone out, she tried shouting to the other girl, but never heard a reply or a bang or a knock of acknowledgement. Maybe she wasn't there anymore, or maybe she just couldn't hear Charley's calls.

Whatever the reason, Charley didn't hear anything of the other girl again.

328

Every day he brought her food and emptied the bucket. He told her he was very happy she was here and that he loved her. She knew it wasn't true. He loved something he was pretending she was... a sister who had died or something.

As time went on, she got craftier at playing the game with him. She'd ask about when she was little, or when Christina was little, and he'd tell her some story or other, like the time she went missing and he looked all over the house for her, until he'd found her sleeping in the little cupboard in the alcove. A few days later Charley would bring it up again as if it was her memory. Small things like that never failed to make him smile.

All the while, she hoped she was gaining his trust and he would eventually let his guard down. Maybe even let her off the chain.

For a good while, things went on like that, every day like the one before, and it may have continued to do so.

If she hadn't tried to escape.

Chapter Thirty-One

Gary searched the kitchen, yanking out drawers and checking along the greasy tops.

Nothing.

He tried the living room, searching high and low for spare keys or a landline. Marsden probably used a mobile, but Gary still needed to check the entire house, just in case.

Up on the landing, the dirty, musty stench grew stronger, pervading his throat and sinuses.

He entered the first bedroom. The bed covers were thrown back, the sheets stained and dirty. He didn't initially take much notice of the torn papers strewn around, but he did see the eyelets screwed into the walls. He curled his finger into one and pulled at it thoughtfully.

An eyelet on the other side of the bed had a chain padlocked to it. He examined it, running the chain through his hands to the steel hinged loop at the other end.

A torn piece of paper caught his eye, bright red and black. He flipped a couple of other pieces and found more parts from a painting of a ladybird. He recognised it immediately and knew that Charley had painted it. While she was imprisoned, chained to this wall, she'd painted pictures of home.

Emotion swelled inside him and he had to turn his face away. He couldn't afford to dwell on the ordeal she'd endured all these lost months. He had to find a way to call for help, or to get her out of that hole. He cursed himself for coming here without a phone. What had he been thinking?

Or maybe that had been the idea all along.

The next room was dark as night. He flicked on the light and discovered a cast iron bathtub with a rusty brown tear-drop stain from a dripping tap. The one window had a chipboard sheet nailed over it. The bottom panel of the door was marked with dusty shoe prints, and a chunk of wood was ripped out of the frame. Someone had kicked it in. He wondered what might have happened here.

When he opened the door to the next room, he had to step back, gagging at the stink of something old and rotten.

Thin cotton curtains allowed light to seep through, staining the room in an eerie yellow glow. He fumbled around the doorway and found the sticky plastic casing of the light switch. He flicked the switch a few times, but nothing happened.

He waited on the threshold for his eyes to adjust to the gloom. The smell was like an old potato sack, earthy and rotten. But beneath that hung the putrid smell of decay. Covering his mouth with his sleeve, he went inside.

The room contained an old-fashioned double bed and tall oak headboard. The bed was unmade, the covers ruffled. To his right stood a wardrobe, the doors open and draped with multilayers of drab, old-fashioned women's clothes.

Looking out of place among five vases of shrivelled brown flowers on the dressing table, stood a claw hammer, resting on its scarred head, the wooden handle stained with dark patches.

Gary edged nearer to the bed. He had thought the covers were just ruffled, but on closer inspection, he realised there was something thin lying beneath them, something that looked suspiciously like a body.

This was no bedroom.

It was a crypt.

331

A mausoleum.

As he came closer, he felt like the walls were closing in around him, his nerves tightening like piano strings. Halfway between the bed and the door was about as far as he was prepared to go. He raised himself on tiptoe, craning his neck to see over the ruffled blankets.

Gary covered his mouth.

The faces of two mummified corpses lay huddled together, their rotted heads resting in putrid stains of brown, red, and green. Dark leathery flesh peeled away from the facial bones, the scalps shrunken and detached from the white domes of the skulls. Long brown hair sprouted from the dried scalp of one body, the other was short and white and tinged with dirty yellow. Gary recognised the nicotine stained hair immediately.

Marsden senior's facial bones were shattered, the nose and upper mandible caved inward.

He looked again at the hammer on the dressing table.

The other body must be the mother's. He couldn't see what her injuries were, but he wasn't getting any closer to find out.

Then something moved in Marsden's empty eye socket. Something white and insect-like with long feelers.

It was a moth.

A second emerged from his mouth, followed by another and another. They walked and crawled and crept out of his broken face, some taking to the air, the soft sound of their wings like whispers in the still room, others tumbling onto the pillow where they flapped and writhed as if barely alive.

Gary remembered his dream and began to inch away, retreating all the way out of the oppressive crypt of a bedroom. Only when he was back out on the landing did he release the breath he'd been holding.

If mother and father were dead, only the son could have killed them and laid the corpses in bed together. So it must follow that the son was the Goldilocks Killer, not the father, as

332

he had first thought.

Gary remembered them coming to the house. The son had been lean and strong even then; it was impossible to predict how he might have grown.

There was no more time to waste. He had to get Charley out of that pit before Marsden junior returned.

Chapter Thirty-Two

One day he had asked if she would cook for him. Charley had made cupcakes with her mother one Father's Day and her dad usually let her toss a pancake on Shrove Tuesday, but that seemed more like having fun than real cooking. She'd made eggs and toast and heated stuff in a pan, but that was about as far as her culinary adventures had taken her.

When she explained that she couldn't cook he had laughed and said it was about time she learned. Instead of taking prepared meals up to her, he began taking her down to the kitchen to teach her how to prepare it.

Each time she worked herself up, imagining all kinds of scenarios in which she could turn cookery lessons into an escape, but he kept her chained to his belt and checked her constantly.

After a time of only letting her watch him, he encouraged her to take part in the preparation, but always under his close supervision. Perversely, Charley began to look forward to the sessions as a distraction from reading, drawing or staring longingly out of the window. She'd asked for a TV or a radio, but he wouldn't allow it. She figured it was because he didn't want her to know what was going on outside her four walls. He wanted to be her entire world.

Sometimes he'd stand behind her while showing her how to

do something, separating the yolk from an egg, for example, or correcting the way she used the vegetable peeler. The worst part about it was that he'd move real close, encircling her with his arms, hands over hers. Closer than he should be—closer than she felt comfortable—his breathing becoming ragged as he pressed himself against her.

When she felt him losing control, she'd take a step back and push him away from her. She'd turn to look him in the face and ask a question about what she was doing. She'd deliberately ask it wrong because he loved so much to correct her. He'd tut at how silly she was, take over and demonstrate. Most importantly for Charley though, the moment would pass.

But then came the time that her question didn't make him stop. When she turned to look at him, his eyes were dark and lustful, his lips wet. He pressed her against the table, pinning her there. She tried to push his hands away, but he was much too strong.

He tried to kiss her, his bristly chin scraping her cheek, his horrible breath in her face.

"Stop," she begged. "Please stop."

But he wouldn't stop. She turned her face away, but he followed her with his ugly lips.

"No," she whimpered. "Please, I'm Christina...I'm your *sister*." And when that didn't stop him, she used something she'd been saving, something she had understood from things he had said to her, and other things that he hadn't. "Stop it!" she screamed at him. "You promised you wouldn't do this to me anymore!"

He jumped back from her, his expression shocked. He tilted his face away in shame.

Charley smoothed out the dress, her heart thumping, hands shaking. Her eyes were full of tears, but she refused to let them fall.

"I'm sorry," he said. "I'm...I struggle...with thoughts...

335

emotions."

"I know," she said, doing her best to keep her voice calm and even. She had seized control of the situation and didn't want to lose it. "But it's alright now. It's just that you...you can't touch me like that. That's not what brothers and sisters do."

He grabbed his face in his long bony hands and pinched the flesh. "I'm sorry!" he cried, and dramatically fell to his knees before her. He clawed at her, pulling her to him, his face pressed to her stomach. "I'm sorry! Please forgive me, Christina. It isn't me, it's *him*! He makes me do it!" He looked up at her, his face a horrible contorted mask of misery. "He told me he'd cut it off if I didn't do it to you! He pulled out my thing and put a knife under it and said he'd cut it off if I didn't use it like a man!"

Charley didn't know what to do. She leaned away from him, her hands on the table, looking down at this craziness. She had wanted him to stop, but hadn't expected this reaction.

"And I did it!" he cried. "I did it to you...and all those other... things. I'm sorry, Chrissy, I'm so sorry." He hugged his face to her belly, his arms tightly around her, his tears wetting the dress. "And while I was doing it to you, you used to whisper to me, 'It's alright, Will, it's okay. It's not your fault. I know it's not your fault'. I loved you so much, my sister. I'm so sorry for what we did to you."

"Will?" Charley said quietly. It was the first time she'd ever used his name.

He hitched a few sobs and grew quiet.

"Will?"

He looked up at her, his eyes and nose streaming, his mouth wet and hanging open.

"*He* isn't here now. *He* isn't making you do anything anymore. You can stop it now. You don't have to keep me here. You can let me go. I won't tell anyone about you, I promise. Just...let me go."

336

He searched her eyes, head moving minutely. For a second she thought he would do it. For one fleeting moment she thought he would unchain her and let her leave, but instead, he seized her in a frighteningly powerful grasp, his hot face against her stomach.

"No!" he shouted. "I can't! He *is* here, he's always here! He won't let you go. He won't ever let you go! He'd kill you before I could ever let you go!"

Charley closed her eyes and knew that she would never be able to talk him into releasing her. She would have to continue to survive, make him trust her and hope for the chance to escape.

That chance came sooner than she thought it would.

After the incident, he appeared to mellow some, allowing her downstairs more often and relaxing around her. More importantly though, her ploy had worked, and he didn't touch her inappropriately anymore.

Whenever he went out of the house for any substantial amount of time, he still locked her in the pit, until the day he announced he would teach her how to make the steak and ale pie she once said she enjoyed. He told her he needed to go out to get some ingredients for it.

Charley pretended to be excited, but prepared herself to spend the next hour or so in the chilly darkness of the pit.

He looked at her carefully and said, "I don't need to lock you up this time, do I? You'll be good?"

Charley had to catch her breath and nodded quickly.

He smiled. "You know, one day you might be able to come to the shops with me. We could go out together like we used to."

"Wow, that would be so cool," she said, and smiled

disarmingly. "You can trust me, Will. I don't know why you don't already. I'm not going to run away or anything. I like it here. You're my big brother and I...I love you. You take care of me."

He looked at her for so long that she began to wonder if she had pushed too far. She'd never told him she loved him before, and she'd gone and stumbled over saying it. After all, she wasn't his sister and surely somewhere deep inside he must know that?

"Hmm," he mused. "Maybe next time."

He left, and a little while later she heard the front door close and the faint sound of an engine fade away. She waited a while, listening in case it was just a test and he was silently waiting on the stairs to see what she'd do.

Once she was certain he really had gone, she spent some time carefully examining her chains, the padlocks and the eyelet in the wall. She'd checked them before, but not thoroughly, because she never knew when he might walk in. If he caught her, she'd surely lose any trust she'd built with him and would end up back in the pit.

She tried to twist the eyelet but it was screwed in tight. She wondered if she could dig out the plaster around the bolt, but she didn't have anything to dig with.

In the end she sat on the bed and just waited for him to return.

She heard the van's engine, and a short time later he came into the bedroom and told her everything was ready. She waited for him to unhook the chain at the wall and attach it to his belt, but he didn't. Instead, he told her to sit on the bed. He lifted her foot and looked gravely at her. "If I take this off, I can trust you, can't I?" he asked. "The way you can trust me now?"

Charley nodded, hardly believing he was actually going to unchain her.

But sure enough, he unlocked the small padlock at her ankle

338

and opened the shackle. The flesh was red and sore where the metal had chaffed her skin, but it didn't matter, *she was free of the tether!* Inside she was soaring, her heart pounding so fast. Her leg felt light and free.

On the way to the kitchen, her mind raced around at a million miles an hour. This could be her one and only chance to escape. She had to do something. He'd taken the chain off this time, but he would surely put it back on after the cookery lesson and there was no guarantee that he'd ever take it off again.

She stood by in the kitchen while he showed her the ingredients to make the pie. When he looked away from her, Charley checked the back door. She'd looked at it before, but had always been tethered, so it had been little more than a cursory glance. Now, she saw a key in the lock. Would he leave it unlocked? If not, could she unlock it and get out before he realised what was happening? An old mop leaned against the door, a crumpled cardboard box full of old newspapers on the floor in front of it. It didn't look like the back door was used much. What if the lock was stiff, or if the door was stuck?

"Are you listening to me?"

Charley jumped. "Um, yes."

"What are you doing over there then? Come closer where you can see."

Charley moved a step nearer and saw the paring knife next to the chopping board. Her heart felt as if it was about to explode from her chest.

"First thing we need to do is trim the meat and dice it. You know what dicing is?"

Charley shook her head. She knew what it meant, but hadn't really heard the question.

"Dicing is when you cut something into cubes," he lectured, "like the dice we used to play board games with. Do you remember when we used to play Ludo?"

Charley nodded.

339

He smiled. "We should do that again, you know? Would you like to play Ludo again?"

Charley nodded.

"Anyway, you need all the pieces roughly the same size so that they cook evenly."

Charley nodded, all wide-eyed, as if he was imparting great words of wisdom.

"Here, I'll show you." He picked up the knife and demonstrated by cutting off a strip of meat.

Charley watched him work, trying to gauge how relaxed he was. Maybe this was a test. Maybe he was watching her too.

Yet he seemed focused on cutting the meat, talking, but not once looking at her. She glanced around the kitchen for something she might be able to use against him. But the only lethal looking weapon was right there in his hand.

He glanced up and frowned. "What are you hanging back for? Don't you want to learn?"

She moved right up beside him.

He offered her the knife. "You think you can do that?"

Charley tried to say 'yes', but her mouth was dry as cardboard.

"Take it then," he said, extending the knife toward her. "Come on, it's nothing to be afraid of."

Charley gripped the plastic handle and stared at it. It was only about three inches long, pointed. If she stabbed him with it, would that be enough?

He moved around the back of her, to the left, allowing her to take his place at the chopping board. "Go on," he prompted. "Careful you don't cut yourself."

As if in a dream, she moved the knife toward the meat, but every sense and nerve in her body was directed at the man standing beside her.

Close enough, more than close enough.

She placed the fingers of her left hand on the steak. It was

340

cold and wet and viscous.

"Trim that bit of fat first," he said, pointing. "The white part."

Charley moved the tip of the blade to the divide between the white rind of fat and the red meat. Her pulse thundered in her ears. Cold air sucked into her throat, her chest visibly rising and falling.

She tightened her fist around the handle of the knife.

"Come on, don't be scared," he told her.

She could do it now, right now while he suspected nothing.

But she turned to look at him instead.

He was smiling, and said something that she didn't hear for the blood pounding in her ears.

Then his smile vanished, and she knew he'd realized his dreadful mistake.

NOW!

Charley whirled, left leg moving out, body turning, shoulder coming around. She wasn't big or strong, but her adrenaline-fuelled attack carried enough force to slam him a step backwards.

Her fist bounced off his chest and for a second it seemed as if she'd lost the knife and had only punched him instead of stabbing him.

He cried out, his hands rising like startled birds. He gaped down at himself, the knife protruding from his upper-chest, buried right to the hilt. No blood. Just a black plastic handle sticking out of his chest. Somehow it looked absurd.

He looked dazedly from the knife to Charley. "Why?" he asked.

His face was so ridiculously pained and betrayed, that for a fleeting moment, Charley felt guilty.

And then she ran.

In her panicked flight, she didn't even think about the back door. All she knew was that the knife hadn't killed him, and she had to get as far away from him as she could.

She sped back down the hall to the front door and yanked frantically on the handle. It wouldn't open. She turned the latch, but still it wouldn't budge. It must be locked some other way too, a bolt or...

"Christina!"

She whimpered at the rage in his voice. There wasn't a bolt! She tried it again, but something she couldn't see was preventing the door from opening.

She had to find another way out!

He lurched into the hallway, his shoulder bashing the doorway and knocking him sideways.

"Christina!"

She sprinted up the stairs, taking them two at a time, and headed for the bathroom, the only room she knew for certain had a lock on it. She slammed the door and slid the small brass bolt home. It wasn't much, but it might offer her a little time.

The window was screwed down, so she grabbed the ceramic soap dish and hurled it straight through the frosted glass. The window exploded outward, leaving a gaping, jagged hole. Cold fresh air rushed inside.

"Christina!"

With panic racing through her, she grabbed a long plastic back scrub and knocked out as much of the remaining shards from the frame as she could.

"CHRISTINA!"

Frighteningly close. Too close. Loud and raging.

She threw the scrub aside and leaned over the sink to look at the drop. Below the ledge jutted a mossy, slate roof that was narrow and steep. She clambered up onto the sink, rising to full height and bracing herself with a hand against the ceiling. Cautiously, she extended her bare foot through the broken window and placed it on the outside sill. Tiny needles of glass stabbed the ball of her foot, but she gritted her teeth and

342

ignored them.

The door handle rattled. "Christina? Christina! Open the door!" He rattled it again. "You fucking little bitch! Open this door right now!"

Despite the raging panic, Charley forced herself to stay in control. She ducked under the glass shards still in the frame and threaded the rest of her body out onto the ledge.

The cold air chilled her like spring water fresh from the mountain. She hadn't breathed fresh air for so long that it burned her lungs.

Marsden kicked the door. *BOOM!*

She prayed the bolt would hold just a little longer.

Clinging tightly to the frame, being careful not to cut herself, she extended her left foot downward, her right knee bending, as she attempted to reach the small roof below.

An even louder bang against the door shook the house. The frame split but somehow the latch still held. With the next kick, he would be in.

Charley stretched down with her foot as far as she could, but her toes couldn't reach the roof!

Another heavy kick ripped a chunk of wood from the jamb. The door flew open, struck the wall and bounced back. He kicked it wide again and saw her out on the ledge. His eyes grew wide and terrified, as if she was a small child in danger.

"Christina!" he screamed and ran at her, his hands reaching out to drag her back inside.

Charley let go.

She felt his hands grasped for her as she dropped straight down onto the slate roof, skinning her bare knees, before sliding helplessly down the mossy incline toward the drop. As she went over, she grabbed onto the old cast iron guttering; which might have held her if the timber it was screwed to hadn't been rotten. Her weight ripped out the support brackets and she plummeted another eight feet or so to the ground. The heavy gutter crashed down with a dull clang, narrowly missing her.

She landed loose and messy, the grassy earth below the window cushioning the fall a little. She checked herself. Nothing seemed to be broken, but her left thigh and arm hurt from the landing, and her knees were bleeding over the black and green slime she'd picked up from her slide down the roof.

Marsden leaned out of the broken window. "Christina! Oh my God! Are you alright? Stay where you are!"

He disappeared back into the house, but she wasn't about to wait for him. Behind her, darkness stretched away to distant winking lights that seemed about a million miles away. She scrambled to her feet and ran around the house, limping and staggering a little, sick and dizzy from the fall.

An unlit path led away. There was nothing but trees and bushes, no other houses or buildings, no neighbours. No one was going to help her. The road was the only way out of there.

She was on her own.

Charley ran as fast as she could along the dirt road, her left leg threatening to give way with each stride. The cold wind billowed her thin dress and ruffled her hair. Loose stones and the textured earth dug painfully into the soles of her bare feet, but she couldn't slow, couldn't weaken.

She snatched a glance back over her shoulder. He was nowhere in sight. Maybe he'd gone to the back door, expecting her to have waited for him.

But then she heard him shout, "Christina!"

She hobbled faster, harder, holding onto her hurt leg, her arm aching.

Next came the growl of an engine.

Charley whimpered. She hadn't even reached those trees yet. Maybe she had been too hasty in her decision. Maybe if she'd waited a little longer, he might have left her in the house alone and unchained, and then she could have escaped at her leisure. Or perhaps he might have taken her to the shops with him as he had promised and she could have raised the alarm.

But it was too late now. She was running for her life.

The van quickly closed the gap between them, roaring right up behind her before he braked hard. The wheels locked, the tyres sliding on the damp dirt.

"Christina! Stop!"

She kept going. Kept pushing. Didn't look back.

The engine roared again and the van raced by her, half off the path. He braked, the backend sliding sideways, the tyres throwing up earth and stones.

He jumped out. "Christina!"

Charley veered right, off the road and into the long grass, hoping he would come around the front of the van before realising she'd gone around the back. But as she limped past the back doors, he was right there, lunging, his strong hands catching her and spinning her around.

Charley screamed and fought as hard as she could, lashing out with her fists. He grabbed her arms in painfully strong fingers and shook her.

"Christina! Stop it! Stop it!"

The knife was still sticking out of his chest. A little blood had leaked from the wound and soaked into his shirt.

Charley grabbed the handle and twisted it.

Marsden threw back his head and screamed, but he wouldn't let go of her. She hung on and twisted the knife the other way.

Still screaming, he drew back his fist, and then everything went black.

Consciousness rose slowly to the surface, like lazy bubbles in a fish tank, and with them exploded the pain. Pain with horns and teeth. Pain that bit and chewed. Her arm and thigh ached,

345

bruised to the bone, but the grinding hot throb in her tight face was both terrible and immense.

When she tried to open her eyes, only the right one worked. The other remained tightly shut. Her vision was blurred, but she already knew she was back in the pit. Both doors above her were open. The eight windows were ebony. She had no way of knowing how long she had been unconscious.

She tried to lick her dry, shrivelled lips, but her tongue was glued to the roof of her gooey mouth. Her back and limbs screamed in protest when she tried to move, her head swirling with pain when she tried to lift it.

"I'm cold," she whispered weakly. "So cold."

She hugged her arms across her chest and realised she was dressed only in her vest and underwear. The summer dress was gone.

"Help me," she whispered weakly. "Please. Help me. Daddy. Please, help me."

"No one's coming to help you," Marsden said, from somewhere out of view. "Your filthy daddy doesn't care about you. No one's looking for you. No one misses you. No one cares about you. I was the only one."

"You're a liar!" She tried to shout it, but her throat hurt, and the words crashed through her fractured face like stabbing knives.

"Am I?"

Yes you are, Charley thought. *My mum and dad miss me and are looking for me. My dad will never stop looking for me. Ever.* But her face hurt too much to speak it out loud.

"You betrayed me, Christina. I thought you were different this time. I thought I could trust you and that you trusted me."

Charley wasn't interested in his craziness anymore. The façade lay in tatters. The actors out of their costumes. "My face hurts," she whimpered, but the words were malformed - *ay hace urts* - as she tried not to move her lips or jaw too much.

346

"So does my fucking chest," he sneered. "I had to put four stitches into it."

He appeared at the edge of the pit, standing high, almost as if he was at the top of a tall mountain, peering down at her. He was bare-chested, the undressed wound puckered with amateur self-stitching that would surely heal in an ugly raised and twisted scar. Aside from the freshly inflicted wound, his torso was covered in old scars, burns and blemishes.

"You're going to pay for sticking this blade in me. I'm going to make you suffer, you little bitch." He raised the knife, his jaw tight, his face twisting in a grotesque sneer. "I'm going to stick this in your sweet little pussy and slit you wide. Then I'll pull out your insides and hold them up where you can see them, until the light goes out of your eyes."

Charley lay there, helpless and in pain while he stood with his arms outstretched, his head back, and his hands curled into claws.

He dropped his arms. "But now," he said, his grin cruel and crazy. "Now."

He jumped down into the pit and unbuttoned his jeans. "Now I'm going to do to you what I should have done that day in the kitchen." He climbed on top of her, his weight crushing her, the pressure making her face feel like it was going to explode.

"Please," she whispered, but it was no use. She had nothing left. There wasn't anything she could say that would stop him now.

His excited, foul breath was in her face. She turned away and closed her eyes, letting her mind drift from the horror. She thought about her mum and her dad, about Mister Whiskers. She imagined her room with her name on the door and all her things. They would all still be there waiting for her.

A single tear trickled from the corner of her eye. *And that's all*, she thought, *that's the only tear I'm going to cry over this.*

She looked defiantly into his face, refusing to cower.

He pushed himself up to gaze mockingly down at her, his eyes cold and black and full of lust. The skin around his wound was fiery red and inflamed. Four black sutures tugged the flesh together.

"Aw, are you crying?"

She let her hand creep to the floor of the pit and rubbed it across the concrete, her fingers picking up a fine layer of gritty dirt.

"Don't worry," he said, his livery lips stretching into a gloating grin. "This won't take long."

He looked between them, pushing his jeans further down.

Charley jammed her fingers into the chest wound, twisting them deep into the muscle.

The shock on his face and the shrillness of his scream was the most satisfying thing Charley had ever witnessed.

The stitches burst and the wound split wide.

He tried to push away, but her fingers hooked under the skin, stretching it out like a rubber sheet.

Blood ran fast and hot down her arm.

Still screaming, he tore her hand away and scrambled into the corner like a kicked dog. He peered down at the blood streaming down his chest, his mouth a downward curve of pain. He cupped the ragged hole, his hand trembling, the raw meat of the wound speckled with the dirt she'd picked up off the concrete.

"You fucking little *BITCH!*" he screamed, his eyes burning with hatred.

"Yeah," Charley said weakly. "And don't you fucking forget it."

He grasped the barred door with one hand, his other still protecting the wound, and pulled himself to his feet. He made a move toward her, maybe to kick her, then grimaced and stepped back, gingerly holding his chest. His torso was slick

348

with sweat.

She smiled. He was crying. She'd made him cry.

"You were *nothing* like Christina," he screamed at her. "You never fooled me! Never! I knew what you were up to all the time! I'm going to make you suffer, bitch! I'm going to enjoy killing you!"

Charley closed her eyes. A thick, corded pulse of pain throbbed through her head and face. She hovered at the edge of darkness, about to pass out, but had the strength to whisper one last thing to enrage him even more.

"Yeah, yeah," she mocked. "Bring it on."

He climbed out of the pit, blood spattering the grey concrete, and slammed both doors down over her.

In the cool darkness, Charley managed to smile before she slipped out of consciousness.

No matter what happened now, she'd won.

Charley drifted in and out of sleep with no idea if she'd been lying there for hours or days. Her body was an aching misery from head to foot, and she was so thirsty and hungry. It felt like the end.

Maybe I'll die tonight, she thought, and the notion of dying hardly concerned her. The pain was intense enough to make her not care anymore. Maybe she would fall asleep and not wake up again. It would be over, and her suffering would end.

Light on her eyelids made her wonder if he'd come back while she was asleep and opened the doors. But when she cracked open her one good eye, she found the pit closed, but filled with a strange, shimmering glow.

A young blonde-haired girl sat cross-legged, by her side, looking down on her with sad blue eyes.

Charley opened her mouth to ask who she was and what she

was doing here, but the little girl placed a finger to her rosebud lips.

Shhhhh.

The whisper seemed to come from nowhere and everywhere.

Emma.

I'm Emma.

Emma.

Hang on, Charley.

He was lost, but he's coming for you now.

"Daddy?" Charley whispered.

The little girl nodded.

He's coming, Charley, just hang on. Hang on a little longer.

Charley closed her eyes and wondered if she was dreaming, or maybe even hallucinating.

Hang on, Charley.

Just a little longer.

When she opened her eye again, the little girl was gone.

The next time she awoke, it was to the sound of the outer door opening. Light poured into her one good eye like needles. She dragged the thin quilt over her face.

This is it, she thought. *He's here to rape me and kill me as he said he would.*

But then she heard an unfamiliar, yet familiar, voice.

"Hey! Vicky! I'm gonna get you out of here."

That wasn't him.

It was...she knew that voice...could it be? She pushed the quilt down and squinted at the blurry figure silhouetted against the artificial light.

"Oh my God," he uttered, but she didn't know why.

"Daddy?" she asked.

350

For a moment, he didn't answer, seeming to sway a little. "No, I'm not your daddy," he told her, "but I'm going to get you out of here. I'm going to get you back to your daddy."

And then she knew it *was* his voice, it was her dad's voice. He had come for her just as the little blonde-haired girl had said he would. Just as she always knew he would.

But he didn't know it was her, he didn't recognise her.

"Daddy," she whispered, her throat dry and hoarse, "it's me...it's Charley."

His eyes widened, and then he leaned onto the bars to look more closely at her.

"Charley?" he asked carefully, as if her name might crumble to nothing.

She nodded, tears flowing at just hearing him say her name again.

"Dad," she cried. "It's me, it's Charley."

He fell onto the bars, scrambled over them, his hands reaching for her. "Charley, oh my God! Oh my God! Is it really you?"

Despite the pain and her weakness, she raised herself up to tenderly touch his fingers. "It's really me," she whispered. "I knew you'd come. I always knew you'd come and find me. You promised me you would."

He grasped her hand, crying. His grip warm and strong and protective. She'd never seen him cry before, she didn't like it.

"Oh my God, Charley! I can't believe it! I can't believe it's you. My sweet pea, my poor baby!"

Charley closed her eyes as he gently cupped the good side of her face. It made the other side hurt, but she didn't care. His touch was everything.

He was here.

Her dad was here.

Now everything would be alright.

Chapter Thirty-Three

Gary hurried back to the sitting room and peered through the hazy grey window. The dirt road was deserted. He ran a hand through his hair and turned back to the room. With no key or phone, he had no choice but to find a way to break Charley out of that hole, and fast.

As he stood there thinking about what he should do, Marsden's white Transit van appeared from behind the copse of trees and began its way toward the house.

If Gary had taken one more glance behind him, he would have seen it, but instead, he rushed back down the hall to the workshop.

"Did you find it?" Charley asked hopefully when he appeared at the edge of the pit.

"No, Sweetheart," he replied, "but I'm going to find another way to get you out."

He rummaged through the tools again, spotting a big crowbar hiding in the corner between the wall and the workbench. It was a heavy duty, hexagonal bar with a flat, wedge at one end and a goose-necked vee for extracting nails at the other. He hefted the bar in his hands, savouring the weight, and returned to the pit.

He forced the wedge end of the crowbar into the gap between the steel door frame and the concrete next to the lower hinge and pried.

Nothing much moved.

He tried again, repeatedly yanking the crowbar back and forth in fast, hard jerks in an attempt to loosen the bolts. When he checked the hinge plate, he found it had gained a couple of millimetre play on the bolts.

"Is it working?" Charley asked.

Gary gave her a nervous smile. "I think so."

The gap between the hinge plate and the concrete still wasn't wide enough to accommodate the wedge, so he went back to work on the frame, yanking backwards and forwards, leaning on the bar and grunting with effort. Pinpricks of sweat broke out across his forehead.

He checked the progress. The hinge plate had moved a tiny bit more, but he couldn't call it progress. The steel wedge was still too thick to squeeze into the gap.

What about a hammer?

Maybe he could pound the crowbar into the gap and then he should be able to lever the bolts right out of the concrete.

Or maybe he could simply smash the concrete around the bolts!

He let the crowbar fall to the ground with a heavy clang and turned away.

"Where are you going?" Charley asked.

"Just need a hammer," he told her.

He found a weighty lump hammer and brought it back.

"Cover your eyes, Charley, I'm going to smash the concrete."

Charley turned her face away.

Gary pounded the concrete, shattering it into a mosaic of broken chunks. When he could see two of the three steel rawl plugs, he tried pulling the corner of the cage door, but it still held-fast. He brought the hammer down a few more times and the hinge broke free of its mooring.

He grinned triumphantly, ready to move over to the other hinge. "We've got this, Charley! I'll have you out of there in a few seconds."

Charley smiled up at him, but then her face changed and her eyes widened in alarm.

"*DAD, LOOK OUT!*" she cried, and then the world seemed to explode, and the bars rushed up to meet him.

Chapter Thirty-Four

Fractured light, like piercing white knives, sliced through his brain, while ribbons of colour looped around and burst apart like fireworks behind his eyelids.

Someone slapped his face, hard and sharp.

"Come on, wake up. You aren't hurt that bad."

Gary raised his head, waves of sickly pain radiating from the back of his skull, and managed to focus on the man sitting on one of the partially-stripped Queen Anne chairs. His face was long, thin, and he was wearing the same black wool hat he wore on the day he strangled poor Emma to death. He'd filled out some, but Gary still recognised the boy who had collected the desk with his father.

The son of Marsden.

The face of the Goldilocks Killer.

"What were you planning on doing with this?" he asked, raising the knife Gary had brought with him.

Gary swallowed. Nothing he could say was going to sound good.

He couldn't move his arms and felt terribly constricted. When he looked down at himself, he found he was tied to the other chair, the rope coiled tightly around his body from his shoulders right down to his waist. His hands poked out from the fold of his lap, wrists bound with blue nylon cord, palms together as if in prayer.

Marsden gripped Gary's jaw in a strong grasp and shook it violently. "Look at me!" he spat. "What are you doing here?" He was agitated, his face greasy, eyes darting. "How did you find me? *How did you find me?*"

Gary tore his face from Marsden's grasp. "Charley!" he cried, the ropes creaking as he strained to look behind him.

"I'm here, Dad! I'm okay."

Marsden grabbed his jaw again and yanked his face forwards. "Oh, don't you worry about her. It's yourself you need to worry about now."

Gary's eyes rolled, his eyelids flickering.

"I know who you are," Marsden sneered. "You're the *father*. The dirty father. Well who has all the power now? Who can make who do those...those *disgusting* things? You think I liked it? You think I liked what you made me do to her?"

"I didn't make you do anything," Gary said.

"*YES, YOU DID!*" Marsden roared. "She was twelve! She was my sister and you made me do all those things to her. Then you left her in the pit to die!"

"It wasn't me," Gary told him. "I'm not your father."

Marsden rose up out of his seat and grabbed Gary by the throat, squeezing hard. "Don't fucking lie to me!"

Just as a ring of darkness began to gather at the edges of Gary's vision, Marsden let go and slapped him solidly around the face. Gary's ears rang.

"*HOW DID YOU FIND ME?*" Marsden screamed, spraying spittle into Gary's face.

Gary's lips stretched across is gritted teeth. "You wouldn't believe me if I told you."

Marsden sat back down. "Wouldn't I?" His tongue slipped out and moistened his dark lips. "Who else knows you're here?"

Gary hesitated.

"Don't lie to me!" Marsden warned. He put the knife to one

side and raised a flat, broad, wood chisel. "You see this? If you lie to me, I'll hurt you with it!" He grabbed a handful of Gary's hair and yanked his head back. The chisel's razor-edge pressed into his throat, shaving off a sliver of skin. "Who else knows you're here? *Who else?"*

"A friend knows!" Gary blurted. He was taking a risk but had to buy some time.

Marsden let go of his hair and regarded him carefully. "A friend? What friend? The tall one? Where is he? What was the plan? You come here and look around and then what?"

Gary tried to think, but the pain bouncing around his head dulled his wits. "I told him...if he didn't...it *I* didn't...contact him after a certain amount of time, he should call the police."

Marsden glanced toward the door and its small windows. "How much time?"

Gary didn't reply.

Marsden half rose off the chair again. *"HOW MUCH FUCKING TIME!"*

"About an hour!" Gary cried. "About an hour."

Marsden took a phone out of his pocket and checked the time. "An hour?" He dragged the chair over to the double doors and climbed onto the seat so he could peer out through the windows. "I don't see anyone coming," he said. "An hour from when?"

Gary tried to gather time, the time he had set off, the time he had arrived, the time he'd spent looking around the house. The minutes had gotten away from him. The truth was that he had no idea what time it was or how long he'd been here.

"You've been out cold for twenty minutes," Marsden said. "And it looks like you've done plenty while you've been here, snooping around and smashing up my place!" He turned away from the window to look at him. "I think you're lying to me."

"I'm not. Lance will have called the police by now; they'll be here any minute."

357

Marsden jumped down from the chair. "Fucking 'Lance'. I don't think so." He slid the hat off his head and tossed it onto the workbench. "I think you're lying." He dragged the chair back to Gary and sat down. "So now I'm going to have to hurt you."

Marsden grasped Gary's ankle and slipped off one of his shoes.

Gary panted rapidly. "What are you going to do?"

"That little game you used to play with a darning needle, or sometimes a pair of pliers, if you were in a real bad mood."

"Look… that wasn't me. I'm not your–"

"*SHUT YOUR FUCKING MOUTH!*"

Gary shrank back.

Marsden pressed a hand into Gary's shoulder, staring intensely into his eyes. "Just be quiet and take it like a man."

Gary tried to stay calm as Marsden stripped the shoe and sock from his other foot, but when the cold edge of the chisel touched his skin, he panicked, fighting against the ropes and trying to twist his foot away.

Marsden sprang up, his face red and angry, an ugly blue vein bulging across his forehead like a twisted root. He grabbed Gary's face and held it firm, his nails digging into his cheek. The chisel hovered a few millimetres from his eye. "Move your foot again and I'll take your fucking eye out and feed it to that little bitch!"

Gary swallowed hard and placed his feet back on the gritty, cold concrete.

Marsden smiled. "That's better. That's a good boy. That's a good little boy."

The razor edge of the chisel pressed into the knuckle of his big toe.

"This little piggy went to market," Marsden rhymed.

The chisel slid to the next toe.

"This little piggy stayed home."

358

Gary glanced frantically around him.

"This little piggy had roast beef, and this little piggy had none."

Marsden raised his head to look at Gary. Grinning, he said, "And *this* little piggy went *weeeeeee...*"

Gary screamed and strained against his ropes, gasping in agony at the split of flesh and the crack of bone. Worms of darkness wriggled at the edges of his vision and it was only Charley's hysterical voice shouting, '*Dad! Dad!*' that brought him back again.

"*Jesus, oh Jesus,*" Gary gasped.

Marsden sat back on the chair, a small pink ball of flesh between his finger and thumb. "Lie to me again and I might cut off something more useful than your little toe. Do you understand me?"

Gary stared at him, his breath rushing through gritted teeth. Silver ribbons of sweat streamed down the sides of his face.

Marsden examined the bloody toe, rolling it between his finger and thumb. He offered it to Gary. "Eat it."

Gary shook his head.

"I said 'eat it'!" Marsden tried to force the toe into Gary's mouth, but he squeezed his lips together and turned his face away. "Eat it, or I'll start cutting pieces off her and feeding them to you instead."

Gary stopped resisting. Shaking, breathing hard, he let his quivering lips part.

Marsden thumbed the toe into Gary's mouth.

"Now swallow it."

The toe was warm, and gritty with dust from the floor. The coppery tang of blood smeared his tongue. His own blood. The toe rolled to the back of his throat like a nub of gristle. He heaved, clenching down the nausea and swallowed, feeling the hard ball of flesh and bone squeeze all the way down his oesophagus and into his stomach.

Marsden looked him over with a satisfaction that gradually turned into curiosity.

"You shouldn't have come here," he said. "This is *my* place. You thought you were going to be the *big hero*? Save Christina?" His face suddenly filled with confusion. "Christina?" He grasped his forehead. "No, no," he whispered. "Not Christina. Christina's dead. Christina's..." His face crumpled. "I only wanted to make it up to her. I just wanted us to be like we used to be. But they were all liars! Pretending, every one of them. They tried to fool me, but I saw through them. I saw through them *every time*. And then *he* told me it was time to make them suffer."

Oh my God, Gary thought, *he's completely insane.*

"I'm going to make you suffer for what you did to me. And you're going to suffer for what you did to Christina. I'm going to cut and stab and burn you, just like you did to me! You bastard! *Just like you did to me!*"

Gary shook his head. "I didn't touch you. It wasn't me."

"*SHUT UP!*" He pointed at the pit. "She's yours, isn't she? That lying slutty little bitch! I'm going to fuck her! I'm going to fuck her and then I'm going to gut her like the slutty little bitch she is!" He grabbed Gary's face. "What do you think about that, *Mister Hero?* What do you think about *that?*"

Gary shook his face out of Marsden's hand. "You touch her, and I'll fucking kill you!"

Marsden jabbed the chisel under Gary's chin, the blade cutting into the flesh. He held it there, staring into Gary's eyes, chest steadily rising and falling.

Gary stared defiantly back at him, refusing to shrink away from the stinging blade. Thick blood oozed down his neck and into the hollow of his throat.

Marsden let the chisel fall away, as if he'd suddenly become bored with the game. He took out his phone and looked at the screen. "I have something I need to do."

360

He checked the ropes, inspecting the knots, and testing the cords around his legs. He nodded, satisfied with his work.

"When I come back, you're going to die screaming."

He strolled off, taking Gary's kitchen knife with him, and climbed the stairs.

When he'd gone, Gary let his head fall back, relieved for this respite, however brief it might be. "Oh my God," he groaned. Rivers of cold sweat streamed down the sides of his face. His foot throbbed like a mouth full of rotted teeth and his head felt as if it might split apart at any second.

"Dad? Dad? Are you okay?" Charley's voice, small and afraid.

"I'm okay, Sweet Pea," he called. "I'm okay. Don't worry about me."

I have to get out of this! For Charley's sake. I have to fucking get out!

He strained against the ropes, teeth gritted, twisting and writhing, but no matter how hard he fought, he couldn't loosen his bindings.

"Dad?"

He stopped struggling and slumped, exhausted. He was going to die horribly in this stinking place and leave his daughter to the vile purposes of this monster.

What kind of a man was he? What kind of a *father* was he?

"Daddy?"

"I'm sorry, Charley," Gary said. He couldn't turn his head enough to see her. "I've messed everything up."

"Dad, Emma's here."

Gary searched the workshop and spotted her standing quietly by the stairs. Dozens of white moths danced and fluttered above and around her. More crawled over her blue coat, the walls, and stair rail.

He stared at her fearfully, not knowing what to expect.

She slowly raised a small hand and gently placed it on her

361

chest. She took in a long, deep breath, her chest and shoulders rising, held it for a few seconds, and then let it all out again, her chest and shoulders falling.

She took another, chest expanding, held it, and let it out again.

Gary shook his head, not understanding what she was showing him. Was she making some reference to him trying to resuscitate her?

Emma pointed at him. Breathed in again, held it, let it out.

"I think she wants you to do what's she's doing, Dad, breathe like she's breathing."

Gary copied her, filling his lungs and grimacing as the creaking ropes tightened. She held the breath and so did Gary. The rope stretched taut across his chest and cut into his shoulders. She let the breath out again, and Gary followed suit, forcing all the air from his lungs.

His eyes widened as the ropes slipped a little.

Emma took another deep breath and Gary followed suit, closing his eyes and concentrating, inflating his chest until the rope cut into his shoulders. When he let it out, the bindings slipped another fraction.

Gary closed his eyes and kept breathing, feeling the rope slacken bit by bit. His head swam and his fingers tingled as they had that day at the park. The breaths and the compressions, the dizzying nausea. That long dark highway that had seemed to stretch out forever.

Only this time it was working. It *was* making a difference. This time he *could* save his little girl.

He opened his eyes, almost cackling with nervous laughter at how much the ropes had loosened. He wriggled his body, coaxing the uppermost loops off his shoulders.

He looked for Emma, but she was no longer standing beside the stairs. Only a few moths remained.

Gary went back to work on the ropes.

With no idea how long it might be before Marsden returned, he had to work quickly to free himself. He pushed on the floor with the balls of his feet, lifting himself. The ropes had slackened, but he was still bound to the tall chair back.

He leaned into the ropes, hoping to loosen them more than they already were. He froze. Besides the alarming amount of blood leaking from the stub of his severed toe, he saw that Marsden had left the chisel lying there on the floor.

Gary's mind raced. He needed to get a hold of that chisel. He had to get down on the floor somehow. Tipping the chair over was the only way.

What if it went wrong and he got stuck there?

Yeah? Well what if you just wait for him to come back and let him kill both you and Charley instead?

He rocked from side to side, using his upper body to get the chair moving. The two right legs lifted, but nowhere near tipping point, and fell back. He kept trying, finding the right timing, repeating the motion until he gave the ground a good push with his uninjured foot.

Time seemed to slow down, his foot off the floor, his butt sliding on the seat, the ropes pulling at him. He braced himself, but the impact was far more violent than he had expected from such a relatively short fall. His head whiplashed against the concrete, hard enough for him to see stars. A thick wave of pain surged through him and settled sickeningly in his gut.

He spared a second to let the nausea subside, then began shuffling himself and the chair clockwise, inch by inch, toward the chisel.

Come on! he urged himself, his eyes constantly flicking toward the stairs. *Just a little more.*

He heard a noise. The television?

Footsteps.

He was coming back!

Gary renewed his efforts, trying to bunny hop off his

shoulder and drag the rest of him with it. But it was too slow. He wasn't going to make it before Marsden walked down the stairs and discovered him, mid-escape.

COME ON, YOU FUCKING LOSER!

Another sound like the quiet click of a cupboard door closing. More footsteps.

Gary stopped and listened, expecting to see Marsden come striding down the steps at any moment. He waited, sweat in his eyes, his breathing harsh and ragged.

When I come back, you're going to die screaming.

The sound of the television grew muffled and all was quiet again.

He couldn't believe it.

There was still time!

Gary wriggled and shuffled himself into position. The chisel was within his reach, but the ropes around his waist weren't loose enough for him to grasp it. Grunting with effort, he stretched out, turning his body, straining his muscles. His fingertips touched the wooden handle. He tried to draw the chisel toward him, but his hand was slick with sweat. He curled his fingers, the nail of his middle finger finding a small chip in the grain. As he drew the chisel toward him, a thin splinter slid under his fingernail like a hot needle. A rind of blood seeped from under his nail and beaded on his fingertip. He gritted his teeth as the splinter drove deeper into his nail bed. The pain was excruciating, but he couldn't let go when he was so close. He lifted the handle, praying that the splinter wouldn't break, secured it with his thumb and drew it into his palm. He closed his fist triumphantly around it.

YES!

He took a breather. Sweat stung his eyes; the groove of his back hot and slick.

He flipped the blade toward himself, holding it with both hands, and made firm cutting motions across the bindings. The chisel's keen edge sliced through the rope, the coils falling away, one by one, until his torso was free of the chair. He trapped the chisel between his knees and drew the nylon cord around his wrists quickly back and forth across the blade. The chisel slipped a few times, but finally, the rope gave way and he was able to untie his legs.

He got to his feet, his whole body throbbing intensely. He tried to pull the splinter out, but it broke, leaving most of it buried in his nail bed. Nothing he could do about it. He checked his foot. Blood still leaked from the raw stump where his little toe used to be. He didn't have time to deal with it. Marsden could return at any moment.

He limped over to Charley, his limbs protesting. "I'm going upstairs."

There was no protest from her this time, but her eyes shone with fear. She looked at the chisel in his hand and knew what he was going to do. What he *had* to do.

"Be careful, Dad," she whispered.

It was hard to break away and leave her, but he stood up straight and tested some weight on his injured foot. A sharp pain shot through his instep. He'd have to walk on his heel.

"I'll be back for you soon," he promised, hoping to God it was true.

He limped to the stairs, each step driving a spike of pain through his injured foot and a small spurt of blood from the stump. He climbed the wooden risers quietly and crept into the empty kitchen.

TV sound filtered in from the front room. The steak was gone from the chopping board, and the knives too. He had the chisel, but another knife might come in handy.

He opened the drawer, remembering from when he'd searched for the key. He ignored the chef's knife and opted for a utility knife with a black handle instead. It felt good in his hand and the blade was narrow.

365

Knife in one hand, chisel in the other, he limped to the hall door and listened. *The Simpsons* theme tune played. He leaned against the jamb, opening the door just enough so that he could peek down the hall.

A drop of sweat ran into his eye and he wiped it away.

The hall was empty.

Using the wall to steady himself, he limped along, a greasy line of bloody heel prints, like red commas, marking his path.

A floorboard creaked, and he froze, but the Simpson's theme was growing to a crescendo.

He eased up to the living room door, keeping his body close to the wall. Shivering, face streaming with perspiration, he peeped carefully around the frame.

The TV was playing to an empty room.

"Oh shit," Gary whispered.

Marsden had righted the sofa, but everything else was much as he had left it. The box of clothes was still out on the floor, the broken door lying on the carpet along with splinters of wood from the smashed top.

Gary looked behind him at the staircase. Maybe Marsden had gone up there. Should he go into the living room and wait for him? Hide behind the door and jump him as he came in?

But what if he's just gone to the loo before heading back to the workshop.

It didn't matter. If that happened, he would quietly follow and take him out down the hall or in the kitchen. He'd still have the advantage.

He stepped into the living room, planning to hide behind the door, and immediately saw Marsden standing with his back to him at the rear of the room.

Gary froze.

Marsden turned toward him, but he was looking at something in his hands. Gary stepped quietly back around the doorway and against the wall in the hall.

366

He took a couple of steadying breaths before risking a peek around the jamb.

Marsden was now in front of the TV with his back to Gary. On the flat screen, Homer was dreaming of doughnuts.

He was watching the fucking Simpsons!

Not only that, the red 'recording' light showed on the front of the DVD player.

That was what he had left for? To record an episode of the Simpsons?

Marsden chuckled and raised something to his mouth. Gary leaned out a little to get a better look, and saw him slicing pieces off an apple with a paring knife.

Gary wiped more sweat from his eyes and wondered how he should handle this. Should he try to creep up on him? What if a board creaked or a shadow alerted him?

Could he take him anyway?

He had to. If he failed, he wouldn't be the only one to pay the price. He *had* to get this right for Charley.

He squeezed his eyes tight and gritted his teeth.

Come on, he urged himself.

The knife came up with another slice of apple. Marsden took it off the blade and chewed.

He started to leave, his eyes still on the TV screen. In another second it would be too late.

Gary rushed him.

It should have worked. He had two blades, the element of surprise, and Marsden was facing away from him, but when his injured foot came down on the varnished part of the floor, his blood-slicked heel slid out from under him, squeaking across the polished surface. His leg skidded out in front of him, his back muscles screaming as he went down on the knee of his good leg.

Marsden whirled, his startled expression twisting quickly into a snarl of rage.

367

Gary was half up when Marsden barrelled into him, carrying him back a couple of steps and slamming him into the open door. He saw a flash of steel and tried to turn his body, but his shoulder lit up in agony as the knife punctured the hollow beneath his clavicle and pierced a nerve cluster there. His hand went into spasm and he lost the chisel, his fingers convulsing while burning electric shocks of pain raced up and down his arm.

Marsden yanked the blade free, spraying a fine line of red drops across the wall.

Gary shoved off the door, the two of them twisting around together. His toes caught under a ruck in the carpet and he fell, bringing Marsden down on top of him.

With his left arm useless, he was as good as fighting with one arm tied behind his back. He lashed out with the knife, but Marsden caught Gary's wrist and forced it to the floor, kneeling on the forearm, grinding the muscles and forcing Gary's hand to open.

The killer slid the knife toward the middle of the room and shifted his weight, getting his knee up onto Gary's chest and pressing the knife into his throat.

"Tricky, tricky," Marsden gasped, sucking air through gritted teeth.

He delivered two stunning blows to Gary's face. Something cracked inside Gary's head, his nose burst, and a Milky Way of stars exploded before he lost focus and slipped into inky blackness, his eyes rolling under waves of unconsciousness.

When he came to again, Marsden was dragging him across the floor by the scruff of his clothes. He caught a glimpse of the chef's knife among the DVDs, but the killer sent it spinning up against the skirting board with the toe of his boot.

"Come into my place and wreck it, would you?" Marsden shouted, spittle flying. "Come in and think you can kill *me?*"

Pain screamed from every fibre of Gary's body. His left arm

368

lay useless on the carpet. Blood in the back of his throat choked him. Tooth fragments, like pieces of shattered ceramic, littered his mouth.

Marsden grabbed a handful of the clothes from the cardboard box. "You liked my souvenirs?" he asked. "Her stuff's in here." He found Charley's purple cap and sat it on his head. "What do you think? Maybe I'll make her wear it when I fuck her."

He knocked the cap off his head and repositioned himself, pressing the knife into Gary's throat. "Yeah. Tricky. Sneaky. Just like always. I think I need to finish you right now, before you surprise me again."

Marsden leaned in and Gary felt the blade drag at the flesh of his throat, felt the burning pain of the skin opening. In that moment, he was filled with the same horror and regret that he'd felt in his dream, knowing that this was how it ended. Knowing that he'd failed Charley once more.

We all die alone.

Marsden stopped and looked at him more closely. "Just how *did* you find me?"

Gary blinked slowly and smiled despite the pain and the hot blood streaming from his wounds. "Emma showed me."

"Emma?" Marsden frowned. "Who's Emma?"

"You know," Gary said. "Emma."

Marsden gave him a narrow, puzzled look.

A white moth landed on his chest. As he peered down at it, another landed on his cheek. He shook it off, flicking at it with his free hand. More appeared from out of nowhere. They flapped and swarmed around his head, fluttering and bumping and scuttling across his face. They invaded his open mouth, their dry legs and bodies on his lips and tongue, worming into the space between his lips and gums. More crawled into his ears and nostrils.

He panicked, shouting and forgetting about Gary; spitting

out moths, thrashing his head around and lashing out with his arms.

And then Emma's strangled, shrieking visage emerged before him, moths crawling all over her face, her eyes screaming, the whites full of blood.

Marsden let out a terrified scream of his own, his hands crossing over his face. His t-shirt rose to reveal his scarred, pasty white stomach over the waistband of his jeans.

Gary grabbed the long splinter of wood from the shattered cupboard top and plunged it deep into Marsden's exposed flesh. Marsden gaped in shock, his scream of terror transforming into a high-pitched shriek of pain and disbelief.

The killer toppled backwards, the wooden shard sliding out of his stomach, the splinters dragging something pink and fleshy out with them. He clutched at the glistening pink tube hanging out of his wound; retching and convulsing on the insects that had squeezed their soft bodies into his sinuses, and down the back of his throat.

Gary rolled over and got to his knees, his head swirling. Blood streamed from the wound in his shoulder and the cuts in his neck. He saw the chisel lying among the debris and grabbed it.

Marsden saw him and lashed out with the knife, despite his predicament.

Gary fell inside the attacking arm and slid the chisel under the killer's ribcage, into his heart. Marsden stiffened, his back arching, his eyes bulging, his mouth a huge, twisting cavern full of writhing insects.

Gary lay on him, his face so close to Marsden's that he could smell his foul breath mixed with the dry, musty stink of the moths. The handle of the chisel jumped in his hand with each beat of the heart muscle.

"This is for all those girls you murdered," Gary sneered, and twisted the chisel, knowing the wide flat blade would tear the

370

heart muscle wide. He rolled away, taking the chisel with him.

The damage was done. There was no turning back. Bright red blood spurted from the hole in the killer's chest

Marsden uttered a shriek of terrible starkness, like the screams of murdered children. He groped at his chest, tearing at his shirt as gouts of blood gushed and spluttered between his grasping fingers.

Small, shadowy hands—children's hands—clawed at the killer's throat and body.

Marsden's eyes widened in terror, his features twisting into a hideous freak of a face. He arched his back, his chest rising, the hole in his chest gaping.

Gary hoped he was seeing what hell had in store for him.

Then the Goldilocks Killer fell dead.

Gary collapsed too, his face lined with pain, his broken teeth singing at the cold air rushing over the exposed nerves.

Something had short-circuited when Marsden stabbed him, because his arm didn't work anymore. His shoulder was alight with burning pain, his arm hanging loosely, the palm numb, fingers twitching and tingling.

He crawled over to Marsden's body, each movement wringing pain from every joint and muscle. The killer lay, his sightless eyes wide-open. Moths lay dead and dying around the killer's body. Gary retrieved the phone from his pocket and peeled back the blood-soaked shirt to find the necklace Charley had told him about. He yanked the key, snapping the chain easily.

Grimacing, he climbed unsteadily to his feet. His arm hung uselessly, like the power had been unplugged. Weird sparkly sensations ran through it.

He slid along the wall, past his bloody heel prints on the floor; staggered through the kitchen and stumbled down the stairs, collapsing onto his knees in the workshop.

"Dad!" Charley cried.

Gary closed his eyes and caught his breath. "I'm here," he gasped. "I'm okay. I'm here."

He forced himself up and leaned against the wall. Right by him was the tripod stand with the sheet covering a bulbous shape sitting on it. He pulled the cloth, letting it slide off and onto the floor. It was a woodcarving, a portrait sculpture of a girl who looked much like Charley, only the girl in the sculpture had long curly hair. Gary blinked at it a few times. It was beautiful, the artistry and the detail remarkable.

"Dad?"

"Yes, I'm here," he said. He staggered over to the pit and dropped to his knees.

Charlie saw how injured and in pain her father was. "Oh my God, Dad. What happened?"

"We're safe now," he told her. "You don't have to be afraid of him anymore. No one needs to be afraid of him anymore."

With his one good hand, he manipulated the lock and inserted the key, feeling the satisfying click of the mechanism snapping open. He unhooked it from the hasp and threw it to one side.

He didn't have strength enough to lift the cage door all the way, so Charley helped him raise it enough for him to get his knee under, the gap wide enough for Charley to wriggle through. Once she was clear, he jerked his knee from under the door and it dropped with a final resounding clang.

Charley threw her arms around him, crying and hugging him fiercely. Gary hugged her back with his good arm, kissing her and telling her how much he loved her. It hurt both of them, but neither cared.

Eventually she eased away from him and wiped her eyes. "Your arm..." she said, seeing the blood and the limb hanging uselessly from his shoulder.

Gary nodded and took Marsden's phone out of his pocket. "Yeah I know," he said. "We'll call for an ambulance in a minute, but there's something we have to do first."

Charley didn't understand as he turned on the phone's display.

"Do you know your mum's number?" he asked.

Charley's face crumpled into tears.

She recited the number and Gary keyed it in. It rang once, twice, three times. Gary thought about the times he'd scolded Fiona for answering numbers she didn't know. Maybe this was one of the few times she was going to take notice of him, the only time he wanted...

"Hello?"

Her voice, hesitant, wary.

"Fiona, it's me, it's Gary."

She must have heard the pain in his voice. "Gary? Are you okay? You sound..."

"Fee, just listen..." And then he found he couldn't tell her for the huge swell of emotion that swept away his power to speak.

"Gary, what is it? What's happened?"

Trembling, he took a moment while the tide sucked back. "Fiona," he said, "I've found her."

The line went quiet. He could imagine her face, her searching eyes.

"What?" she asked. "What did you say?"

"I've found her, Fee. I've found Charley. She's alive."

"What? *You've what?* Gary? What are you saying? *She's alive?* What are you...?"

"I've found her, Fee. She's right here with me now. Do you want to speak to her?"

It was a stupid question.

He handed the phone to Charley, who was crying so hard she could barely speak. She pressed the phone to the good side of her face. "Mum!" she cried. "Mum, I love you! I love you so much!"

Gary heard Fiona crying and saying Charley's name over

373

and over. He wished they could be with her right now, together, a family again. But that would come.

Across the workshop, he saw Emma standing by the stairs, watching them. Moths danced and swirled in the spread of white light above her head. Just a little girl wearing a blue coat and white socks pulled up to the knees. A little girl to whom he owed so much.

He smiled at her and held Charley close. It wasn't revenge she had wanted. *This* was what she had wanted.

"Thank you," Gary whispered.

She smiled shyly and inclined her head in a way much too old for her years. Then, like a wisp of dawn fog, she followed the moths into the light and was gone.

Gary closed his eyes and held Charley to him, the smothering agony of the months without her lifting and freeing him of its soul-crushing weight.

The way ahead would not be easy, but for right now, just holding her was enough.

Where do you get your ideas?

It's a question perhaps asked too often of authors, but I thought some readers might be interested in how Dead Petals came to be.

Ideas come from anywhere and everywhere. News stories, anecdotes, little 'what if' muses that float around in an author's mind looking for somewhere fertile to land. Sometimes we have to work at it, digging the story, bit by bit, like a fossil from the ground, as Stephen King once aptly described it.

The seed for Dead Petals dropped from the tree and took root immediately, though it would be years before it grew into the story found within the pages of this book.

Back in 2005, the company I had worked at for eighteen years was closing and I was being made redundant. I was forty-five and afraid that my prospects for finding another job weren't that great.

One warm summer's day, feeling low, I took a walk around the block and sat in a little garden area just off the roadside. As I sat there feeling sorry for myself, a small child ducked out of the bushes and stood there staring at me, as small children often do. He was far too young to be out on his own, but I couldn't see any parents about, until a couple of mums with pushchairs walked by and called him back to them.

I smiled and nodded, but the old story machine had already started up (it was better maintained back then), the gears grinding, the oily pistons pumping.

What if that hadn't been a child who had just wandered away from his mother?

What if that child had been here with a message for me?

What if that child had been a ghost?

What if it was the ghost of a child who was trying to tell me he was being murdered just a few yards away from where I sat?

It was enough for me to sit down that night at the word processor and over the next few weeks I wrote a short story version of it. The short story began with the ghostly child on the park, and went through to the end, including Gary finding his missing daughter.

I'd had a story called Halloween Eddie's published in an anthology called Wicked Karnival's Halloween Horrors, and they were looking for submissions for a new anthology to be called Raw Meat. I decided to submit Dead Petals.

The editor, Tom Moran, read it and enjoyed it, but felt there was something missing. He thought some parts were encapsulated, and that it ended too quickly. More importantly, he told me he believed the material was too ambitious for a short story, and if I developed it a bit more, it had the potential to be one hell of a novella (his words not mine).

At the time I was only disappointed not to have gotten into the anthology. I dismissed his advice. It was a 5,000 word short story. A novella needed to be a minimum of 40,000 words. No way. The story was done. There was no more.

Or so I thought.

I lost interest in writing after a run of rejections (I know, don't start) and took my creative fix by returning to sculpting, though Dead Petals continued to simmer at the back of my mind. The core concept of the ghost child pointing to where she was being murdered still intrigued me.

377

It took about 10 years before the obvious answer hit me. *Why not tell the story of what happened to Gary and his family* before *that day at the park?*

After some research, I started writing about this happy family whose lives are torn apart when their daughter goes missing. That initial short story grew, and soon I had surpassed that seemingly impossible 40,000 word mark and I still had more to say.

I used to go for a walk at lunch time at work (yeah, I got another job) to think about scenes and make up dialogue. The story grew and grew, and though I had wanted to keep it under 100K, the story dictated otherwise, and about nine drafts and a professional edit later, the manuscript finally weighed in at a hundred and three thousand words.

The moths, they came in the final edit.

I'm glad I waited for them.

Alan I'Anson, March 31, 2019

Coming Soon

The Dark Destiny

Dreams of an old house and a faceless man.
The stirring of memories best left forgotten.
The re-awakening of psychic abilities long dormant.

Jack Freeman has lost his way.
Following the death of his wife, he has wandered, unsettled and
unsatisfied, always feeling that something important is missing
from his life.

When bad news draws him back to his old home town of
Gableton, the place of his darkest memories, he discovers the
truth about the faceless man, and finds the answers to questions
someone has desperately tried to make him forget.

The path to Jack's destiny is revealed once more, but does he
have the strength to follow it to its dark conclusion?

Printed in Great Britain
by Amazon